Praise for the novels of Sally Worboyes

'Unbridled passions run riot' *Daily Mail*

'A rich, vivid, three-dimensional, gutsy narrative which has you turning the pages into the early hours' *Eastern Daily Press*

'Sizzles with passion' *Guardian*

'An excellent book combining humour and passion' *Telegraph and Argus*

'A ripping yarn' *Bury Free Press*

'Here is a vivid evocation of a way of life' *East Anglian Daily Times*

About Sally Worboyes

Sally Worboyes was born and grew up in Stepney with four brothers and sisters, and she brings some of the raw history of her own family background to her East End sagas. She now lives in Norfolk with her husband, with whom she has three grown-up children. She has written several plays for BBC Radio 4 and Anglia Television. She also adapted her own play and novel, *Wild Hops*, as a musical for production at the Mermaid Theatre.

SALLY WORBOYES

Down by
Tobacco Dock

CORONET BOOKS
Hodder & Stoughton

Copyright © 2003 by Sally Worboyes

First published in Great Britain in 2003 by Hodder and Stoughton
A division of Hodder Headline

The right of Sally Worboyes to be identified as the Author of the
Work has been asserted by her in accordance with the Copyright,
Designs and Patents Act 1988.

A Coronet paperback

3 5 7 9 10 8 6 4

A CIP catalogue record for this title is available from the
British Library

ISBN 0340 82450 6

Typese   mited,

For Lin Redmond, Margaret McGregor
and Sally Lipka

ACKNOWLEDGEMENTS

My thanks to Emma Longhurst for her unyielding determination to get me to the signings on time!

Also, my special thanks to the artist, Gordon Crabb, for bringing alive my books with his spectacular paintings of our characters.

Preface

In 1546 Walter Bertram, in his early twenties, had a passion for sailing on the beautiful River Thames, and had secured himself a position as ship's navigator. His favourite trips had been to the east of London, and especially to Wapping and Ratcliffe, where, on one occasion, his ship was to be equipped before sailing from Limehouse to Guyana. During his short stay ashore he had met and fallen in love with a local clergyman's daughter and together, against the wishes of both families, they had settled by Shadwell Basin, where at that time most of the eight thousand dwellings in the area were small and wood-framed, infilled with bricks. Between that period and the time when Victoria was crowned Queen great changes came about, and soon after she came to the throne a light was shed on her impoverished subjects, who were mostly living in the rural countryside in small cottages which were damp, draughty and in bad repair, lit only by candles or tin oil lamps, with scraps of canvas covering empty window panes. There were no inside lavatories or proper drains, and all water had to be pulled from a deep well or monotonously carried in buckets from nearby rivers.

In towns, and especially in some parts of London, things were no better, with only one communal standpipe at the end of filthy, lopsided streets, bordered on either side by decaying dwellings in the worst of conditions. There were no drains or sewers and death caused by disease was never far away.

It came as no shock to Victoria's subjects when a report, printed in a national newspaper, told of children who, from the age of seven, were working in coal mines, textile mills, factories and the smaller cottage industries such as lace-making, glue-making and straw-plaiting. It was also common knowledge that boys who were continually being forced to make a paltry living by sweeping chimneys – like those working underground in the coal mines – could expect a premature and slow, painful death from soot in the lungs. At the age of twelve many girls hired as domestic live-in servants or kitchen maids were working twelve hours a day at a stretch for pitifully low wages.

In the very early years of Queen Victoria's reign questions were being asked about the working and living conditions of the children of the poor, and the horrors of the fate that befell them were made public. Many of these children had lost limbs through unguarded and broken machinery in factories, were frequently beaten for falling into an exhausted and malnourished slumber at looms, and were growing into adulthood crippled from labouring for long hours, bent over their work. For the very first time in Britain attempts were being made to change conditions, and a law was passed restricting the hours a child could legally work.

The arrival of steam engines was encouraging, bringing about change and new hope of a huge increase in manufacturing which would greatly affect the way people lived. Industries that had previously relied on small cottage manufacture, such as hand spinning and weaving, were gradually being revolutionised by machines powered by water, and huge, sprawling factories appeared almost overnight in the towns and especially in the capital, creating work for labourers who came to London in their droves to work in them.

Unfortunately, cheap accommodation rapidly provided by new employers showed little thought and bad workmanship. The row upon row of houses offered little fresh air or daylight. These new homes were to become the slum dwellings, with woodworm eating into the soft timber and rain trickling through the scantily tiled rooftops. In the east of London in particular the emphasis was on fast construction rather than comfort – hence the continuing lack of utilities. Shared standpipes remained at the end of streets and turnings, and still there were no proper sewage facilities or drains. For the lucky ones, lime-filled lavatories (holes in the ground) were placed inside small tin huts in back yards.

A cholera epidemic in 1848 was in a sense a blessing in disguise for it resulted in Parliament being forced to take notice and to address the problems of waste disposal. The slow, tedious work of building a system deep beneath the Embankment began, and eventually London's sewage was taken downstream before it could flow into the Thames.

During the construction Londoners referred to this period as the time of the great stink, owing to the foul smell emitted from the mud flats of the River Thames at low tide, but at least something positive was being done. Things looked promising in other areas too. The structure that housed the Great Exhibition of 1857, Crystal Palace, came to fruition and was seen as a revolutionary and breathtaking achievement, a monument to glass and iron production and manufacturing.

New factories continued to attract thousands of workers into towns and cities, but the work available was badly paid, unpleasant and often entailed long hours and hazardous working conditions. So although things for the country were changing for the good, for the low-paid working classes and their children there was little difference in their quality of life. The invention of something as simple as the sewing machine by Isaac Singer at this time did, however, create a huge wave of mass production, which changed the way people dressed and inevitably produced more cast-offs for those who wore rags. Far more clothes could be purchased very cheaply in second-hand shops.

But the streets of London, and especially East London, were still no cleaner thanks to dense pollution from the new factory chimneys, which made life worse for street beggars and the unemployed homeless. Orphans and destitute children were still having to shelter at night wherever they could, mostly in filthy marketplaces, sleeping under tarpaulin in the bitterly cold and foggy winters and during the stifling hot summers among rotting food that was too putrid to be sold or eaten.

Fortunately, the intervention of two men made a great impact on the lives of the destitute. Dr Barnardo opened his first children's home, having witnessed worsening conditions during his work in and around Whitechapel, and William Booth created the Salvation Army, which provided night shelters, hostels and soup kitchens for the starving poor.

More new and improved laws were gradually passed. Women, and children under the age of ten, were no longer labouring in the coal mines and children's working hours were reduced to a limit of ten hours a day. Machinery was made safer for its operators.

By 1870 Parliament had decreed that all children between the ages of five and ten should go to school. School boards or committees were set up and many new schools were built. Mothers in poor families welcomed the change with open arms – their children were being taken into account where education was concerned, and there was at last new hope for a better and fairer Britain.

I

1876

As dawn broke over the rooftops of 11 Kelly's Yard in Shadwell, East London, Maria Bertram stirred in her sleep as she turned to breathe in the fragrance of scented honeysuckle wafting in through the open window. Hers was a small, stuffy bedroom shared with her brother and sister. In her semi-conscious state she hung on drowsily to the remnants of her dreams until they faded and merged with the chattering song of a blackbird perched near by and the gentle whimpering of her younger brother lying on a cot mattress on the floor beside her bed.

Reaching across to him, Maria touched his shoulder, murmuring sleepily, 'It's all right, Willy . . . only a dream . . . turn over and it'll go away.'

'Did I wet the bed, Ria?' mumbled the sleepy five-year-old, his sloping green eyes flickering half open and peering at her. 'Did I wet the bed?' This anxiety was nothing new and Maria was quite used to hearing her brother talking in this half-awake state, especially at first light.

Once up, dressed and ready to face the day, relieved at having passed another night without shaming himself, Willy seemed to have no worries whatsoever. He depended for the most part on his eight-year-old sister Daisy to look out for him once she had come home from morning school. A shy boy and a little slow on the uptake, he hadn't really a care in the world other than the fear of wetting the bed. This had happened only three times since he had been out of a napkin cloth, but still the fear of disgracing himself and giving his hard-working mother extra washing haunted him.

Slipping her arm beneath her brother's warm and sleepy body, Maria felt the sheet, which was also warm and damp, but from his perspiration and nothing else. With her hand on his arm, she leaned forward and whispered, 'No, Willy . . . 'course you never wet the bed. Do you need the chamber pot?'

'No . . . don't need to . . .' He yawned, curling up and mumbling something before returning to his childish dreams. 'Night-night, Ria.'

'It's nearly morning, sweetheart. Soon be time to get up,' she whispered, smiling. The lad was already back in his world of dreams despite having had a good night's rest – this five-year-old seemed to need more than eight hours' sleep, with his eyes shut tight against the world. His dreams were always vivid and he was forever describing them, especially to his sister Daisy, who wasn't in the least bit interested and hardly ever listened to his long-drawn-out ramblings.

Carefully lifting wisps of sweaty brown hair off his face with the tips of her fingers, Maria watched as his breathing became even and relaxed now that he was back in his world of fantasy and magic. Then, sinking her head back into her pillow, she stifled a yawn, listening for the sounds of a new day beginning outside. As she slowly remembered that she had something special to look forward to later that day, a warm glow spread through her and she let her thoughts flow. She hadn't heard the low, whining sound of the local brewery hooter marking the seventh hour, and until she did she could afford to lie back and enjoy this precious time of day when she was all by herself – her thoughts entirely her own. Of course, she could hear distant clamour in the surrounding streets and courtyards as early workers began their day and pedlars called out, promoting their wares, but it all drifted above her head, and the dawn chorus of early risers, dogs and town birds could have been miles away for all the notice she took.

The familiar echoing clip-clop of the carthorse's hoofs on the cobblestones as it came into the yard was a welcome reminder that she was due for a rummage through the rag-and-bone man's pile of second-hand clothes. Maria's only working skirt was beginning to wear at the hem and her Sunday frock, previously salvaged from one of Olly Black's bundles on one of his returns from a Hampstead run, was too frivolous to comply with the rules of Bollards & Co., the shop-fitting company in Commercial Road. She had been lucky to secure her position as a filing clerk and general office girl Friday in the otherwise male-dominated offices, and couldn't afford to be dismissed over the breaking of a silly rule. Neither did she want to draw unwanted attention to herself since she was already walking a fine line by having broken another of the company rules, which had resulted in a handsome colleague asking her to meet him secretly. Maria had admired the young gentleman, John Cunningham, who had finally plucked up the courage to invite her to go for a walk in Shadwell Green this coming Sunday. Up until then they had simply smiled cautiously at each other and exchanged a few snatched words on passing when Maria delivered the morning post to the architects' department, where he was employed as an apprentice and runner to a team of draughtsmen.

Bollards, an old and archaic firm, had clear and strict rules, the breaking of which resulted in dire consequences for the employee who ignored or even bent them. Under no circumstances were clerical staff to mix with the shop floor workers, and within the office block the inflexible rule of no talking was to be obeyed at all times.

Properly awake and alert, with the sun streaming in through the gap between the two pieces of moth-eaten, faded floral curtain, Maria pictured herself, dressed in a summer gown with matching bonnet, John Cunningham by her side, strolling through the gardens on a breezy summer's day with only the song of birds for company. Of course, this was just wistful fantasy, but such dreams were all the more important for seeming unattainable. It was Maria's way of coping with the drudgery of everyday life in a cramped and dilapidated house with barely enough money coming in to feed and clothe herself, her two younger siblings and her exhausted widowed mother.

In reality, Shadwell Green would be a noisy place,

with scruffy children letting off steam, shrieking and yelling at one another and enjoying a rough-and-tumble or getting into a real fight. Here in this corner of East London, wild half-starved dogs would also take refuge, barking continuously, darting all over the place or simply lying in the shade, dying. Drunks would argue viciously over a drop of cheap gin or be stretched out on the grass in the shade of a tree, out for the count. But for the majority of the people living in and around Shadwell, Wapping and Stepney, these gardens were a place to get away and appreciate the sense of being in the countryside – albeit a very noisy little piece of heaven.

Bringing herself firmly back to earth, Maria pictured what she might be wearing if her neighbour Olly should have nothing in his ramshackle wooden cart to suit her taste and thin purse. She had only one long grey skirt and jacket to her name, and two blouses which she had worn as her work uniform and which John Cunningham had seen many times. Her second-hand and extremely outmoded Sunday outfit wouldn't do for this romantic rendezvous; apart from anything else it was far too puerile and tight around the sleeves. If all else failed she would have to find a way to liven up her standard outfit. She thought that her preferred linen blouse with the lace-trimmed collar and cuffs would benefit from a new ribbon under the collar, a lovely red silk ribbon with a matching band sewn on to her straw bonnet.

She glanced across the small bedroom, her eyes resting on the skinny eight-year-old, Daisy, who was kicking off her bed sheet and cursing under her breath.

Maria imagined her sister's freckled face screwing up if she were to present her with a tiny matching red bow to clip into her long, unkempt corkscrew curls. Sleeping soundly again in the corner of the room on a mattress, her tangled brown hair strewn all over the place, Daisy was dead to the world, lying on top of her flannelette sheet in her worn and stitched knickers and bodice, her white legs akimbo.

Looking from her to Willy, Maria made herself a promise, as she had so many times before, that one day she would earn enough money to buy them nice new things to wear instead of always having to forage through the rag-and-bone man's sack. Her sister Daisy was boyish and a street raker, hardly ever indoors and someone who didn't really much care that she had only one drab old frock which hung unevenly around her ankles beneath her grey patched pinafores, or that her thick black stockings had been restitched time and time again and were hanging together by threads.

For three years now, since their father had died from tuberculosis, day-to-day living had been hard for the family. Between Maria and her mother they could manage to keep a roof, albeit a leaking one, over their heads, food on the table and clothes on their backs. Maria's mother, Liza, a good, hard-working woman, somehow managed to make ends meet, but at the turn of a week the shillings earned, after rent had been deducted, amounted to very little when piled on the table.

At least here in Kelly's Yard, where Maria and her sister and brother had been born, she could be sure that her neighbours would, should the hour of need arrive, be there with good cheer and well-meant advice and bread if they were hungry. There was an unspoken camaraderie in this small, close-knit place which surfaced when one of the families, through no fault of their own, could no longer cope without a helping hand. Neighbours would then pull together until the family in question was more or less capable of staving off hunger pains and could pay their rent.

Over the years there had been occasions when there had been nothing any of them could do to save a family that had hit rock bottom. When it came to this their fate could only be left in the hands of the good Lord to see them through a period in the much dreaded and feared workhouse. Overriding terror of that wretched place lurked in the shadows and was a reminder to those fortunate enough to have some kind of a roof over their heads.

Fully aware of their lot, they nevertheless had no time for envy of the greedy privileged who, by ill-gotten gains or otherwise, lived in comfort and luxury with more money than they or their extended families could possibly spend in many lifetimes. Time, experience and life had taught them that to lose sleep over the injustices of the world helped not one iota and did little other than cause anger and frustration.

Those less fortunate than Maria's family, who slept rough in filthy streets, were in the main too far gone down the slippery slope and too downtrodden to be angry. The poor, only just existing above the poverty line in and around the docks, could often be seen bending over a few sticks of burning wood, cooking a meal in a tin from scraps of food they had begged, stolen or picked up in the markets.

The plea of the poverty-stricken fell on deaf ears as a rule, and the handful of those in a position to speak out and condemn capitalism were quickly branded by their peers with the patronising label 'misguided philanthropist'.

With the grim reality around her, and the hint of worse times to come for the people of Shadwell and Wapping, Maria was in no doubt that her birthplace was slowly changing, and that it was only a matter of time before all of them in Kelly's Yard and the surrounding courts faced eviction. Family homes were family homes, no matter how small and lacking, and she could envisage hundreds of mothers and children sobbing when they saw their own morsel of heritage razed to the ground to make way for grander, taller buildings. Whether offices or grand town houses were to be built on the sites made no difference when a home was being smashed into rubble. To the Shadwellians, Shadwell was *theirs*. To those born and bred in Wapping, then *Wapping* was theirs. This bond was also felt by those living in Stepney, Bethnal Green, Hackney, Bow, Whitechapel and by those who for generations had lived and worked alongside the river or close to it on both sides, in Blackwall Reach, Greenwich, Limehouse, Surrey, Rotherhithe – the entire double bend of the River Thames from Blackwall to the Tower of London. This was their river, their River Thames.

Dilapidated homes were, for reasons of gain and not welfare, gradually and slowly being possessed and demolished to make space for avenues of select houses. For Britain this was a time of peak industrial wealth. But the rich were becoming richer and the poor poorer; the impoverished ignored or conveniently forgotten while wealthy merchants and noble country landlords saw their bank balances rise. Not satisfied with owning grand sprawling countryside estates elsewhere, certain members of the gentry, who could not afford a home in the wealthier parts of London but wanted splendid town houses and mansions designed and built for them to provide a residence in the capital, opted for riverside homes.

It was becoming even more fashionable to have a London place to be frequented by the gentry in the 'season', as the aristocratic and wealthy referred to it, or simply to come to see and be seen by peers and hopefully be invited to attend lavish balls with other frustrated, aspiring upper-class parents desperate to rid themselves of their adult children. To secure marriages within families of either wealth, title or both, remained the everlasting dream.

Maria, whose only education had come from her father, was intelligent and wise enough to realise that land in East London was cheap and its proximity to the city caused it to be sought after as a place in which to build these grand homes set around tree-lined squares and illuminated romantically at nightfall by gas light. To accommodate this influx of society, crumbling hovels, which had at least given a roof to impoverished families, had been, and still were being, razed to the ground by astute prosperous landlords – landlords who were in some instances forced to offer alternative accommodation to those they were making homeless. No one dare turn down the alternative flea pits tendered for fear of being thrown into the work-house or on to the overcrowded and filthy streets to battle with death. The promise of new charity trust housing was sincere, but it was anyone's guess as to whether or not the dream would come to fruition or whether priorities would simply continue to work in favour of the influential rich.

As she left for work, stepping around a fresh pile of steaming horse manure, compliments of the rag-and-bone man's old mare, Maria came face to face with Charlie, the cart-pusher, a short man with thick grey hair growing only on the sides of his head and poking out beneath his battered old trilby. He was struggling with a loaded barrow, pushing the stubborn wooden cartwheels hard over the cobbled stones, his shoulders bent from years of hard, laborious work. Beads of perspiration were trickling down his face and neck and soaking into his grubby red (and what could almost be passed for white) neckerchief. Stopping for a well-earned breather, he eased the now useless tiny butt of a roll-up from the corner of his mouth and dropped it to the ground. 'D'yer reckon it's gonna rain, Maria? I couldn't 'alf do with a July shower,' he gasped.

'No such luck, Charlie.' Maria smiled. 'It's gonna

be a scorcher, I reckon. Why don't you stop off for five minutes and 'ave a cup of coffee with Mum?'

'More'n my life's worth, ducks. A jug of water'll do me. Some for inside and some for out.' He pushed the moth-eaten brim of his hat off his forehead and nodded towards the water tap. 'Second thoughts, I'll fill a bucket an' pour it over meself. Is the rat-catcher abaht?'

'Dunno. Go and see if the traps are set,' she said, walking away and calling back over her shoulder, 'Olly Black's in 'is stable sortin' out 'is old rags. He'll know. And tell 'im to clear away this morning's parcel! It stinks!'

At the sound of his master's name, the old carthorse in the stable whinnied loudly, bringing the rag-and-bone merchant from the back of the stables to check on the fuss. Shielding his eyes from the sunlight, he peered across at Charlie and waved him over with a surreptitious hand gesture, as if he had something very secret and special to show him. It was an old trick he had learned somewhere and one that everyone who knew Olly smiled at.

''Course Olly'll know,' Charlie replied, giving her a sly wink. 'Knows everyfing, that one . . . or so he likes to think. On yer way then, cock. Don't wanna lose time or you'll end up wiv no work, no hat and broken shoes!'

Laughing at him and his funny expressions, Maria was unaware that she was being watched from the window of one of the rooms above the stable by someone who was thought to be a rather mysterious young man. This was Steffan Tremain, who lived there with his father. The father, a man in his late forties, had the vague air of a gentleman, but since he had not once spoken to any of his neighbours in the yard they could only surmise from his and his son's shabby old tailored clothes and demeanour that they were from a very different walk of life.

Mr Tremain's dour expression was deliberate. He preferred to give a silent message – *Speak not one word to me*. His son, tall and lean with a gentle face, light blue eyes and fair hair, who was coming up to his twenty-first birthday, was no easier to fathom. To his neighbours he appeared to be shy and withdrawn with an aura that aroused curiosity but at the same time did nothing to invite suspicion. The very fact that he seemed unable to look anyone in the eye stirred bemused compassion rather than concern.

Father and son had been living in drab rooms above the stable for two years and were each employed at London railway stations, the young man leaving the house at mid-morning at exactly the same time, except on Sundays, and returning late in the evening, while his father seemed to come and go with no particular routine.

Steffan, who was still watching Maria, imagined himself, as he had so many times before, enjoying a conversation with his neighbours, and especially with the lovely girl who lived with her colourful family in the yard. He knew her name. He had heard her called by it. Maria.

There had been several occasions when this out-
wardly introverted young man had timed his leaving
the yard to coincide with Maria departing for work so
that he might walk beside her and begin a conversation.
So far, however, his instincts had stopped him. His
father would only spoil things. Since the day some six
years ago when Steffan's mother had left their home in
the country and his father had dragged him to London
away from his place of birth in Essex, Steffan Tremain
had had little choice other than to keep himself to
himself, which was very much against his character.
Had he not been blessed with his mother's calm, strong
temperament he would by now be so downtrodden as
to have lost all hope of right triumphing over wrong.
But now, having almost reached the landmark age,
the thought of which had kept him going through
the darkest of times, he was ready to walk away from
his overbearing father, who had always ruled with the
birch and had now become a pathetic responsibility
and burden.

On the frightening and unhappy journey from Saffron Walden, when Steffan was just fourteen years old,
Mr Tremain had instructed his son, and forcefully so,
that whatever happened they were from then on to
keep themselves to themselves and on no account let
anyone know who they were or where they had come
from. At that time Steffan had had no idea of his fate
or that his father was facing a term in prison, and that
he would have to make his own way until the two-year
sentence had been served.

*   *   *

Aware that the very good-looking and polite young man who she had still not yet spoken to was watching her, Maria felt herself blush. This was not the first time she had found herself thinking that she would like to break through the invisible barrier that he seemed to need to keep between himself and those living in Kelly's Yard. Not wishing to embarrass him, she made a pretence of not having caught his eye and hitched up her skirt to avoid the hem sweeping the dirty cobblestones.

'Got to stop off at the cobbler's one day this week . . .' she murmured self-consciously. 'Can't go on an outing with John Cunningham in worn-down heels.' Her thought went from her boots to her bonnet and the new ribbons she was going to buy. She still had the sense that her every move was being observed and her every word listened to, right up until the moment she strode out of the yard and through the half-moon passage, out of sight.

'You couldn't 'ave come on a better day, Charlie!' said the rag-and-bone man, creeping forward and looking around. 'I've got a little something out the back that'll do you a turn or two,' he continued, talking behind his hand. 'Got it from a posh old girl up West London. Was 'er husband's, be all accounts. 'Andsome, thick worsted frock-coat, as long as you like and in lovely condition. Smells beautiful, it do – pure mothball. I've got a couple of top hats an' all. Gawd . . . what a show you'd give the neighbours, eh?' He chuckled, leaning back and admiring the skinny old man.

'What do he want wiv a bleedin' fick coat in July, you silly sod!' Olly's wife, Angel, was carrying her workbench from inside her front room, where it was used as a kitchen table. 'Keep it for 'im till November comes round. He can put sixpence down and pay the shilling once it's on 'is back.'

'And what if it's sold before then?'

'Please God it will be and we can 'ave some lard on our bread.' Angel the matchbox-maker grinned, unloading her work materials from a tin box and setting them up as she had done for several years. Strips of magenta paper and thin pieces of wood, once in neat piles, would be pasted together with a small brush and then thrown on the ground to dry before Angel set to and formed pyramids of trays and lids. Her matchboxes would then be tied with string, and sent back to the factory. In summertime the warm air would dry the woman's work, but in the winter a tiny glowing coal fire in the corner of her kitchen cum living room would be kept in day and night – a pathetic attempt to dry the boxes as well as warm her aching bones.

'You've always got dripping for your bread, wife, so you have! And meat on the plate once if not twice a week!' called Olly from the stable, loud enough for all those living in the yard to hear.

'And a bleeding great goose at Christmas!' laughed one of the other women from an upstairs window.

'You come across any towels from them fancy hotels yet, Olly?' yelled another. 'Promises won't dry us, will they?'

'And impatience won't bring rewards! If my old man says he's gonna get a batch of nice big white towels, he will! Be nice money, an' all!'

'Tuppence a towel, I was told, Angel!'

'Well, you was told wrong, then, wasn't you!' Olly answered for his wife. 'Sixpence is what I said . . . and we're not talking about worn-out and threadbare!'

'Only when he's talking about 'is pockets he's talking worn-out and threadbare!' cackled Angel, enjoying herself.

'You've never gone short, woman! I see you all right and you know it! No holes in your boots!'

'Not much boot around the holes, more like!'

And so the good-natured banter between husband and wife continued, and Angel Black, mother of three sons, settled herself on a purpose-made box by her bench, legs wide apart and with a waft of her own familiar smell coming from under her layers of grubby clothes.

Their chatter was going over Charlie's head. He was thinking about Maria and how much she reminded him of his late wife when she had been young and carefree. Similar light brown eyes, big and smiling, same thick dark brown hair and eyebrows.

'Never mind the overcoat, then,' said Olly, flapping a hand. 'Come on out the back of the stable and rummage through the shirts, Charlie. All wrapped up in a bundle they are, and as white as snow itself.'

'Not today, mate.' Charlie winked, nice and friendly. 'When me boat comes in I'll 'ave a change of ward-robe.' With that he slapped the man on the shoulder and laughed. 'When me ship comes in I'll buy the bloomin' lot off yer!'

'Well, won't that be a fine thing.' Olly grinned. 'And per'aps you'll buy us a castle to live in. Move us lot out of this dump and ship us off to a castle in Scotland. That'd do me.'

'Why,' said Charlie, pulling his hat down over his eyes, shielding them from the sun, 'this is a lovely little place to be. Always fancy I'm in a different part of town when I come in 'ere. It's a sort of pleasant grubby world of its own, wouldn't you say?'

'Well, I s'pose you could say that, Charlie,' replied his mate, rubbing his chin thoughtfully. 'Yes . . . now you come to mention it it's not altogether a pigsty, is it? The drains tend to pong a bit at times and 'orse shit hums on a warm day, but then we don't really smell it any more. Used to it, you see. And you won't see finer honeysuckle than that one creeping up Maria's mother's wall. Liza Bertram planted that in that old barrel years ago and now look at it. Beau'iful!' He shook his head thoughtfully. 'Funny old world . . . out of stinking manure comes the lovely scent of honeysuckle.'

Leaving Olly to look about himself with a touch of renewed pride and satisfaction, Charlie pushed his cart into the rat-catcher's section of the stable and unloaded three drums of poison into the iron lock-up, thinking that perhaps he shouldn't have praised the yard as a decent place to live but privately admire it and give nothing away. He quite fancied Olly's little two-up, two-down himself. Or one like it. As he rested for a while in the shade, the smell of the fresh bales of straw made him feel like a five-minute kip next to the old mare. The ramshackle stable wasn't as clean as it might have been but there was a homely feel to the place and the two rows of crumbling red-brick houses squaring up to the stables did give Kelly's Yard a special kind of atmosphere. And there had to be a reason why those who were born here or had moved in never moved out, unless it was on the back of the undertaker's wagon.

Kelly's Yard was, however, under threat. Daughters and sons had for generations been taking over the tiny houses from their mothers and fathers once they had passed away. Now a dark cloud hovered over this yard. Not that the tenants had an inkling that ominous clouds were gathering over the future of their homes. And so they continued as they had always done, the men repairing leaking rooftops, gutters and broken windows as best they could, the women taking it in turns to scrub the communal lavatory block to one side of the stable, which was strictly for the use of those living in the yard.

A standpipe with an attached water tap ran along the outside wall of the privies, and in the very far corner of the yard was the shared cook-house, with three back-to-back old brick fireplaces and an iron bar across each from which to hang a stew pot. Beneath the bar, the fireplace housed rusty iron grates on which a heavy pot-roaster could be held securely above the flames, spreading delicious wafts of roasting potatoes and parsnips on cooking day, and, if a family was very lucky, a small piece of fatted roasting meat or wild rabbit brought back by Olly after one of his Essex rounds.

Fuel for the fires, small logs and offcuts, was piled in one corner of the stable, and fresh loads were brought in fortnightly by horse and cart from Wanstead by Olly, who had lived in the yard at number six all his life. Fuel wasn't dirt cheap or easy to come by, so for reasons of economy fires were lit only on Mondays for the washing of laundry in tin baths and again on Saturdays, when they were kept in until the early hours of the next morning and the last of the families, according to their rota held by Sophie Marcovitch, the rat-catcher's wife, had had their turn at cooking.

Left to simmer on the Sunday embers was always an enormous black pot in which at least five or six round plump suet puddings simmered. Flavoured with snips of bacon fat or small squares of cheese, or sweetened with figs, a slice of boiled pudding each day, toasted or cold, was not only tasty and filling, but nutritious.

Only those who lived in Kelly's Yard and their visitors had reason to come in through the half-moon passageway, and when a stranger happened to saunter through into the yard, somebody living in one of the tiny houses would appear protectively at a window or in a doorway, watching suspiciously. The stranger, usually a gentleman from the city or the country, would then either offer a polite smile and leave or ask directions to somewhere else.

Maria had yet to meet one of these fine gentlemen she had heard about, and she had sometimes wondered what their reaction might be if she were to invite one of them in to see that, poor though they were, their homes were kept clean despite the circumstances in which they had to manage. She wanted to offer a glimpse of the inside of the homes they seemed to find so fascinating from the outside, so they could leave with a new perspective on a world that so far they had only read about in a work of fiction or in the exaggerated prose of newspaper columns.

Although her family house was very small and the furniture purchased from second-hand shops, it was homely, with the living space occupied by two worn and creaky fireside chairs, a square dining table and two ill-matching high-backed chairs. The old mirror in its carved frame and two old oil paintings of the Suffolk countryside in the autumn had been purchased by Maria's father long ago when he had seen them stacked with others in an old junk shop and bought them for no more than a shilling for the lot.

In her mother's living room, where the only light at night was from a small oil lamp, Maria sometimes imagined a gentleman of means in one of the fireside chairs enjoying a cup of tea by the burning coals on a winter's day. It was no more than a fancy, but to her the pictures conjured up in her own mind were as vivid as those she saw in the real world daily, and more preferable.

To see gentlemen in fine clothes coming into this poor man's yard was not so unusual but neither was it that common. Journalists, writers, men of the press and painters had become intrigued by the people in this dark and mysterious part of London so close to the docks and the River Thames, and the way they coped with poverty and hunger. To Maria's mind, the fact that they ventured where others from the same class dared not tread showed that there was some hope that they were not entirely self-absorbed and might actually register the injustice in the huge gap between the fabulously wealthy and the pitifully poor.

As in most other places in East London, in Shadwell and Wapping families were so large that they spilled out on to the streets. Mostly unwashed and wearing dirty, shabby clothes, they loitered, argued, joked or squatted cross-legged on filthy pavements by litter-filled gutters, playing cards. To an outsider not used to the sight or the area, they would indeed look a touch menacing. But anyone who spent time in their company, listening to them, would soon realise that these tough, unfortunate people, given half a chance, would much sooner be inside a decent warm, dry home or working, especially on freezing cold winter evenings. Should anyone criticise her neighbours, Maria would have no qualms whatsoever about being totally honest and pointing out that the dwellings in which they 'lived' had enough space only for makeshift beds on damp stone floors. In reality 'home' meant a bed for the night and no more. 'Possessions' were for the wealthy, who took them for granted, but here they had to make do with the very bare necessities, which they did sometimes, and with good reason, resent.

The children, with their active imaginations, made the very most of the shiny worn-down cobblestones, often playing their own invented outside games while their mothers sat by their front doors toiling over their piecework. Making the most of things was one way to avoid falling into the trap of wretchedness and the sense of being downtrodden, which inevitably bred a mean, resentful spirit. Even though the occasional row or fist fight broke out, in general peace reigned in Kelly's Yard.

Living as people did cheek by jowl, with ever-increasing broods crammed into overcrowded rooms, infections spread fast, and the sound of coughing during the winter months was as common as the sound of the wind whistling through and around this tiny corner of London town. The families living in the yard, so far as Maria was concerned, were by and large a good-natured bunch, but it wasn't all camaraderie and light banter. There were occasions when tempers were high and spirits low. The people living here were no distance from the Thames and the docks, and so they had seen their fair share of the illnesses and diseases common to the area, and there was often a need for them to pull together when a neighbour was mourning for a lost loved one or friend. It was not unusual for the dying to be very young. The winters were harshly cruel and biting and the summers just as wicked as the temperature soared and stifled the rancid air, accelerating the breeding of disease-spreading flies and rats.

Maria often felt lucky that her sister Daisy and her brother Willy were now just old and strong enough to fight off most infections, and that her mother, though tired and worn out, especially since her husband had died, was still relatively robust, if a little malnourished.

Fortunately rats weren't a problem for Maria's family or for her neighbour. At number six lived old Jacob Marcovitch, the rat-catcher, who took pride in the fact that his neighbours rarely caught sight of this hated and feared vermin. Mice and cockroaches were something else. Mice were left to the stray cats, who would otherwise starve to death without this source of food, and thereby cause more disease to spread from their maggot-ridden remains. Cockroaches, the biggest problem of all, had to be tackled when spotted. This was Jacob's way of seeing things, and no one argued with the old gentleman, who, at the crack of dawn each morning and before he went out on his rounds, would check and reset his rat traps, and every night before turning in would repeat the same pattern.

To his mind, Jacob's work was his vocation. His wife Sophie, the mattress-filler, was responsible for looking after their three grown sons, apart from those times when punishment was required to be meted out. By working outside, stuffing mattresses for a local factory, Sophie Marcovitch could on a good day make seven pence while her neighbour, Angel Black, wife of the rag-and-bone man, whose rough and large hands were always busy making matchboxes, toiled all hours for a penny a gross. The rest of the women living in the yard, Maria's mother Liza included, worked outside their houses on wooden chairs or the doorstep engaged in outwork such as brush-making and belt-finishing. During the bitter or wet winter months, when the weather made it impossible and the drains were too overpowering, the women had to manage inside their cramped dwellings as best they could, with their materials spread about them, taking up the little space there was.

Although most of the children in Shadwell attended the paupers' school for two or three hours in the nearby mission hall in Trinity Square, St George's in the East, they still had to find ways of making a few pennies. Older brothers and sisters who were too young to find proper work would scavenge in the markets for bruised fruit and vegetables or tout for odd jobs, carrying sacks of coal or helping street vendors to pack up their wares and clear away rubbish. Those children too frail or timid to beg would run home after their lessons to look after baby brothers or sisters, allowing their mothers to work faster on their back-bending outwork, without distraction. Jacob the rat-catcher and his wife Sophie, however, were more fortunate. They had sent their boys off to work in a tin box factory in Wapping once they had marked their eighth birthday, where they now had a job for life. Their uncle had been working at the factory since he was a boy and was in a position to pull strings when relatives' lads came of age.

Other fathers, who had not absconded or been press-ganged on a ship or imprisoned, worked from dawn to dusk for small reward in the nearby docks, markets and factories. Stealing from those who were better off had become a normal way of life, and going outside the area to take from rich folk who could well afford to be charitable but lacked benevolence did not seem ungodly to those on the breadline. From a very early age the children living in Kelly's Yard, like thousands of others elsewhere, learned how to slip and slide, duck and dive, in order to fetch home 'the bacon' – food for their families. Canny and naturally born wayward children went on to more lucrative crime, picking pockets and pogues and squeezing in through the tiny windows of big houses in and out of the area.

By her open doorway on this fine morning, with steaming tea in a chipped blue-and-white enamelled mug on the window sill, sat the rat-catcher's wife, Sophie, a short, round woman in her early forties. Her thinning hair scuffed back with pins and with dark rings around her eyes, she looked older than her years from worry and hard work, but she was nearly always in fair spirits and enjoyed nothing more than to give advice about oncoming perils. With all three of her sons now earning a living of sorts, four or so shillings a week, she had expected to be able to take life a little easier, but as history had proved over and over again, the lads' earnings, even now that they were older, were only enough to clothe and boot themselves, with a little left over for a beer or two at the local taverns, which meant Mother still had to supply most of their food.

Sophie drank down her tea in one go and then, with a pile of horsehair and flock by her right hand and gripping the open end of the mattress cover with her left, she began her work. As if she were a human machine she started with great expertise to feed the stuffing into the thick twill cover, with a little made-up tune running through her head. Within minutes of getting into her slow and even rhythm she began to sing quietly as she worked . . .

'One two three, one two three, here we go . . .
Stuffing the mattress before we sew.
Shove in a sparrow and what do you know,
Someone might lose a smelly toe.
Shove in a blackbird and my oh my,
Someone could end up with only one eye.
Shove in a bird with a beak sharp as rock
And someone might end up with a right bleedin'
    cock . . . les
and winkles for Sunday tea . . .
Mother-in-law says you *will* invite me—'

'Oi, oi, oi!' Jacob's voice came booming from inside the house. 'You leave my mother out of it! You could learn something from her!'

With the other women joining in the ditty and adding their own lines ad hoc, the yard was in full swing. This communal singing, with various tunes from silly made-up ditties to popular songs of the day, echoing through the yard, would go on until it was time for a tea break. It all helped to ease the burning deep pain in their shoulders or lower backs, and at the same time make light of the repetitive and mind-numbing work which gave little financial reward. Carried away with a ballad, they relaxed while they worked and thought of nothing more than the lyrics of the chosen song, allowing all cares and woes to float away.

So immersed were they in their own world the women hardly noticed the middle-aged, austere gentleman who lived above the smelly stables coming down the wooden steps, his head held high and wearing his usual attire of black shabby coat, striped trousers and stale-tobacco-smelling bowler hat. Striding through the yard, paying no attention to the women whatsoever, he went through the half-moon passage as if they were invisible and soundless. Even though they had jollied up their song for his benefit, still he had ignored them and stepped up his pace, eager to get away from this awful place and to Fenchurch Street railway station, where he was employed as a porter.

'What d'yer reckons to 'im, then, Sophie?' Angel Black grinned, one eye on the interloper as he disappeared through the archway. 'Is he a prince or a pauper just like us lot?'

'Neither, I shouldn't think,' said her friend, pushing a long thick needle through a mattress she had stuffed and was knotting. 'No . . . that one's got the eyebrows of a murderer. Dark and thick and so close together they meet in the middle. Wouldn't want to meet 'im on a lonely night.'

'A murderer?' Liza Bertram, trimming the bristles of a newly made hairbrush, chuckled. 'Too feeble for that. It takes a strong man to kill a person. My Maria feels sorry for the man . . . and his son. Says they're like ducks out of water.'

'Each to their own, Liza. Each to their own. You can't say we've not given that man and his son a fair chance. Olly's tried to engage 'im in conversation many a time, but he either shakes 'is head or gives him a certain look which is a touch on the snooty side.'

'Olly engages everyone, Sophie. Always got somefing to sell.'

'And what's wrong wiv that, Liza Bertram, may I enquire!'

'Nuffing wrong with it, Angel Black. Your 'usband has a living to make and he works every minute God sends . . . all I'm saying is—'

'Well, for my money,' Sophie cut in, her own thoughts still uppermost in her mind, 'I would say that I wouldn't be too certain that he's not a murderer. No. I wouldn't be too slack over it. You tell your Maria to keep out of 'is way, Liza.'

'Ha!' Liza smiled, lifting her eyes to meet Sophie's. 'And you think that strong-headed daughter of mine would take notice?'

'I would say so. She's not an obstinate girl. Got vigour, that's all . . . and that's no bad thing. She'll work 'er way out of this place . . . you mark my words. I wish one of my sons would court and marry your girl. Lucky the chap who gets your Maria, Liza . . . oh, yes, lucky the chap.'

'Don't know about your Daisy, though, Liza. Little minx,' said Angel Black, tying string around a container of finished matchboxes. 'That frisky little mare'll end up running all the lads out of this court the way she goes on. Eight years old and frightens the life out of the lads if they would but admit it. Needs a little bit of harnessing, that one.'

'She is a little cow . . . we all know that . . . but she's

honest and that's no bad thing. God knows we could do with some honesty in our lives. Would that things were as good as they used to be.' Sophie smiled wistfully and slowly shook her head, enjoying a little bit of nostalgia. 'My poor mother, may she be resting in peace, would turn in her grave should she see the way things have turned out. She always said that life for her children would be much better than it had been for her. I'm not so sure.' She sighed, looking about herself. 'I think we were better off then than we are now. We always had a piece of fruit every day, no matter what.'

'Well, you would 'ave done,' said Angel. 'Your dad was a porter in Spitalfields fruit market. I doubt you ever saw a bit of meat, though.'

'My Maria'll be all right,' said Liza, warding off an argument between her two neighbours, who were always at each other, looking for a squabble, baiting and scoring points. 'A bit high spirited, that's all. Bright as a button, though. She could end up running the country. And wouldn't that be something to boast about? A woman running the men out of government.'

'What a different world this would be if that were the case,' said Sophie, always eager to put the world to rights. 'They're gonna stop public execution, you know,' she said, shaking her head. 'And it could be this year. Don't know what they fink they're doin'. You'd think they'd know better. There'll be more murders,' she added, gravely. 'More murders. What kind of a world will it be in the future? I don't think I want grandchildren. How could I sleep at night worrying over them?'

'Why do you say that?' Liza looked up from her work, disturbed momentarily by this talk of the dark and morbid side of life. 'Why would abolishing penny-a-look hangings cause more murders? That's daft. It's sickening to watch, anyway.'

'You think so?' Sophie kept her head down and concentrated on her sewing.

'Come on, you torment.' Angel Black grinned. 'What're you thinking? What've you heard?'

'Who says I'm thinking about it? It's out of my mind,' Sophie said, flapping her hand and putting on a droll face. 'I've put it from my mind already. But I will say this and you can think on it. Don't the very thought of 'aving one of your own being hanged for everyone to see and anyone to throw rotten fruit at make your blood run cold? And if you 'ad sons who might do anything to stop their kids from starving to death, wouldn't you drum it into them from birth that they must never kill, no matter what the circumstances?'

''Course we would, Sophie! And so would you.'

'But not everyone's the same, are they? No. If some women didn't 'ave to think of their sons hanging in public they might be inclined to turn a blind eye if their sons was murdering for money.' She raised her eyes and looked from one to the other. 'Wouldn't you do anything you could to stop one of your sons thieving at any cost, if they was to face being hanged with all your neighbours there to see? With strangers chucking rotten fruit at someone you cherished. A husband, a child, a nephew. Could you bear to see that . . . and with a mob of strangers cheering the hangman?'

''Course we couldn't bear it! Silly, daft thing to say!
No mother wants to see one of her own—'

'I rest my case,' murmured Sophie, 'I rest my case.
But I will say one more thing before I thank you to
drop the matter. Some people, not all, I grant you, but
some people might relax a bit with regard to what they
encourage and what they don't encourage if they knew
their sons could be hanged for everyone to see. Now
do you see what I'm saying? What I'm getting at?'

Liza and Angel looked at each other and shrugged.
'Kind of . . .' murmured Angel, irritated by her neighbour's self-assured conviction. 'But I still don't agree
with you. The sooner they stop public execution the
better.'

'Well, you never was one to think too deeply about
fings, was you?' Sophie sniffed. 'The list of hangings
will rise to double once they execute in a dark and
closed place where there are no witnesses and nosy
parkers to see what's exactly what. Never mind all the
rest I've said.'

'*Shut your trap, Mrs Marcovitch!*' The sudden shrill
voice of Daisy rang out from her open bedroom
window. 'I've got gutsache and I'm trying to get to
sleep! Stop effin well goin' on abaht murderers!' The
clanking shut of the window caused the women to
wince. Too much force and the glass that was still in
some of the small rotten frames would fall out.

'Yes.' Angel smiled, her eyes on Liza. 'Your Daisy'll
sort the men from the boys all right.'

'The girl should be at school,' snapped Sophie.
'You'd best keep your eye on that one, Liza Bertram,

before she brings trouble to your doorstep. And fetch trouble she will. Yes, I should keep a close eye on that one.'

'Oh, I will, Sophie Marcovitch, I will.'

'And Maria. She likes to think she's above everyone in the yard just because she's one of the first batch of women to be taken on to do the work of gentlemen. Women working in stuffy smoke-filled offices side by side whisky-supping so-called gentlemen and learning shorthand.' She shook her head solemnly. 'Whatever next? I dread to think.'

'At least she's not out there gaming herself like some I could mention, Mrs Marcovitch. Your nieces would do well to take a leaf out of Maria's book,' said Liza, constraining her anger.

Ignoring that, Sophie smiled and slowly raised her eyes, looking from one woman to the other. 'Look at yourselves. Working the fingers raw . . . and for what? For a few coppers to buy a loaf of bread and dripping. Face it, we're stuck in a human machine that every now and then tumbles about a bit and promises something better, but we all end up in the same place . . . Poverty Place – always 'aving to make do.'

'Which is why I'm proud of Maria . . . for using her brain instead of her body. And we'll end it there, if you don't mind. Let's wait and see where she'll be in five years' time, shall we?'

'Please God we'll still be alive and not six feet under feeding the rats. There'll be another plague, you see if I'm wrong. The Black Death didn't go away . . . it just lies waiting, like all the killer germs do. Living in this filth and decay the way we do, I expect one of us will be the first to go down with it.'

Glancing at each other with a wry smile on their faces, Liza and Angel suddenly burst out laughing.

'Sure . . . make light of it the pair of you. Laugh and the Devil laughs with you.'

'You're a tonic, Sophie, whether you know it or not.' Liza chuckled, wiping a tear from the corner of her eye. 'You're funny and don't know it.'

With a different tone in her voice, Sophie the mattress-filler picked up on her ditty with a change to the lyrics . . .

'One two three, one two three, watch your step,
Jump on thin ice and you're bound to get wet,
Drowning in water but still let's not fret,
'Cos Liza and Angel are on a good bet,
No harm will accost them 'cos . . . *they're* carved
    from jet!'

2

A week had passed since Maria had enjoyed her pleasant afternoon with John Cunningham and now she was at a loss to understand why he appeared to have been avoiding her at work. When going into the architects' office with the post, she had been disappointed that he had either kept his head down or returned her smile with no more than a polite nod. Had they been seen talking, she wondered, and if so had John been warned not to associate with a colleague? Or was it a simple case of him not wishing to encourage her? All of these thoughts were swimming through her mind as she brushed out her long wavy hair and tried to fathom the reason behind his change of attitude and cool manner. He had acted as if he had enjoyed their time together on the day, and she had felt comfortable in his company, chatting freely about all manner of things on that warm Sunday afternoon. And as they took leave of each other fondly, she had believed that he had felt the same as herself and that a promising friendship at the least had been forged.

Engrossed in their conversation, they had strolled through the noisy Shadwell Green oblivious to everything going on around them, and had then continued on to the bustling riverside, to watch the unloading of cargo ships in Tobacco Dock, with the barges coming in and going out. It had been John's idea for them to steal into a very old timber-and-brick waterside warehouse, an enticing building which looked as if it had come straight out of a Grimm fairy tale. The ramshackle building abutted the river when the tide was in and the mud when the tide was out. Inside, the panelled rooms were discoloured with the dirt and smoke of over a hundred years. The wooden floorboards and staircase, although in a state of decay, had once been good solid oak timbers. From below and above they had heard the squeaking and scuffling of the grey rats, which had proved too much to bear, and both Maria and John had made a very quick departure, laughing and shrieking with terror.

Gazing at her reflection in the small cracked mirror, Maria wondered whether perhaps she had talked too much during their afternoon out and shouldn't have been so eager to fill silent pauses. Or maybe she had asked too many questions? Whatever the case, the young man, with his good looks and polite ways, had managed to warm her heart and work his way into her dreams.

'The trouble with you, Maria Bertram,' she murmured, talking to her reflection and pulling her thick hair up into a plait, 'is that you're not used to being alone in a young man's company and it's time you was.'

'Why you talking to yerself, Ria?' sniffed Daisy, coming into the living room in search of a lost stocking.

'Miss Fartarse says it's a sign of madness when any of us does it.'

'Well, maybe I'm going loony, then, eh? Your teacher must know about these things.'

'Bats in the belfry,' Daisy playfully taunted as she crawled under the table to retrieve the missing item of clothing which was covered in dust. 'That's what the fart says about folk who talks to 'emselves.'

'Is that right? Well, she'll 'ave something else to say to you if you don't give your hair a good brushing. We'll 'ave to cut the lot off soon,' said Maria, spreading a little cold cream on her face.

'Good,' said Daisy, lying on the floor and pulling on her thick black stocking, 'and if you don't I will. I'll find the scissors one of these days.'

Watching her sister on the floor with one leg up in the air, pulling at her stocking so that the hole in the heel came under her foot, Maria shook her head despairingly. 'You don't need to wear stockings in weather like this. No one'll see your bare leg under your skirt. Take 'em off.'

'You don't know what dirty Dick's like. He looks up our skirts and sniffs our knickers and then pinches the pink bit.'

Momentarily stunned by this sudden revelation, Maria demanded to know more. 'Which *pink* bit exactly?'

'Between our drawers and our garters, what d'yer fink? The tops of our legs, Maria!' Daisy screwed her nose and curled her lip. 'He's a dirty rude 'orrid boy!'

'Well, I should say he is,' said Maria, suppressing hearty laughter. 'Is Willy up yet?'

'No, and he's pissed the bed so he won't get up out of it. Finks I don't know but I can smell it up there.'

'Daisy, how many times 'as Mum told you not to use that kind of language? It's not very ladylike.'

'How should I know 'ow many times she's said it? I can't count up to an 'undred. I *can* read, though, and I look up all the bad words in Miss Fartarse's dicshunary. If a word's in there you're allowed to say it and piss is in there.'

Staring into her sister's stubborn, freckled, sunburned face, Maria stopped herself from smiling. 'But Miss *Faintheart*,' she said, emphasising the correct name, 'didn't know what words you was looking up, did she now?'

'Never asked. And she gimme a sweet out of 'er pocket for reading the dicshunary wivout being told to. I spat it out, though, when she wasn't looking. It tasted of the way her skirts smell.'

'You carry on like this, swearing and cursing and being rude, and you'll be in serious trouble at school.'

'Good. They can send me 'ome as punishment. Anyway, her clothes do smell. She farts all the time, that's why – speshally when she sits dahn. We always know when she's gonna do it 'cos she lifts 'alf 'er arse and wrinkles 'er lips up tight. And it bleedin' stinks an' all. Spreads right fru the room.'

'Stop it, Dai,' said Maria, 'it's not funny.'

'Arse is in the dicshunary an' all. So's shit. It's what Miss Fingy needs. A good shit. That's what dirty

Dick says. D'yer fink there's summink wrong with 'er stomach that she'll die of?' she asked gravely.

'And why do you say that?' said Maria, beginning to take Daisy seriously. 'Is there talk of 'er being ill?'

'Dunno. She smells of beer as well. Reeks of it.'

The loud voice of their mother calling from upstairs stopped Daisy short. 'She's gonna effin' well try and brush me 'air, Ria! She is!' A look of sheer panic and fear was in Daisy's light blue eyes. 'It'll effin' well kill me!'

'Stop swearing!'

'It's Saturday. I always say what I want on Saturdays 'cos Sundays is religious. Anyhow, you should fink yerself lucky I only said effin'!' Leaving her sister to stare after her, Daisy stomped up the narrow wooden staircase, the heels of her boots crashing on every wooden tread. 'The proper word's in the dicshunary so I could've used that!' she shouted back over her shoulder. 'And you can ask all the others if you don't believe me! I showed it to 'em! Shocked, they was! Never stopped goin' on abaht it!'

As she left the house later that morning Maria's mind was back on John Cunningham and whether she should ignore him or find an opportunity to ask why he was so reticent, or behaving so coolly towards her. Immersed in her thoughts, she hadn't noticed the rag-and-bone man lurking in the stable measuring a length of lead piping.

Having heard her come out of her house, and having been waiting for her, Olly called her name quietly, his tone belying any attempt he might have been making to cover his zeal for an idea that had come to him while unloading odds and ends from his cart. 'Maria . . .' he hissed from the shadows. 'Spare a minute, will you, cock?'

'So long as it is only a minute, Olly,' she said, stepping into the stable. 'I'm on my way to Whitechapel to see someone about some work in Covent Garden of a Saturday.'

'Deary, deary me,' he said, taking off his cap and scratching his head. 'You're gonna end up living the life, Maria, I can see that. Covent Garden, eh? You'll find a different sort of people there, you know. From top brass to . . . well, you know, ladies of the night, as it were.' He shuffled from one foot to the other, a touch embarrassed, his cheeks a little flushed. 'So what will you do, then, for work, that is?'

'Sell flowers, what else? On a stall. Our tea lady at work knows a Whitechapel flower seller who runs a stall in Covent Garden. She told me there was a job going there so I mustn't be late and miss the boat.'

'It's my favourite market, you know, Covent Garden. Oh, yus. I tout my trade round that area whenever I can. Get some decent stuff at times an' all. Lovely place. Spring or summer there's always the smell of sweet flowers in the air. 'Course you don't wanna be late, Maria, girl,' he said, looking around and taking her arm. 'It's yer opinion I'm after. You being educated an' that.'

'I'm not educated. I work in an office, that's all.'

'Yes, yes, yes,' he said, impatiently wiggling a finger at her, 'but it's all up there.' He tapped the side of his temple. 'Brains, you see. You've got 'em else they would never 'ave taken you on at them offices, now, would they?'

'So it's my brain you're after, is it, and not my sweet lips?' She was gently teasing him. He was so easy to bait it seemed hardly fair, but no one could resist poking a bit of fun at this lovely tout, who took pride in the fact that his family had been in rags and bones for generations. 'And I wouldn't 'ave thought I could advise you, Olly. What with you bein' a businessman. Your own boss, so to speak.'

'Ne' mind all that now,' he said, feeling rather flattered and drawing her into a far corner, where he stacked and piled his old iron bits and bobs. 'I've 'ad such a cracking idea and I've bin wondering ever since I've bin back from me rounds as to why I never thought of it before. Why any of us never came up with the idea. Especially you . . . with all your brains.'

'Well, there we are, then, Olly,' she said, winking at him. 'Just goes to show who's the dark horse, don't it.'

'How d'yer mean?' he said in an affronted tone while picking up a fixing that had come with the bundle of lead piping. 'I'm no dark horse. Honest and open, me. Always 'ave bin, always will be. What made you say a fing like that?'

'Never mind. So what 'ave you got as a bargain this time?'

'No, no, no, Maria.' He sighed. 'I'm not talking shop.' Again he tapped his temple. 'I'm talking bright ideas. New ideas. And one in particular that could make things better for all of us round our way.'

'Well, that'd be something. Go on, then. Be quick, though.'

With a sly smile on his face he mopped his sweaty brow. 'The town 'all clock 'asn't struck the hour of eight yet and it's scorchin' already. Makes you fancy a nice cold shower, wouldn't you say?'

Maria looked from his twinkling eyes to the lead pipe in his hand. 'Wash your body and your clothes at the same time? Is that it?'

The man tapped the side of his long straight nose. 'Not quite, Maria, not quite.' He moved his mouth to her ear and excitedly whispered his glorious vision. 'What about a private little corrugated tin shed with a latch door which bolts from the inside with another little shed adjoining, into which you could toss over and hook your clothes, so they wouldn't get wet.' He checked his surroundings again to make absolute certain no one was eavesdropping or lip-reading. 'Our very own personal and private shower room like the ones you see up the new municipal baths. I've bin racking my brains over it since dawn when the idea first came into my mind.'

'When you picked up that old lead piping, you mean?'

'That's right. So what d'yer say? Would the others pay tuppence for a private shower?'

'If you supplied Sunlight soap and a towel they might.'

'A towel!' he shrieked, stepping back and staring into her face. 'Are you barmy as well as beautiful? A shower and a towel and soap and all for tuppence?'

'Olly, I'm gonna 'ave to get off now. I'll talk to you about it later on when I get home. But don't give me half a story.' She grinned knowingly. 'I've spotted the bundles of white towels on the back of your cart that you've picked up this morning for next to nothing. How much was you gonna charge for use of a towel?'

Rubbing his chin and looking a bit sheepish, he admitted, grudgingly, 'Penny ha'penny a loan. But that's only so's I can cover the cost of the laundry.'

'I'll talk to you about it later on, Olly,' she said, walking quickly away. 'It's a good idea if it'll work!'

'So you'd appreciate the service, then!' he called after her.

'Might do, Olly!' she replied cheekily as she disappeared through the narrow archway and out into the bustling, noisy streets, leaving him to believe he had won her over with this new idea of his.

From his room above the stables, standing by the open window, hidden by the piece of curtain, Steffan Tremain, who watched out for Maria each morning, was smiling to himself. As he did most of the conversations going on in the yard, Steffan had overheard this one too, and it amused him. He had also learned where Maria was going. To the new Whitechapel people's market, which he had been meaning to visit again himself. The thought of perhaps bumping into her there brought a different smile to his face. But this momentary sense of cheerfulness was about to be dashed, for his father had come out of his bedroom

and crept up behind him. The odour of stale perspiration and beer was not in itself a give-away since
in these rooms this familiar smell always hung heavy
in the air, whether the mean-spirited man was in the
room or not.

'Does it amuse you to look down pitifully on poverty
and filth, Steffan?' he suddenly barked, startling the
twenty-year-old. 'Is this the way you fill the hours spent
in this unbearable place?'

What else is there? thought Steffan, who could
hardly bear to be in the same room as his father. 'I
no longer see the poverty as much as I used to, Father,
and since we live in worse rooms than our neighbours,
I never pity them. I see people who must rise above it
all and rise above it with a smile, albeit a grim one, or
be imprisoned in their own world of misery.'

'There is a grain of sense in what you say and it
would serve you well to heed it. Your disposition is
far from sunny.'

'Would that I had something to cheer me within
these four walls,' Steffan replied, trying to suppress
his anger and loathing. To rankle his father would be
to play into his hands since he was, quite obviously, in
one of his goading moods and looking for a reason to
lash out.

'You don't have to make it your prison. There is a
far, far better place away from here. A good walk and
a short train journey will take you where the air is fresh
and the people more in keeping with your birth.'

'Indeed. But at least in this part of London, whether
I know anyone or not, I am in a crowd of real people.

"Salt of the earth" is how you've referred to them in the past, before we moved to London. And that's the reason why I go out for a stroll most evenings.'

'Mmm . . .' was his father's apathetic reply as he put a light to his pipe and drew on it. 'I've often wondered what it is that lures you out into the night to trudge through these appalling backstreets and for hours on end.'

'I do not trudge, Father,' Steffan said quietly, wishing to maintain an even mood. 'I simply go out and take the air when it is too humid to be inside, and I like walking. You may not believe it but I find solace in a quiet stroll—'

'Good Lord. I was right. You are losing your sense of reality. How can it be quiet in this hellhole? With the continuing rattle of countless vehicles – hansom cabs, decrepit old stagecoaches, wagons and hackney carriages – and cockneys who are the only ones who can understand what they are saying or rather yelling and screeching at the top of their voices.'

'There are quiet places too. Not many people walk around old churches and tombstones.'

'No, I shouldn't think they do.' His father laughed, and in truth he had not much to laugh over. He had lost everything, including his soul, through his lust for women, drink and gambling. 'At least when I go out, boy, it is for a reason. I cannot abide the people who I must live among here in this God-forsaken part of London. Would that I could look at them without disgust filling my very soul.' His tone became more vicious and resentful as he warmed to his favourite topic and made no effort to hide his loathing.

'Would that the sun never shone here and they were forever in the dark, unseen. At least in the dark I do not have to look at them in passing. You, on the other hand, appear to have an affinity with these animals – which accounts for why you watch them so much. Ha! Watch and admire. But then I always did say that you had your mother's blood in your veins. Were it not for my generosity and compassion she would still be nothing more than a paid servant – probably she has gone back to that trade whence she came, wherever she happens to be now. If indeed she is still alive.'

'A governess, Father. There is a huge difference and it is eminently respectable.' Finding it difficult not to scream at this contemptuous man, Steffan clenched his hands and used every bit of his will-power not to rise to his bait. To use his beloved mother as a stick to beat him was a tactic he so often practised when all else failed.

'You think so?' His father was sprawling in the one and only armchair now, his legs stretched out as he stared up at the ceiling, puffing on his pipe.

'I know so, as do you.'

The man slowly nodded, a sardonic grin on his face. 'Well then, let us hope, for the sake of the family name, that she governs in a respectful house, if indeed she governs at all. She may well be a scullery maid, for all we know. Or worse still, a common whore.' His face bright red from the cheap gin he had already consumed, he began to chuckle. 'A very common whore.'

'I doubt that very much.'

'Do you indeed? My, my, how opinionated we are today. I trust that your pathetic little stationmaster hasn't been kicking your arse, boy? Could that be the reason for this defiant mood, perchance?'

'No. I get on quite well with him as a matter of fact.'

'Oh, how interesting. I cannot abide the fellow, and I think I can safely say that he knows it.' A self-satisfied smile spread across his face. 'Well then, what brings on this dour mood?'

'It isn't me in a mood, it is you.'

'Really? How so? I feel exactly the same as I always do . . . almost.'

'Exactly. You are always in this mood.' Turning to face his father, Steffan clenched his jaw and glared at him, at his red-rimmed eyes, determined that he would not let this man, who had whipped him yet again out of a cheerful mood into a very low one, get the better of him. 'I take it you won't be in for supper this evening?'

'You take it correctly and it begs a question. Why ask? I *believe* I go out and stay out of a Saturday night and have done so for the past two years?' He paused and gave his son a calculated look. 'Well, am I right, boy? Or is it my mind that is getting lost and not yours?'

'I was merely checking . . .' Steffan said through gritted teeth. 'To make absolutely certain that I would not have your company this evening should I decide to stay at home.'

'You can be sure of it, my boy. It is the weekend. A time when *normal* men go out and attend to their animal instincts. A good woman would soon sort you out.'

Enough had been said, and there was no more Steffan could do other than make his escape. Anywhere in the world was better than this room with this man. He much preferred to roam the streets during his free hours until it was time for him to clock in at the railway station at Hackney Wick where he worked.

'You should take a leaf from my book, Steffan,' said his father while topping up his glass of gin. 'I shan't be back until morning. I prefer to see characters who come out into the streets at night rather than those people out there, who you seem to admire.' He sipped his drink and shook his head disdainfully. 'A damn good woman for a night would do you the world of good.'

Leaving his father to his own devices, Steffan went into his room, brushed down his shabby clothes and smartened himself as best he could. Then, turning the key in the lock so as not to allow his father entry while he was out, he made to leave – but his father had not done with him yet.

With a half-full bottle of cheap gin to his lips, he pushed his puffy red face close to his son's, grinning menacingly. 'I shouldn't bed that little whore from number eleven, if I were you. She has the look of a woman with the clap. Syphilis at the very least, I would have thought.'

Pulling his face away from the reeking breath, Steffan replied in a flat tone, giving his father no reason to fly off the handle. 'I don't know who you mean.'

'Ooooh, I think you do.' His father pointed a finger and winked at his son. 'I've seen you . . . lusting through the window, with one hand down your trousers.' He clicked his teeth and winked approvingly. 'Dirty little bugger.'

Repulsed and almost unable to hold his temper, Steffan clenched his teeth, murmuring, 'You're disgusting.'

'What was that?' snarled his father, putting a hand to one ear, spoiling for a fight. 'Come again, boy?'

'I said you're disgusting.' The slight nervous tremble in Steffan's voice gave him away, and when his father grinned broadly at him, showing his clenched teeth, he knew what was coming. He stepped back but the large-framed man was already upon him and there was no time to make his escape. To try to fight this giant of a man who, when in this state of drunkenness, had the strength of a wild bear was all but suicidal.

Pulling a thick arm back as far as he was able, Steffan's father, his eyes blazing, landed an almighty back-hander on his son's face, sending him reeling across the room and crashing to the floor.

Raising his eyes to see whether his father was done or whether his boot was about to find his ribs, Steffan was relieved to see him lumbering towards his chipped washing bowl and plunging his hand into the much-used cold, grimy water, mumbling, 'Little bastard. Filthy little bastard.'

Pulling himself to his feet, dazed and unsteady,

Steffan stared at the rounded broad shoulders of the loathsome man. Memories of how he had sometimes reduced his mother to a trembling wreck came flooding back, as did the last words she had whispered to him the night she ran away: '*Stay by your father's side, my darling, so that I may track you down and come back for you when I'm able.*'

His face burning hot, and throbbing with pain, Steffan left the lodgings and made his way down the wooden steps, steadying himself on the iron balustrade, grateful that he had got away with only one blow.

His original plan for this afternoon had been to take a stroll to Victoria Park in Hackney, where there was to be an open-air performance of *Macbeth* by a travelling theatre group for tuppence a bench seat. But this plan was far from his mind now. All he wanted was to find somewhere close by to sit down, where he could rest against a wall and wait for the throbbing in his face and head to ease off. The tears behind his eyes were not born of pain but of frustration and a deep sense of loss and isolation.

At times like this his thoughts always turned to his mother – what she had gone through and how much he badly wanted to be held tightly by her, to smell her soft soap scent again, and talk to her, ordinary, everyday conversation. In the past, when he was much younger, they had often sat by a blazing fire in bitter winters when snow was thick on the ground, with her telling him of her days as a child, tales which he had loved to hear.

Steffan had missed his mother so much during their

six years apart, and had been painfully lonely in his own empty, silent world, even when in the thick of the hustle and bustle of London street life. There had been times when he had longed simply to have someone to talk to, but since he was sworn to secrecy over the family scandal that had led to bankruptcy and caused his father to go to prison, he had had no choice other than to stay silent. Not being inclined to fabricate a story to explain why he was living in this part of London, he chose to stay in his own isolated world until such time as he could live the way he chose.

At least today was Saturday, and he would have the rooms to himself the long night through, with no fear of being disturbed. There had been times, when his father was in one of his moods, when Steffan could hardly bear to listen to him pacing up and down the floor during the night, which could go on for fifteen minutes or three hours. It was almost as if he were trying to walk off the injustices that he believed life had dealt him. All that Steffan could do at times like these was lie very still in his bed, hoping his father would not come in, spoiling for an argument and the opportunity to take out his frustration on his son. There had been days when Steffan had felt as if he were living on a precipice, and on occasions he had even vaguely welcomed the release that death would eventually bring him, especially when his father, maddened by alcohol, would rant and rage as to how he had suffered and how he had only been trying to be a good husband and father and how his mother was to blame for everything. Steffan had heard this so many times that he could now let the words go over his head. As the years had dragged on he had begun to think that his father was losing his mind and all sense of logic through his perpetual drinking of cheap gin.

The drinking had not begun with his arrest over his huge debts. On the contrary, his debts had come from the drinking and his irresponsible behaviour in having mistresses that he entertained extravagantly and his gambling, which had once been an obsession. Along with the alcohol he had also taken laudanum, which had been the last straw as far as his mother had been concerned. That she could leave her young son without any word as to where she might be contacted seemed cruel in everyone's eyes except Steffan's, for he was the only one who knew the truth. His own welfare was no more enhanced for his mother being there, and since she had gone away penniless he knew she could not possibly have taken care of him and would most likely have believed that his paternal grandparents would take her boy into the fold. How wrong she had been. His father had dragged him away before they could make any claims on him. At that point in his father's life Steffan had suddenly become his prop.

It had come as something of a surprise to the family when Steffan's mother had fled from her husband, but a numbing shock when Steffan's father was arrested the following year for debts which had nothing to do with her leaving. Having spent two miserable years incarcerated in the Marshalsea Prison, with too much time to think, the loathsome man had convinced himself that the boy's mother, his own selfish wife, had been the cause of his downfall and had found all kinds of reasons for laying the blame for everything at her feet.

Having run away from the dictatorial, brutish man long before his arrest and internment, the distraught woman had made no contact and had seemingly disappeared into thin air. Steffan's only hope was that she might still be in hiding, somewhere in Thaxted, Essex, her place of birth, where her lower-middle-class family were still living, with the exception of his maternal grandmother, who, now in her eightieth year, was residing within the lovely cottage gardens of Whitaker's Almshouses in Loughton. The gentle, kind old lady had been living in the tenement cottage for over two decades. As a child Steffan used to visit her with his mother, travelling by stagecoach from Saffron Walden en route to London.

The promise he had made to himself, that he would go against his father's ruling of not contacting his mother's family and paying the old woman a visit, was forever in his thoughts. Older now and more mature, with a mind of his own and growing stronger in character, he was ready to break that injunction. Soon he would be twenty-one, and to his mind, with the little savings he had managed to hide away, his next birthday would be the milestone at which he would set out on his own to do whatever he wanted. Most importantly, he was determined to find his mother, and to do that he must call on her grandmother first. Should he find his mother, he would be the happiest person in the world. When she ran away from his father she had left behind a heartbroken child. She and Steffan had been so close, and he felt sure that wherever she was she too would be thinking of him and pining for her only son, her only child.

When his father had been imprisoned Steffan had been fourteen years old and in a complete and utter state of despair. He had been dragged to London by his father and made homeless. Taking a room in a decaying lodging house, wedged in between crumbling old buildings near the river, he was shoulder to shoulder with the prison in which his father had been interned. In return for free lodgings in this place and a weekly wage of five shillings, he became a barge-cleaner and rat-trapper. The rats and the filth had turned out to be a blessing in disguise, for they allowed Steffan to earn a living and gave him a roof over his head.

Miserable and very lonely, he had had no choice but to put his education and family behind him and accept that he had to think and behave like an adult instead of a fourteen-year-old, part of a warm family. Working for a living had not worried him – in fact he had looked forward to it until the dire reality of where he would be working shattered him. With no brothers or sisters for comfort and his cousins suddenly out of his life, he had felt as if he was far from any centre of human warmth, with no one to talk to. All of his family during that dark period of his life had either been taken from him, had left of their own accord, or, as in the case of his grandparents, *he* had been dragged away from *them*.

Of course, Steffan had his memories of very happy

times at home when his cousins had made impromptu visits or attended the numerous dinner parties that his mother, against the wishes of her husband, had often arranged. The very opposite to her husband, Steffan's gracious and gentle mother was a social and fun-loving person, who maintained excellent housekeeping accounts and always made certain they were in credit. She did not live above her means – it was his father who bankrupted and broke up the family.

Before he fully realised it, Steffan was at the noisy Tobacco Dock, with all the hustle and bustle going on around him. Taking refuge on a narrow flight of wooden steps leading up to a black-tarred weatherboarded warehouse, with his head in his hands, he closed his eyes and tried to imagine himself invisible.

'Nuffing in the world is as bad as all that, son.' A fatherly voice sent waves of mixed emotions through his body and soul. Slowly raising his eyes to meet the gaze of the sympathetic and kind face, he swallowed the lump in his throat.

'No. Nuffing's that bad.' The stranger smiled. 'Love's young dream let you down, 'as she, or 'as someone picked yer pocket?'

'Not quite.' Steffan smiled. 'In fact, nothing like that at all, sir.'

'Sir, eh? Well then, aren't you the polite lad.' He pushed a hand into Steffan's and shook it, taking him by surprise. 'The name's Wilkie Crow. Not from these parts, are you?'

'Mine's Steffan Tremain and no, I'm not from these

parts, but I've been living in Kelly's Yard for nigh on two years.'

'Ah, so you're in reduced circumstances. And where did you live before coming into this jungle?'

'Saffron Walden . . . in Essex.'

'Thought as much. Up from the country. Well, if you can take my company, I'll pull a half-pint for yer.' He nodded towards a tavern which from the outside looked like a very rough place. A very rough place indeed. 'It's a working-man's tavern but you won't feel out of place. You've got the appearance of a young gentleman down at heel. That goes some way round 'ere, son. Come on. Up you get. If there's a dog or cock fight goin' on out in the back yard you must close yer eyes to it. You look a bit on the soft side for all of that. Gambling's part and parcel down this way. Fink you can stomach the place? It's generally only the working men during the day. At night it turns into a dancing saloon and you can guess the rest,' Crow said, winking and smiling, showing unusually good teeth compared to most people Steffan had seen so far in this part of the world.

Pleased to have found a friendly person to talk to, Steffan allowed himself to be led into the tavern and felt himself relaxing into the surroundings. 'I've lived in worse places before coming to Shadwell but I do feel a fish out of water, I must admit. It's a friendly place but I don't seem to make friends too easily.'

'Well, you 'ave to give and take, son. And since you're the interloper, as it were, you've got to do most of the giving till they accept yer. A smile and a nod goes a very long way, as does patience. You don't wanna go barging in, but then agen you don't want to appear offhand. D'yer get my drift?'

'I do.' He looked at Wilkie Crow and smiled. 'I thought that's what I'd been doing. Obviously I must have been getting *something* wrong.'

'I think you must 'ave, son, I think you must 'ave.' For a second, Wilkie was allowing the softer side of his otherwise tough character to get the better of him. But then a sudden and fierce argument breaking out on a table close by over a game of cards brought him out of his balmy mood. 'You can't afford to be too squishy around 'ere,' he said, with an eye on the two men, who were sparring up to each other across the small table.

Looking directly at the men, Steffan raised an eyebrow and then turned back to his newly made acquaintance. 'Someone's not happy.'

'Look away, son. Look away. And close your ears. The language you are about to hear—'

'I've heard before. Like I said – I've lived in worse places.'

'Mmm. Well, if you'll excuse me.' Wilkie smiled and rose from his chair. 'I have a little bit of business to attend to while you nurse that swollen face. But don't go away.' With that the man walked over to the small marble-topped table where a fight was about to break out and grabbed each of the men by the collar and brought their heads together. 'Next time, gentlemen, your nuts will collide wiv a very loud bang,' snarled Wilkie. 'Now play like good boys or get out.

Understood, gentlemen?' He then released the men and sauntered slowly to the bar.

Glancing around, Steffan could see that he had indeed strolled into a rough alehouse. The characters sitting around one grubby table in a corner of the bar, playing cards, took no notice of the fracas whatsoever, and neither, it seemed, did they care about the mess on their table – a small round table filled with dirty ashtrays, beer glasses, half-eaten meat pies on newspaper, and in the middle of the mess a mound of pennies. One thing was clear – Wilkie Crow commanded respect in this small corner of London, where even the hardest of men might think twice before venturing on to what appeared to be his territory.

'Sorry about that,' said Wilkie, joining him again, with a pitcher of ale in each hand, 'and don't look so serious. You soon get used to it. Have to keep 'em in order, you see. Good behaviour's very important down this way. Don't wanna attract the law, do we?'

'No.' Steffan smiled. 'I shouldn't think so.' He had already learned from his time living next to the prison that while the majority of policemen were on a par with the dim-witted, a few others were a very good match for villains. 'I thought that living in London would be exciting, but once you're in it and not looking on from the outside . . .'

'It's as dull as your ditch water?' Wilkie chuckled. 'I can't believe that,' he said, putting his ale to his lips.

'Well, no, that's not what I meant. Not exactly. But at least I can tell the difference between an ordinary woman and a prostitute now. I had a few of them wink at me when I first arrived in this area and thought they were just being friendly cockneys.'

Roaring with laughter, Wilkie slapped his knee. 'Well, if I was you, son, I would stay on the safe side of the road and not smile at any of the women, unless they smile at you first, that is. Then you must waste no time. A Shadwellian lady,' he added, using a mock-posh voice, 'must be made to feel like a queen.'

'I'll remember that.' Steffan smiled. 'It seems that my wits have dulled since I've been in London, when really they should have sharpened.'

'You need to get out and about more, I expect. You've a lot to learn, but you'll get there. Never a dull moment round these parts, even if you're not too clever at mixing in. A big town can be a bit on the lonely side, though. Yes, I've heard that said more'n once.' Sipping his beer and studying Steffan's immature face, he gave him a wink. 'You'll be all right once you've got a few lines on yer face. You'll see that most folk round this way don't sit and talk as we're doing, unless they're discussing a bit of business, or 'aving an argument. No time to sit and debate, you see. Time is money and money's a bit thin on the ground.' He chuckled warmly.

'And that's why everyone speaks so quickly and in a sort of verbal shorthand.'

'You've got it. That and . . . well, you don't always want any old Tom, Dick or Harry to get the gist of your conversation.' He winked at Steffan again and sipped his beer. 'We're not expected to say anything intelligent in any case. Wealth buys a lot of things, son, but it can't buy a quick brain. Do you play cards?'

'Only when I was a child . . . and then only with my mother.'

'Well then, I should keep your hands in your pockets and watch for a few months before anyone gets you round the table.' He sipped his beer again and started to laugh quietly. 'Talk about easy meat. They'd 'ave you for dinner, all right.'

'Well, there you are. That's why I keep on the fringe of things. I just don't fit in – pure and simple.'

'You will in time,' Wilkie said, 'you will. I'll introduce you to one or two regulars and pass the word not to strip you. So you live in Kelly's Yard, eh? Jacob's all right. The Jew. I should think you get on with him. His missus is a pain in the neck, though. Solemn Sophie, always talking life down as if she's on a different planet from the rest of us.'

'I think I know who you mean.' Steffan laughed. 'I haven't spoken to any of my neighbours but I hear them call out to each other and watch from my room. Angel Black is married to the rag-and-bone man – Olly. And Maria is the daughter of the widow Bertram. Maria's younger sister is called Daisy and her smaller brother Willy.'

'Mmmm.' Wilkie Crow smiled. 'You've paid attention to the prettiest girl around Shadwell so you're not that slow on the uptake. She'll be snapped up by one of your lot, mark my words. Got blue blood in 'er veins 'as Maria. A throwback from some prince or the other 'aving a bit on the side.

'So they don't talk to you, eh?' Wilkie scratched the side of his head and rolled his eyes. 'Always acted as if they're a bit above anyone outside smelly Kelly's Yard. Gawd knows why.'

'I did pause once on my way through the yard to make conversation but they made me feel as if I were some kind of an apparition. Gazed at me with a faraway, puzzled expression on their faces.' Steffan sipped his ale and shrugged as if he were bemused by it all. 'They always go quiet when I walk through the yard.'

Bursting into laughter, Wilkie put up an apologetic hand. 'I'm sorry, son. I don't mean to mock yer. They just don't know quite what to say to someone like yerself, I expect. For all their airs and graces they don't know quite the right way to talk to a gentleman. That should tell you something.'

'Is that how they see me, do you think?'

'It's how you see yerself, innit?' said Wilkie, wiping his nose on his red-and-blue neckerchief.

'Not really, no. I'm a square pin in a round hole, I suppose. That's how it feels, at any rate. Even the street beggars never return my smile.'

'They're probably too weak to say anything, son.' Wilkie grinned, amused by this young man's naivety. 'Still, there you are. It's the way of the world and we'll leave it there. I'm not one for debating the whys and wherefores. Waste of time.'

'I wasn't shocked by the beggars. We had very poor people coming into Saffron Walden from the villages who were living on bread and milk. But here, in this part of London, I can't help feeling for those who live in the shadows with nothing other than a bottle of physic to slowly bring an end to their miserable lives. They know they're dying and wait patiently for the end.'

'Yes, well, like I say, no point in wasting time on what we know and can't do much about. You're not exactly living the life yerself. Them rooms above the stables ain't exactly Buckingham Palace, are they?' He smiled, raising an eyebrow.

'No. They're damp, dark but not *quite* condemned. But they are marginally better than our previous lodgings which were in Back Lane over Bethnal Green.'

'Oooh dear.' Wilkie chuckled. 'Next door to the madhouse. You were a fish out of water there, I should fink. Mind you, it's a Jew's paradise a stone's throw either way. Luck of the Jews is wot they say. Little public greens all round 'em. Think they're a bit above us Shadwellians, do them in the suburbia, as they like to refer to it.

'So there we are, you're on the rise agen, eh? You meet a better class of people in Shadwell, not that the Bethnal Greeners would agree.' He swallowed the remains of his beer with one eye on this naive young man's face. It was hard not to continually laugh at the poor bugger who, to Wilkie's mind, would be a fish out of water in London no matter where he hung his hat.

'I suppose there are just too many people in big towns,' said Steffan, preoccupied with his own thoughts. 'It's bursting at the seams. Too many coming from overseas hoping for a better life, I expect.' Glancing into his companion's face, he leaned a little closer to him and lowered his voice. 'I hadn't realised how many opium dens there were. I looked in through a filthy window in Limehouse and saw old Chinamen and women in a stupor, lounging about the smoke-filled room while a young woman blew on a strange sort of a pipe to kindle it. Do you think that—'

'Now you listen to me,' said Wilkie, cutting in and leaning forward, his face almost touching Steffan's. 'You carry on roaming through them kinds of back-streets and you're liable to get your throat slit. Some folks in this neighbourhood will kill you for the shoes on your feet, never mind your coat and cap. You're an intelligent lad, so don't act like a silly boy up from the country. You'll score no points for it and to survive in this part of the world you need points. D'yer get my drift?'

'I think I do.' Steffan smiled. 'It's sinking in.'

'It's no smiling matter, son. Act like a first-class fool and I'll 'ave no more to do wiv yer. Time's too precious to waste on idle talk. Time's money.'

'I suppose I listened to wrong heed I was given before I left my home as a boy.'

'And what might that have bin?'

'That in London there's crime, starvation, misery. That it's a savage place but you just have to get used to it and not perpetually worry that your throat might be slit for the shoes on your feet.'

'Ha! Well, that shows what country bumpkins know! You *will* get your throat slit if you go down the wrong alleyway, and you, my friend, are too naive to know which ones they are. Now leave it at that. Least said sooner mended.' With that Wilkie stood up, squeezed Steffan's shoulder and winked at him, smiling. 'I should stick to places you're more used to, son.'

Leaving Steffan to gaze after him, and hoping the word naive had struck a chord, Wilkie Crow walked away with mixed feelings about this young man who had a great deal to learn, even though he was educated. The fact that he had no idea that his father was a regular visitor to the establishment where they had just enjoyed an ale together was a clear indication that he should be discouraged from returning, should he appear again, and Wilkie didn't think he would. Who exactly the lad was had not been difficult to fathom. The penny had dropped once he said he lived in Kelly's Yard. His father was not only a regular in this corner of Shadwell but someone who enjoyed his drink and a game of cards, was a compulsive gambler and someone who had a penchant for oriental women. Whether it was because they were cheaper to bed or not was neither here nor there. The 'City Gent', as the man had been nicknamed from the very beginning, had never given his name and was by now used to anyone down Tobacco Dock calling him 'Gent'. Neither had he given his address, but Wilkie in his wisdom had had him followed after his first visit and had got the gist of his circumstances straight away. In this shady part of London, should a stranger come into the fold, they were treated with suspicion until more was known about them – where they lived and worked. City Gent had passed the test, and so this stranger from another walk of life was allowed into Shadwell's small, lawless world, provided he behaved himself according to their rules.

More importantly the well-spoken Gent was a decent card player and an excellent bluff at poker, and he was willing to pay for the services of the team of prostitutes run by old Sarah Kenny. The pompous fellow had even joined Wilkie's little loan club.

In a slightly more enlightened mood, with the pain to his face now gone and only a faint red swelling to be seen, Steffan made his way through the backstreets until he was out on Commercial Road East and passing through Sidney Street. Here, where it was quieter, he replayed the short conversation that had made such an impression on him. He wasn't sure why the man in Tobacco Dock should have been so friendly, but it now made him question his own behaviour. Had he, all these years of living in poverty, amid people from a different class, appeared to have been a touch above himself without realising it? Had he given the people a proper chance to befriend him? Had he seen things from their point of view? One thing that was becoming clear was that if he were to continue to live and work here, he must make more of an effort to be part of the local way of life, which he now understood a little better, making him feel less like an outsider.

Better to hear the voice of ridicule or scorn than not to hear anything at all was the thought going through his mind. From now on he would no longer accept people treating him as if he were invisible. He had as much right to walk these streets as anyone else, and henceforth he would speak to strangers as Wilkie had spoken to him, without any inhibitions and with the same confidence he had had when he was in his home town, Saffron Walden, all those years ago.

Arriving in the noisy and active Whitechapel, he crossed the busy wide road, weaving between the fast-moving traffic – horse-drawn carts, trams, old stagecoaches and hansom cabs and an open-topped petrol-driven horseless carriage with a wealthy family seated inside. This was a truly rare glimpse of luxury in this area.

Steffan could easily picture his father in wealthier days, before the debts and prison, smugly driving such a vehicle, and found himself smiling at the irony. His mother, who deserved the luxury, would not have wanted it, and his father, who did not deserve it, would without a shadow of doubt have relished the attention and show of wealth. He would certainly have been one of the very first to purchase the new gleaming beast and flaunt it for all it was worth. He could almost hear him bragging vulgarly in his gentleman's club and see him pulling up outside his personal tailors in Saffron Walden, swollen with puffed-up pride and relishing the envy his new toy provoked.

Once safely across the busy thoroughfare and in the midst of the hustle and bustle of the Whitechapel market, which rang with the echoing cries of the street vendors and was heavy with the delicious aroma of sizzling sausages, boiled bacon and pot-roast potatoes, Steffan began to feel hungry. Easing his way through the throng of shoppers, he made his way towards a place where a mix of people, Londoners and foreign immigrants, mostly German, were clustered in small groups around various market stalls, haggling and beating down the stall-holders in loud voices as they picked over their wares. He paused by a place where shoppers were milling around talking and lunching on bowls of tuppeny soup, potatoes and bread, a real Saturday treat for those who lived in the old crumbling back-to-back houses in and around the squalid streets of Whitechapel and Aldgate. These were the people who lived in perpetual fear of disease from the filth which permeated the area, and where the foul smell of disease and death hung in every dingy corner of every alleyway and courtyard.

Catching sight of a familiar figure, Steffan ordered his soup and bread and watched from a short distance away. Daisy Bertram, younger sister of the lovely Maria, was holding her small brother's hand as they went from one person to another, selecting only those shoppers or visitors to the area who were better dressed than the poor and ragged. Keeping his distance, and spooning his soup from the small cracked bowl, he watched them, trying to work out exactly what they were up to. The reaction of the people they approached was not outright dismissal, and the children were smiling, with no expression of ill will. He was intrigued. When he saw an elderly gentleman of clean but shabby appearance smile and hand Daisy a penny, he realised that they were in fact begging. But begging with a difference. Close enough to hear, and at pains not be noticed, he listened intently as Daisy approached two well-dressed middle-aged ladies walking side by side, arm in arm.

'Scuse me, ma'am,' said Daisy, offering a penny piece. 'Could you please give me change of two ha'pennies for this penny 'cos I 'ave to share it wiv my little bruvver? I want to buy a crust of bread wiv mine, yer see, and he wants to waste 'is on a sugar stick.'

Steffan was amused. This was a very artful way of begging without actually begging. Any man or woman who could afford to give a penny so cheerfully to skinny waifs such as these two was not going to be able to resist.

Looking slyly at them again, enjoying the show they put on as they accepted a coin from the women and returned their expression of compassion with a grateful angelic smile, Steffan marvelled at their intelligence and wit. They were appealing for money rather than pleading, and it worked. They were managing to touch the magnanimous side of people's nature, which a run-of-the-mill beggar might not.

On seeing an elderly gentleman dip his hand into his pocket and pass over a penny coin, Steffan moved closer, but kept his back to them as he looked into the window of a well-appointed grocer's shop, which displayed packaged foods in colourful tins, jars and cardboard containers. This shop was out of place in this poor district, and yet inside he could see women lining up at the counter. In wealthier parts of London he had seen the new packaged goods, and when he had been living in Saffron Walden as a child his mother had, on several occasions, taken him into a cooperative grocery store. He hardly expected to see another of these stores, albeit much smaller, in Whitechapel.

As he returned his empty soup bowl and spoon to the vendor, another familiar figure caught his eye. At a nearby baker's stall, Maria, shopping for her mother, was buying a loaf of bread. He felt sure that she couldn't possibly know what her sister and brother were up to, and without thinking he turned quickly away from the soup stall and found the children in the midst of the crowds farther along. Gripping Willy's hand, Daisy was about to approach a gentleman wearing a top hat and smart frock-coat. Steffan placed a gentle hand on her shoulder and whispered into her ear, 'Daisy . . . your sister is coming this way.'

Spinning on her heels, wide eyed and startled, she stared into Steffan's face, recognising him as the madman from the yard. 'I won't say a word about what you're up to,' he quickly added to put her at ease. 'I just thought you should know.' He nodded in the direction of Maria, who was heading towards them. 'I think she's spotted us,' he said, smiling. Then, giving the frightened Willy a reassuring wink, he whispered, 'I'll not say a word.'

'Daisy? What are you doing in Whitechapel?' said Maria, aware of Steffan's presence and blushing for no reason she could think of. 'Did Mum send you to find me?'

'No,' said Daisy, her eyes wide and innocent. 'Me an' Willy reckoned it was time we came and 'ad a look at how to shop in the market for when you're working down Covent Garden of a Saturday. 'Cos you won't 'ave time to shop for us then, will yer?'

'Oh.' Maria sighed, relieved that they were not up to mischief. Catching a certain look in Daisy's eyes, she turned her attention to Steffan. 'Hello,' she said, smiling politely and hoping her blushing cheeks were not too obvious. 'They've not been giving you any trouble, I hope?'

'No. Of course not,' was his relaxed answer. 'I recognised them from Kelly's Yard and stopped to say hello.'

'Oh, of course,' said Maria, avoiding his eyes, 'you live above the stables. I recognise you now.' Again she felt herself blush, but this time she did know why. She was pretending that she hadn't placed him straight away. 'Well, that's something. I wouldn't like to think that Daisy might 'ave cheeked you. She can be a bit lippy at times.'

'Bleedin' cheek,' murmured Daisy. 'That's what you get for trying to 'elp out.'

'What was it like, Ria?' said Willy, squinting up at his precious big sister and wiping his nose on the cuff of his sleeve. 'In the Covent garden. Was it like a park wiv flowers and grass everywhere?'

'No.' Maria smiled. 'It's not much different to this place, Wills, but they sell mostly flowers. Specially the bit where I'll be working.'

'So you got the work, then?' exclaimed Daisy, her face lighting up. 'Wot about me? Did you say that you 'ad a sister at home who'll work 'er fingers to the bone?'

'No, I never. You find your own employment, miss.'

'Well, I will, then!' Daisy said, grabbing Willy's hand again. 'Come on. We'll ask up the 'ardware shop. I've 'eard they need a skivvy.' With that she dragged Willy away, leaving Maria and Steffan to gaze fondly after them.

'She has guts . . . I will say that.'

'Do you think so? I would call it something else but I'll give 'er the benefit of the doubt.' She slowly turned to look into Steffan's face and noticed that he had been hurt. 'I was just going into the coffee shop. You can join me if you like.'

'I would like to. Thank you very much.' He held out his hand and spoke quietly. 'My name's Steffan. Steffan Tremain.'

'Mine's Maria. Maria Bertram.'

'I know, and I'm pleased to meet you properly, Maria, instead of just passing as neighbours. Are you sure you don't mind my joining you?'

'I wouldn't 'ave asked, would I, if I minded,' she said, smiling, all inhibitions suddenly gone. 'Come on.'

Believing Steffan to be shy and self-conscious, she tried to think of something to say that might help him relax. She couldn't think of anything, but it didn't seem to matter. This was a busy market day, and with so many people about, and so much going on around them, there could hardly be embarrassing silences.

As he opened the coffee-shop door for her in a natural and easy manner she found that her opinion of him was changing. She had thought him to be a little superior, but was now wondering whether she had been too judgmental and unfair in appraising him before they had even spoken. Maybe he hadn't been snubbing them all this time but was too polite to push his way into a world where he felt he didn't belong. If she were truly honest with herself, Maria would have to admit that neither she nor the others had been altogether fair or hospitable, even though there had always been an air of mystery surrounding him and his father. Now, with her curiosity piqued, she wanted to know more about him. One thing was for certain . . . she felt easy in his company.

Settled at a small round table by the window in the busy coffee shop, she glanced through a dirty window to the back yard while Steffan ordered their coffee. She told herself not to fire questions at him but wait for him to open up the conversation. Her impression of him, after all was said and done, had changed within a very short space of time, which in itself was unnerving. Questions were flying through her mind. Why should she suddenly feel as if she had known him for a long time? Why was she warming so instantaneously to his manner, his honest, open face and gentle smile? He was taller than she'd thought too. Taller and more mature. And those eyes, those expressive light blue eyes, one minute sad and the next laughing.

'What happened to your father, Maria?' she heard him say, almost as if he were speaking from another world and not the one she was in. Pushing her fleeting intimate thoughts from her mind, she brought herself back to the present moment as his voice continued to drift across her. He had asked her a question. She tipped her head forward a little and paid attention, while her inner voice whispered, *His hair is much lighter too.*

'I know from the conversations in the yard that he died a relatively young man. Was it an accident or illness?'

'Tuberculosis,' she murmured, open to any question he wanted to ask no matter how intimate or personal. 'How did you know he'd died?' she heard herself say. 'He could have left us, for all you know.'

He shrugged and his expression became sad. 'It can be very lonely at times in those rooms so I suppose I've got into the habit of listening to the conversations below, and sometimes I involve myself as if I'm part of it all. Putting my views forward. A participant in debates with no one listening.' He quietly chuckled, amused by himself. 'I've learnt everything about everybody from listening to Sophie and Angel in my unsoundproof room.'

'Well then, you could probably tell me a thing or two,' she said, touched by his honesty. 'You know more about my family and neighbours than I know about yours.'

'That's true,' he said, in a low, soft voice which abruptly changed to one more serious and matter-of-fact. 'My mother left my father and he brought me to London against the wishes of my grandparents, who I was very close to. That was six years ago. I've seen none of my family since then. I could be dead for all they know.'

'But surely you kept in touch?'

'No. My father forbade it at first and I could see his reasons . . . then. He'd brought shame on the family name, and once we were in London things went from bad to worse. He insisted they shouldn't know just how bad it was, and that if they found out my grandmother would probably have a heart attack.' Glancing up at the young girl who had fetched their hot drinks to the table, he nodded a polite thank-you as she put them down and left.

'And your mother?' said Maria, sipping her coffee.

'I wouldn't know where to start looking for her. I did write to my maternal grandmother when we first came to London and she wrote back saying she didn't know where her daughter had escaped to. I could tell that she had cried while writing to me, and I didn't have the heart to tell her what I was going through. She couldn't have done much about my situation, if anything. So I thought it best to let her forget me.'

Her eyes cast down, Maria was suddenly overcome with a rush of compassion for someone who she could so easily have befriended before now, instead of going along with others in their belief that strangers were to be kept at arm's length until they knocked on your own front door. 'I'm sorry,' she whispered, lowering her eyes. 'I didn't realise that you were so sad.' Embarrassed by her own words, she felt the blood rush to her cheeks and couldn't think of anything else to say to him.

'I'm not sad any more, Maria. I intend to find my mother, and soon. I shall go to my grandmother in Loughton first. Now that I can present a less pathetic figure. Much better they don't know what I've been through. It's all over, in any case. I'm all right now.' He looked at her and offered a faint smile. 'I look all right, don't I? I don't look as if I've been living in hell?'

'No, of course not. And you *haven't*. We're not that bad, and I know Kelly's Yard's not a palace but—'

'I didn't mean that. I meant before I came here, and in particular when I first came to London. My life in Shadwell has been good in comparison to that.' He sipped his coffee and waited for the next question, but it was not forthcoming. Clearly Maria was waiting for him to tell her more – the expression on her face was evidence of that.

'Living above a stable's not as bad as living next door to the prison, cleaning barges and killing rats to pay the rent money, and it's better than the lodgings we shared in Back Lane over Bethnal Green way.'

'You lived next door to a prison? Whatever for? Was your father the warden? Is that the reason why?'

'No.' Steffan laughed. 'He would probably have liked that, mind you. Yes, he would have loved it, in fact. You could say that he's on the side of dictatorship.'

'Do you know what I think?' said Maria, leaning back in her chair and smiling at him. 'I think that you're kidding me, Steffan Tremain. Telling pork pies. Why would anyone choose to live of all places next to a prison?' She sipped her coffee and held his gaze. 'You've got a dry sense of humour ... I will say that.'

A thoughtful expression replaced his smile and there

was a different look in his eyes. A look of relaxed honesty. 'What makes you think I chose it?'

'You mean you were forced, then?'

'Circumstances forced me to it, yes. And before you ask, I live in Kelly's Yard out of choice by comparison. It's not only affordable rent but well situated for work. When we first came I imagined I'd be labouring in one of the riverside wharfs and was prepared for it, but by a stroke of luck my father bumped into an old chum and business colleague here in London and he put a word in at the railway for the both of us. I work at Hackney Wick station and my father at Fenchurch Street.'

Maria was intrigued. He clearly didn't want to elaborate further as to why he had lodged by a prison, and she could only presume from this that his family had fallen from grace, as the gossips would have it. 'A friend in need is a friend indeed.' She smiled, for want of anything else to say to him.

Sensing her embarrassment, Steffan smoothly changed the mood and turned the conversation away from his personal life. 'Sophie the mattress-filler and Angel Black are very funny. I'm not sure if she knows it or not. I love listening to her . . . to all of them, in fact. Those rooms we live in were not built for the purpose of living. They've been botched and nowhere near good enough to make them soundproof. Far from it.'

'You poor devil.' She chuckled. 'Having to listen to all of that *and* put up with the smell.'

'It's not too bad if you keep the windows shut. And *you* have to put up with it too.'

'I've grown up with it, though. There's the difference. You've known a different life, if I'm not mistaken.'

'You're not mistaken, no, but it seems like an age ago. I lived next to the prison so I could visit my father and because it came with work, which allowed me to pay the rent and earn enough to keep the wolf from my door. I was miserable and I was lonely but I got through it.'

'Your father was in prison?' Maria could hardly believe it.

'Yes. For two years. I could have lived in the prison as many other families who had nowhere to go did but I chose not to. He was bound over until he could pay his debts. He had to stay until he could claim release under the Insolvent Debtors Act. My grandfather wouldn't forgive him for the way he had behaved and the shame he had brought on the family. I knew he would never pay the debts – they were quite a few thousand pounds – and had no idea how long the sentence would be. It turned out to be two years.'

'Your father was in *prison* and you lived next door so as to be able to visit him every day?' said Maria, finding his story too incredible to believe, and yet she could see he was telling the truth.

'I was fourteen at the time and frightened at being alone in London. At least he wasn't as far away as my mother or my grandparents,' he said. Leaning back in his chair, he turned his head slightly to avoid her searching eyes, her warm, telling brown eyes. 'We moved a few times between him being released and coming to Shadwell. I suppose you could say we've settled into a routine at last. A rather monotonous routine but a stable one at least . . . if you'll excuse the pun.' Sipping his coffee again and looking at her, he said, 'But I do like it in the yard. It's lively and the people are funny. Down-to-earth.'

Stunned by his casual telling of something so shocking, Maria did her best to act natural and decided to keep off the subject of jail. 'So how long do you think you'll stay for? Always?'

'No. I shall be moving on when the time's right . . . in search of my mother. Not that my father has any idea of that. I'm an only child, Maria,' he said, looking into her eyes. 'I want to find my mother.'

'I'm sure you must,' Maria murmured, feeling peculiarly close to someone that really she had only just met.

'Don't be downhearted over it,' he said, quietly laughing. 'I will find her. When the time's right. I'm not miserable any more over it, so why should you be?'

'I'm not, I'm not,' she said, shaking her head slowly. 'It's just that it must 'ave been lonely living all by yourself at that age, in a strange area, and not knowing a soul. It must 'ave been!'

'It was at times. Yes, there were times when I could hardly bear it. But it doesn't matter any more. I went out for long walks and that helped. I got through it, Maria . . . I got through it and here I am to prove it. Here with you, happy and carefree and telling you things about my miserable past to depress you. I apologise.'

'I'm glad you told me.' She laid the tips of her

fingers on his hand, murmuring, 'Now that we've broken the ice . . . let's be friends, Steffan. We are close neighbours, after all.'

'I'd like that very much, Maria,' he said, gazing into her eyes and sending a rush of love through her.

Drawing breath, Steffan took her hand in his and brought it to his lips, brushing a kiss across her fingers. 'You're kind and sweet and I'm getting emotional and so I'm going to change the subject. Your sister Daisy is a gem and very funny.'

'No, she's not – she's a minx,' said Maria, slipping her hand out of his. 'Won't do as she's told and doesn't give tuppence what people think.'

'I know.' He grinned. 'That's why she's funny. I expect your mother found it hard looking after all three of you once she was made a widow?'

'At first. But we manage now. We don't go hungry, but I s'pose you could say we live like paupers. But that'll change in time. Once we're all earning a living. Willy can start working as soon as he's eight if we wanted but Mum's keeping 'im on at school till he's ten and then he'll go to the tin box factory in Wapping where Sophie's sons work. A relative of hers will put in a good word for 'im. Daisy could walk out of school any time and find factory work but she won't. She'll stop there till she's ten. She'd miss all the books and the learning and she knows it.

'The work I found in Covent Garden of a Saturday will help in the meantime. Every shilling counts, especially when you have a plan.'

'And you have one?'

'Mum does and I go along with it. It's what Dad wanted and what he would have made happen. We'll take a train ride up to the North of England and start a new life. Now you know why every shilling counts.'

'I know already, Maria. I of all people know the value of money. It shouldn't be the way it is but that's life. A healthy bank account gives you the freedom to live the way you want.'

'Oh, I don't expect we'll 'ave a bank account.' She laughed. 'Just enough to keep us warm in the winter with food in our bellies. That's all we're after. And a healthier way of life closer to the countryside. It may be a pipe dream but it keeps us going.'

'There's nothing wrong with holding on to dreams. It's what kept me going when I was at my lowest ebb, soon after I left Saffron Walden, where I was very happy.'

'Before the embarrassment?'

'Yes, before the lives of my family crumbled.'

'It must 'ave been so different from the way we all live in Kelly's Yard,' said Maria. 'Really different.'

'It was,' he replied with a faraway look clouding his face.

'I've never been out of London . . . all I know of other ways of life is what I read when I'm in the public library. Olly's second-hand penny novels are nothing to go by.'

Steffan leaned back in his chair, admiring wisps of soft golden-brown hair that had tumbled loose and framed her face. 'Saffron Walden is the most beautiful place in the world. Our house, timber framed with woodland gardens, had two-thirds of its land in Thaxted parish and one third in Broxted parish.'

'So you lived on the border in utter disorder.'

'As it turned out, we did, yes. Not that my mother and I knew what my father was really up to. But then, as they say, ignorance is bliss. We enjoyed our time living in Essex.'

'I would love to live in the country,' she murmured, 'I really would.'

'Well . . . if I were to choose anywhere I think it would be Thaxted in Essex. Small leafy lanes leading to windmills and small farms, a rustic barn-like church, the hustle and bustle in the market square and . . . according to folklore Dick Turpin was born close by in one of the old inns. Apparently he was a rather gay young man about town. Quick tempered and lacked enterprise, if you can believe that.'

'I can believe anything.' Maria laughed. 'Enough goes on in these parts to take any stardust out of your eyes. Anyone else famous live there?'

'Not that I know of. That's my only claim to fame. While you, born and bred here in this part of London which is steeped in history and famous people . . .'

'Lot of good it does us,' she said, interrupting his flow.

'Oh, don't be too quick to put it down. Saffron Walden may have lovely old houses and there were no pickpockets, swindlers and forgers mingling with the crowds, but it lacks London colour. It was all very proper there. Even the beggars coming in from the countryside were polite. But London is unique. I've walked all over it, I should think, and it's so vastly different in parts. Yes, there is the mud, dirt, damp, fog and rats, but it's a wonderfully historic town.

'The historic buildings are fascinating. Northumberland House in the Strand was my favourite, with the elegant lion holding sway above the parapet. I was lucky to see that building before they demolished it. I think my favourite, though, are the eighteenth-century carvings of Gog and Magog at the Guildhall.'

'Gog and Magog?' Maria chuckled. 'Man and wife, were they?'

'Hardly. In the Old Testament Gog is a prince in the land of Magog, who leads the barbarian tribes of the North in an assault on Israel. In Genesis Magog is the son of Japheth, living north of Israel. In the New Testament the names reappear as nations that make war on the Kingdom of Christ.'

'Sounds like I should read the Bible more often. And if you really think that looking at old buildings is more interesting than living in the countryside and studying nature, your Saffron Walden must have been a little bit on the stuffy side?'

'No . . . just very different to London.' He leaned forward and looked directly into her eyes, ready to tease her. 'It's called Saffron Walden because of the crocuses which were originally grown there to produce the saffron herb, which was smuggled into this country from Greece and grown in sufficient quantities to merit the town changing its name from Chepyng Walden to Saffron Walden in the sixteenth century.' He leaned back again and smiled. 'So you see . . . I *am* proud of our history. But are you proud of your London's architecture? I don't think you are.'

'I've never thought about it. It's too boring. But . . . did you know that a sailor coming in from abroad sold an unknown plant at the Prospect of Whitby and a local market gardener who purchased it named it fuchsia?'

'I didn't know that; but I do know that the Prospect was once the gruesome setting for the public execution of pirates and one of the most famous to be hanged there was Captain Kidd.'

'Yeah, that's common knowledge. But not many people know about the stolen plant that became the fuchsia. Only locals know that. Our river front might be decrepit but it's famous *and* the stench has gone now. Now that they've got the Embankment in full swing.'

'You're proud of where you live, Maria, and that's good. Not everyone is that lucky.'

'If you say so. What sort of a house did you live in before London? Did you have servants? A butler?'

'No. We had an orphan girl, Molly, who lived in, and a couple of women who used to come in from a nearby village . . . oh, and there was a cook who shared the attic rooms with Molly and there was the old laundress who came in daily.' A huge smile spread across his face and his blue eyes were shining. 'You could easily imagine *she'd* stepped straight out of the seventeenth century. She spoke in Old English and was forever taking snuff and was all doom and gloom. The first time she told me that the world was coming to an end I was terrified. I must have been about four years old but I remember it to this day. Sophie in the yard reminds me of her.

'And she never spoke with a worried voice but with a kind of mirth, as if she relished the day when we would all be blown to smithereens – according to her version of the Bible, rich and poor together suffering the same indignities.'

'Does sound a bit like Sophie Marcovitch in the yard. She never sees the bright side of anything.'

'Exactly. I love listening to her. She's so funny – she brightens my day.'

'What about a nanny? Did you have one of them fussing over you?'

'No. I spent most of my early years in the company of my mother and my paternal grandfather. He took me everywhere – to the blacksmith, the carpenter, the oar-maker, the rope-maker. The list is endless. He wanted me to see how things were made and who made them. I loved those outings.'

'But you must 'ave had a governess? All rich children do, don't they?'

'Most, I suppose,' he said, reflectively, 'but not me. Once I was old enough I went to an ordinary school. My mother was my first teacher. Taught me *and* let me draw and paint for an hour each day. My father was against that, of course. So we kept my sketches and paintings hidden away. He ruled with the birch, I'm afraid. My mother, on the other hand, was loving and thoughtful and the most unselfish person. She always put herself last.' There was an emotional pause as Steffan closed his eyes and pressed his lips together.

Gently squeezing his hand, Maria whispered, 'You don't have to go on telling me about it if it's too upsetting. I shouldn't have asked. I'm sorry.'

'It's all right,' he said, withdrawing his hand and covering his face. 'Give me a minute. It's just that I've not spoken properly like this to anyone in a very long time.'

'Well, there we are, then. Maybe the time's come for it. You can't bottle up grief all your life. It's not right. And anyway, it's what the tear ducts are for. Have a cry, if you want to.'

'No. I don't need to,' he said, pulling a handkerchief from his pocket and composing himself. 'It's so good being able to talk, I can't tell you.'

'Of course it is.' Maria sat quietly and waited for him to either clamp up or go on.

'To be honest with you, I've not really had a proper conversation with anyone since I was fourteen, if you can believe that. Well . . . except for earlier today. Someone called Wilkie Crow spoke to me as if I was a real person and not invisible.' Again he only just managed to control his feelings. 'A few words exchanged in a shop or at the railway station is all there's been.' He blotted his watery eyes and took a long deep breath. 'That's better. It all seems to be pouring out today. I expect that's what it is.'

'It's all right. You don't 'ave to apologise.'

'I'm not . . . at least, I don't think I am. But I've kept you long enough,' he said, clearing his throat, 'and I'm due at the railway in just over an hour.'

'It's a fair walk to Hackney Wick from Whitechapel.'

Maria smiled. 'So you had best go. But we will do this again, Steffan. And you've got to break this daft idea that you're not part of the yard – and don't tell me that you've not bin thinking that way because I can tell that you must have.' She leaned back in her chair and held his gaze, murmuring, 'Knock and the door shall be opened?'

'Yes . . . you're right. You're right. I just—' He flapped a hand and smiled properly again. 'Let's leave it at that for now.'

'I agree. And if it's of any help I'll just say this and no more. I've not had a conversation like this, ever. Not ever, Steffan. The banter in the yard is good for different reasons but it's nothing like this. Now, go away before I start to cry.'

'So we're proper friends, then? As well as neighbours?'

'We're whatever you want us to be,' she said without thinking, and then quickly checked herself. 'Except man and wife, of course. I wouldn't want you for a husband.'

'And I wouldn't want you for a wife.' He laughed.

'Now then. I'm leaving first instead of you because I reckon you need five minutes sitting here by yourself,' said Maria, rising from her chair. 'I'll see you in the yard later on. Mum'll be worrying where I've got to with the shopping. If you see that brother and sister of mine, send 'em straight home for me. They'll listen to you.'

'Do you really think so?'

'Wouldn't say it otherwise. I can always tell by the way they are with certain people.' Adjusting her straw bonnet, she said, 'That Daisy'll get Willy into bad habits if we're not careful. She doesn't care what she does, that's the trouble.'

Steffan splayed his hands. 'And who's to say she's not right?'

'I am. And another thing. I want to hear more about your mum and your grandparents, so don't go clamping up again. I'm a nosy cow, that's my trouble.' With that, Maria left the coffee shop and Steffan to himself.

After enjoying a few reflective moments by himself, Steffan, feeling like a different person and with a lighter spring in his step, made his way through the people's market oblivious to the hustle and bustle going on around him. He was remembering the first time he had caught sight of Maria from his window. He could hardly believe that he had all but told her his life story in one sitting and after having only just introduced himself. He supposed it was all down to the girl, who had in her own natural way brought him out of himself and drawn him into not only thinking about his past, but talking about it. He felt as if a thick heavy cloud which had engulfed him since the day his mother had left was beginning to lift. As the memories of his home in Saffron Walden and the years he had spent there continued to flood back, it felt to him as if a heavy locked door had begun to slowly open, allowing a thin stream of sunny light to filter through.

His thoughts turned to those who had been part of the family scene, and especially to the gardener, the kind, elderly Lenny, who was forever picking up Celtic and Roman artefacts and bringing them in to show him. With one recollection sparking off another, he recalled the day when Lenny had brought him here to London by railway and taken him on a short sightseeing tour. Curiously, the place he remembered most vividly was Smithfield. The point of the visit to the meat market had been for the old gentleman to meet up with his brother for their once-a-year reunion, and at the same time give Steffan a short tour of a world he had no inkling of. To see pickled tongues, oxtails, pig's trotters and sheep's head was repulsive to a six-year-old, but at the same time fascinating. Sickening though the smell had been, it had not put him off. The carcasses of dead animals hanging row upon row had provoked his young creative mind, and for a few months afterwards his drawings had been a touch gruesome. Although he had obeyed his mother's concerned edict that he draw more pleasant subjects, those earlier impressions had stayed with him. The subjects he had chosen to draw or paint were not only of the animal kingdom but of men and women too.

One particular memory caused him to smile as he recalled his paternal grandfather roaring with laughter and slapping his knee when Steffan had related the butchery he had seen in Smithfield and asked which of the animals they might be having for dinner that evening. His Grandfather Tremain was so unlike Steffan's father that it now seemed almost impossible that they were father and son. His grandfather had always been one for cracking jokes and telling long-drawn-out stories of when he was a boy; frightening tales of how very strict *his* parents had been and how they had forever been saying how easy children had it. Steffan's father had told no such stories and had hardly ever made a jest or laughed, except for those times when he was being facetious and was in high spirits from drinking too much.

His gracious Grandmother Tremain, who simply adored Steffan, was a calm, content woman, happy to let her husband spend enjoyable hours settled in his favourite armchair in his study, puffing at his pipe and reading his favourite author, Charles Dickens, and his much-loved poetry by Alfred Tennyson. It was in this room that the warm and kindly gentleman had begun telling his grandson stories to make his hair curl.

Steffan's favourite family outings had almost certainly been when his father had been absent and when his grandfather had ferried himself, his mother and grandmother in his beloved boat downriver, mooring at riverside inns where, after lunch, Steffan would be allowed to watch the ships, schooners, barges and yachts sailing by and draw pictures of the river traffic or people on the river bank under the watchful eye of the caring adults. His love for drawing and painting had never left him, and this gift had been his saving grace while living alone in those dingy, cold rooms into which the sunshine never penetrated. The only window faced a very tall and old crumbling damp wall. With no company, and his father in the grimmest prison imaginable, he had used his private solitude to sketch and paint away the hours, which would otherwise have dragged slowly by.

Preoccupied by his memories, Steffan was only partially aware of the people around him, and when he felt someone pulling sharply on his coat sleeve, he stopped abruptly in his tracks, causing a flower seller walking behind him to almost drop her basket. Apologising profusely to the woman, he turned round to see Daisy and Willy staring up at him.

'Fanks for not telling Fish-face what we was up to,' said Daisy. 'She would 'ave took our money away, you know.'

'Well,' said Steffan, only just managing to keep a straight face, 'I didn't know that but I do know that she wouldn't have been too pleased to see her brother and sister begging.'

'We wasn't begging! We was gettin' change, that's all! It's not our fault if people wanna give us money, is it?'

'That's one way of looking at it, I suppose.'

''Course it is. I'm sixpence better off and Willy's got threepence. We're goin' up the fairground to spend it.' With one eye closed and her nose wrinkled, she peered at him, saying, 'You ain't gonna tell Maria, are yer?'

'No. It's none of my business, and besides, I'm not one for telling tales out of school. I shan't say anything, but should you really be going to the fairground by yourselves?'

She looked oddly at him. 'Whyever not?'

'Do you think you'll be safe without a guardian?'

''Course we will.' She chuckled. 'The sort of bad men you're finking abaht 'ang around the work'ouses if they wanna take children and make 'em their slaves an' that. They're the ones who get dragged off, not us. We ain't bleedin' work'ouse kids, are we? We've got a proper 'ome an' a muvver.'

Steffan seemed to be learning more in one day about

this part of London and the way things worked in the slums than in two years of having lived in Kelly's Yard. 'Well, just be careful is all I'm saying. There's far more traffic on the streets nowadays. You don't want to be trampled by horses.'

Curling her top lip and eyeing him with uncertainty, Daisy murmured, 'I've never seen anyone trampled. Never in me life.'

'I'm pleased to hear it.' He tipped his hat and turned away, smiling.

'Oi, mister!' called Daisy suddenly.

Turning slowly round and just managing to keep a straight face, he looked back at their seemingly angelic expressions. 'Yes?'

'Have you got two farvings for a ha'penny, please, sir? Only I want to share this ha'penny wiv this poor little orphan I found crying in a shop doorway.'

'Yes, I have, thank you. And I'm keeping them, if it's all the same to you.'

'Tight bugger,' murmured Daisy, watching him walk away.

'D'yer fink he'll tell on us, Dai?'

'Nar. He's all right. Warned us that Maria was abaht, didn't he? Bit soft in the 'ead, that's all.' She gripped her brother's hand tighter and dragged him along, weaving him through the crowds. 'He'll soon learn.'

'Where we goin' now, Dai? To the funfair?'

'Nar, not yet. We ain't earned enough for rides and toffee apples.'

3

---◆---

As Maria dressed for work on this sunny August morning, she found herself thinking of her father, who had been drifting in and out of her dreams on and off throughout the night. She was remembering the times when he would read to her before bedtime and on Sunday afternoons. Up until she was ten years old she had been an only child, and life had seemed carefree. Her father, William, had been in full-time employment, and her mother was working in a tiny basement hat-making factory in Cambridgeheath to which Maria would be taken each day; she was paid threepence and a currant bun for sweeping up the felt cuttings. Six months after her sister Daisy had been born, once she was weaned off the breast, their mother returned to her former employment at the milliner's, but this time leaving Maria at home to look after her baby sister. It was not until the birth of Willy that Liza stopped going to work altogether and Maria went out into the working world, employed for various small businesses as bookkeeper and note-taker until she finally secured the position she had been working towards in a much larger company, Bollards.

Light in spirit at having been able to revive those

memories of happy times without feeling the pain of having lost her beloved father, Maria strolled through the half-moon passage and out into the long, winding cobbled street which ran almost all the way down to the river. She was oblivious to the people milling around. Charlie the cart-pusher, on seeing her, called out her name and beckoned her over.

'Whatever's the matter, Charlie?' she said, moving closer to him and looking around. 'Why are all these people out so early? Has there bin an accident?'

The old boy pushed back his battered trilby and dabbed his sweat-beaded brow. 'Has there bin an accident? Well, I would like to think so, Maria,' he said, shaking his head. 'I would like to think it was an accident but that's not what they're saying. 'Course, I 'aven't seen it m'self so I couldn't say for certain or speak the truth. But there . . . who can speak the truth when no one ever sees a thing when it comes down to murder?' He pushed his friendly face a little closer to Maria's. 'The loud-mouths go silent when it's a serious business. Petrified of their own shadows are them that are only too quick to shout and swear and curse when there's no reason. When there's something more pressing to attend to they're the ones who slip into the shadows, hiding and watching in fear.'

'Charlie? What are you goin' on about?' snapped Maria, knowing she would be in serious trouble if she was late for work. 'I don't 'ave many minutes but now you've got me thinking I must know what's happened! You've something awful to tell me?'

'Well, no, you don't want to be late for work, Maria.

They'll sack you for less. You go on and I'll see you later on wiv a full report. I can't say fairer than that, can I?'

'Is it a dreadful accident, then? Is this why the crowds 'ave come out? Morbid sightseeing?'

'Well, I hope so and that's all I can say. We 'aven't 'ad a murder down in Tobacco Dock before and I wouldn't like to think we've got one now.'

'Murder? But I thought you were—'

'Joshing? No. No, I wouldn't jest over such a thing, Maria. But you get off to work and leave the fact-finding to me.' With that he pulled the brim of his hat down to shield his eyes from the sun. 'Go on now. Your muvver needs your wages. Four mouths to feed . . . that's more than enough to worry over.'

Stunned by what she might learn, Maria looked about herself at the excited gathering crowds and spotted Olly the rag-and-bone man in the centre of a small noisy group of people who clearly had the look of fear in their eyes but were nevertheless fired up. Olly was as usual the centre of attention. Hoping she might get a short rundown from him of what all the hysteria was about, she eased her way through until she was close enough to catch his eye. But Olly had a new audience today. Rich as well as poor. Word spread quickly when murder was on the lips, and he was entertaining a few wealthy outsiders and doing his best to draw them into the yard and to the back of the stable.

Pulling on Olly's sleeve as she came up to him, Maria demanded to know what was going on. His eyes narrowed as he put his lips to her ear and confided, 'Business is business, Maria. A crowd's bin drawn so leave me be, there's a good girl. This may well turn out to be a blessing in disguise for me. Don't forget it's not just old rags I collect from wealthy areas. I've quite a few bits and bobs tucked away. Other people's junk 'as sometimes turned out to be a nice little earner. Get my drift?' Giving her a wink, he pushed his shoulders back and sported the look of a businessman.

'I see what you're saying, Olly, but the place is buzzing and they're talking about a murder. What's going on?'

'Well, be all accounts they've pulled a penny farthing out of the river down by Miller's Wharf late last night. Now there's talk of dragging out a body which is part-way trapped under an oyster boat. They say it's the body of a woman seen riding the bicycle. A posh sightseer or summink.' His sharp, dark brown eyes were darting from one punter to another as he spoke. Posh sightseers rumoured to be murdered would bring more posh and rich people into the area and Olly could smell moneyed people a mile off.

Maria pulled her neighbour to one side. 'Olly, posh people don't *buy* second-'and clothes – they *give* 'em away. And posh people don't ride bicycles down by the river at night. Especially not a lady.'

''Course they don't buy clothes, Maria,' he said, speaking out of the corner of his mouth. 'I know that. It's my antiques I'm baiting 'em to. This could go on for weeks. Your Daisy still indoors, is she?'

'She's not up yet, Olly, and when she is she'll be

flying out of the yard, late for school. And you haven't got antiques, just old junk. Why do you ask about Daisy?'

'Gonna get 'er to 'elp set up my old market stall out the back and make a nice show of me bric-a-brac and antiques. How comes she's still going to school, in any case? They shove 'em out once they've turned eight. Should be earning a living be now.'

'She does find work here and there but she wants to keep on learning. You haven't *got* any antiques, Olly.'

''Course I 'ave! All hidden away in boxes, mind. You can pick up some good stuff if you've got a good eye,' he said, giving her a sly wink. 'You can fetch them old paintings down, if you like. Get a few bob for them, you will. I won't charge much commission. Learning what exactly?'

'Anything she can. You told Dad they weren't worth the canvas they're painted on.'

'Well, yes . . . but that was when he was alive and not short of a penny. I wouldn't short-change a widow, Maria. You should know me better'n that.' He leaned back and peered at her. 'You mean that little cow Daisy likes school?'

'No, she likes learning. Takes after Dad. I hope there's not been a murder, Olly,' she said, looking around and suddenly worried by the ever-increasing mob. Their faces were filled with fear, anger and lust for more information. 'Has the body of a woman really been pulled out of the river? Is that why more people are pouring in?'

'It's wot I 'eard,' he said. 'And there's no smoke

wivout fire. Look at this lot. Shot out of the woodwork, wouldn't you say?'

Catching sight of two policemen in the crowd, Maria tensed. 'Well, let Mum and Daisy know for me, will you? And keep an eye out for Willy, he—'

'Stop worrying your pretty head over it. Olly's 'ere. No harm'll come to anyone from our yard, don't you worry. Asking for trouble, wasn't she? Flaunting 'er silks and satins and no doubt a string of pearls round 'er neck. Won't be there now, though, will they? Be lining some thief-in-the-night's pocket.'

'Oh God . . . it makes my blood run cold. You will let Mum know right away, won't you?'

'Yes, yes, yes. I'll get in the yard and announce the news to them who 'aven't come out by now to see wot it's all about.' Shaking his head, he walked through the alley into the yard, reluctant to leave possible customers behind. 'The trouble wiv you, Olly Black,' he murmured, 'is that you was born to be a businessman but people keep stopping you from being one!'

Arriving at Bollards at sixes and sevens, having walked far too quickly with the bright morning sun in her eyes, and out of breath, Maria entered the factory, leaned on a wall in the dimly lit entrance and collected herself. The nightwatchman, out of uniform and back in his ordinary clothes, gave her a cautious look. 'You're seven minutes late, Maria. This is never like you. What 'appened? Is your mother ill?'

'No,' said Maria, drawing a long breath, her eyes closed. 'I'll be all right in a minute, once I get my breath back. I walked as fast as I could to get 'ere on time. Now I've got a terrible stitch in my side.'

'You must come up with a good reason for this,' said the worldly gentleman, who had been working in this place for years and had witnessed people in tears of joy after being hired and the faces of misery when wretched souls had been fired. 'The road to hell is paved with good intentions. That's the motto in this place. If you use a weak excuse you'll be out on your ear. Mark my words.'

'I know.' Straightening and sporting a confident expression, she said, 'I'll be all right. Stop worrying. Go on. Off you go. You look dog tired. See you tomorrow morning.'

'Well, I shall hope for the best and prepare for the worst,' he replied ominously. He tipped his cap and turned away to push open the heavy timber-and-glass double doors, his expression one of sympathy.

'So shall I,' said Maria in a quiet voice, 'so shall I.'

On her arrival on the third floor, she found Miss Drake, a grey-haired spinster in her mid-forties, waiting for her, hands clasped in a devout fashion and a look of remonstration on her ashen face, which looked as if it had never seen the light of day. In cold silence this thin woman, dressed in an immaculate brown blouse with a high stiff collar and matching skirts, waited. Her steely grey eyes glaring out over her pince-nez were directed at Maria's flushed face. Waiting for an explanation, the woman lifted one eyebrow a fraction. 'Silence is not necessarily a virtue, Miss Bertram!'

'I'm sorry to be so late, Miss Drake.'

'Reason?' snapped the woman.

'There's been a *murder!*' said Maria, losing a little of her control. 'Close to where I live.'

'I asked you for a reason for being late, Miss Bertram. And since *you* are not the victim of this so-called murder it is not a reason. You will make up the time by working through your twenty-minute lunch break and stay a further twenty minutes after the bell as a penance.'

Forced to look at this cold and hateful woman for a few seconds, Maria felt a strong desire to speak her mind and turn away from this austere place, but she could not afford to do what she wanted. Instead she brought to mind something that Angel Black from the yard had once told her: 'When face to face with them that fancy they're above you imagine 'em wivout any clothes on, or on the lav.' The thought of Miss Drake in her altogether unwittingly brought a faint smile to her lips. 'I accept my penalty, Miss Drake, and wish to be excused so that I may be a good employee and get to my work.'

This intelligent and polite reply was spoken with a voice tinged with apology which disarmed the hardened woman but did not crack her invisible armour. 'Tell that to Mr Clarkson, who is waiting in his office. And I should wipe the smile from your face, madam. The chief of personnel need not tolerate defiance and contempt as I must.' She then turned away and, with one leg marginally shorter than the other, marched along a corridor, her footsteps echoing. And now Maria, feeling very much alone in a world that suddenly felt alien to her, had to face her superior, Mr Clarkson. Tapping softly on his office door, she could feel her heart beating faster and beads of sweat breaking out on the palms of her hands. Listening intently, she thought she heard a sound coming from inside the room but couldn't quite be certain. She tapped again, this time with a little more conviction. The thunderous roar of her senior's voice caused her to freeze on the spot. 'Come in, damn you!'

With trembling fingers she turned the brass handle of the heavy mahogany door and slowly pushed it open, fearing this man as if he were a hunter waiting with a gun.

'Are you deaf as *well* as a bad timekeeper, young lady?'

'No, sir. I just wasn't sure whether I heard your voice or not and I didn't want to intrude or disturb you.'

A loud grunt was his reply as he glanced at a note on his desk.

'Kindly take a seat, Miss Bertram. This is not a railway station.'

'Yes, sir,' murmured Maria, forcing back her tears. 'There is a reason why I was late, sir . . .'

Flashing a look of disapproval, he silenced her. 'You have much to learn, young lady. In these offices, you speak only when you are spoken to and furthermore you do not speak with your colleagues while in this building.' He tapped a black book lying to one side of the desk. 'And please do not attempt to deny it. It's written in the book. You were seen. One complaint over your conduct is serious enough. Now we have another rule broken. You arrive late into these premises looking somewhat dishevelled and ill at ease, which does not bode well, Miss Bertram. It does not bode well at all!'

'I apologise for speaking to a colleague, sir, and that shan't happen again. As for my timekeeping, I have not once been a minute late before. In fact I have made it a principle to be here a few minutes early. This morning I could not make my way through the streets surrounding the place where I live. It was crowded with journalists and policemen, to say nothing of all the neighbours.'

'How so?' he said, his tone surprisingly changed at the mention of police and journalists.

'There's talk of a murder, sir. Of a woman whose penny farthing was pulled out of the river in the night and the body of that woman now trapped in the river, halfway under a boat.'

'I see,' he said, rubbing his chin and avoiding her eyes in case she should see the glint in his own. This talk of murder was causing a rush of adrenalin. 'Well, obviously you will have avoided asking questions at the scene of the crime, since it would take up too much of your time, so I assume that all you tell me is from hearsay?'

'Yes, sir. Although the police would not be there without good reason. I was very worried for my widowed mother and my eight-year-old sister. I wanted to go back home and tell them to stay inside but I couldn't do that. I couldn't let Miss Drake down so badly.'

'So you resisted a strong family commitment for the sake of the firm. I commend you, Miss Bertram!' Smiling, he looked from her pretty face to her shapely body. 'I shall see to it that this particular late mark be removed from the book. I'm a fair man – always have been; always will be. But on the matter of conversing and wasting the time of one of our most promising draughtsmen I stand firm. We'll have no more of it. Is that understood?'

'Yes, sir.'

'Very well, then. You may take your leave. And please instruct Miss Drake to send out the messenger for the latest edition. I should like to read up on this dramatic turn of events. Murders such as this do not happen on the hour every day.'

'Yes, sir. Thank you, sir,' said Maria, eager to be out of this room and away from this man's leering eyes.

Slyly watching her as she turned and walked across the office, he felt the blood rushing to his prized possession, now a little stiff from imagining her unclothed body and the smoothness of her skin. He shifted in his seat and cleared his throat. Maria turned back to face him. 'I shouldn't take that woman too much to heart, if I were you,' he said, his voice soft and intimate. 'Miss Drake has not experienced the warmth a husband brings. Her heart is as cold as her bed and she will bring that chill into this building with her.' He looked directly into Maria's eyes, a lecherous smile on his face. 'But of course, that must be strictly between the two of us, my dear.'

Lowering her eyes, with one hand on the door

handle, Maria could hardly believe the sudden change in her superior. He was talking to her almost conspiratorially, and as if she were his equal. 'You're a good girl, Maria.' He smiled, his eyes on her breasts. 'Excellent bookkeeper and your handwriting is a work of art. You'll go far.'

'Thank you, sir,' she said, taken aback by his change of mood. 'I do try my best.'

'Ye-es . . . I'm sure you do. Come in and see me first thing tomorrow and give an update on what's going on down there by the river. Better to hear it firsthand. The press have a way of blowing things out of proportion.'

'Yes, sir, they do.'

'Good. Good girl. Agreeable girl. I like that. Excellent. Off you go. Keep the wheels oiled and turning.' Beneath his desk and within his trousers his pride was swelling and almost at bursting point. The beads of sweat on his brow and the heavy breathing should have been a give-away, but Maria would never have thought, not in a million years, that a distinguished gentleman of Mr Clarkson's standing could be as lecherous and rude as certain types from her own walk of life. She had much to learn of those classes above her own.

Arriving home later that day, and anxious to find out more of what had actually happened in Miller's Wharf, Maria could see her sister in the yard in the midst of a small crowd, thoroughly enjoying all the dark conversations and talk of murder between the neighbours and people who lived outside the yard. The scene reminded her of when she was three years old and people had gathered in the yard when Queen Victoria's husband Albert had died of typhoid. The Queen's famous words at that time came flooding back: 'My life as a happy person is ended!' She wondered who might now be feeling just as distraught over the murdered woman. She made her way over to her sister and was disheartened to see excitement in her face. Her eyes were wide with amazement, her unruly long corkscrew curls all over the place.

'You ain't *never* gonna guess in a million years wot's bleedin' well 'appened down by the docks, Ria!'

'I think I do know, Daisy, and it's nothing to be excited over or to celebrate. That could be me pulled out of that river. How would you feel then?'

'I wasn't bein' excited over it! I'm bleedin' well frightened for me life! And when you was late back from work I said you must 'ave bin strangled. Willy's still in the lav with the door bolted, crying 'is eyes out 'cos he believed me! How was I to know he'd believe you was the one murdered? Mum's on 'er bed wiv the curtain closed wiv one of 'er 'eadaches so I couldn't let Willy go in to 'er, could I?'

'Daisy's right, Maria,' said Angel Black, who was sitting outside and in front of her small work table, clearing away her materials for another day. 'Will's bin in there for a good ten minutes, sobbing for yer. That little mare's frightened the life out of 'im.'

'I ain't a bleedin' mare, am I? You nosy parker!'

Cross with her sister, Maria slapped her across the

arm. 'Now you just apologise to Mrs Black, Daisy Bertram. This minute!'

Her lip curled down, Daisy went quiet. 'Didn't 'ave to 'it me so 'ard, did yer?' The hard glare from her sister took the last of the steam from her engine. 'She knows I never meant it.'

'Who's *she*? The cat's mother?'

'Angel knew I never meant it!'

'Mrs Black to you, miss!'

'All right, Ria! No need to shout at me!' Daisy turned to the rag-and-bone man's wife, saying, 'I'm sorry. You ain't the nosy parker . . . Sophie Marcovitch is.'

This pleased Angel more than a thousand apologies could. 'Well, that's all right, then. We're all a bit upset, I should say. Yes . . . we're all a bit mixed up and down in the mouth over this.' She turned to Maria and shrugged. 'Lovely-looking woman, by all accounts. No more than thirty if that, so they say. She worked for some newspaper or the other in Fleet Street and they say she was gonna do a story on this business of pulling down slums to make way for another mansion 'ouse. Our yard's on the drawing board as well, by all accounts.'

'Our yard?' said Maria, shocked. 'Kelly's Yard to be razed to the ground?'

'So the rumour that's spreading like fire goes. Anyway, you'd best get little Willy out of the lav. I'm not the only one who needs a pee. And chuck some earth and lime down for us. My Olly's left a full bucket by the side of the lav.'

Leaving Daisy with Angel, Maria went across to the

one and only lavatory in the yard to rescue Willy from his sorrows.

'D'yer want a bit of chocolate, Mrs Black?' said Daisy, offering a handful of broken pieces. 'Have a bit and then you'll know I'm sorry, won't yer? Cost me a penny for a bag. Swept a bleedin' long gutter for that penny an' all.'

Angel peered at the small chunks of brown stuff. 'You mustn't eat that, Daisy. Give you gripe and the runs, that will.'

''Course it won't,' she growled, her lip curling again. 'It's bleedin' good chocolate, that!'

Angel took a piece from her and pressed it between her fingers. 'No. You mustn't eat this and you must tell your mother where you bought it. This is melted-down candle wax mixed wiv paint and a little sugar. I 'ope to God you never bought any toffee from this place. That'll be made up of sugar sweepings from the factories as well – which 'as bin peed on by cats and dogs and boiled down. Never mind mice droppings and bugs.'

As she stared up at the woman, Daisy's jaw dropped. 'Me and Willy eat the toffee between us.'

'Well then, maybe that's why he's still in the lav? Chuck that in the dustbin and let your muvver know. You might need the poor doctor.'

'I ain't bleedin' well chucking it away! I'm taking it back!'

'The vendor won't be there tomorrow. He'll be off in some other market wiv 'is box of dirty tricks. Put it down to experience, Daisy, and *learn* by it.'

'So I'm to throw it away, then?'

'Where no other child will pick it up. When I was a girl it wasn't only chocolate and toffee they cheated on. Used tea leaves was collected and dried out agen and sold as fresh and Cheddar cheese was dyed red and sold as Gloucester. They caught my mother wiv that once but they never caught 'er twice. Brand labels on the food's put the price up but at least you can trust what you're buying. Not that it matters to any of us. We 'ave to rely on the markets for third-grade food.'

'Don't sound fair to me, Mrs Black. I'm gonna do somefing about that when I'm old enough. I can read, you know.'

'I know.' Angel looked at Daisy through tired eyes. 'Things might be different in ten years' time. Who knows? And who cares, anyway? Ten years on I'll be ten foot under!' At least the smile was back on her face.

'Wot about murders? Was there any like this one they're talking about when you was little?'

'Oh dear.' Angel sighed. 'Fings you ask. I would 'ave to rack my brain to remember that far back.' She dipped her hand deep into her skirt pocket and pulled out a ragged pack of cards and settled herself to play a game of patience amid the turmoil and noise. It was one way of putting worry to one side and restoring calm. 'I pity the family of that poor girl,' she murmured, slapping her cards down on the table in unexposed rows with the end card showing.

'Can you play bezique?' said Daisy, looking over Angel's shoulder.

'I can. But we'd need two packs of cards.'

'All right . . . I might fetch ours dahn later on when this lot 'ave gone and challenge yer. I'm good at cards.'

'I bet you are.' Angel chuckled. 'I bet my last shilling you are.'

'I don't 'ave to go to school, y'know. I'm eight and can do wot I like.'

'And what do you like, Daisy?'

'Not bleedin' school, that's for sure. It's a very harsh place,' she said, mimicking something she had overheard. 'They tell us to know our place and to aspire to higher fings. I fink I know wot that means. I like to learn as much as I can. And it's free. I use their slate and chalk to work out me sums and practise me 'andwriting and sometimes we get to do a bit of drawing as well. Paper's free an' all. You can't bring the pencil 'ome, though. I'm gonna be a very important person when I grow up. Own me own shop probably.'

'Well, mind you chuck away that candle wax that goes by the name of chocolate, then. Otherwise you might not grow up.'

''Course I will,' said Daisy, turning away and heading for her mother's place. Once inside and away from the others, she stuffed the handful of sweet bits into her mouth and munched them as fast as she could before Maria or her mother came in to stop her. Angel Black was a nice lady but she talked a lot and was bound to let it slip about the wax and brown dye.

Coming into the house just minutes afterwards, Maria had Willy in her arms, his face buried in her shoulder, still weeping. She had managed to coax him out of the lavatory but hadn't managed to persuade him that the murderer was probably miles away by now, and from a different part of London. She settled him on an armchair and gently pushed his sweaty hair off his face.

'I bet he shit 'is trousers,' said Daisy. 'Frightened out of 'is life he was, and you wasn't 'ere to comfort 'im. Was you wiv that bloke from above the stables? He's not back yet either. I saw you both in the coffee shop 'olding hands. Did you kiss 'im an' all?'

'They . . . they wasn't . . . kissing,' sobbed Willy. 'Stop f . . . fibbing, Daisy.'

'They was 'olding bleedin' hands, though, and lookin' at each other up close. He might 'ave 'ad his hand up Maria's skirt, for all I know.'

'Any more, Daisy, and you'll get another slap! Dirty little cow.'

Daisy rolled her eyes and went back outside. The crowd hadn't grown and neither had it shrunk, but it had changed. Some outsiders had left and others had arrived. Standing with her hands on her hips, glaring at the busybodies, she pursed her lips and then opened her mouth to yell something, but Sophie Marcovitch was outside her front door now, drinking a glass of water, giving Daisy a silent message to keep quiet. Marching over to her, she slumped down on the woman's doorstep within hearing distance of both Angel and Sophie.

'Bleedin' cheek! Coming into our yard to do their bleedin' gossiping!' Daisy looked around, her expression full of contempt. Raising her voice, she said, 'Someone'd best put a padlock on the lavatory door before one of this lot pisses in our pot!' The place suddenly went quiet as they all turned to look at the scruffy urchin squatting on the edge of the doorstep, her legs wide apart and the hem of her skirts dangling in the dirt. 'Why don't you all go where you live! This is our 'ome, if you don't mind! Get dahn the soddin' river and talk abaht the murder there! There might be another dead body laying in the oyster boat for you to ogle at!' She then pointed a finger at a small, skinny Yiddish man who was sheltering in the shade of his rotund wife's body. 'I bet he did it! I bet he's the murderer! Look – he's half frightened to death that you might 'ang 'im!'

Her last remark had an immediate effect. Couple by couple, small groups sauntered out, whispering behind their hands and throwing Daisy black looks. Once the last of the outsiders had gone, a peal of laughter rang out from number eleven. Liza Bertram had heard her charming daughter and it amused her, especially since she alone had managed to rid the yard of the noisy gossips. They knew who was to blame for luring them in – Angel's husband, the ever-industrious Olly Black, who was lurking in the darkness of the stable. When he finally did come out, sporting an expression of intense mental agony, he gazed up at the sky and waited for the dressing-down from Sophie, the rat-catcher's wife . . . and if not from her, from his own sweet love, Angel. Then, of course, he had the minx Daisy to contend with.

'Worthwhile, was it, Olly?' Sophie smiled, her voice echoing through the yard. 'Scraped in a few coppers, did you?'

'Ah, not so bad . . . not so bad. Mustn't grumble. Sold a little mirror and a scent bottle that's bin knocking around for ages.' Unable to contain himself, he had to boast further. 'I got rid of some old bric-a-brac and did rather well on them old Charles Dickens *Pickwick Papers* which only cost me a penny a piece.'

'How much did yer get for 'em, then?' said Daisy, screwing up her nose.

'Tuppence a piece and threepence off the final price if the lady bought the lot. Yes,' he said, majestically, 'I did all right there. You mark what I'm saying, young Daisy. It may not sound much making a penny on *Pickwick Papers* but it's a very good profit, all said and done. One hundred per cent profit.'

'How many did you get rid of?' asked his wife, who had been the one to put them into an old tin trunk and away from nibbling mice in the first place. 'All of 'em?'

'All thirty of them, wife, so I did.' He smiled. Then, with his hands clasped behind his back and in the manner of a true gentleman, he paced the yard. 'We shall be out of this place in a year or so at this rate. I shall 'ave enough for a deposit on a little cottage in the countryside. That I shall. Where there's muck there's money, and where's there's money there's muck. Remember that, Daisy, and you'll end up a very rich woman. You've got years on your side. Whereas I'm nearly an old man.'

'Well, we are honoured to be in your company, sir,' said his wife, 'indeed we are. Why, when we first met you was no more than a fearful young man with a limp. Now look at you. King of the castle.'

'And you shall be his queen!' Sophie laughed, giving Olly a sideways glance. 'Oh, you're a lovely man, Olly. There I was down in the dumps and you've pulled me right out of 'em!'

'Now then, now then,' said Olly, sporting an honest and frank expression. 'No need for any of us to be down, Sophie. We'll 'ave none of that.' He pushed his hand deep into his pocket and pulled out half a crown. 'Fetch two pitchers of ale from the tavern, Daisy Bertram! And take a penny for going!' He flicked the coin towards her and she caught it effortlessly.

'Wot abaht four hot pies? One for each of us.' Daisy knew when she was on to a good thing. 'I'm certain a successful businessman like yerself can afford to treat three 'ungry ladies to hot pies, sir.'

'Well, yes, there's a mark of truth in wot you say, child.' He dug deeper and pulled out a shilling. 'Return the pitchers to the barman once we 'ave emptied them and you can keep the two farthings deposit.' Smiling and tipping his cap at the women, he returned to his hideaway at the rear of the stable where he intended to smoke his pipe and enjoy this moment in the sun. What he had refrained from telling the women was that he had also managed to sell a rather tarnished but pure silver Georgian pocket watch complete with an ornate matching double chain and a box of assorted and only slightly damaged Cranberry and Bristol glass ornaments. All, of course, for a fair price! His total income on this happy day had amounted to six pounds, eleven shillings and threepence. He had made his fortune at last!

While Olly sat bathing in his own sunshine in the privacy of his little shaded world in the back of the stable, Maria arrived, having heard everything through the open bedroom window. She had comforted Willy and left him with a very old picture book to look at, with a promise of a story later on. Her mother remained inside. Maria joined the women, a burning question on her mind which, if she were to sleep at all this night, she had to know the answer to.

'You're looking a little flushed, Maria,' said Sophie Marcovitch, shifting along her narrow wooden bench and making room for her neighbour's daughter. 'Not going down with anyfing, I should 'ope.'

'I'm burning up, Mrs Marcovitch, I will admit that,' was her reply as she sat beside the woman. 'Burning inside and out.'

Placing a hand on Maria's forehead, Sophie shrugged. 'You 'aven't got a temperature, so I take it this business of murder's playing havoc?'

'I'm upset about that, it's true . . . but I've got to admit that there's something else that's worrying me.' She leaned forward and turned to face Angel, who was sitting with her face to the waning sun. 'It's something you said earlier, Mrs Black. About the woman . . . the journalist . . . and why she was in the area.'

'Yes. The woman was one of them socialists, according to a copper, and was gonna write a piece damning the plans they've got for Shadwell. According to another journalist who was here today, the mansion 'ouse is to be the beginning of a much bigger plan for the future. To change the face of the docks and tart it up.'

'Well,' said Maria, 'I won't deny that our riverside does need urgent attention. Some of them old rat-infested buildings are a death trap. But you said that our yard was to be pulled down as well as the streets around us?'

'It's only what I 'eard, child. Rumour ain't fact.'

'No, but by the time it is fact it'll be too late to do anything about it. We must find out more and lose no time on it. If they pull our yard down where shall we live?'

'In a lovely new tenement flat with running water,' said Sophie with a wink, 'and a siphonic lavatory to draw away the sewage. One lavatory between four flats, granted, but it's still a big improvement on what we're making do wiv now.'

'So you're for it, Sophie . . . is that what you're saying?'

'Implying, Maria. There's a difference. I've not give it much thought what with the murder and all the comings and goings. There are more immediate fings to think about. Any one of us could be next. You never can tell with a maniac.'

'Sounds like a fairy tale to me,' said Angel Black, gazing out on a world of her own. 'Running water inside and a lavatory that draws away sewage. A brand spanking new place to live in wiv no vermin, no damp, no leaking roof. Two bedrooms and a little snug and a kitchen. Heaven-scented days, they'd be. It's just a fairy tale, Maria. Take no heed.'

'We're all giving ourselves a hot flush about everyfing and nuffing,' murmured Sophie. 'I should set your mind to work as to immediate plans, Maria.'

'Such as?' Maria could see that Sophie Marcovitch was drifting into one of her doom-and-gloom moods.

'Such as us women only going about two by two for a while . . . till they catch the raving lunatic.' She shook her head gravely. 'There's no accounting for some folk. Look at that Helen Abercromby case. That poor young woman was struck dead after coming 'ome after a pleasant trip to the theatre. Poisoned by a maniac who had poisoned time and time again before her and gone undetected. Then there was the murder aboard the train on the North London Line between Bow and Hackney Wick. Horrid murder, they called it, and so it was. Poor lad was only seventeen years old.'

'Best not dwell on it, Sophie,' said Angel Black, knowing there was little chance of stopping her neighbour once she got going. 'We'll all be 'aving nightmares at this rate.'

'The worse to my mind was that poor young woman, Harriet Lane, in the Mile End Road—'

'Yes, all right, Sophie!' Angel knew she was wasting her time. Sophie's trance-like expression was on her face.

'An uncle of mine lodged in a room next door at

the time,' she continued. 'Two brothers plotting and planning to bring about 'er death when all the time she believed them both to love and want 'er. An educated girl as well.'

'Yes, I do remember that one,' said Angel. 'Wasn't so long ago, to my recollection. Two years, I should fink. That was one to remind us about, but if you could leave it there.'

'That's right . . .' murmured Sophie. 'It was two years ago this summer. Who would 'ave thought it of Henry Wainright? Came from a very prosperous family as well. Inherited 'is father's brush-making business in Whitechapel Road and a share of a considerable fortune.'

'Yep, and he lost it all in the end. We know!'

'Then he goes and murders that poor innocent girl,' said Sophie, shaking her head sadly. 'My brother went to that hanging. It drew a big crowd, be all accounts.'

'Oh, please . . . I've gone icy cold,' whispered Maria. 'Can't we change the subject?'

'The Ratcliffe Highway murders were the worst this century will ever see. In one hour that maniac 'ad murdered the Marr family, the Williamson family and that servant lad, James Biggs—'

'That's enough!' Angel stood up. 'We'll 'ave no more of it. Say something cheerful or say nothing at all!' The look of remonstration on her face did the trick – it finally silenced her neighbour. 'You've frightened the wits out of poor Maria,' Angel added, her voice softer.

'I am frightened now, Angel, you're right. I've got goose pimples.'

'You won't be the only one, child.' Sophie shuddered and looked around. 'Listen . . .'

There was a moment of quiet as the three of them cocked an ear. 'Listen to what, Sophie?' Maria finally whispered.

'To the silence. There's no one on the streets. Doors and windows will be locked and bolted this night, you can bank on that.'

Again the three of them sat in silence until the sound of echoing footsteps coming from the half-moon alley leading into the yard gripped them. Footsteps which seemed to strike the flagstones with determination and defiance. Looking from one to the other, the women sat rigid, afraid to move a muscle. The striking appearance of Steffan's father in his long coat and top hat was an eerie sight as he came into the yard, strode past the women and ascended the wooden steps leading to his rooms above the stable.

'His eyebrows are too close together,' whispered Sophie. 'I said it before and I'll say it agen. The man's got the mark of a murderer on that forehead. Them black eyebrows all but meet in the middle.'

Maria shivered at the remark and thought of her father, no longer there to protect and reassure his family. The sudden change in circumstances when he had passed away had obviously taken its toll, and she felt it was at times like these when her mother would miss his protective ways and watchful eye most. Especially now, when she would feel the full weight of the burden of taking care of the children alone. Maria was fully aware that her mother had buried her grief over the years and channelled her energies into working hard to make up for the loss of her husband's income and support. She had borne her cross well without complaint or self-pity, even though she had been understandably low in spirits for months after her husband's death. The support and friendship from the yard had helped all of them to come to terms with, and get used to, the heartbreaking loss of the warm and gentle man they had loved so dearly. William Bertram had always held firm to the belief that one day he would move his flock away from London altogether, to the industrial North of England, and in particular to Stoke, where he felt sure he would find employment as accounts clerk in one of the expanding successful potteries. He had read that small houses were being built close to new factories for employees. There was little doubt that William Bertram would have seen his plans come to fruition had he not fallen fatally ill.

Engaged as an accounts clerk in the post office, he had been a dedicated employee who could leave family ties behind him when at work and the worries of the office at his desk when he came home in the evenings to enjoy time with his family, often sitting by the fireside in winter and outside in summer, first with Maria curled on his lap, reading to her from picture books, and then Daisy and Willy. He read stories of giants and goblins, fairies and beanstalks, lost forests and giant-slayers. Maria's all-time favourite stories had been 'Little Red Riding Hood' and 'The Three Bears'.

Without them realising it, their father had been artfully coaching his children to read.

The body of the young woman dragged from the river had by now been identified as that of Rose Cranfield, who was lodging alone in Kentish Town. As the dismal truth slowly emerged in the press, fear among the Shadwellians grew. During a thorough police search of the murdered woman's home, her personal diary had been discovered, and although not giving too much away, it suggested that she had not, as at first believed, come to Shadwell to report on plans for the area, but was in fact in search of her unnamed lover. It seemed she had recently been cast off for a second and last time after a relationship lasting some ten years. The woman had not seen her lover for six years until he had turned up again out of the blue. She had every reason to be angry. She had written in her diary that she had gleaned from the man whom she had loved and lost twice that he had temporarily taken rooms at an inn by the river in Shadwell, and that he and two other business colleagues were about to make a substantial shipping investment. He had come into town from his country estate to survey the area and to conduct his business. It was also apparent from her writings that when her lover had first disappeared without a word, the broken-hearted woman whom he had once kept in the style of a lady had drifted into prostitution in order to pay her rent and bills, and before long it had become a way of life.

From the many dilapidated taverns, inns and gin

houses down by the docks, Rose Cranfield had selected
the River Inn as her residence, staying in one of its
jumbled, run-down rooms over the busy public bar.
The narrow wooden steps going up to a badly lit old
timber balcony led into the lodging rooms, which had
a sinister and malevolent feel about them and would
cause anyone unfamiliar with the area to shudder.
Miss Cranfield had parked her bicycle by the small
fishing boats moored close to the harbour master's
rooms. Whether the woman had realised it or not,
here was a place where local prostitutes procured their
sixpenny-trick clients, paying the landlord half of their
earnings.

Two hours before her tragic end the murdered
woman had concocted a story to explain her presence
in the area to the barman. It appeared that the reasons
she gave as to why she, a smartly dressed lady, was
in this grim and harsh corner of London had been
convincing. She had told of a rumour she had heard
through the grapevine that vast changes were planned
for the docks in Shadwell and farther south towards
St Katharine's docks, close to the Tower of London.
The woman had embroidered her convincing tale,
saying she wrote articles for the freethinking *National
Reformer*. She knew that the area was a place where
homeless women could at least earn enough at their
illicit trade to feed themselves, and that if it were
to be pulled down they would face an even more
destitute life.

Rose Cranfield had been living a clandestine life in
Kentish Town as a courtesan to gentlemen of means,

and by the time her long-lost love had chosen to return after years of silence she had put him out of her mind and out of her heart. Her rented basement flat, originally leased by her father in order that she could live in London and be employed by middle-class families as a private music and English tutor, was where she entertained her clients. A discreet advertisement placed in *The Times*, which overtly gave nothing away but said everything to the type of man who knew that she was exactly what they were in search of, soon paid off. Her client list had grown rapidly, and she soon realised that her gentlemen much preferred to come to her sparse but comfortable lodgings rather than be lured into some dark alley by those less fortunate prostitutes who had no choice but to do their business in back alleys.

As her diary progressed it revealed a great deal about the murdered woman's life. Each and every one of her 'lovers' was made to feel as if he was more special than any other. She listened patiently to pillow talk as they poured their hearts out to her in bed after lovemaking. It was clear that for this service they were only too pleased to pay three guineas a visit.

Her life had seemingly fallen into place, and on the whole Rose had been content with it. She had a regular income and appreciated the safety of working from home, and the fact that she could more or less pick her clients comforted her. Naturally, after the surprise visit from the one man she thought she'd never see again, she felt as if her world were turned upside down. All of a sudden, nothing made sense as she fought with her conflicting emotions. The anger that she had always planned to express should he one day return, bubbled to the surface but all too quickly disappeared as the sheer joy of seeing his face again overcame her.

Following a long night of passionate lovemaking, and an account as to why he had had to stay away for so long, her sweetheart had left her believing that he would return the following week, and would resume his role as unlawful husband, paying her rent and her bills once again, provided she gave up prostitution. The soft-hearted, gullible woman had listened to her lover's heart-rending lies and been deeply moved by the compassion he had supposedly shown his wife, who, he had told her, had finally slipped away after he had nursed her through a long illness. Rose Cranfield had welcomed her lover back with open arms. Not only had she taken him back into her bed and believed his atrocious lies, but she had loaned him five pounds when, on one occasion, he had shown deep embarrassment at having no money because he had arrived at the bank five minutes after it had closed. The beguiled woman had had no reason to doubt his integrity, for her much-adored lover, who had falsely given his name as Howard Traverse, had always been very generous throughout their earlier years together, when he had been full of promises to divorce his wife and remarry. And she had believed every word he had uttered. It was anger at her own naivety which drove her to hire a penny farthing bicycle for the day and come in search of someone she had finally realised to be a cheat, an impostor and a snake in the grass. His ardent promises had come to nothing, and this woman was not prepared to have her heart broken twice by the same lover. She had been determined to find and expose him.

Wrapped up in his own self-importance, her lover had known little of her history, despite their years together. He had not been in the least motivated to ask about her family or upbringing, and she was too polite to force the information upon him. In fact Rose Cranfield had been born to a middle-class family living in Sevenoaks, Kent. She had had a happy childhood with her brothers and sisters, who were now involved in the running of the family business – a string of grocery shops, the largest of which was in their own country town, the others in neighbouring Tunbridge Wells, Tonbridge and Maidstone. Although the deceased had written regularly to her family and had travelled by train five or six times a year to visit, she had never mentioned her secret life and they continued to believe that she had been a private governess employed by three different homes to teach the children of wealthy London folk. Coming to London once the police had notified them as to the death and the suspicious circumstances surrounding it, her parents had been mortified to learn of the life their daughter had been leading. In a state of shock, and struck by grief at the knowledge of her having been strangled and dumped into the filthy River Thames, they vowed that they would find the murderer themselves if the police failed, their major concern being that, while a murder in Sevenoaks would be a rare thing indeed, here in this ungodly part of London it was almost commonplace, especially when it involved those women who made themselves vulnerable by prostituting themselves to men from all walks of life who left no means of being traced.

The horror of their daughter's body having been found tangled in foul-smelling mooring ropes and heavy chains not far from the very inn where she had sat talking to the bartender was almost too much to bear. Leaving their sons to run their business in Kent, they had booked themselves into a small hotel in Bloomsbury, with every reason to privately oversee the efficiency of the police inquiry and with every intention of keeping the press informed. In short, whoever murdered their daughter was going to be brought to justice and hanged – come hell or high water!

4

With talk of murder on everyone's lips in and around Kelly's Yard, Maria was more concerned for her mother than for herself. She spent most of her time away from home at the factory. Her walk to and from work took one and half hours from her day, on top of the nine-hour shift at Bollards. This meant that by the time she arrived home in the evenings all she wanted after her supper was to curl up and read, her one and only pastime. Liza, on the other hand, spent all her time in Shadwell, working alongside the other women in the yard on her piecework, in the house, or shopping in the local market, and Daisy, when she wasn't at school, could usually be found rooting around Shadwell for casual work or playing in the streets and alleyways. Her shy younger brother Willy was content to be close to his mother, hanging on to her skirts when trouble was in the air.

Sitting on the edge of her narrow iron bed, lacing up her worn ankle boots, Maria glanced at her sister, lying sound asleep, spread-eagled on top of her mattress, and a wave of maternal love swept through her. Daisy looked like a comical angel when she was out for the count, and it was never easy having to disturb her, but given her desire to soak up as much knowledge as possible school was essential and encouragement to attend regularly of the utmost importance. Her elderly teacher had often said that this wiry child had a brain like a sponge but that the Devil himself had hold of her spirit, which would be her downfall. Daisy and Maria had often laughed over this and other doom-filled predictions from this devout Christian woman, who read the Bible aloud in class each morning for fifteen minutes. Maria learned from Daisy that, during this session, the eight-year-old took the opportunity for a nap. Religious Education clearly was not Daisy's subject.

Ready for work at last, Maria tiptoed over to her sister, so as not to wake Willy, and gently shook her, whispering, 'Time to wake up, Dai.'

Turning over and groaning quietly, Daisy lifted her eyelids a fraction, peered at Maria and then closed them again. 'I've got the gutsache. I ain't goin' to school.'

'No, you 'aven't,' whispered Maria. 'Come on. Don't wake Willy up. Be a good girl and see to yerself. Mum's downstairs and she's got some porridge on the go.'

Knowing that Daisy would soon drag herself up from her mattress, Maria crept out of the bedroom and down the narrow winding staircase.

'Madam's awake and I'm gonna 'ave to fly, Mum.'

'No, you're not, Maria. There's a bowl of porridge there for you and it's cooled down enough for you to eat. You can't do a decent day's work on an empty stomach.' Liza pulled a chair from under the old pine table and tapped the back of it. 'Come on. Five minutes won't make you late, I know.'

'That's true enough,' said Maria, reluctantly sitting down. 'Will you be taking Daisy to school again this morning? Or do you feel easier about things now that the place is crawling with policemen and reporters?'

'No. I've given up trying. Yesterday was the last day I could get away with. She'll be all right in any case. Knowing her she'd give the swine a kick in the shins and bring 'im down. Anyway, they say that the police 'ave an inkling as to who killed the poor woman.'

'You never said.' Maria looked up into her mother's face. 'Why didn't you tell me that last night?'

'Because I only heard it this morning. Sophie popped in and told me.'

'So why the glum face, then? Or is it someone we know?'

'No . . . well, not exactly. Anyhow,' said her mother elusively, sitting down at the table to eat her breakfast, 'it's only hearsay. And from Sophie at that.'

'Well, who is it, then?' Maria was beginning to feel nervous about her mother's evasiveness.

'It's not so much who it was as where the man's from. They're saying he's local.'

'And?' said Maria, spooning her porridge.

'There's to be a house-to-house enquiry. According to Sophie our yard is where they'll be coming today. We're all to be questioned.' Turning her face away from Maria's questioning eyes, the woman shuddered.

'It makes my blood run cold to think a murderer may be among us.'

'Sophie's not worried about any of her sons, is she?'

'No, of course not. Fancy saying a thing like that. What if she heard you, Maria?' Glancing out of the open doorway, Liza checked to see who was about. 'It won't be anyone in this yard, but it's bad enough to think it might be someone just outside of it. That poor woman, by all accounts, came here in search of her sweet'eart and gets strangled for her pains! Strangled and thrown into the river like an old bundle of clothes.' Her eyes were full of worry. 'You will look about you on your way 'ome from work, won't you?'

'It's not the winter, Mum. It's still daylight at seven o'clock, don't forget. Stop worrying. It'd be different if it was November time, then I would be frightened for my life. Let's hope they catch the man, then we can all stop worrying.'

Maria left for work, not entirely convinced by her own words, which had been more to ease her mother's mind than what she felt to be the truth. She was frightened, but there seemed little point in adding to the worry by admitting it. There were, after all, many places in which a maniac could hide in these parts: unlit coal yards and stables, candlelit gin taverns and decrepit premises used as opium dens, dark and winding streets and alleyways lit only by spasmodic street lamps and cast into blackness when the oil had burned dry. There was the constant sound of the echoing footsteps that had over the years worn rough stones smooth and glossy. She had to pass homeless people who slept under sacks in courtyards and back alleyways, having mixed feelings about their presence – half pity and half fear.

At the main door of Bollards, five minutes early, Maria saw for the first time since her warning over lateness the chief of personnel, Mr Clarkson, and was taken aback at how short he was. She had previously only seen him seated behind his leather-topped desk. Adding to her sense of surprise, he gave her a smile that had a hint of familiarity about it, and then, surprising her further, he pulled on the brass handle of the heavy door and said, 'After you, my dear.'

'Why, thank you, sir.' Maria smiled.

'My pleasure, Miss Bertram,' was his slick response.

Once inside, he pulled the lift bell and moved closer to her, smiling, beads of perspiration showing on his forehead. 'Five minutes early,' he said approvingly. 'Well done. Any more news on who the murderer might be, my dear?'

'No, sir. But the word in the streets is that he is a local man.'

'Tut tut,' he murmured, shaking his head. 'We may have to make arrangements to have you delivered safely home until they've nailed the man.' Thoughtful for a few seconds, he then looked into her face. 'Yes, I think we might have to think very seriously about it. My regular cab man could make a short detour, I'm sure. Come and see me at ten this morning and we'll sort something out.'

'Oh, I'll be all right, sir,' said Maria, on her guard,

not entirely at ease with the likely reason for his protective offer. 'It's not as if it's the winter and pitch black when I walk home.'

'Those who choose to kill for pleasure, Miss Bertram, will find a way whether it is pitch black or bright sunshine. From what I read in the newspaper report, the imprints on the woman's neck show the mark of a man who knew exactly what he was doing. You may well have a serial murderer as a neighbour.' He turned his head slightly and smiled at her again. 'Why not join me in the gentlemen's lift today, Miss Bertram?'

'I am obliged to you, sir, but I don't think that Miss Drake would be too pleased. I don't mind taking the stairs. It's exercise, after all. But thank you for offering.'

'Oh, stop being so proper, child,' he said, giving her a mock scolding look. 'I offer you a ride and you turn me down? You do have a very pretty neck, my dear, but I promise you, my hands shall not go anywhere near it.'

'Oh, but I wasn't thinking anything of the sort, Mr Clarkson! Truly I wasn't.'

'Come come, my dear. I was joshing. At Bollards we are proud of our female staff, small though the numbers are. And we like to take good care of them. I shouldn't sleep at night if I had the least bit worry that we had neglected your welfare in the face of a murderer on the loose. Ours is an established firm which looks after its ladies. And although I shouldn't pat myself on the back, I was the first chief of personnel in any of the local factories to have put forward the idea of employing female clerical staff in our offices.'

Maria smiled although she knew otherwise. She was quite aware that more and more factories were employing women to work alongside men in their clerks' departments. The local biscuit manufacturer, Meredith and Drew, were employing secretaries who had undergone lessons in shorthand and note-taking.

'It was very good of you, sir, to put forward the new idea. Annie Besant would salute you, I'm sure of it.'

'Well, well, my dear. You keep up with your politics, I see. I am impressed. Annie Besant . . .' he mused. 'A highly intelligent freethinker but a ravishing beauty nonetheless.'

The sound of the lift crashing to a halt and the double doors opening stopped the conversation there and the sour expression on the lift man's face caused Maria to smile. This tiny mechanical lift was strictly for gentlemen. 'After you, my dear,' said Mr Clarkson, sweeping a hand through the air.

Once inside the small space, with this man standing so close, Maria had a strong sense of something not quite right, as if she was being manipulated in some way. There had to be a reason for the chief of personnel to allow her to join him in the lift when she would normally be expected to walk up the stairs. She had a strong feeling that she was going to have to share his hackney carriage this evening whether she liked it or not.

Once out of the lift, with Mr Clarkson trailing in her shadow, she came face to face with Miss Drake, there as usual to catch latecomers. Maria offered a faint smile which was returned with no more than a frozen expression and a look of scepticism in the steely grey eyes. This was out of order and most definitely against the rules. Maria had dared to use the lift which was strictly for management only and, worse still, Mr Clarkson had an air of euphoria about him and was overly polite. He was now shepherding Miss Bertram towards the swing-doors.

'Good morning, Miss Drake,' he called over his shoulder.

'Good morning, sir. Good morning, Miss Bertram.'

'Good morning, Miss Drake.'

As they passed through the swing-doors into the long corridor, Mr Clarkson whispered in Maria's ear. 'My cab waits by the side entrance of the building, Miss Bertram. Tell the driver that Mr Clarkson has given you permission to board and I shall join you at five minutes past six.' With that he tipped his bowler hat, smiled and strode off along the corridor towards his private offices, leaving Maria rooted to the spot, confused by the whole episode.

Once she had disrobed and was in the post sorting room alone with her thoughts, she recalled the scene from the moment she had entered the building to Mr Clarkson striding away, humming a quiet tune, his briefcase under one arm and his silver-tipped walking cane in the other hand. Why did she not trust this gentleman who had kindly offered to see her safely to Shadwell? The short journey was hardly out of his way and little harm could come to her in a two-seater hansom cab, and yet the worry was not shifting – if anything it was building.

Inside this safe and familiar place, which she felt to be her territory, she filed the morning mail into the various small wooden cubicles, then withdrew each bundle and secured it with a thick rubber band. When she came to those in the cubby-hole marked 'Drawing Office and Architects' Department' she paused, thinking of John Cunningham. During the occasion when they had walked out together they had been comfortable in each other's company and had felt no inhibitions where conversation was concerned, and right then she felt the need for his company and his sound advice, despite his recent behaviour, which had been rather discouraging. Glancing through the tiny square window in the door of the post room, which was there for Miss Drake to spy through, Maria could hear no sound of footsteps in the empty corridor. Quickly scribbling on her notepad, she wrote:

> *Dear John*
> *I need to speak with you.*
> *Shall we meet in the turning opposite in the coffee house during our lunch break?*
> *Your friend and colleague, Maria*

It was with trepidation that Maria sat by the window of the small Italian coffee and sandwich shop. Having optimistically ordered two coffees, she watched as a poor, wretched family, with the aid of the driver of a horse and rickety cart, loaded up their sticks of furniture on to a removal van, and couldn't help thinking how lucky she and her family had been after her father had passed away. It could so easily have been a different story if she had not been old enough to earn a living or her mother not able to take in home work with too many children to look after. The dirty and bedraggled family, who had obviously up until now managed to scrape by in this ill-kept place infested by rats, thieves and prostitutes, were, like so many other large families in this district, being evicted into the streets or, worst of all, into the workhouse.

Watching the barefoot children coming in and out of the lodgings, she guessed there must be seven or eight of them. No doubt their fate would be similar to that of hundreds of others. They would be split up, the mother going into a workhouse with her very small children, the father into a debtors' prison for rent arrears, the children above eight years old considered able to fend for themselves in the filthy streets and alleyways, sharing a tarpaulin in one of the markets at night, begging and stealing food simply to stay alive.

The expression on the face of the mother was one of despair and defeat. She looked as if she had gone through years of desperation and was now at her lowest ebb. Maria had seen this before, but still it affected her as it affected anyone in the area when a neighbour had fallen on hard times. It was a constant reminder of what could so easily happen to them.

The familiar voice of John Cunningham, who had come into the café and was standing behind her, watching through the window, did little to dispel the depressed mood that had filled this tiny place. None could ignore what was going on outside the house opposite.

'It's the same old story,' murmured John. 'The rich get fatter and the poor die younger.'

'Bless me if you ain't a cheerful soul,' said an elderly gentleman, speaking over his shoulder. 'Fond of dancing on graves as well, are yer?' The robust laughter which filled the café was in some ways a relief. 'Still,' continued the humorous gentleman, 'they can't take the future from us, can they? That'll always be there waitin'.' He sniffed and gave John the once-over. 'Well, take a seat, young man, before you root to the spot. Can't abide people making our little palace untidy. Begging your pardon for saying so.'

John pulled up a chair and sat down. 'I appreciate your honesty, sir,' he said before turning to face Maria and raising an eyebrow.

'Well . . . I must be off!' shouted another old gentleman, who must have thought that either everyone was as deaf as himself or that he was not deaf at all. He pulled on his cap, saying, 'Late to work makes an early grave!' He then winked at his tea-drinking companion, an old tramp who had nothing to lose in life but time. 'Make a lovely couple, don't they?' He turned and grinned at Maria and John. 'Better to marry women than murder 'em.' He grinned, showing his few remaining tobacco-stained teeth. 'Or . . . is it the other way round? Can't quite remember.'

'It's the other way round, Charlie, no fear,' cackled the old woman behind the serving counter. ''Cos you know that we'll be the death of you if you're not the death of us first.'

'The point is, sir,' chuckled a heavily busted midwife sitting at the next table, 'wivout us ladies there'd be no birfs and none of you lot'd be 'ere to tell a tale!'

Leaning forward, his voice quiet, John tried his best to blank out the asides and quips flying across the room from one old East Ender to another. 'What made you choose this place, Maria? It's awful.'

'It's the closest and we haven't got much time. You mustn't be late back. I want your advice about something . . . well, something that's a touch embarrassing.'

'Go on.'

'Have you much to do with Mr Clarkson? The chief of personnel?'

'No.' John smiled. 'Been sniffing around your skirts, has he?'

Shocked by his direct manner, Maria straightened in her chair. 'Not exactly. Why, does he 'ave a reputation for it?'

John had a serious expression on his face. 'Listen to what I'm about to say and mark my words. If he has made subtle advances of *any* kind—'

'He's offered to share 'is cab,' she said, interrupting him, 'after work. And he's been a bit over-familiar. But he's done nothing untoward. It's just—'

'Exactly my point. He never does at first.'

'Shush! Keep your voice down,' whispered Maria. 'Someone in this place might work at Bollards.'

'I doubt it. Look . . . he's begun the chase. You must get out now before he ruins your reputation.'

Maria leaned her face closer to his. 'Surely not, John? It can't be that bad.'

'He will try to bed you; and if you refuse him you will be accused of being a tease or a prostitute. You'll be sacked and without a testimony. I've seen it happen, as have those in my office before me.'

As much as Maria wanted to believe that John was thinking of her welfare, doubts were floating into her mind. This conversation was a little too raw, even though his delivery had not been exactly coarse. Why, having given her the cold shoulder, should he now be so concerned about her welfare? 'So I really must leave Bollards? Because of this man, John?'

'Yes. Just quietly hand in your two-week notice. Make an excuse. Any excuse. Say you've enjoyed working for the firm but . . . oh, I don't know, say you're moving out of the area. That your father's been offered work elsewhere—'

'My dad's dead, John. I thought I told you that.'

'Of course. I am sorry. Really sorry. It's just that—'

'I understand. It's been a while since we first talked. Anyone could be forgiven for forgetting.' Quickly changing the subject, she picked up the conversation. 'I s'pose I could say my mother wants us to move and be closer to her family in South London.'

'Yes. I should do that. And during your time working through your notice you could slip out at lunch-times and look for another post in the area. It won't be difficult now that you're experienced in shorthand note-taking *and* a trusted employee where private and business mail is concerned. That will count for a lot.' He leaned back in his chair and studied her face. 'The man's a scoundrel but a very clever one. The directors know what he's like but better to sack a girl than put a black mark on a gentleman's character.'

'Well, that's hardly fair. Maybe I should expose him gradually. Or let him show his true colours himself. I'm not as silly as I may look.'

'No. But then neither is he.' He nodded at the poor family across the street, who were piled on the cart along with their belongings. 'And *neither* are they, as silly as they might look to some. It's an unfair world we live in, Maria. Forget that just for one day and you'll be sharply reminded of it the next.'

'Well, I suppose I do look on the bright side of things and maybe that's as bad as you looking at the worst it could be. But thank you for the advice. I will take it. I don't really feel as if I want to work there now.'

'You must act sooner rather than later, and when it's time to go home today leave by the front door, the way you always do. Then once you're home why not write a polite note addressed to Mr Clarkson? Say that you've so much on your mind, what with a murderer on the loose and being so close at hand, that you rushed away and forgot all about his kind offer. Thank him for it and then say that as it's turned out you felt very safe walking home and feel it might unbalance you if you ride in a cab one day and walk the next.'

'Unbalance?' She frowned, smiling. 'That sounds a bit far-fetched.'

'Not really, Maria. You're used to walking and you're used to the route. It's familiar and it's your home ground. To ride one day, protected, and then have to walk all the other times, forever checking the shadows, could shatter your confidence. Oh, just say anything you like, but get out of his clutches before it's too late! You don't have a choice now that the rogue's marked you for his own. Trust me. I saw what happened to a seventeen-year-old girl. She was sent packing as if she were a common whore, and it nearly destroyed her.'

Maria finished her coffee and spoke with conviction. 'All right, John. I will take your advice. I appreciate it. Thank you.'

'Good.' He relaxed, studying her face. 'How are you fixed for this coming Sunday afternoon?'

'For that stroll in Shadwell Green?'

'Why not?'

'No reason that I can think of.'

'Good. There is something else I would like to talk to you about. We'll find a nice quiet bench somewhere.'

Unable to resist teasing him, she said, 'Chance'd be a fine thing. A *quiet* bench? In Shadwell? Wake up, Mr Know-all!'

'Well . . . at least we can always sit on the grass under the shade of a tree,' he said, aroused by her response. 'Or we could go to a park near your home?' So far he hadn't told her where he lived or anything about his home life, and she was curious to know more. 'I'm sure you told me where you lived but . . . I've forgotten,' she fibbed.

'Camden Town. Sunday at three, then? By the gate into Shadwell Green.'

'Sunday at three. Now then, shall I leave first or will you? God forbid that we should be seen together and in broad daylight.'

'God forbid.' He smiled, and then left the dingy coffee house.

Once John was out of view, Maria asked for a glass of water. She needed a little time to herself to think things through. Mr Clarkson had made her flesh creep, it was true, but to hand in her notice over it seemed a rather strong reaction, and even though she had gone along with John, she had been sceptical as to his motives. But what these motives might be she had no idea. Uncertainties about him were building. She wondered why he had all but ignored her since their afternoon out and why he had been so adamant that she should leave Bollards. There had been a look in his eyes almost defying her to differ with him. A look that could almost wilt a rose . . . but it was fleeting, and now she couldn't be sure whether she had imagined it or not. The problem was, now that he had sown the seed of doubt in her mind over Mr Clarkson, she really didn't feel comfortable about working in those offices. She decided to sleep on it and, as her father would always say, see what the morning brought to mind.

With luck on her side, Maria slipped quietly out of the office later on, once work had ended, having seen no sign of Mr Clarkson loitering in a dark corner, as she had imagined all afternoon since listening to John. Back in her own part of Shadwell after a brisk walk home, she was hardly surprised to find her neighbours outside in the yard, gossiping. This was fast becoming a familiar scene since the murder, the only difference this evening being that she could see no sign of any news reporters, who had been around quite a bit. She hoped that the interest focused on Kelly's Yard was on the wane.

There were, however, two policemen standing either side of the half-moon passage and an inspector in the yard, at that precise moment talking, or rather listening, to Sophie Marcovitch. The other neighbours, including her own mother and Daisy, were in smaller groups, while Willy was standing very still and staring up at the uniformed policemen, waiting for them to talk to him. So far the only response from one of them in reply to his shy hello had been: 'Run along, sonny. Off home with you.'

It was Sophie's voice which Maria could hear above the others. She was on her soap box and enjoying it. 'Well, of course, it's not for me to cast aspersions, and who am I to in any case? We might be short of money in this yard but we're not short of brains. No, sir, if there was to be a motto placed over the passage entrance into this yard it would be this: "An idle brain is the Devil's workshop!" Make of that what you will!'

Gently pulling her mother away from a small group of women, Maria whispered into her ear, 'What's happening?'

Her arms folded, Liza turned and walked slowly away from the neighbours to where she and Maria could not be heard. 'I'm not sure if this visit is simply routine, Maria, or something worse. Sophie's casting doubt over the gentleman and his son above the stable and Angel's been doing her best to whitewash her own sons' characters. The others are speculating as usual.'

Maria cast a worried glance around the yard, but when her eyes found her small, scruffy brother staring up at the policeman, she quietly laughed. 'Look at that Willy. He's loving it.'

'And so's Daisy. She's been shadowing the inspector as if he was royalty, and chucking in her own ha'penny-worth now and then. He tells her to run along and she does, but only to pass on to one of the others what she says she's heard.'

'But this is more than a routine check. I know they've been goin' door to door all around Shadwell but . . .' She shrugged and then shivered. 'This feels horribly serious.'

'I know. I would say the point of all of this is the shabby genteels. I believe they're waiting for one of them to arrive. And if I'm correct it's the older gentleman they're wishing to talk to . . . about his son.'

'They don't suspect Steffan, surely?'

'Well, it has to be someone, Maria. Just because they live on top of us don't mean to say they couldn't be murderers. And so that's his name, is it? Steffan. And how would you know that?'

'I've spoken to him, and he's as gentle as a lamb. He treated me to a coffee in Whitechapel.' She refrained from telling her mother that his father had in fact been in prison. She couldn't break this confidence, not even to her own mother. 'Has the inspector questioned you?'

'Not yet. I think he's been waiting for you to come home so he could see us both at the same time. Madam piped up that you and the lad were sweethearts.'

'She never did say such a thing! It'll be all round the yard by now. What if he got to hear it? I'd die of embarrassment. We're not sweethearts!'

'Choose your words carefully, Maria. Don't be too defensive. Our neighbours are frightened for their own and a touch wary of you if the truth be told. You working alongside gentlemen and now making friends with that young man. It doesn't go down too well when it's piled up for the count. Their sons and daughters not being able to get out of the rat nest.'

'Well, I'm hardly out of it, am I? We live in this yard too.'

Glancing over Maria's shoulder, Liza could see that the others were looking their way and knew that she had drawn attention by pulling her daughter aside for a quiet word. 'Well, maybe so, but everyone's in a very strange mood is all I can say. Can't you feel it, Maria? You could cut the atmosphere with a knife.

'They're scared. Frightened that there's a murderer in our midst and worried that their own might be pulled aside and questioned for it. There's no murderer here, we know . . . but there are thieves who come and go and who prefer to keep out of the limelight.'

'There's trouble *everywhere* in Shadwell and the police know that,' said Maria, looking around at the serious faces of the neighbours. At this time of day in the summertime they were usually enjoying a quiet singsong, a favourite melody. 'No . . . there's more to this than meets the eye.'

'Well, we're about to find out, sweetheart. Keep your temper even, there's a good girl. We don't want no trouble.'

Before Maria could answer, the imposing Inspector Barcroft was walking towards them, and judging by the expression on his face he had already had enough of the people in this yard. Or, more to the point, Sophie had in her cunning way managed to make him wish this particular job had gone to a colleague rather than himself. Her aim was to see the back of the police altogether.

'Good evening, madam,' said the inspector, addressing Liza. 'I wonder if we might go inside for a few private words. I'm investigating the murder of a Miss Rose Cranfield.' His eyes flashed from Liza to Maria, and when he saw that she was a little flushed he held his stony gaze on her. 'I take it you have no objection, madam?'

'No, sir. None whatsoever.' Maria could feel her throat becoming parched. Having walked briskly home from work on this humid summer's day, she longed for nothing more than a glass of water, or better still a fresh cup of weak tea. The presence of this intimidating gentleman she could do without.

Showing the inspector into her home, Liza caught a glimpse of Sophie, who was looking her way and hoping to get her attention. The message she passed, with a quick movement of one hand clenched into a fist, meant one thing and one thing only. Close ranks, give nothing away, stay silent. Sophie had from childhood had a great fear of the law, which was no wonder since her seven brothers were on the wrong side of it and her mother had been interrogated many times.

'Would you like a cup of tea, sir?' said Liza with a polite smile. 'The kettle's on the oil burner and almost to the boil.'

A look of relief spread across the tired and somewhat frustrated face of the inspector. 'Well, as a matter of fact I would. It's been a long afternoon. Thank you.'

'I'm sure it must have been,' she said, giving him a knowing look and a faint smile. 'Sophie Marcovitch and Angel Black relish a little excitement. Not that they glory in murder, no. It's the uniforms of your officers that excite them. They respect the uniform and, if I'm honest, they're a bit attracted by it.'

'As many will be, Mrs Bertram . . . as many will be. Do you mind if I take the weight from my feet?'

'No, of course not. I was forgetting my manners, sir.' She pulled a chair out from under their tiny dining table. 'Would you mind if the tea's black, sir? Black and sweet. I've enough sugar but the little milk left in the churn had curdled in this heat, I'm afraid.'

'I would prefer it that way, madam, thank you.' He nodded politely at her and then turned his attention to Maria, who was rinsing her hands in a small stone bowl of cold water. 'Your sister, Daisy, was telling me earlier that you and the lad above the stables are to be engaged, Miss Bertram. Am I to congratulate you?'

Maria glanced at her mother, who was shaking her head. 'I'm sorry, sir, but really you mustn't take any notice of what Daisy says. She lives in a fantasy world and plays games in this real one.'

'So I'm to take it that you've not been walking out with the young man?'

'You are, sir, yes.' Maria smiled, pouring boiling water from the kettle into the teapot. 'I don't get much time to walk out with anyone. We work all the hours God sends. My mother's a widow . . . but I'm sure you must know that already since you know our names.'

'Yes . . . I did glean that much from a neighbour who referred to your mother as the widow Bertram. I hadn't meant to offend you.'

'Offend me, sir? Why, no . . . why should I take offence?' Maria knew that this man was playing cat and mouse with them and a flush of anger was rising. 'There's no shame in my mother having been left a widow—'

'I'm sure that's not what the gentleman meant, Maria . . .' warned Liza.

'No shame in that and no shame in working her fingers to the bone to make ends meet.'

'Indeed not,' said the inspector, accepting his much-needed cup of tea. 'So would you say that you are neighbourly with Steffan Tremain and no more than that?'

'I should say that was about right, sir. Yes.'

'But you've never even spoken to the lad, Maria. Or rather he's never spoken to you.' Liza turned to the inspector. 'He keeps himself very much to himself. The father too. But then, you would expect that. Them coming from a better class of family.'

'I have spoken to Steffan, as a matter of fact. I bumped into him in Whitechapel market and he treated me to a cup of coffee. He's not as offhand as we thought. Shy, that's all . . . and a bit out of his realm in this smelly yard.'

'Maria . . . this is our family home. It may not be a palace but it is our home.'

'And it does smell of horse manure . . .' Maria smiled. 'Fresh horse manure. Be truthful and shame the Devil.'

The inspector cleared his throat loudly to get their attention back. Privately he was enjoying his break in this house, away from the prying eyes, the gossips and the ragged children who had been trailing him and his police sergeants all day. 'What about the lad's father? Would you say that he's been as offhand to you as to the others in the yard, Mrs Bertram?' The gentleman sipped his tea, checked her expression and waited.

'I don't think he's offhand, just more used to a different way of life and different people. He wouldn't be the first of the wealthy to 'ave fallen, sir. You read it in the newspaper on a regular basis. Bankruptcy and such.'

'And you know nothing of his past?'

'Certainly not. If a neighbour prefers privacy, then so be it. Even Sophie Marcovitch wouldn't go so far as to pry into someone's past, sir. Live and let live, as the saying is.'

Inspector Barcroft shifted his eyes from Liza to Maria. 'And you, madam? During your coffee respite did you talk on an intimate level or discuss the weather?'

'Both,' said Maria, 'but if you mean did he tell me about his father being in the debtors' prison . . . he did, sir. I found that very sad.' She raised her eyes to meet the inspector's. 'I take it you already knew about that?'

'Yes, Miss Bertram. We have to check police records if we're to carry out a thorough investigation of murder efficiently. I beg your pardon if I appeared to be playing the fox. It was not my intention.'

'I never did think for one minute that it was, sir. You have your work to do.'

'And what of the lad? Steffan Tremain. Did he say why he's living with his father here in Shadwell and not with the family in the country?'

'His grandparents?' Maria shrugged. 'When his father was arrested, he felt duty bound to lodge in rooms next to the prison so he could visit him. His mother had left home without a trace some time before the arrest.'

'It seems you know a great deal more about those two than you've let on, Maria,' said Liza, a little disappointed with her daughter. 'Was it meant to be a kept secret?'

'No. But that kind of a conversation is personal. I just never thought to repeat it to you or anyone. There was nothing secret about it. We just met up in the market by chance and had coffee together, that's all.'

'And you found nothing odd about the young man?'

'No. Nothing odd whatsoever. He's just a shy person until you get him talking. A lonely person too. I shall be his friend from now on. Now that we've introduced ourselves. If my mother agrees I might ask him if he'd like to play cards with us one evening.'

'And Mr Tremain senior?'

'I couldn't really comment, sir. I've never spoken to the man. I will say that from appearances I don't much take to him. Not because he's posh or on the haughty side but . . . well, least said sooner mended. Put it that way.'

'You might feel nervous if you were to meet him in a lonely street on a dark night?'

'No, I wouldn't say that. I wouldn't say that at all. He's just not one of us.'

'But neither is his son, Miss Bertram.'

'No . . . but he's more responsive, if you know what I mean. Not pushy but doesn't snub you either.'

'And if you were to meet him in a dark street while walking alone?'

'Now that I've got to know 'im . . . I'd greet him the same way as I greet my other neighbours in the yard.'

'But you wouldn't have felt comfortable if you hadn't got to know him over a cup of coffee. Whereas when I asked about his father, you showed no concern whatsoever. Am I to take it that you've taken coffee with him too? Before you bumped into his son in Whitechapel?'

'Of course not. I've never spoken to the man.'

'Thank you, Miss Bertram. I think that will be all for now.' He stood up and smiled politely at Liza. 'Thank you for your time and hospitality, madam. The tea was most welcome.'

'I take it that we won't 'ave to live too long in fear that there might be another murder?' said Maria. 'Some people say that history tells us that a second murder to cover tracks often follows a first.'

'History tells us nothing of the sort, Miss Bertram. Speculation and fear set their own record which we must pass over if we are to keep a healthy balance of mind. But if it helps to ease your worry, I will say that, all things considered, strangers do not wander aimlessly into courtyards, backstreets or night-houses and low taverns in an area such as this, looking for someone to strangle.'

'So we must accept that it's someone local who killed that poor woman, then?'

'Until we have arrested, tried and convicted the culprit, we must not accept or presume too much.'

'But you just said that no outsider would come in looking to murder someone. Begging your pardon, sir, but surely that implies that it's one of our own people you've set your sights on?'

'You are quick on the uptake, Miss Bertram, but you are not a police officer.' He smiled. 'I shouldn't trouble your mind over this too much. Experience tells me that would-be detectives or amateur sleuths become not only a nuisance to the cause of justice but dangerous when they begin to gather small amounts of knowledge.' Pulling on his hat, he bade Liza good evening and offered a curt nod to Maria.

In their small and silent room Maria and Liza simply gazed at each other, each of them feeling as if Maria had been cross-examined . . . as if she were on the list of suspects. Sophie coming through the open door brought them back into the real world.

Shaking her head solemnly, Sophie murmured, 'They've gone at last. Too long by my reckoning. Too many questions . . . and mostly centred around those two oddballs up there who never open their curtains. We must all throw the bolts on our doors from now on, Liza. Our little yard is not the safe place it once was.'

'It's no more perilous than it's ever been,' said Liza, quietly, her slim fingers beginning to tremble. 'Although my husband's only ambition in life was to move us away from here.'

'And you think we don't 'ave the same aspirations? That everyone in this slum don't want to get out of it?'

'Well, I don't know . . .'

'No . . . well, just you think on it and don't be so lofty. You're no different from the rest of us. We would all like something better for our children and grandchildren. Claw as much as we try we won't see a different sky. This is our lot and no one gives a fig. The outside world sees us as vermin. Vermin, Liza . . . and nothing more than that. We're of the same flesh and blood and 'aven't bin as lucky as others but at the end of the day bad luck or misfortune don't melt the cold 'earts of them who are comfortable in their own feathered bed.'

Liza raised her eyes apologetically and gazed into her neighbour's face. Everything she said was right and anyone who stopped to think for longer than a minute or so would have to face the grim truth. But the truth was all around them, and the only way to keep going in this life was to hold very tightly on to hope. Hope and, by the grace of God, a touch of good fortune.

'No one cares is what you're saying, Sophie. And yes, you're right. But are we really to sit back and accept it all and live this way? Is all of our anger and strength really gone?'

'No. It's sitting on the back burner waiting for someone to light the match.' Sophie turned her attention to Maria, who was staring down at the dusty stone floor. 'It's the young and strong-willed that we must put our faith in. Your children and mine. All the slum children. We've managed to drag them through thus far. Now they must take up the cause and scream and shout until someone takes notice. They must band together and go to Parliament, to the Prime Minister; even the Queen of England, if needs be.'

Liza followed Sophie's gaze and viewed her daughter in a different light. As she sat on the faded worn chair across the room, she might have been in a different world. Could her daughter really find the strength needed to fight for them all, or was she resigned, like her mother, to letting things be?

'It'll be the likes of your Maria or Daisy, once she's mature enough to be taken seriously. Give the girl five more years and she'll be out there with the banner, screaming for fair play among all men and women and not just the privileged.'

'No,' murmured Maria, 'you're wrong, Sophie. Daisy's the next link in the chain after me and I come after you and Mum.' She looked up and smiled. 'You're not done yet, Sophie Marcovitch. And nor is Mum. At nineteen I'm only just beginning and Daisy's not far behind me. If you want us to go to the Prime Minister waving banners and screaming then we will, but you'll have to be there with us. And Angel and the other women in this yard and those outside of it. Let the reporters come in sniffing for a murder story to sell their newspapers. Welcome them. Make a big pot of tea and draw 'em in. But the story they'll hear won't be the one they came for.'

'That wouldn't work, Maria,' said Liza. 'We're not sensational enough for them.'

'No, Mum, we're not. Not in this mood. Sophie's right. We're gonna 'ave to show our mettle. But we must plan it properly. Come up with something to excite them.' She became thoughtful, her mind turning over. The women could see from her eyes and expressions that she was best left to it. They didn't have long to wait. A smile slowly spread across Maria's face, a radiant smile full of a new understanding. 'It's time we stood up and were counted. We're not vermin. We didn't choose this way of life. The men won't go along with it for fear of making things worse, but we mustn't let them stop us. We'll go to every factory gate. Give me a soap box to stand on and I'll bring them all to attention. If there's to be a change in the way we, the scum of society, are seen, we must show that underneath the rags and the look of death coming we do 'ave brains, and feelings, and spirit . . . and ambition. I've always felt that something wasn't right, but now I see what to do about it.'

'That's more like it, Maria. That's the spirit! You've

bin a while waking up, and if it 'ad to take a murder in our Shadwell then we can say somefing good 'as come out of somefing terrible.' Cackling, and rather pleased with herself, Sophie began her favourite pastime . . . singing ad lib.

'One two three, one two three, what are we not?
Vermin nor beggars nor shamed of our lot.
One two three, one two three, give us our health,
A clean place to live and a small share of wealth!'

Encouraging Liza and Maria to join in, she repeated the small verse and artfully led them out into the yard where she easily drew in the others until they were all singing loudly and cavorting about the place in high spirits. It was young Willy who finally quietened them by standing on top of a dustbin and yelling at the top of his voice, 'Get Jacob Marcovitch! The rat-catcher! Fetch 'im quick!'

'*Mr* Marcovitch,' said Sophie, 'is out on business. Catching royal rats nesting in posh 'omes in Westminster. Why?'

His face creasing up and his bottom lip curling, Willy could not stop the tears from pouring out. He looked terrified. 'There's . . . there's . . . in the stable . . . big, big grey rat . . . and . . . and . . . lots of pink baby ones.' The dustbin lid was beginning to rattle under his trembling body.

'That's all right, cock,' said Charlie the cart-pusher, going to his aid. 'Come on down,' he went on, holding out his arms. 'Uncle Jacob'll be back soon and'll put paid to that nest. Good boy for spotting it and for lettin' us know.' Willy buried his head in Charlie's shoulder as the old gentleman passed him over to Maria.

With her arms on her hips, Sophie looked around at the others and was determined not to let their spirits fall because of one nest of rats. With her short fat arms outstretched, she began to dance around the yard again, singing, and soon had the others joining in both song and dance until their voices could be heard echoing round the streets surrounding Kelly's Yard . . .

'One two three, one two three, what do we care?
We've rats in the stable and fleas in our hair!
No soles to our shoes and our feet are all bare,
But . . . one two three, one two three . . . life isn't fair.
Come, you posh ladies, come into the lair,
See what you see . . . and tell us it's fair.
One two three, one two three, we . . . *do* bleedin' care!'

The following day at Bollards, Maria was tense, feeling the strain of trying to behave normally. She had written a polite letter to Mr Clarkson and taken it in when she had delivered his daily post. Fortunately he was in a meeting with the directors at the time so she hadn't had to face him. It was now the middle of the afternoon and she was due to go in and see Miss Drake as she had arranged that morning. She hadn't given a reason as to why she wished to see her, and the smug expression on the woman's face spoke volumes. Maria had a strong feeling that Miss Drake was under the impression that she wanted either to lodge a complaint or ask for a raise in salary. Either would give the austere woman a weapon. A complaint could be seen as disloyalty to the company, provoking instant dismissal, and a request for a raise was likely to be turned down flat for no given reason. The latter would be Miss Drake's first choice, as she usually relished delivering the inevitable sermon that followed, enjoying it more than any of her duties at Bollards. It was unclear whether it was the female staff or the young male upstarts whom she saw as a threat to her position, but to Maria it was neither here nor there. The point was that the woman firmly believed herself to be their superior, enjoying the role and determined not to let anyone usurp her.

As she arrived at the door with the woman's name slotted into a long, narrow brass frame above the words 'Four minutes is one too many', Maria went cold, as if a ghost had walked over her grave. This was Miss Drake's motto, one she had placed there herself. Taking a deep breath, she reminded herself that this woman was no different from any other under her austere clothing, and stripped of her work title would be no match for the wit and brains of Maria. She tapped quietly on the door and waited for the thin, cold instruction from within, the unwaveringly cold command. 'Enter!'

Inside the small office it was chilly even on this sunny day. The green blinds had been pulled down to all but shut out the light. Maria stole a quick look at the stony expression on the woman's face, which only confirmed her fears that this meeting would be brief, to the point and anything but easy.

'Well, Miss Bertram? Time and tide wait for no man.'

Clearing her throat, Maria stretched to her full height and reeled off her words. 'I would like to offer two weeks' notice of my intention to leave my position at Bollards, Miss Drake.'

Clearly taken aback by this unexpected statement, Miss Drake was momentarily at a loss for words, but within seconds had composed herself and regained her haughty manner. 'This is rather sudden, Miss Bertram. We thought you were happy here at Bollards. We have certainly given you no reason to be otherwise.'

'My mother's been asked by her sister if she would like to live in her spacious lodgings in North London and it may be the case that she accepts. If it does not turn out to be so, if either my aunt or my mother has a change of heart, I will have given up the employment that I have enjoyed here at Bollards unnecessarily. On the other hand, I cannot take the risk of not giving my two-week notice now should we move away, as I will need to seek further employment. I would rather not make the journey from North London for the very reason you have your blinds drawn, Miss Drake. Commercial Road is extremely busy, as will be all the roads across London to here.'

'Well, you've obviously prepared your speech. At least that's something. I shall have to speak to Mr Clarkson to see if he will give his permission.'

'Give his permission, Miss Drake? I don't understand.'

'There has to be a good reason for your leaving, Miss Bertram. We have the name and reputation of this firm to think of. You have signed a binding contract.'

'But I read nothing in it to say that I may not leave provided I give—'

'Well, perhaps you didn't read between the lines! You have been working here for three years, Miss Bertram! That is time enough for you to have found out more than is good for the firm. For all we know you may seek employment with our main competitor.' A smug smile of satisfaction spread across the woman's face as her shoulders relaxed. She had found a reason for not immediately accepting this resignation. 'I shall see you in this office Monday morning at eight thirty sharp. I shall give you my answer then.'

Unsettled by the brief and rather one-sided meeting, Maria walked back to her office, wondering why the woman had managed to make her feel as if she were a criminal. The sense of being trapped in this place was growing. Not only had she Mr Clarkson to contend with but Miss Drake too. Her emotions would have her running from the building, but her instincts were telling her otherwise. She was going to have to grit her teeth and work through this day feeling the burden of worry in her soul. It was as if the firm had its claws fixed around her, holding her tightly in its grasp, and she had the uneasy feeling that she would not be released easily.

5

On a blisteringly hot Saturday afternoon, Maria sat outside her open front door, staring at the picture on the front page of her newspaper, and found herself unable to believe that the beautiful woman she had been reading about could be lying on a slab in the mortuary. The report on the murder confirmed all the speculation as to where Rose Cranfield was from and why someone of a different class, wearing good clothes, should be riding a bicycle in a God-forsaken dark place where rats bred among the thick dirt in the old slumped buildings lurching over the river. Reading on, Maria felt anger rising as the report seemed to condone the killing: 'She, the woman scorned, had indeed come looking for the man who had all but broken her heart. Revenge must have been on the woman's mind. Could it be that this killing was an act of self-defence?'

'Maria?' The soft, quiet voice of Steffan brought her back sharply into the real world.

'Steffan!' she said, a touch startled. 'I didn't realise you were there.' She slapped the newspaper angrily with the back of her hand. 'This is dreadful. They're all but blaming the poor cow for having got herself strangled and then dumped in the river!'

'Sensational stories that stir the reader sell well.' He smiled, admiring the anger in her eyes and on her beautiful face. 'In my paper they completely dismissed the theory of the hunt of the scorned lover. On one of the placards at the railway station it states that the search for the mystery man is under way. You're reacting exactly how you're meant to, Maria. I only believe a third of what gets reported, and even then I take it with a pinch of salt.'

'I s'pose you're right,' she said. 'But *this* is wrong! How dare they print stuff like this? What must her family feel like? If it makes *my* blood boil what must it be doin' to them?'

'Destroying their souls, I imagine . . . as it did to my grandparents when they read about their son. Grossly exaggerated, of course. Not that my father didn't deserve what he got.'

'Oh, Steffan.' Maria sighed, slowly shaking her head. 'I am so sorry. You know what it's like to see your family name ruined in the newspapers. I wasn't thinking.' She lifted herself from the chair, placed a hand on his shoulder and smiled. 'It's just that I get so angry when people are condemned in print and can't fight back.' Then, without thinking who might be watching or caring what anyone might say, she put her arms around him and whispered another brief apology before brushing a kiss across his cheek.

'It's all right, Maria.' He smiled, taking both her hands in his and giving her a long reassuring look. 'You couldn't hurt my feelings if you tried.' For a few moments they held each other's gaze, as if they were the only ones in the yard, or in the world for that matter. 'And anyway, indignation is no bad thing – it brings anger to the surface, which is much better than having it stay inside eating away at you.'

'Steffan, you're always so calm and placid and I love you for it. Come on, let's go for a walk to a quieter part of the river. To King James's Stairs near the park.'

Surprised by her sudden offer, he had no time to mask his joy, which almost gave away his true feelings for her. The fact that she had just mentioned the word love had touched a chord deep inside him. 'That sounds like a lovely idea.' He smiled, his blue eyes twinkling, momentarily lost for words, then said, 'Shouldn't you lock the door?' He knew that eyes were watching from windows and was aware that the women sitting outside had gone rather quiet.

'We lost the key years ago. We 'aven't got anything worth stealing in any case, and strangers, should they come in, are warned off with a glare. Mum'll be back soon anyway – she's gone down to the municipal baths to see how much it costs to do a copper of washing, and Daisy's out with Willy, probably down by the river driving Wilkie mad. They love it down there.'

'Didn't you play there too when you were their age?'

'I did, Steffan,' said Maria, returning his smile. 'I wasn't as daring an explorer as Daisy, but I did play with my friends down by the lock, you're right.' She slipped her arm through his, giving her neighbours something to talk about.

Arm in arm, with no thoughts as to what the others

were thinking now, they strolled from the yard into the entrance to the half-moon alley. Glancing back over her shoulder, Maria checked her two favourite neighbours to see that Sophie was almost smiling with a look of approval on her face and Angel, with her arms folded, was also looking their way and chuckling. Steffan, however, had eyes only for Maria – the neighbours had become invisible.

'It's a pity the river's not cleaner,' he said. 'In this heat a swim would be refreshing.'

'We never did that. Dad used to take me for a very long walk all the way to the Tower and to the muddy beach. The river opens up more there and it was thought to be safer, provided bathers only went in for a shallow paddle.'

'Perhaps we could do that one day – go for a paddle on the edge of the beach?'

'We could take some jam sandwiches and sherbet water and have a picnic.'

'That would be lovely,' he said, trying his best not to look or sound too eager. In truth he wanted to grip her by the waist, lift her high in the air and spin her around for all the neighbours to see. This emotion was very new to him and to repress it seemed wrong. But as with so many emotions in his life, repress it he did.

Watching from the stable, where they had been rummaging through Olly's latest collection of second-hand clothes collected from his rounds in Islington, Sophie and Angel returned each other's silent looks of mild concern. Ever since the police had come in to question them, their main focus of attention having seemed to be the 'would-be' gentleman and his son, they had been left with the growing idea that one or the other of them might be under suspicion. Or even that perhaps they could both have been involved. They knew nothing of the father and son's past and had often wondered what they were doing, living in these surroundings. Up until now they had been viewed as odd but harmless interlopers who must have fallen from grace and into debt. This was a common phenomenon – the East End of London was full of shabby genteels in the same position. Sophie had speculated that the murdered woman may have had something to do with the strange pair, and Angel had the notion that it was the son rather than the father who had something to hide.

With an eye on the two women, Olly sat in a corner of the stable on a bale of straw, contemplating what their next move might be. He had listened to their continuous deliberations on the topic and was fed up with hearing them. To his mind there was nothing suspicious about the father and son living over the stable – like hundreds of others in their circumstances they may well have been made bankrupt and have come here simply to scrape a living. He had enough understanding of human nature to think that perhaps their reluctance to get to know their neighbours arose from embarrassment, not from any malicious or sinister feelings which they were now accused of harbouring.

During his lifetime, Olly had travelled all over London, as a boy assisting his father on his rounds and later, when he could afford to buy his own horse and dilapidated cart, setting out on his own, and had seen his fair share of life's injustices. He had witnessed the rise of a small number of young men who had been born into poverty and had used their wits and intelligence to their advantage: the renowned 'water rats', who robbed the shipping in the Thames; those who owned the old iron and rag shops, which were notorious for fencing stolen goods, or the public houses and beer shops that were little more than a rendezvous for highwaymen, housebreakers, card-sharps and counterfeit coiners. The richest by far were the latter – counterfeit coining had long since been a huge industry, with men from all walks of life involved in this highly lucrative but incredibly risky business. One mint alone had been found to have produced two thousand pounds' worth of bad half-crowns in seven years. The 'smasher', or passer of coins, lurked near every inn yard, and most experienced hackney coachmen had a counterfeit in his hand to return to the unsuspecting fare unwary enough to offer him a good one.

But this side of life was not women's talk, and Olly had always kept certain dealings that he knew about to himself. The women would talk till doomsday about how the rich were getting richer and the poor poorer, but in certain circumstances the opposite was the case. To Olly's way of thinking things had changed little and would continue in much the same way, the wheeling and dealing in the Stock Exchange being no match for the shadier wheeling and dealing that went on in the streets. To him the police were a joke, next to useless when it came to burglary and housebreaking, which were daily occurrences. He knew from what he had heard and seen in various parts of London that the system was inefficient and corrupt, and the police watch nightly patrolling the streets was for the most part comprised of aged dodgers whose income came largely from bribery. His own grandfather many years ago had told him tales of constables going out into the streets and giving unsuspecting beggars pennies in order to arrest them and claim a ten-pound reward. Things had changed since then, but not as much as the Metropolitan Police would have people believe. He smiled at the memory of the grinning, leathery face of his grandfather, but that smile quickly dissolved when his formidable wife called out to him.

'Stop daydreaming, Olly, and come out 'ere into the light! We've somefing to discuss!'

'Leave me be, woman!' was his reply. 'I've been up and about since half past four this morning earning a living! I'm kipping with me eyes open!'

'You'll kip wiv 'em black and blue if you don't move yer arse!'

Reluctantly dragging himself up with a sigh, he slowly stepped forward into the light, but remained under the shade of the abutting roof. 'Be careful, woman . . . I'm too tired for your quips and asides.'

'Come over 'ere!' she whispered loudly. 'What I've to say's not for everyone's ears!'

Making a show of dragging his tired body to where the two women were sitting, outside Sophie's front door, he emerged as if he were on the verge of collapse.

'Go on, then. What's your theory today? The father or the son?'

'What d'yer reckon to Maria walking out with that young man?'

Uttering a long-drawn-out sigh, Olly scratched the inside of his ear. 'Who said they're walking out?'

'We just saw it wiv our eyes, so we did!' said Sophie. 'Whispering and smiling at one another they was. Liza will 'ave a purple fit.'

'How many times 'ave you seen 'em walking together?' Olly sniffed, his eyelids half closed. 'Go on. How many?'

'A first time is generally followed by a second, as you well know!'

'So only the once, then,' he said conclusively. He waved a hand at the women and went back inside to his hideaway, his retreat, where he would stretch out on the bales of hay and enjoy a nap.

'All the same, men are,' said Sophie, shaking her head. 'Can't be bothered to think straight about what's under their own noses.'

'He's tired after a long day, that's all,' said Angel, determined not to let anyone else but herself put her husband down, especially not Sophie.

'So should we 'ave a word with Liza when she gets back from shopping?'

'No, Sophie. Best leave it. You know what a madam she can be. Fancies 'erself as being a touch above us lot, so it'll only add another feather to her cap if she finks that her daughter's caught the son of a gentleman.'

'Ha,' cackled Sophie, 'the son of a penniless one ain't

gonna do her much good, is it? It's money that counts
at the end of the day. *Money.* I mean to say . . . where're
'is friends and family?' She nodded towards the rooms
above the stable. 'They 'aven't exactly bailed 'im out
of any trouble he might've 'ad, money-wise. No. They
talk of breeding and class but should one of 'em fall . . .
you can bet your last penny they'll see no more than
cold shoulders and closed doors. And that gentleman
has fallen, trust me. The mark's on his face. I pity
the son.'

'Whereas we do 'elp each other out when the shadow
falls.'

'Indeed. And may that never change.'

'Do you still believe him to be capable? Of . . . you
know?'

'Murder? I do, Angel. It's them eyebrows. Can't say
about 'is eyes, mind. The man never lifts them for us
to see. If that's not secretive I don't know what is.'

Angel shuddered. 'Oh . . . you make my blood run
cold at times.'

'Yes. And you love it.'

After a pleasant walk with Steffan, and feeling better for telling him about having given in her notice
at Bollards, she left him down by the river on his
way to see if Wilkie Crow was around. Surprised at
the way he had found her tale about her lecherous
superior humorous, she almost felt foolish for taking
it so seriously, and began to wonder whether John
Cunningham might have been overreacting. But the
wheels had been set in motion and her notice handed

in. For reasons which Maria couldn't quite fathom, she wasn't worried about having acted so swiftly now, and had no more doubts as to whether she had perhaps jumped the gun. It simply felt right to leave. Soon she would pen a letter to the employment officer at Meredith and Drew, which was closer to home and, according to one or two of her neighbours outside the yard who were employed in the biscuit factory, it wasn't too bad a place to work. With the building being only forty years old it was less sombre than places like Bollards.

Pleased to see Wilkie at his regular table outside the Ship's Anchor, Steffan approached quietly, since the man had his eyes closed and his face to the sun. Pulling up a chair, he coughed politely to let his new friend know that he was there, should he not be sleeping. Without opening his eyes, or changing his position, Wilkie smiled and said, 'Hello, Steffan, lad. I was only finking about you yesterday and wondering if you'd come back to see us.'

'How are you, Mr Crow? Weary from the heat?'

'No. I'm never weary till my 'ead hits the pillow at night. Can't afford to be. I might look as if I'm being idle, son, but my brain's at work.'

'Oh . . . and I've disturbed you. I'm sorry.'

'Do I look disturbed, lad?'

'No,' chuckled Steffan, 'you don't.'

'Well, that's good, then. Mustn't look what we're not, must we?'

'May I buy you an ale?'

Wilkie smiled. 'Yes, son, you may. What a polite lad you are. Would that my six sons were as polite as you.' Stretching, Wilkie stood up. 'Best if I get the drinks pulled. Joseph'll rob you blind if you go up to the bar.'

'The prices *are* chalked up, Mr Crow—'

'Wilkie to you, son. We're on first-name terms, don't forget. And never underestimate a man serving drinks. They sport a gormless expression on purpose.'

'I know, Wilkie. I've not *just* come up from the country, don't forget. I've been in London since I was fourteen.' Steffan pulled a half-crown from his trouser pocket.

'Well, of course you 'ave! And that's long enough to be one of us,' said Wilkie, looking furtively around. 'But I'll go to the bar in any case 'cos I like to keep a check, if you get my drift.'

His attention suddenly diverted, Steffan leaned forward, peering farther along the river bank. 'Isn't that Maria's small brother?'

'Yes . . . I should say it is.'

'And the gentleman?'

'Oh, I shouldn't concern yerself, lad.' Wilkie's tone had changed from friendly to authoritative. 'A pint, was it?'

'But Wilkie . . . the gentleman has his hand and they're walking off together. Do you know him?'

'Like I said, lad, don't concern yerself. You just sit and take the sun.' With that Wilkie went to the bar and looked around again until a roguish-looking man wearing a battered trilby and a ragged tail-coat gave him a nod and a wink.

Left by himself, Steffan felt anxious for the five-year-old Willy. Something was not right. Turning his head towards the route homeward to the yard, he saw Daisy coming along, peering into dark loading bays and other old buildings and sheds. Ignoring Wilkie's advice he called out to her. 'Daisy! Over here! Are you looking for your brother?'

'I am, yeah,' she said, arriving at his side. 'Little bleeder slipped out of me sight, didn't he?' She looked up at him, one eye closed against the bright sunshine. 'Have yer seen 'im, then?'

'Yes, I have.' He turned and nodded towards Willy and the gentleman, who were walking into the distance. 'Would that be someone you know? The gentleman holding his hand?'

'No, it bleedin' well wouldn't!' snapped Daisy. Losing no time, she tore past Steffan and raced along the quay, leaving Steffan to stare after her and wonder what went on down here by the river.

'You're gonna 'ave to do as you're asked, lad. Until you get to learn the ropes, and that won't be for a while if today's anyfing to go by.'

'But Wilkie,' urged Steffan, 'look at Daisy! She must sense danger – she's faster than a hare in a chase! Who is that man?'

Scratching his ear, Wilkie sighed. 'Come on. I s'pose this way you'll learn quicker. Stop looking so worried. You did the right fing, all considered. Come on.' He turned and pushed his face close to Steffan's. 'But this time . . . don't go shooting your mouth off. Keep shtum. Look, listen and learn.'

Shoving his hands into his old frock-coat pockets, Wilkie sauntered off in Daisy's footsteps, whistling. Puzzled by his lack of urgency, Steffan began to follow, realising that there was more to Wilkie than he liked to let on. Rough-looking men, young and old, were by now sauntering out from dark corners. Steffan counted five in all. With a twist of his hand, Wilkie gave them a message to fall back, almost as if he wanted Daisy to get to her brother before they did. Then, once they were a stone's throw from Daisy, her brother and the gentleman, Wilkie stopped in his tracks and motioned for the others to do the same. He looked at Steffan and sniffed.

'We'll let Daisy 'ave this one.' He then winked and put a finger to his lips when he saw Steffan's mouth open to say something.

Daisy's voice rang out above the sounds of boats coming and going, mooring and unloading. 'Oi! Where d'yer fink you're taking my bruvver to?'

Stopping short, the man spun around and stared distastefully down at what he considered to be a stupid, ragged, unruly urchin. 'Are you addressing *me*, young lady?'

'Well, you're the one 'olding me bruvver's 'and! Where d'you fink you're taking 'im to?'

'It's all right, Daisy,' said Willy, his voice a little shaky. 'He said he was going to take me to a chocolate shop to buy somefing for Mum. It's a long way away but he's gonna fetch me back by a proper 'ansom cab!'

Glancing suspiciously at the stranger, Daisy demanded, 'And why would you wanna be buying my
muvver chocolates? You don't even know 'er!'

'It's a way of thanking your brother, my dear.' The
man beamed naively. 'You see . . . I very carelessly
dropped my wallet and as I turned on hearing it hit the
floor he was there, retrieving it for me. Now that kind
of honesty deserves a reward, wouldn't you say?'

'Bollocks. You was taking 'im away.' She tugged at
Willy's free hand and pulled him from the man's grip.
'So,' she said, pushing Willy away and taking one step
closer to the man, who, by now, looked edgy, having
seen the array of rogues loitering but keeping their
distance, 'you was gonna take my bruvver to buy
chocolates, was yer?'

'Indeed I was,' the man replied nervously, glancing
over her shoulder at the approaching roughnecks, and
especially at one who was carrying a docker's hook
with a very sharp pointed end. 'As a reward for being
honest,' he added. Flashing a look at her and then at
the men, he pulled his handkerchief from his sleeve and
mopped his brow. 'A much-deserved reward,' he mut-
tered, his full attention now on the men and stepping
back from Daisy, who was far too close for his liking.

'Daisy, I want to go 'ome!' cried Willy, and the tears
cascaded down his grubby cheeks. 'I want Mum!'

The posh villain was by now terrified, having fully
realised that he was about to be, at the very least,
disrobed. Terrified, he tilted his head to one side,
grinned falsely at Daisy and took a step backwards.
'I meant no harm to your brother, little girl—'

'Liar!' screeched Daisy. 'Liar! Liar! Liar!' She took a step forward, her eyes fiery with rage, her face red and angry. 'You're one of *them*!' she snarled. 'I can smell your sort a mile off. You smell of scented soap and I smell of wee and that can't be right, *can* it? It should be the other way round, *shouldn't* it?' She slowly inched her way farther forward as he edged his way back from her, getting closer all the while to the edge of the quay.

'What is it you want?' he asked, drawing back from what he considered to be the Devil's child. Almost in tears, he just managed to say, 'Is it money? Are you a beggar? You want a sixpence, is that it?' Catching the sullen look of the skulking men, his face and collar now soaked with sweat, he withdrew a white-lace-edged purse from his sleeve. 'I always give to the beggars,' he cried, his voice going up an octave or two. 'Or a shilling perhaps? Would that help to make you more cheerful, you poor unfortunate—?'

'I'm not bleedin' poor, fank you very much!'

'Daisy, stop it!' wailed Willy, his bottom lip trembling. 'He was being kind to me.'

'Shut up, Willy,' said Daisy, taking a final, determined step forward, causing the almost fainting man to pull farther away from her. His heels at the edge of the quay-side, he lost his balance, and as his arms flew up as if to grab on to thin air he tumbled backwards into the murky river below, his seedy life flashing before him.

The silence was suddenly followed by a chorus of laughter, which rang through the wharf and

along Tobacco Dock as workers of all kinds –
boat-builders, warehouse workers, anchor smiths
and others – emerged to see what the fuss was about.
As the bedraggled gentleman called out for help, the
hardened East London men looked to Wilkie and his
small gang for a sign. With a jerk of the head, a silent
message was instantly conveyed. *Go back to work.*

Within no time, apart from the noise of a mechanical
conveyor belt rolling in a nearby warehouse and a
ship's hooter in the background, the dockside was
silent. A second gesture from Wilkie Crow instructed
the men to go about their work as normal, and suddenly, apart from the hustle and bustle of a normal
working day, the only human voice that could be heard
was that of the drowning man as his shrill screams for
help echoed.

'Off you go, Daisy,' Wilkie said firmly. 'Get yerself
and Willy away 'ome. I'll do me best to save the poor
man.' Then, tousling Willy's unkempt hair, he winked
at him. 'Don't you worry, sonny boy. The man'll be all
right, but learn from it, eh? Never go off wiv someone
you don't know, man or woman.'

'I won't!' cried Willy, shaking his head furiously. 'I
won't ever do it agen!'

'Good boy.' He turned to Daisy. 'Go on, you little
cow. Sling your hook.'

'I never touched 'im, Wilkie! On my life I never!'
screeched Daisy.

'I know that. We all know that.' He looked sternly
down at her. 'Go on. Off you go home.'

Grabbing her brother's hand, Daisy lost no time and

sped along the quay-side, with Willy trying to keep up, his little legs working overtime to try to match her pace.

Coming out of the shadows where he had been hanging back quietly, Steffan approached Wilkie, saying, 'I don't understand. Why have they all vanished? There's a man drowning, for God's sake!'

'Is there?' Wilkie asked innocently, glancing casually into the river. The man was no longer calling out but struggling to make it to one of the oyster boats moored near by. 'No, he's all right. A gentleman like him will know how to swim. Probably got his own private baths where he's practised since he was a kid. Come on inside the tavern. We'll wet our whistles there.'

'Wilkie!' Steffan insisted. 'The man is drowning!'

Leaning forward, Wilkie glared into Steffan's eyes and spoke in a low voice. 'Go inside the tavern or never show yer face down 'ere again.'

Feeling confused and agitated, Steffan resisted the urge to go to the aid of the man and grabbed his new friend's arm. 'I don't know what's going on here . . . but if you don't order your men out of their hiding places to drag that poor devil out I shall go in myself!'

'Poor devil? Tut tut, lad. You've still got sand in yer eyes and in your ears. If you'd 'ave looked and listened and used yer brain from the second you arrived and saw me sunning meself as if I've no work to do or no living to make, you might 'ave followed events with a bit more of a clue.' He turned away and walked back to the tavern with Steffan following in his footsteps.

'I'm in the dark, I'll admit that, but a life is at stake here and—'

'But nothing, son. Finish your ale before it goes flat.'

'I can't do that. I have to go and help before it's too late. Standing by doing nothing is the same as murder!'

Wilkie drew breath and sucked his teeth, his tone now urgent and full of venom. 'You just don't learn that quick, do yer. Having the gentleman in the river is preferable to us finding young Willy's corpse in a month or so. That filthy bastard would have violated his little body and left him for dead, all used up. Now do you get my drift?'

Steffan narrowed his eyes and gazed questioningly but more calmly into Wilkie's face. 'How do you know that?'

'We can smell them coming from a mile off, son.'

Steffan turned away but Wilkie grabbed his collar and turned him back to face him. 'That's right, Steffan, lad. They come down to places like Tobacco Dock and stroll through as if they're on their way to somewhere, but they're not. They come looking. Some like little girls. Some like little boys. Some like both. But any of 'em that come searching in this neck of the woods never find their way home.'

'But you must have seen Willy walking away with the man? Why didn't you call him back?'

'Because the man was spotted at the south end of the dock and word sped through to the north end up by St James's Walk. Our little lads working along the river can run with the speed of a race'orse. The message goes round, gets passed on, and we sit and wait. If they pass through without approaching a child playing we leave well alone.'

'So Willy was some kind of a trap?'

'No. You're not listening. We don't need a decoy. Thousands of kids 'ave gone missing from these parts over the decades and the authorities do sod-all about it. So we've 'ad to set up our own policing, if you get my drift. And by now I would 'ope that you do, lad.'

'I think I am getting the picture,' murmured Steffan, mopping his brow, feeling sick at the thought of what might have been, and slightly embarrassed over his naivety. He knew he must start trusting the people from the world he now belonged to if he was to be really accepted as one of them.

'Good. Daisy being Daisy had to do what she did. She knows what 'appens to them that go missing and she loves 'er little bruvver more'n a mother could love 'er son. She did mess things a bit 'cos it's better to follow these bastards before they meet their end. There's a network who pass a child from one to the other, and the only ones who're gonna ever break into it and blow the lot of 'em to smithereens is the likes of ourselves.' With that Wilkie turned away, went outside and calmly and blandly yelled, 'MAN OVERBOARD!'

Watching from inside the open-fronted tavern, Steffan could hardly believe his own eyes. Men came out from nowhere and made a show about saving the man, who by now was already dead. The shrill sound of a policeman's whistle followed. 'My God . . .' murmured Steffan to himself in awe. 'They are organised.'

A Bow Street Runner stood on the dockside, the buttons on his uniform glinting in the sunshine, chatting to Wilkie while two of his men used a hooked pole to drag the corpse from the river. Leaving formalities to others, Wilkie came back in, sat down and drained his remaining ale in one go.

'You've organised your own policing, Wilkie,' said Steffan, now seeing the truth and Wilkie's considerable power in this place. 'You're a law unto yourselves.'

'Have to be, son. No one gives a fig about us. Shadwellians don't pay taxes, do we? So none of the government's filthy lucre will be spent on us.'

'Of course the poor don't pay tax. They don't earn enough to be taxed. From what I've seen all the families are on the breadline, if they're lucky.'

'Good. You're catching on.' Wilkie ordered two more ales. 'Bit slow on the uptake but then I s'pose you would be. Not born and bred, so it's not in the blood. That's understandable,' he conceded agreeably.

'What do yer want us to do wiv the body, Wilkie?' A young roguish-looking man had come in. 'Put it on the back of a cart and dump it at the 'ospital?'

'What does our policeman say about that?'

'Eh?'

'Well, he is the law. Check wiv 'im first and then dump it on the cart and get it out of 'ere before I take my knife to that throat.'

'Oh, right, yeah.' The lad grinned as light dawned. 'Gotta do it all law and orderly, eh?'

'Off you go, then, lad. Over and done wiv. You saw what 'appened,' he prompted meaningfully.

'Oh, yeah . . . we all saw it. The gent was leaning over the river watching the rats and he leaned too far and fell in.'

'And his purse is where it should be?'

'Oh, yeah. Our policeman checked that straight away. Weren't much in it, though.'

'A gentleman always carries an amount of money, lad.'

'Oh, yeah. There was a gold sovereign and a couple of half-crowns.'

'And the rest of it? You're not giving your statement now,' he pressed.

'Um . . .' murmured the lad, concentrating. 'I'm not sure.'

'And the *rest* of it?'

'Oh, yeah . . . I was forgettin'. It's in my pocket. Four gold sovereigns. The others'll vouch for it,' he fretted.

'No need. Put it in the kitty, boy.'

''Course I will, Wilkie. Why, that's what I come in for.' He withdrew the gold coins and pushed them into a big wooden money box in the shape of a boat, marked 'Poverty Pittance for the Poor. Give generously'. Tipping his cap, the man turned away a touch shamefaced and limped as if his bad leg were giving him pain.

'You're limping on the wrong foot!' Wilkie called after him, breaking into laughter.

'I seem to learn so much in such a short time when

I come down here,' said Steffan, still feeling a little in awe of the place and its people.

'Which is how it should be if you intend to stay. But maybe this will change your mind?'

'No, I don't think so. On the contrary. I'm beginning to feel like one of you at last. I might never leave.' He looked around at the hustle and bustle on the dockside. On the river a ship was just coming into view. 'Having no pressures from any side is not something to take for granted, Wilkie.'

'I'm sure. So what's the word in the yard as to the murdered woman?'

'I've no idea. I don't invite myself into their conversations. The opposite in fact. It still goes quiet when I pass through, especially so since the murder.'

'They'll soon tire of it. But you see the difference?' Wilkie assumed an innocent and slightly dispassionate tone. 'The unfortunate gentleman who was sadly drowned 'ere today and the lady from a middle-class family who gets herself murdered will no doubt be given a full inquiry for the sake of the poor bereaved wealthy families. Whereas had it been one of our women strangled, all we'd see is one of the doddery old coppers. There's the rub and there's the reason why we must be our own judge and jury.' He looked slyly at Steffan's face for his reaction.

'"Only when left and right hand rule as one will success be achieved,"' murmured Steffan, 'and you've worked that out and put it into practice. Government could learn from this small world you've created between yourselves, Wilkie.'

'You try telling them so. But so long as the government's nose is kept out of our business we'll keep our noses out of theirs and get on with it. The Metropolitan Police as well, for that matter. Whoever came in and murdered that woman 'ad best not return to gloat. We don't want Scotland Yard crawling all over the place for much longer. You never know with that lot. They might deem it fit to turn up six times or not even bother to come agen.'

Steffan tried to curb his disbelief, asking, 'But they will *now*, surely?'

'Wot, over that drowning?' Wilkie laughed. 'I doubt it. Who in his right mind would want to push a gentleman into the river? And for no reason? His purse 'as not bin stolen and there'll be no incriminating bruises on his body. The man fell into the river! And that's what the post-mortem will show. No doubt he'll be short of a few other valuables before he's stitched up again. So everyone gains by it.' He grinned. 'Even the medical students.'

Waiting for Steffan's reaction to his cynical comment, Wilkie sniffed and put his face to the sun, eyes closed. As the silent minutes ticked by, he wondered whether it might be time to confess to knowing Steffan's father. The fact that Wilkie had guessed on first meeting Steffan that he and the Gent were father and son was neither here nor there, and normally he would keep quiet about it until one or the other of them deigned to mention the fact in passing. Neither of them so far had mentioned the other, which seemed odd to Wilkie. And now that a woman had been murdered on his patch, Wilkie's mind was working differently concerning father and son, who both appeared to be on the list of possible suspects. He was wary of the pair of them and wanted to find out as much as he could without giving away too much himself. He needed to know a little about their past, but decided not to broach the subject just yet. His silence had paid off and, as he had hoped, had so far encouraged Steffan to make conversation. If he didn't mention the recent murder again then something was up, to his mind.

Seemingly lost in thought, Steffan suddenly piped up, 'So you don't think the police will come and ask questions about that man? If they believe it to have been an accident, Wilkie?'

'I doubt it, lad. Unless of course they think this second drowning in a very short space of time might be linked to the first one.' Wilkie looked slyly at Steffan, who was now staring into the river. '*We* know it wasn't linked, so if they do come sniffing we can 'ave a bit of fun with 'em. Nothing I enjoy more than baiting and teasing the Bow Street Runners. I hear they've bin spending more time in Kelly's Yard than you'd expect. Why d'yer reckon that might be?'

'Have they?' Steffan sounded mildly surprised. 'I didn't know that.'

'That's wot I 'eard.' Wilkie averted his gaze from Steffan and continued. 'From the tone of your voice I take it they've not cross-examined you yet.'

'No, Wilkie, they haven't. I don't spend much time in my lodgings, it's true, but they've not knocked on our door as yet, to my knowledge. I've not seen hide nor hair of the police. Nor has my father. At least, he's not said anything to me, and I'm sure he would have done.'

'Strange, that,' replied Wilkie, rubbing his chin. 'From what they say your name's been on their lips more than once. I would 'ave thought they'd 'ave made it their business to find you at 'ome . . . or at work.'

Steffan looked genuinely agitated but managed to keep his voice calm. 'Why? I don't understand. Why would *our* names be on their lips?'

'I said *your* name, but now you mention it I'm sure they will be keen to have a word with your old man as well. It's beyond me. But then . . . they wouldn't link you or your father to the woman for no reason, would they? As it turns out, and if we're to believe wot we read in the newspapers, she came looking for someone while posing as a reporter. Don't know why she'd want to lie to 'er own diary. Can't imagine anyone'd do that. Be rather daft, wouldn't it? Defeat the object of 'aving a secret diary. But then she needn't 'ave lied to us dahn 'ere, come to that. Saying she was a reporter when she wasn't.' Wilkie sniffed and gazed down at the floor, shaking his head. 'No . . . there was no need for her to lie to us. We're pretty open an' honest about the life we lead.'

'I see what you're getting at now, Wilkie,' murmured Steffan, preoccupied. He was thinking about his father and the lie of a life he had led and was still leading. He knew he used whores – the man had never made a secret of it and had openly encouraged Steffan to do the same – but he couldn't believe that this woman could possibly be one of them. No. His father was many things, but a murderer? Never. He felt sure of it, and more calm now. 'Well, I've nothing to hide, Wilkie. If the police want to speak to me they know where I am.'

''Course they do! So you've got nuffing to worry your 'ead over, 'ave yer? They play cat and mouse now and then. I wouldn't worry abaht it.'

'I'm not. Well, at least, I wasn't' – he grinned ruefully – 'till now. Maybe I should go to them. To the station.'

'You could do. They'd drop dead from shock but . . . it might save 'em troubling you at 'ome. Then agen,' Wilkie said, scratching the inside of his ear, 'it might look as if . . .'

'I protest too much?'

'Summink like that, I s'pose. Yeah. No. I should leave fings be, lad,' he said, having considered the options. 'Forget I ever said anyfing,' he added amiably.

'I don't think I can now. I'll ask in the yard. See if they've all been questioned.' Steffan stood up to leave. 'I hope you don't mind me bringing this up again, Wilkie, but, well, you don't seem the least bit put out over this latest incident. I mean to say . . . is it something that happens frequently?'

'What incident might that be?'

'The drowned man.'

'Oh, that.' He shrugged. 'No. No, that was unfortunate. But like I say, Daisy will as Daisy wants. Normally, the skunk would 'ave bin dealt wiv away from these parts. But there. You don't wanna worry yer 'ead over that. It's forgotten as far as us lot dahn 'ere are concerned. Don't know about Daisy, though. Will 'er lot praise 'er for ridding the world of one more of them or will she get a caning? Can never tell and it's not worth the debate, lad. We're all the better off for it and another five-year-old's bin saved. I should go around smiling over it, if I was you. Sport that half-and-half expression or give the wrong opinion and folk will fancy you don't agree wiv the way we do fings around Shadwell. And that wouldn't be healthy. You don't want that, lad. Unless, of course, you are finking of moving on after all?'

This speech from Wilkie had been deliberately engineered to get to this point. From what he had heard from the easy talkers in the neighbourhood, the finger of guilt was pointing at either Steffan or his father for the murder, and until they had proved themselves innocent in their neighbours' eyes their every move would be watched without them having any idea of it.

'No, I'm not moving on,' said Steffan. 'I told you, I'm beginning to feel at home at last. Thanks mainly to you . . . and Maria.'

Wilkie saw the flicker of love in the lad's eyes and smiled, saying, 'You've got a few miles to go yet, son, but I would say that you are beginning to meet and mould to our ways . . . just.'

In Kelly's Yard, Maria was outside listening to Daisy giving her account of what had happened down by the river. By now Willy had stopped crying and was very quiet, watching his sister's expression while Liza grilled her as to how her brother had managed to wander off without her. Willy had already received a smack on the back of the leg from Liza for going off with a stranger.

'I can't watch 'im all the bleedin' seconds God sends me, can I!' cried Daisy, her face saving her from a good slapping. Liza knew her child well enough to realise she was very upset by the turn of events. 'And it wasn't my fault the man fell in the river! You can ask Wilkie Crow or any of the others!'

'I never said it was your fault,' her mother replied, 'I'm just saying that if you'd kept a closer eye on your brother none of this would 'ave happened! Now go inside the both of you and calm down!'

Taking Willy's hand, Daisy tossed back her hair defiantly and smeared the tears from her face with the back of her hand as she moved out of harm's way, before adding, 'I would 'ave pushed the bugger in anyway even if he never fell.' The slamming shut of her front door brought a wry smile to Liza's face as she raised her eyes skyward and also a quiet chuckle from Maria.

'That spirit of 'ers is either gonna be 'er downfall or will be the success of 'er,' said Sophie, laughing. 'I wouldn't like to gamble on which it might be.'

'But you look here, ladies,' said Angel, 'this really is no laughing matter. I dread to think what could 'ave happened had Daisy not seen 'im in time.'

'Or what's goin' on in this world all the time with

none of us 'aving a clue about it,' Sophie chimed in. 'Wilkie and the lads are sharp and on their toes when one of that lot appear but them poor children who sleep rough over Whitechapel and in Aldgate . . .' She shook her head solemnly as her words trailed off. 'I dread to think.'

'If we could but rely on the coppers it would be somefing,' murmured Angel. 'But I've heard that one or two of them are not opposed to having their way with a child themselves.'

'Oh, come on, Angel!' snapped Liza. 'Don't say such things. If we can't respect the law then who can we trust?'

'That's just my point,' she said, becoming more animated and warming to her subject. 'We can't trust any of 'em. Politicians nor the law, nor royalty. We're nothing to them. Nothing. Never mind we're flesh and blood. It's where we are in society that counts, our place, and we're counted in with wild animals or rats so far as they're concerned. Let's not fool ourselves and believe otherwise. It's a fact and always 'as bin.'

'Well, we're everything to each other and that counts for a lot in my book,' said Sophie. 'Now then, I must string and tie my mattresses ready for collection or there'll be nuffing for me to toss into the stew pot this evening.'

'And I must be off to Pierhead to scrub them floors,' said Angel.

'How's the work down there going?' asked Liza, with the idea that she might try for a few hours' work cleaning inside the government building. 'It's a very big place, the Customs House, isn't it?'

'There's enough work down there for us all, Liza, but it's hard work and all for ninepence an hour. But there we are. Four hours brings in three shillings so it's worth risking housemaid's knee for.'

Running the idea through her mind, Liza nodded, thoughtfully. 'I might pop down there later on and sign on. It's a busy place from what I gather and very noisy. Is that right?'

'I should say so. And filthy with all the mud and grease and so on. But mud and grease give us work so there we are.'

'I wouldn't 'ave thought there was that much dirt inside the buildings, Angel,' said Sophie, pulling string tightly round a rolled mattress. 'Very smart places they are.'

'What? The corridors and stairs want scrubbing twice a day. In the building on either side of the pier. The living quarters are different. They wouldn't employ the likes of us for in there nor in the offices. No. They keep live-in chamber maids for that.'

'Ha! Personal prostitutes that do a bit of dusting on the side, you mean!'

'Well, yes.' Angel grinned. 'That is the case sometimes, so I've heard, but we must turn a blind eye if we're to keep our jobs. And if you were to ask me, I would say that when them old ramshackle buildings at Pierhead were pulled down to make way for the new grand properties it was the beginning of the end of a way of life.'

'I know,' murmured Liza. 'I agree with you, Angel. Ours is not exactly a grand way of life by any means but it's where we live and it's our territory, our patch of London. And what of our yard? Do we know any more yet as to whether we're to be turned out on to the streets? Or have things simply got out of hand? A rumour spread and blown out of all proportion thanks to the newspapers, smoke without fire?'

'There's never smoke wivout fire, Liza. You should know that,' said Sophie, slowly shaking her head. 'But as Jacob was saying, maybe it is a blessing in disguise. Maybe we will be offered new tenement flats. Clean and dry from floor to ceiling. If so, maybe that will be our turning point.'

'I very much doubt it. Have you seen the ones that have already been built? Across the river?' said Liza. 'Just like prisons, they are, and from what I've heard there's nowhere to sit outside, hundreds of steps to climb should you be placed at the top of a four-storey, and hundreds of steps to go down every time you wanted to put rubbish in your dustbin.'

As much as she didn't like hearing this, Sophie had little choice other than to accept Liza's worrying account of the facts. 'Well then,' she said, slowly shaking her head, the look of doom back on her face, 'if all you say is right, we'll have a wicked fight on our hands, so let's not treat it all as humbug. Not if there's a shred of truth in the rumours.'

'And fight we must if we're to keep the little we have. These places might be small but we're not on the streets and if we're too lax over our futures we may well end up like thousands of others, in the workhouse. We mustn't lose hope nor go off the boil. My Maria said she'll storm into Parliament over it. And we were all for that when we spoke previously, I believe.'

'I'm not for laying down quietly and taking it, Liza,' murmured Sophie, slowly rubbing her eyes. 'But don't ask me to lead the way, that's all. Or carry a banner. I'm too weary for all that. Too weary, too past it and too worn out.'

'No, we'll follow the leader and leave the younger ones to fight,' said Liza. 'Maria, Daisy, your sons and any more we can rope in. They can carry the flag, and let's agree to say no more about it until we hear more and for certain.'

'Agreed,' replied Sophie, stretching one shoulder after the other to ease the burning pain.

'Agreed,' murmured Angel, with one eye on her friend, noting that Sophie Marcovitch was looking a little more weary than usual. 'Why don't I make us three a decent cup of strong tea?'

Both Liza and Sophie stared at Angel, disbelieving. They didn't usually make jokes about such things – it was tantamount to cruelty. 'That would be very very nice, Angel,' was the cautious, hopeful reply.

'Well,' said Angel, looking around her and leaning forward, 'close yer mouths 'fore a fly gets in. I found my way into a store cupboard in a room where the secretaries make the governors their morning coffee and afternoon tea. They get two cheese rolls each in the morning with their coffee and chocolate biscuits in the afternoon with their tea. Now I'm not saying I would let you 'ave biscuits if I should ever manage to get my hands on any, but I will share the half a pound of tea with you.'

'Angel, you never did!' whispered Liza incredulously. 'You'll lose the work and worse if they find out!'

'They won't find out. That cupboard's stacked with tea, coffee, sugar . . . and cocoa! And none of it listed!' She stood up, stretched, placed her hands on her hips and smiled at them both. 'Ladies, I think our boat might be in at last – or should I say our ship? And not one ship but more and all packed with good things that we should 'ave been 'aving a share of be now. So what d'yer say to that, Sophie?' Angel smiled, eyeing her friend with caution.

'A cup of tea would be very nice, Angel. It would be wonderful!' Sophie giggled.

'Come on, that's not what I meant. Don't let us down . . . "One two three, one two three . . ."' She cocked an ear and waited for her friend to finish the line and break into one of her ad lib ditties.

'Not now, eh? Tomorrow. We'll sing it tomorrow – when I'm not so worn out.' Sophie turned slowly around and lumbered into her front room, calling quietly behind her, 'Fetch it in for me, eh, Angel? I'm just gonna lie down for ten minutes.'

Glancing at each other worriedly, Liza and Angel fell quiet. They knew when it was time to stay silent and not make a fuss. Sophie was best left to herself at such moments, and they knew to keep their distance, but also to keep an eye on her. The woman had had her fair share of worry during her lifetime, and if truth be known she was still worrying without letting on. She was clearly frightened that she and her husband the rat-catcher might lose their one-up, two-down home. If there were plans afoot for their homes to be possessed and razed to the ground, she of all people would have thought about it at length and come to her own conclusions. In reality there was little any of them could do to stop the powers that be!

The colour had drained from Sophie's face and there had been a look of pain in her eyes that they hadn't seen before. Sophie wasn't herself – not by a long chalk. Exhaustion from too much hard labour alone could bring any woman down to a level that she might not be able to pull herself up from too easily. Most of those here in Shadwell who were living hand to mouth were malnourished, which inevitably meant that resistance to any type of illness, slight or otherwise, was lowered. If Sophie was just suffering from exhaustion then the others could pull together and get her through it. If it was more of a medical problem . . . they were possibly staring death in the face where their friend was concerned. 'I've never known her to lie on her bed during the day, Angel,' murmured Liza, frightened for Sophie and without her usual confidence that things had a way of turning out right in the end.

'No . . . neither 'ave I and maybe that's the trouble. She should. We should all stop for at least twenty minutes and rest our bodies. We mistreat ourselves, that's the trouble. Twenty minutes is no time when you consider how many hours we're up and about.'

'But do we have a choice?'

'Of course we do. Everyone 'as a choice. We push ourselves beyond the limit or we pace ourselves and live longer.'

'Maybe you're right,' said Liza, turning her head to focus on the open doorway into Sophie's house. 'And we mustn't leave it till it's too late.' She glanced at Angel and shrugged. 'Let this be a warning to all three of us and not just to our friend.'

'I agree, Liza. I absolutely agree. The fear that if we stop working we might not be able to get going agen is silly. We must all take it a little easier. We won't starve. Please God we'll never starve.'

By the time Steffan returned from Tobacco Dock there were people from outside buzzing around the yard, having been drawn in by the news that there had been another drowning and eager to know whether this was also a case of murder. Catching Maria's eye, Steffan was pleased when she indicated for him to give her a couple of minutes until she could join him. She was listening to Angel, who was giving her a brief run-down on Sophie and how she was still lying on her bed, drifting in and out of sleep.

Going into the stable, Steffan glanced at Olly's rickety old stall on which he had arranged his bric-a-brac, priced up for the next wave of bargain-hunters coming into Shadwell. To Olly, the news of the latest drowning was a blessing. The world was rid of one more of the worst kind of human beings imaginable *and* he could expect a steady crowd of the morbidly curious over the next few days. It seemed to him that there would always be folk who had money in their purses and not much sense, and who could not resist the chance of picking up an antique on the cheap while also being party to Olly's 'highly confidential' report on the local colour, dark or otherwise, including rumours and suspicions. From his recent experiences he had discovered that the wealthy were not as bright as he had imagined. He could out-fox most and have them departing with a little something that gave him a good profit. It hadn't taken long for Olly to see that his best tactic was to have them believe they were more discerning than he was himself. Had they known that, although illiterate, he had a trunk of tatty second-hand illustrated books depicting porcelain, silver and small pieces of furniture with makers' marks and values, they may not have been quite so eager to part with their shillings. He knew that a chip or crack rendered most pieces of china all but worthless to a collector, and this man's ardent passion was, with the aid of washing soda and his own filler paste recipe, to cleverly conceal the faults. His long hours spent bent over his work table at the back of the stable by the light of an oil lamp were beginning to pay off. Catching sight of Steffan, Olly stepped forward out of the shadows and, with a wave of the hand, beckoned him in.

Pleased that barriers which he thought impenetrable were coming down, Steffan joined his neighbour and smiled. 'This is much better,' he said, looking around. 'Much cooler in this shade.'

''Course it is. Once you get used to the pong it's not

half as bad. But then I should fink you're quite used to it anyway lodging up there in the palace.'

'Palace?' Steffan quietly laughed. 'I wouldn't call it that.'

'Well, no, but them rooms are spacious and you've got, what, three for only you and your father to spread out in? That counts as a palace round this way. Dunno why the rent's so cheap but there we are. Unless the crafty landlord put it up when you moved in.'

'No, I don't think he did. It's cheap but the roof leaks and the wind howls through in the winter.' Steffan was aware of Olly coaxing him towards the stall at the back, which was crammed with a jumble of artefacts that he had to admit looked interesting.

'It's funny you should pick today to come into my little shop, as I now like to call it. If you've a sweet'eart I've just the fing for yer. Cheap at the price and cheaper still 'cos you're one of us, a neighbour.' He picked up a small blue-and-white glass scent bottle. 'Look at that glass. Not a bubble to be seen. Sapphire blue that is. And the top's silver, you know. Georgian silver that is.' He passed it to Steffan, who had no choice but to accept and admire it.

'It's very beautiful. Pity the top is dented.' Making this casual remark was the worst thing he could have done. To Olly it meant he was bartering and the sale was all but clinched.

'Dent? Well, do you know, I never noticed that.' He peered at it more closely but did not take the bottle back. 'Oh . . . now I see it. Well, I s'pose that proves its age. Proves that it's an antique. Although there is a silver hallmark there. A bit worn out but then it would be. It being an antique. I could bring the price down, though, on account of my not noticing that dent when I purchased it. My loss not my customer's is the way I see it. A shilling and a shake of the hand and it's yours. I can't say fairer than that, Mr Tremain.'

Flattered that this man knew his name, and guessing he'd learned it from Maria, Steffan was at a loss as to how to get out of this predicament. A shilling to him meant a few miles closer to his mother come the day when he had enough saved to go in search of her. 'I'm afraid I don't have a sweetheart, Mr Black. Would that I had. If it were the case I would most certainly have been interested in buying this lovely bottle, but as it is—'

'All right,' said Olly, all knowing and familiar, 'I should 'ave known you'd be as shrewd as myself when it came to a deal to be struck. We'll call it ninepence, shall we?'

'It's very good of you but—'

'All right.' Olly grinned, shrugging. 'I 'ave to admire you for it. Sixpence and you can pop it into your pocket for when you do have a sweetheart.'

Seeing no way out of this, Steffan reluctantly thanked him for his generosity, dug his hand into his pocket and pulled out a sixpenny bit, one he would rather have kept than spent on something he had no use for. 'Thank you very much,' he said, shaking Olly's hand.

Pulling him closer, Olly whispered in his ear. 'Lady luck's on your side, lad.' He nodded over Steffan's shoulder at Maria, who was approaching. 'Well, talk of the devil!' he said, overly loudly and purposely so.

'I might not be an angel, Olly, but I don't have horns either.' Maria smiled, looking from him to Steffan.

''Course you don't. And we think you are an angel. Why, Steffan was only just saying so. Look at what he's just bought for yer. Cost 'im a few shillings that did.' He winked at Steffan and went back to his creaky old chair and rocked to and fro, considering his recent sale. He had picked up the bottle in a box of other old scent bottles and powder bowls for next to nothing.

'It's all right, Steffan.' Maria laughed. 'I know him of old. He's cornered you into buying that and then cornered you into believing you have to give it to me. How much did he charge you for it?'

'Not very much at all. And actually, I did buy it for you. As a thank-you for bringing me into the fold, as it were. I doubt that Olly would have befriended me so readily had he not seen us smiling at each other in the yard.'

Maria looked from Steffan to the glass bottle in his hand. 'It's really lovely but I couldn't accept it. You work hard for your money and—'

'Well then, never mind. I'll give it to Daisy instead.' Steffan turned away from her beautiful questioning eyes, embarrassed. He felt as if he had been too forward in offering her a present. 'I owe as much to her and Willy as I do to you. It was because of them that I found you in Whitechapel.'

'Well, if you do give it to our Daisy,' said Maria, having had a change of heart and now wanting the bottle herself, 'don't be disappointed if she sells it on the sly to one of Olly's customers for more than you paid.'

'She wouldn't do that, Maria, would she? You think it's not lovely enough to want to keep?'

'I do, but I can't speak for Madam.' Maria smiled. 'She's got a brain for business inside that scatty head of hers. I think she takes after Dad. Pretty though this may be a full belly to our Daisy is worth its weight in gold.'

'So you do think it's pretty?'

'I told you, Steffan . . .' She glanced at the bottle and shrugged. 'I think it's lovely but . . . well, it doesn't seem right you spending your money on me.'

'It didn't cost the earth, Maria.' He smiled almost apologetically at her.

'Perhaps not, but you need every penny if you're to buy your way out of this yard.'

'Sixpence won't break the bank,' he said, lifting the bottle to the light so that the sun shone through it. 'But if you don't want it—'

'I do want it.'

'Well then, have it.' He pressed it into her hand and cupped hers with his. 'I wish you well when you use it. As use it one day you will, when it will be filled with perfume.'

'Thank you,' said Maria, suppressing the desire to hug him. She kissed him lightly on the cheek, and when he responded by placing his hand around her waist and pulling her closer to him she kissed him again, this time on the lips. Gently breaking away from him, she said, 'I'll keep it for ever, Steffan. Till my dying day. It's beautiful. Thank you.'

'So are you.' He smiled, observing out of the corner of his eye that one or two of the neighbours were looking their way. 'I wonder what the gossips will make of this?'

'Oh, they'll 'ave us down for gettin' married now.' She laughed. 'Take no notice of them.'

'Well,' he said, 'we'll soon find out. Your mother's looking our way now and I think she's going to come over.'

'She don't bite, you know. Stop being so nervous of this lot. Once they've accepted you, you'll be one of us and see things differently.'

As Liza drew close to them, Maria could see that Steffan had folded his arms and his back had straightened. He now sported the look of a young man standing his ground, desperate to get away but willing himself not to run.

At Maria's side, Liza glanced from her to Steffan and waited. 'Come on, Maria, where're your manners?'

'Oh, sorry, Mum. This is Steffan. He lives—'

'I know where he lives, you daft thing. I've not been introduced, that's all. Pleased to meet you properly, Steffan, after all this time.' She smiled as she offered her hand.

'Pleased to meet you too, Mrs Bertram, and I'm sorry now that I hid away for so long,' he said slightly flirtatiously, slipping his hand into hers and gently squeezing it.

'And so are we. I've just heard that I've something to thank you for, Mr Tremain.'

'Really?'

'One of the lads from the dock told me that it was you who alerted Daisy about our Willy going off with the stranger. He said you went against Wilkie Crow's advice. That was very bold of you, and in my book the best deed in any one lifetime.'

'Oh, well, not really,' mumbled Steffan, embarrassed. 'Wilkie and his men had it under control. I learned that afterwards and felt a bit of a fool.'

'That's as may be but it's my little boy we're talking about and I'm none too pleased that they took a chance like that. What if he'd had someone waiting to charge off at speed in a cab? We'd all be feeling very different now had that been the case.'

'No,' said Steffan, his tone definite. 'That wouldn't have happened. Take my word for it. They had men posted along the quay. The man was spotted coming in and word spread like lightning. I still can't believe it myself, Mrs Bertram. But I do assure you, Willy was safe in their hands.'

'Well, maybe so. But thank you all the same. And should you ever feel like a bit of company, you're very welcome in our house. We may only be able to offer you a weak cup of coffee and companionship but it comes with a good heart.'

'I appreciate that, Mrs Bertram,' he replied, looking over her shoulder, uneasy. He could see his father making his way through the gathering in the yard, his face a high colour and his eyes glassy. Not yet early evening and already he was a touch unsteady on his feet. Maria had seen too. She had a fine view of Mr Tremain senior.

'I didn't know you were the hero, Steffan,' teased Maria, impressed by the way he had not mentioned his part in saving Willy from danger, let alone come into the yard bragging about it the way most others would. 'I'll talk with you about that later on. Come on, Mother, time waits for no man,' she said, indicating to Liza with her eyes that it was time for them to part company with Steffan. 'Come on inside the house. We've the suet pudding to knock up, don't forget.'

Maria breathed more easily as she pulled the door of their house to and watched through the small gap. Steffan's father, in an aggressive mood, was standing over his son, a look of contempt on his puffy red face as he quietly berated him. Turning his back abruptly and walking away from him, Steffan went up the wooden steps and into their lodgings, leaving his father barking at thin air.

'Good for you, Steffan,' murmured Maria, 'it's about time.'

'About time for what?' asked Liza, pulling her enormous mixing bowl from her kitchen cupboard.

'That he stood up to that horrid man. His father.'

'Oh? But he seems a real gentleman. What makes you say a thing like that?'

'He's a bully. Steffan can't wait to save enough to move on and get away from 'im.'

'Well now . . . you two seem to have got to know each other. How long's this bin going on?'

'I told you. We bumped into each other last week and went into the coffee shop. He's much more relaxed when he's out of the yard. I don't know why.'

'Well I never. Funny how things turn out.' Liza smiled, scooping flour from a small sack. 'I sat more than once out there making belts and imagining you and that young man walking out. A little fantasy to stop me from worrying over the kind of chap you could end up with, I s'pose.'

'Well, you just go on dreaming, Mum.' Maria laughed. 'He'll marry one of 'is own kind, one day, once he's making his way. Living in this yard with us is a stepping stone, that's all. A stepping stone away from the path he was on and the one he'll find 'is way back to.'

'If you say so, Maria. If you say so.'

Liza began to knead her dough, making a little wish. A wish that she would keep to herself.

6

By the time John Cunningham arrived in Shadwell Green on Sunday he was feeling as if he had been up and about for twenty-four hours instead of nine. He had had his fill of people and was weary from all he had seen, heard and smelt on his trip from Islington to Petticoat Lane by omnibus, and then by foot along Whitechapel and on to Wapping.

It was a typical day for many of London's poor and destitute, especially children, who were making use of the good weather. The park was full of them, scrambling in ancient trees, teasing stray dogs, swatting flies and bees with old rolled-up newspapers, and of course on the lookout for someone to offer services to, whether errand-running or shoe-shining.

Leaning against some iron railings and enjoying a few draws on his pipe, John could not help but wonder why the street urchins in their rags, running barefoot and filthy, appeared to be so much freer in spirit than those children wearing smart, restrictive, Sunday-best clothes who were on their very best behaviour. He felt as if he were watching two worlds merging into one. Here in this park the wealthy and the ragged poor walked in each other's footsteps, breathed in the same air and enjoyed the same scenery. As one would expect, the children did not mix or play together. Nannies or parents shepherding their children would soon put paid to that sort of thing. It simply wasn't done.

But what might happen if there were no adults present? thought John. What if all of the children here were left by themselves to find amusement? Would they play together? He believed they might. Then again history had proved time and time again that a fist fight, nail-scratching and hair-pulling would soon be likely to break out all over the place, and it would be the middle-class children who would return home dishevelled and ragged, without shoes or boots or bonnets, and sporting a beauty of a black eye or two.

Having just been introduced to Petticoat Lane for the very first time, this young man, who lived a fairly quiet existence with his mother, had seen more of the real world in half a day than he had witnessed in his entire lifetime. He had gone to the well-known market-place, a narrow thoroughfare leading to numerous filthy alleys and courts, on a kind of sightseeing tour. The most memorable thing had been the vast number of people who congregated there every Sunday morning, to peddle, purchase or plunder the booty on offer. The whole length of Petticoat Lane, of which half was in Middlesex and the other half in London, presented an ideal situation for rogues, who could fence their stolen goods without too much bother from the police, who were unable to intervene, knowing that criminals dodged from one police patch to another through the winding back streets and courts.

John's trip to the notorious lane had been an eye-opener, to put it mildly. He had been on a fact-finding mission for his mother, who had recently taken a low-rent shopfront in Islington, where she planned to sell good second-hand clothes. She needed to find a source from which she could purchase cheaply, regularly and reliably. In Petticoat Lane John had found a wealth of suppliers selling goods ranging from the tattiest of rags to the finest array of discarded middle-class cast-offs. Much to his amazement there had been just as much bartering on the ancient narrow streets surrounding the lane, between inhabitants and people from outside who had wandered away from the main part of the market to soak up the local atmosphere.

Away from the crowded lanes now, and comfortable in the shade of a tree in Shadwell Green, John enjoyed his packed lunch of cheese-and-pickle sandwiches as he mused over his first visit to Petticoat Lane. He regretted having been too unsettled by the constant shenanigans and the noise and crowds to have managed to purchase a single thing, but at least he had gleaned enough about how things worked to familiarise himself for his return.

The crockery and glass stalls, the pawnbrokers outside their shops inviting people in, the spirited trading all around him – he had loved it all, and could not wait to tell his mother of this wonderful place. He felt as if he had found Aladdin's cave. True, he had had to keep a close check on anything about his person that was not tightly fastened or buttoned down, given the wily street children continually darting in and out of the milling crowds or leaning on a chosen corner of an old warehouse, watching and biding their time with the guile of a fox. The sudden and urgent cry of 'Stop, thief!' which could be heard regularly was received with no more than a shrug from the inhabitants, who saw any toffs coming on to their patch as fair game. This had horrified him at first until he had become used to double-checking the security of his own pockets.

Had he wandered through those same streets on a pleasant Saturday evening he would have thought he had stepped into a completely different world. Saturday evening being near the close of the Jews' Sabbath, the silence which prevailed by comparison to a Sunday morning was more than striking, and in particular in Cutler Street, a stone's throw from Petticoat Lane.

On Saturdays Jewesses, many of them richly dressed, formed gossiping groups, and although places of business, including public houses, were nearly all closed, the area would be filled with a multitude of Jewish families, some in gala costume, enjoying the evening of their day of rest. For the mothers in particular it was a day when a match might be made between a boy from a good Jewish family and one of their own daughters – often lovely young girls with faces of great beauty, transmitted from generation to generation since the days of Moses.

'Look at 'im all done up to the nines!' said a grubby seven-year-old girl as she nudged John with her foot, snapping him out of his thoughts. 'Spare a couple of coppers for two starving kids, can yer, mister? Me brother's terminal.' She nodded at her smaller brother, who was wearing ripped dirty trousers, a shirt far too big for him, with the sleeves cut to the elbows, and odd boots which had the fronts cut away, showing his dirty feet and black toenails. 'You look a proper gentleman, you do. A kindly sort of man. Are yer rich?' The boy sniffed, cuffing his nose.

'No,' said John. 'I can spare a threepenny bit between you. How does that sound?'

'What do we 'ave to do for it?' said the girl, screwing up her nose and peering at him with hardened suspicion, her blue eyes in stark contrast to the grime etched on her face. No one ever *offered* money. It had to be squeezed out of people as a rule.

'Leave me in peace.' He grinned, flicking the coin at the boy, who caught it and ran off laughing. The girl, close on his heels, was cursing him for all she was worth.

John looked around for Maria, at the same time making certain than none of the lads there to pick pockets was too close to him. Content with his own company under the shade of the old oak tree, he watched a tramp with a Bible who had appeared and, with his good book open, had begun pacing up and down, whether reading or reciting something brainwashed into him since childhood wasn't clear. The man was a sight to behold with his battered trilby, his long coat, baggy trousers and aged shoes. His grey-black beard and wiry hair falling to his shoulders brought to mind a character out of one of Mr Charles Dickens' stories. He was totally absorbed in his own world, as if he were the only person there. This old gentleman was known locally as Sid, a harmless, gentle soul who had the natural ability to spread calm.

Farther afield were three gypsy women in layers of washed-out clothes which had once been bright and cheerful. They were picking wild roses growing on a huge rambler climbing against an old brick wall which separated one of the terraced houses from the park. Near by were five or six gypsy children wrapping waxed paper around the stems of roses and carefully plucking off those petals which were not perfect. John knew that as soon as Maria turned up a rose would be offered to him for a penny, for the 'beautiful lady'.

These old Romanies were known to travel all around London (around England, for that matter), and it was easy for John to believe that those here today might be the same travellers who offered their services as fortune-tellers in the markets close to where he lived in North London. He knew that gypsies slept in parks and greens under the stars during spring, summer and autumn, but had no idea where they laid their heads during the bitter winter months, when they would go from door to door all day long selling small bunches of lucky lavender and heather. His mother had once told him, when he was a boy, that the gypsies had small colourful wagons parked on waste ground which were like little palaces.

'Well, you look comfortable enough, Mr Cunningham,' said Maria, coming up behind him. 'I hope I've not kept you waiting. It's not very nice having to hang on a piece of string, is it?'

There was a hint of acerbity in her voice which went

undetected. On her way to the park she had asked herself why she was bothering. After that first time together, when she had believed he had enjoyed his afternoon with her, he had all but ignored her at work. She was not used to fickle people in her world, where black was black and white was white.

'No, I've not been here very long,' said John, shifting along the wide tree trunk to make space for her. 'The grass is quite thick and plush here. I can't think why.'

'I can,' said Maria, inspecting the grass and wondering why he had not responded to her sarcasm. Her neighbours would have pounced on it. 'Dad, bless his heart, always said that dogs giving the trees a watering was the best thing for the grass.'

'I think he might have been pulling your leg, Maria.' John chuckled.

'Very likely. So, John . . . here we are agen. Do you want to know how I got on with handing in my notice?' She settled herself next to him and stretched her legs. 'Oh . . . that's better. You never realise how much your legs ache till you take the weight off 'em.'

'You didn't have any problems, did you?' said John, a concerned look in his eyes. 'They accepted your notice, didn't they?'

Maria shrugged casually, keeping her thoughts to herself – her thoughts being that he was overly concerned about her leaving Bollards because of the lecherous Mr Clarkson. Did he think her so pathetic as not to be able to fight her own corner? To stand and speak the truth?

She withdrew a bottle of home-made sherbet water

from her bag and pulled out the glass stopper. 'I must wait to see if they'll accept my notice, John. Miss Drake hinted that they might not. And to be honest with you, I'm having second thoughts in any case.'

'Why? You must think of your reputation. He could ruin it!'

'If I stay I'll keep out of his way. I'm not as bothered about it as you are. Stop worrying. Why spoil a sunny Sunday thinking about work?' She smiled. 'Or that silly woman, Miss Drake. All that talk of hers about loyalty and confidentiality. She must 'ave a very dull life, is all I can say.'

'Loyalty and confidentiality?' He was peering into her face now, and it was making her feel uncomfortable.

'That's right. She said I may have seen things I could pass on to a competitor.'

'Oh dear. That does sound ominous.'

'What does?' His sombre mood was getting under her skin, to say the least.

'Loyalty and confidentiality. I wonder what they're up to, what they've gleaned for themselves? Maybe we were seen in that café together, talking?'

'You're too worried for your own good,' she said, drinking from the bottle of sherbet water. Offering it to him, she was offended by the way he waved it away, as if he wouldn't want to drink from the same bottle. 'They can't force me to stay there, and they've no reason to make me leave, so . . . the choice is still mine. I probably will stay.'

'I wouldn't be too sure of yourself, Maria. They're

very strict where confidentiality's concerned, which is why I go cold at the thought of what I'm now going to have to tell you. Bollards could do worse than give me the sack if they ever found out what I'm about to say. They could refuse to give me a reference, and I can't afford to let that happen.' He lowered his eyes to the ground and drew a breath. 'I really can't, but at the same time I think you should know. Especially after what you've just told me.'

'Well, spit it out, then.' She chuckled. 'Nothing's that bad when you put the world's troubles on the table to look at.'

'If you did as promised and found work elsewhere it would be different.'

'Well, I might! I don't know. I'm just weighing it all up, that's all.' She looked at him, at his expression. 'You know what I think? I think you're more worried over your job than you are over mine. In case they see us looking at each other at work.' There was a light teasing tone to her voice, but privately she was beginning to believe this might be the case.

'Saving my own skin, you mean,' he said quietly, a hurt expression on his face. 'No, that's not the reason, but . . .' There was a long pause and Maria suddenly felt sorry for him.

'Well, what is it, then? You can tell me. It won't go any farther, you've got my word on it. Come on,' she continued, coaxing him. 'Free time's too precious to waste. This wasn't what I expected. I was looking forward to an easy stroll in this lovely sunny weather, not doom and gloom.'

'Well, you see . . . there is something else that I was worried about, and if you stay at Bollards we wouldn't be able to see each other or even breathe the same air, inside Bollards or out of it.' He looked at her with a little-boy-lost look in his eyes. 'It's to do with Kelly's Yard.'

'Where I live?' Maria could hardly believe it.

'Yes, I'm afraid so.' He lowered his head again and gazed down at the grass. 'There are plans being made. Plans for new buildings are being drawn up in my department and I shall be working on part of them. They're to be almost exactly like those built at Pierhead in Wapping. Government buildings and a customs house with living accommodation and a special house for the harbour master.'

Stunned by this sudden outpouring, Maria could do no more than stare at him, disbelieving. 'Kelly's Yard? It's to be rebuilt and *you've* been working on the plans? You mean it wasn't just a rumour and that woman who was murdered really was going to write an article?'

'I don't know where the leak came from but those in high places are furious.'

'But the police should be told, surely? There might be a connection.'

'No. There isn't.' For the first time that day he was being positive. 'No connection whatsoever. From what I've heard the chief suspect is the ex-lover she came looking for. I'm sorry, Maria. I shouldn't have come out with it so hurriedly. I've shocked you.

'I'm sorry that it's happening. Sorry for your neigh-bours as well as your family. I've been into the yard with one of our surveyors and could tell from the way the women sit outside working and quietly singing that that private place away from the decrepit surrounding streets is all they have to keep up their spirits. Then I met you, of course, and learned where you lived . . .' He sighed and pushed a hand through his hair. 'I hate myself for not telling you straight away. I should have said something before now and had done with it.'

'And that's why you suggested I leave? Not because of Mr Clarkson but because of your job. What I said in jest was the truth?'

'Partly. You see, I was bound by confidentiality. I tried to keep my distance after we'd gone for that walk down by the river and so on. But it wasn't easy, feeling the way I do. And then, of course, you slipped that note to me and I felt as if fate was having her way. I was *meant* to see you again.'

'And now? Now that you know I won't take this sitting down?'

'What do you mean, Maria? You won't take it sitting down?'

'I'll fight to stop it. We all will. And not just them living in our yard but those in the surrounding streets. I'm angry that you told me to leave for the sake of my reputation when there was a different reason for you wanting me to go, but . . . there're more serious things to think about than that. You did what you thought was best so we'll leave it at that.'

'Well . . .' he said. 'That wasn't the only reason—'

'It doesn't matter. I'm angry, and disappointed. I feel as if I've bin badly let down.'

'So you don't want to hear my other reason?'

'No, not now. I've enough to think about. People are planning to smash down my family's home. Sorry if I can't raise a smile, but I'm a bit shocked by it all.'

'You can't stop progress, Maria,' he said, as if he hadn't heard what she had just said. 'There's too much at stake for those involved to take notice of a gaggle of lodgers who want to hang on to decrepit old buildings.'

'A gaggle of lodgers? That's how we're seen? We pay our rent on time, we've improved the place by keeping the drains and lavatories clean, and we grow honeysuckle up the wall. And you may find it 'ard to believe but we don't consider them to be decrepit old buildings.'

'I'm sorry. I didn't mean it to come out like that.' He clasped his head in his hands and sighed. 'I've known about the plans for some twelve months but I haven't known you for that long so—'

'And before you knew me? When you came to the yard? Didn't you feel bad about planning the fate of my neighbours? Couldn't you see that we're a small, tight-knit community? That we're quite proud of the way we live in our yard? It's not just a roof over our heads – it's where we live!'

'I didn't personally plan it, Maria. I'm a junior. I must do as I'm told, and that'll be the same wherever I work until I've passed my exams.'

'And by then you won't care very much about a gaggle of people who don't want to have their homes demolished. You'll be far too important and full of pride for that. By then you won't care! None of the others in positions of power do, so why should you?'

'This is the age of industrial revolution, Maria. Factories need to be built *if* there's to be progress. To build factories we need to knock down buildings that are about to fall down in any case. And we'll need to build tenement blocks so that the factory workers can come in from the countryside and have somewhere to live. It's all part of a master plan.'

'But you will 'ave built something for the locals beforehand? Before you smash their homes to pieces? Or must we all sleep in the streets?'

'There are other places better than streets—'

'Well, you tell that to the poor souls who huddle together, freezing cold in the winter, old and young alike. Huddled up in filthy unused shop doorways so they're not kicked out of the way when it's time to open up because those shops don't open any more! They're on the list of buildings to be demolished too! What 'appened to the people who once ran them? I wonder. Where 'ave they gone? Under the embankment with the rats?'

'I can't blame you for being angry,' John murmured, his eyes fixed on the ground.

'Oh, I'm not angry. No. I expect some nice alms-houses set around a tree-lined square will be flown in for us from heaven so people can enjoy a fair, decent life. Or will all the old worthless buildings be smashed down before there's any thought gone into where we might go and live?'

'People like me are not there to argue the toss over

right and wrong, Maria. If I dare to speak out I would be dismissed on the spot. I realise that makes you angry, and it's no real answer. But we have to face facts – those few who sit at the top of the tree are very strong and powerful. What they say goes, and without the bat of an eyelid. Money speaks all languages.'

Turning away from him, Maria was so angry she was on the verge of tears. Did he really think he needed to tell her that money spoke all languages? Hardly. Deep down she could feel a knot, as if a scream was desperate to escape. A scream of fury and hurt. Steffan came to mind. Steffan and his calm way of going about things. Using every bit of her will-power she pushed from her mind the vision of an empty space with bricks and rubble waiting to be cleared away. She didn't want to think of remnants of her parents' home in the debris, or bits and pieces of Sophie and Angel's things buried in the wreckage.

'You'll be wasting your time and energy if you try to stop it, Maria. It's too far along the road now.'

'Do you think so?' she murmured, gazing out at nothing. 'And will we be rehoused?'

'I don't know. But I'm sure there'll be somewhere for you all to go.'

'Somewhere? Anywhere, I s'pose, so long as we disappear. Well, thank you for letting me know, John.' Her tone was curt and brisk. 'I hope you don't get into trouble for it. Only I really might not leave Bollards now. But I'll keep out of your way, so don't worry.'

'You must do as you feel, Maria. I just wish you'd taken it more seriously when it was first printed in the newspaper. When they found the murdered woman's body in Miller's Wharf.'

'That's right,' said Maria, thinking aloud, 'and it just goes to show. It took the discovery of a dead woman's body in the Thames for the rumour to leak out, and that's all we took it for – a trumped-up story. We believed the real reason for her being there was to track down her lover.'

'I could have been blamed for that leak, you know. Especially since we had been seen talking.'

'Well,' murmured Maria, caught up in her own world, 'whatever happens I'll keep my dignity when I withdraw my notice. I'll heed my dad's advice. No matter what, Maria, he would say, hold tight to your dignity. I can be just as secretive about this as they are, can't I? I'll act as if I know nothing about it.'

'Do you think you could manage that?'

'Oh yes, John, I can manage that. If we are to be thrown out of our homes I'll need to be keeping my ears to the ground so I'll know when they plan to evict us. We won't take this lying down.' She shook her head. 'Parents get old . . . their grown-up children look after them until they die and then *their* offspring do the same for them. Sometimes there are three generations living in the same house. Their roots are there and the rent's affordable for a poor man.

'They can scrape that together, the rent. And they know that there'll always be a lump of coal to keep the hearth warm in winter-time and hot soup to line their stomachs. Not much more than that half the time, but no one complains. Not *really* complains. We all 'ave a moan now and then, but one way or another we manage not to starve.'

'I know all that, Maria. Honestly I do. It's a tight-knit community which, like others, will be dissipated one day whether we like it or not. I felt especially bad when I learned that your mother was a widow.' His eyes were burning into her face, and she was beginning to feel uncomfortable. 'I wanted to see you again, Maria, to tell you the other reason as to why I want you to leave Bollards. It's something I've been battling with since we first met properly. I don't think I could be in the same building and not want to see you but I have to be loyal to my employers and obey their rules.' He raised his eyes to meet hers. 'You see, the thing is . . . I think I love you.'

Stunned by John's sudden untimely confession of love, Maria stayed behind in the park, having said goodbye and watched him slope off. She needed to sit and think. She was confused, and in a worse state for hearing his lying pledge. She couldn't believe that someone would go that far to save their job. There was no doubt in her mind that right up until he walked away from her he had done his utmost to persuade her not to withdraw her notice. But to say he thought he loved her? Surely no one would stoop that low?

She was confused, bewildered and also suspicious of his motives, and couldn't help thinking that he wanted her to leave Bollards in order to protect himself because he was working on the plans for the yard. With her out of the way he could rest more assured that she would not one day behave irrationally and storm into the architects' department and rip up the drawings. Tear them into pieces and announce that she knew of their cloak-and-dagger plan to knock down Kelly's Yard, and not only Kelly's Yard but the surrounding courts as well. He would get the blame for it, she could see that. They already knew that she and John had been talking to each other, and she had been given a black mark for something as insignificant as that!

Determined that she would not stand by and let Bollards see this through without creating a rumpus, and stirring up all those living around her, Maria knew that she would have to be patient and alert and wait to see if the property developers who had bought the land were going to offer decent alternative accommodation. As far as she was concerned, and especially in her present mood, charity almshouses set around a small green were the *only* alternative. That or nothing. None of her neighbours wanted to move into a tenement block now. People from across the river who came in and out of Shadwell on a regular basis said the same thing over and over. Such buildings were more akin to a prison than a place where a family should live, and the South Londoners hated them.

Now that the full significance of what could so easily happen to her family was sinking in, she cursed Bollards for deceiving her. Somewhere in the files were her details, surely including her home address. They must have known all along that a death sentence hung over her family home and ignored the fact. As for John, he might well be a victim of circumstances and may have taken a risk by giving her highly confidential information, but she still wasn't sure whether it was calculated after he realised that she might withdraw her resignation.

The more she thought about it the more things became clearer and her anger grew. This fury was a sentiment foreign to her, a new experience. She felt as if she had been tricked and was still being tricked under the guise of love. It was difficult to believe that anyone would do such a thing simply to save their own neck, but to her mind the cards were stacked that way.

Thinking back to the time in the coffee house, she recalled how adamant John had been that she should hand in her notice and lose no time in doing so. He had without a shadow of doubt made it his business to try his best to persuade her to leave Bollards. Her name had been linked to his, and they had both been given a black mark for talking to each other. The more she thought about it the stronger her conviction grew. But even so, that very thin ray of warmth she had felt on having been told that she was loved by him had not entirely gone away. His face, his penetrating dark blue eyes and husky voice pervaded her very soul. If only it had been Steffan saying it, she thought. If only.

Having made a spur-of-the-moment arrangement to meet up again the following Sunday at the same time and in the same place, after John had said three times that he loved her, she was now wondering whether she had made a mistake. She should not have let herself be persuaded. The nagging sense of doubt had not gone away and if anything had grown stronger.

He had rambled on about how he had been bumping into lamp-posts and waking five or six times during the night with her on his mind, but she found it hard to believe him. She was now very confused indeed.

Having to care for her widowed mother, brother and sister, Maria had put work and earning extra income before anything else, without realising she was doing it. She hadn't thought of romance or socialising with people of her own age or going to a music hall as a treat. It just hadn't occurred to her that she could break her routine of work, eat, sleep, work, with only silly banter between herself and the neighbours as a social break. She had always thought it enough to be within a living family, helping to ensure that they kept their heads above water. Really and truly, Liza, Daisy and Willy were everything to her. Was it possible to love all of them and someone else? Steffan for instance?

Arriving back at the yard she was relieved that the women were in the cook-house lifting boiled suet puddings from the enormous pot and gossiping. She went into the house, treasuring the rare chance to have the place to herself. Daisy was out somewhere in the streets and Willy was in the stable helping Olly sort his new collection of old clothes. Wishing for nothing else but to be alone, she dropped into the armchair, closed her eyes and relived every second, from the moment she had set eyes on John in the park as he sat by the tree in the shade waiting for her, the shadow cast over the yard temporarily forgotten.

Her eyes closed, she began to fantasise about a different life, away from Shadwell and living as a wife to someone like John in a small cottage in the country with climbing roses around the door, flowers in the front garden and vegetables in the back. She visualised their small children running around laughing, and the family cat basking in the sunshine. It was all so perfect and peaceful until the door, which was slightly ajar, suddenly crashed open and Daisy's familiar piercing voice brought her sharply back down to earth.

'I'm gonna be a bleedin' nurse, Maria! I'm gonna go to a proper training school for nurses! At St Thomas's Hospital! So if there's another soddin' Crimean War I can go where Florence Nightingale went and look after the wounded soldiers!'

'Who said so?' said Maria, begrudgingly.

'Fartarse. She was prattling on about Nightingale and the Jamaican Mary Seacole who's a darkie and learned to look after ill people by 'erself wiv no bleeding training! Going on about it in school on Friday and I've just seen 'er over in Sugar Loaf Green, taking a Sunday stroll, so I asked some more about it and—'

'Daisy, slow down!' snapped Maria. 'You're going too quick for me. And you can't be a nurse unless you train. Not in this country anyway. So unless you're gonna sail off to Jamaica you can forget it. People like us 'ave to work for a living. Training without wages is for the wealthy, not us.'

'Well, that's wot I'm trying to *tell* yer! Fartarse said she'd even pay for me to go to the West Indies if I didn't wanna train! She said so!'

'I bet she did.' Maria laughed, ever amused by her

peculiar sister. 'She'd send you to the other side of the blinking moon to be rid of you.'

'No, acshully! You're wrong agen, Maria,' Daisy persisted, stamping her foot in frustration. 'She finks I'd make a good nurse, she said that on Friday in school, and she never says anyfing good abaht me so she must 'ave meant it!'

'Well, that's true,' Maria mused. There was no fear of her sister being devastated when she learned the truth. Daisy bounced back from anything. 'So who's going to fix you up at St Thomas's training centre? Miss Faintheart?'

'I dunno! But when I do go I can get me hands on antiseptic, can't I? And none of us'll get infections and Mum won't die like Dad did! And they give you a uniform as well. All washed and starched for yer!'

'But you love doing sums. There won't be no call for that if you're a nurse.'

'I'll do their bloomin' bookkeeping for 'em an' all! Fartarse said she'd arrange that as well if I go to the West India.'

'West Indies.' Maria studied Daisy's flushed face. Her eyes were shining so brightly she couldn't bear to tell her the hard truth. That Miss Faintheart had been tormenting her. 'Well, sleep on it for a while, Dai, and I'll go and see your teacher and find out more.'

'When? When you goin'?'

'In a week or so.'

'She'll go off the bleedin' boil be then!'

'Well, that's too bad. I've got more important things on my mind right now.'

'Wot . . . more important than my entire life?'

'In a way.'

Daisy curled her top lip and quietly growled. 'You're a lazy cow, that's wot you are. Bin over the bleedin' park agen, ain't yer? Wiv that silly boy lemon from work. He'll get you pregnant, he will!' With that she stormed out of the house and marched through the yard, steaming. 'He'll prick yer when you ain't looking!'

'What was that all about?' asked Liza, coming into the house. She, Sophie and the other women had heard Daisy sounding off.

'Miss Faintheart's human after all, Mum. She's been teasing poor Daisy. Best to let it lie and pretend it never 'appened. Unless she brings it up again, which I doubt she will. You know what she's like. Last year she was definitely gonna be a politician and fight for women's rights. And in between then and now she's fancied herself as an artist, a writer and a furniture maker.'

'I know,' said Liza, rippling with laughter. 'Still . . . at least she's got her sights set high, that's something. Shall I make a fresh pot of coffee?'

'Tea would be nice.'

'Wouldn't it just,' said Liza, raising an eyebrow and lifting the smoke-black kettle from the fireplace. 'But we'll just 'ave to wait till Daisy starts earning properly and Willy's eight years old, unless the price of tea comes down. Unless of course I get myself taken on as a cleaner at Pierhead.'

'You don't 'ave to scrub floors in the little spare time you've got, Mum, just for the price of a pot of tea.'

'Well, that's not exactly what I meant but never mind.' At the doorway she turned around and paused. 'The police 'ave been round agen. They knocked on your new friend's door but got no answer.'

'It's procedure. They've got a job to do. Stop being like the others and making a mountain out of a molehill. No one in this yard murdered that poor woman. No doubt they've bin back more than once to the streets around us as well.'

'Well, yes, there is that. The young lady's parents are pressing for action and you can't really blame 'em. But why would a man not want to face being asked a few questions? Because Steffan's father was in, Maria. He was up there but pretended he wasn't. He's still up there hiding himself away. Don't you think that's a bit odd?'

'No, not really. I don't s'pose he can be bothered with it all. And besides, he might be sound asleep. He works for the railway, don't forget, and might well have been on duty during the night.'

'Maybe,' said Liza, 'we'll see.' She left Maria to stare after her and went outside to the cook-house to put her kettle on the grid.

Privately Maria had to admit that she did find it mysterious that Steffan's father had all but hidden himself away from the police when, as far as she knew, they had not yet interrogated him or Steffan. It hadn't escaped her that the press had claimed that the woman had come looking for a gentleman whom she had once been involved with, one who had returned to hurt, love and leave her again. Steffan had said that his father had been and still was a womaniser. But a murderer? She could hardly believe it. But then no doubt a million people over the centuries had thought the same when they had discovered that someone they knew had killed another person. She ran all that she had learned of this man from Steffan through her mind and felt herself go cold. He was aloof, kept himself to himself and spoke to none of his neighbours; not even a polite greeting came from his lips.

Pushing that from her mind, she recalled the more serious side of her conversation with John and wondered whether she might have to leave Bollards now that she had set the ball rolling. For now she would keep to herself all that she had learned about the plan concerning the yard. Once she was settled into a new position at the biscuit factory, if that was to be her destiny, she would call a meeting of her neighbours. The most pressing and important thing for her now was to find somewhere else to work in case she had to leave Bollards. She had discussed it all with her mother, who at first had been horrified at the thought of her leaving a position others could only dream of one day acquiring, but had finally agreed that Maria should follow her instincts and do what she thought was right. The matter of John Cunningham and Kelly's Yard had not been mentioned.

With all thoughts of romance shelved, Maria decided that she had nothing to lose in going to see Angel Black's friend, who worked at Meredith and Drew and who lived close by. She wanted to know more about the rules of the firm before she wrote in for an appointment, and to find out more about the biscuit factory and who she should ask for by name when seeking an interview.

After enjoying a cup of coffee with Liza, Sophie and Angel, Maria left them to chew the fat over the gentleman above the stables. With the name of the woman she was to call on written on a scrap of brown paper, she made her way to number 6 Mercer Street with all thoughts of Steffan, his father, the lecherous Mr Clarkson at Bollards and the plans for razing her home to the ground left simmering on the back burner.

'One step at a time, Maria,' she told herself, joining the ranks of people who walked the streets mumbling to themselves. 'First things first. A new job and no more horrid Mr Clarkson.' Her thoughts moved on immediately to Steffan. Next on the list was a little chat with him to let him know what the others in the yard were saying about his father before it got out of hand, and before he heard it in a way that would be a hundred times worse. She couldn't be sure whether the police were simply attending to their duties or not. If so, they would surely come back again at their leisure. The fact that she and her mother had been quizzed over both father and son did not necessarily point the finger at either of them.

Stop defending strangers, Maria. The voice of her dead father suddenly swept through her mind and confused her. This hadn't happened before, and she could hardly believe it had happened now. Had it come out of her subconscious? Her own inner voice using that of her father to bring her up sharply? Or was his voice so deeply rooted in her memory that she was simply evoking it herself now when she needed advice? Although she couldn't remember her father having said such a thing before.

She paused by a low brick wall that separated the pavement from a rough piece of ground and sat down for a quiet five minutes by herself. She ran his words through her mind again and could vaguely remember her father saying this to her, but it must have been when she was very small for it to be so faint in her memory. *Stop defending strangers.* Had she been too defensive? Defending Steffan's father of all people without realising it? She would shield Steffan from the gossips whatever they thought. She couldn't imagine him harming a hair on anyone's head. He was a gentle soul who was turned out to fend for himself at a young age and had been lonely in a crowded town. Others who had gone through such suffering as he had would show resentment or bitterness or both, but not Steffan. To be alone day and night, through long winters with little money and lodging in a small, dark room, was to her unimaginable, and yet he had and was no worse a character for it. In fact she couldn't think of anyone else who was so good natured.

She had visualised him more than once living alone in that dingy silent room at the age of fourteen until his father was released from prison. Steffan was a sensitive person to her mind, and one who needed protecting from people like Sophie and Angel when they were on one of their witch-hunts. She remembered when they had stalked two men who were lodging in one of the cheapest and worst inns down by Ropemaker Street in Limehouse. The thieves had come into the area from Blackwall Reach and stolen from two very small and modest family shops in Shakespears Walk, Wapping. To steal from folk who worked all hours God sent to get from one week to the next was a sin, and for their sin the men suffered. Sophie, Angel and Lizzie Wood from Nelly's Row, a turning adjacent to the yard, had caught the two men red-handed with a biscuit tin filled with a week's takings which they had retrieved from under the floorboards of an old couple's shop. This pitiful place displayed a home-made sign painted on a piece of driftwood: '*The everyfing shop*'. Their weapons clutched in their hands, the three women had given chase, and the chase had brought out their animal and territorial instincts. The ferocious beating from three women armed with rolling pins and buckled belts which followed was wicked.

With no reason that she could think of to distrust Steffan, Maria focused on his father and was angry with herself for not having properly listened to or taken notice of the others. Sophie and Angel were known for not pulling their punches, and voiced their opinions openly as a matter of course. And what of the police? Surely they had good reason to focus their attention on the yard? In particular those questions concerning Mr Tremain senior. Why then had *she* not cast doubt in that direction? More to the point, why had she deliberately dismissed the very idea, even though she knew that Mr Tremain displayed the traits of someone who could, out of temper or self-perservation, kill another. Steffan had told her that his father had a violent streak and had beaten him several times, and that his mother had run away from the brute. He had been in the debtors' prison, as had thousands of other men, but unlike so many others he had not incurred debts by falling on bad times through no fault of his own but by womanising, gambling and drinking. They had said in the newspaper that the murdered woman's diary revealed that the man she had come in search of had jilted her some six years before, and Steffan had told her that it had been six years ago that his father went to prison!

With this succession of facts flooding through her mind, Maria lost the urge to go to the woman's house to ask about Meredith and Drew, and felt instead a strong desire to find Steffan and tell him that he and his father had been the object of the police visit and that she herself had been quizzed about him, but she decided against it. There was a knot in the pit of her stomach, but she had to put earning a living first. Meredith and Drew might not have vacancies and she would have to look elsewhere. She had to go and see the woman whether she felt like it or not.

On her way again, she could hardly believe she had been so lax in her thinking. Why had she not put two and two together before now? If the stuck-up drunk, as he was now beginning to be known, had murdered the woman, then the beast was free to roam the streets and no woman was safe. If he had killed once he could do it again, and not only was her mother at risk but her sister Daisy.

It was a well-known fact that those who favoured prostitutes saw young girls as fair game. And if Mr Tremain senior was under suspicion of murder then all the women in the yard were not just at risk, but in jeopardy.

Her mind in a spin, bouncing from one worry to the next, Maria recalled all she had heard from Daisy while they lay in bed the night before, when her sister had told her step by step what had happened in Tobacco Dock when Willy could so easily have been lost to them. Of course she had dreaded to think what might have been, but she hadn't considered what Daisy must have been feeling. She had, after all, been the cause of the man falling into the river – even though she had not laid a finger on him. The poor girl was only eight years old and the incident could give her terrifying nightmares and possibly scar her for life.

Maybe this was the cause of Daisy suddenly wanting to be a nurse? To make up for having caused a man to drown she felt duty-bound to save the lives of others. Not that she would ever admit that to herself, never mind anyone else.

With the welfare of her family uppermost in her mind, Maria continued on her way to Mercer Street, the handsome John Cunningham temporarily forgotten. She had to secure employment if she was to leave Bollards, as leave she would one day. She had no desire to work there now that she knew exactly what kind of plans had been hatched in secret in the architects' department. But she would try to retrieve her resignation. She wasn't quite ready to go yet!

When she arrived she had to push from her mind the thought that her visit might be untimely and she would not be welcomed. She had no idea what the woman she had been recommended to talk to or her family might be like. She would, of course, take her leave politely should the woman reject her outright at the front door.

Approaching the house, she felt a little apprehensive, for no real reason other than the fact that she was imposing herself on complete strangers who, like everyone else living in poor conditions in this part of London, had their own problems and worries to contend with. She knocked lightly on the front door of the terraced house in this well-kept street, where only a few ragged homeless people had established themselves in the doorway of a recently closed down cobbler's shop.

As the door slowly creaked open, the suspicious eyes of a pale and thin fourteen-year-old stared up at her. 'Mum and Dad're out,' was her rehearsed speech.

'Oh . . . not to worry over it,' said Maria. 'I'm Maria Bertram from Kelly's Yard and I came to talk to your mother about the biscuit factory and what it's like working there.'

'Oh,' returned the girl. 'Well, that might be different. Wait there a minute.'

The door was closed on Maria, and while she waited, believing that it might not open to her again, she regretted making this journey. Looking along the street, she could see those who lived the best way they could outside the shoe-mender's staring at her with a lost look of despondency. She had seen hundreds of people down and out, so why should this handful of lost souls make her suddenly feel angry at the injustice? The creaking sound of the door opening once again caused her to remind herself of the reason for her being here. She could find herself jobless if she weren't careful.

'Did yer say yer name was Maria?' the girl asked with no hint of a smile or any expression whatsoever.

'That's right. Maria Bertram.'

'Don't matter abaht the other name. Mum said you was to come in. Did you wanna come in? My dad's in as well.'

'If it's no trouble? I just wanted a few words, that's all,' said Maria, wondering why she was being warned about the girl's father.

'She eiver wants to come in or she don't wanna come in, Dora! Eiver way, shut the bleedin' door before the rats come in!' This was the girl's father.

Unable to suppress a smile, Maria cupped her mouth as she looked into Dora's frightened face. 'He sounds like a character,' she whispered, trying not to giggle.

'We 'aven't got rats,' Dora whispered, her pale face breaking into a shy smile. 'Take no notice. He's all right, Dad. Just shows off a bit, but don't say I said, will yer?'

''Course I won't.'

Following the girl through the narrow unlit passage to the family's small living room out the back, Maria was relieved to see that, although simply furnished, the place was clean, with no atmosphere of misery, dire impoverishment or fear. 'I'm sorry to butt in like this,' she said, addressing the forty-year-old gentleman who sat by the unlit fire, his legs stretched out. 'Mrs Black sent me. She said it would be all right. I only wanted to ask a couple of questions about Meredith and Drew. I'm hoping to find work there.' She glanced at his wife, Polly, and returned a faint smile.

'Well, we ain't gonna bite yer 'ead off for it, gal.' He kicked his eighteen-year-old son on the leg, saying, 'Get up and give the lady a chair.' His eyes went from his lanky son back to Maria. 'Not looking for someone to marry, perchance, are yer?'

'Shut up, Dad,' moaned the lad, before slinking out of the room and slamming the door shut behind him.

'He's got a job down the iron foundry,' continued the man, giving Maria the once-over. 'Ain't that right, Muvver? He might make summing of 'imself, mightn't he? She could do worse.'

'I should say so, but I don't think this young lady is the type to 'ang about the Prospect of Whitby late of a night.'

'Saucy cow.' The man grinned. 'Well, sit yerself down, gal. No one stands on ceremony in my little 'ouse. If it's advice yer after, yer in luck. Words don't cost nuffing and smiles are free an' all.'

'That's true.' Maria chuckled, taking the weight off her feet. 'It's your wife's brains I need to pick.'

'Brains, eh? You 'ear that, Polly. She finks we've got brains. That's a lovely compliment that is – even though it is the plain truth.' The man drew a long breath and stretched out his legs. 'Bin working at that factory for nigh on four years now, ain't you, Poll?'

'Well – I think it must be by now. I mean, it must be. Didn't like it first off. No. Never thought much of it. Too busy with everyone gettin' on wiv it. None of 'em spoke to me at first. No. But that changed once they was used to me. Best not to gossip or that. They don't like that. No. They won't 'ave that. And best not to moan about your employer. Extremely loyal, they are.'

'Loyal, my left foot,' said the man, raising one eyebrow. 'Keepin' in wiv the managers who're there to spy on the workers. No one wants to be put out on their elbow, Poll.' He turned to Maria again and the pride on his face was genuine. 'She's done all right, 'as my Polly. She'll tell yer. Go on, Poll,' he said, filled with pride.

'Oh, well. It's nuffing really,' she half protested, fanning her face. 'Not really, but I'm satisfied.'

'Bin promoted, ain't she? Oh, yeah . . . no flies on my missus. One of the largest biscuit manufacturers in the world and she gets promoted.' He shook his head disbelievingly. 'Just shows yer. Just goes to prove.'

'I used to work in the brewery, you know. Got promoted there an' all, didn't I, Bill?'

'Oh, yeah,' he said, nodding his head with an all-knowing expression on his face. 'Well, she's a worker, you see. A quick worker and wiv a brain to go wiv it. Knows 'ow to work them managers – that's the secret.'

'I used to skylark a bit when I first went out to work after I'd 'ad me babies. Well, it was the freedom, you see. I felt like a single girl agen. Not that I flirted with the men. No. Wouldn't do a fing like that.'

'No need to wiv me under the roof, Poll. No need.' The man turned his head again and peered into Maria's face. 'The lad's got work, you know. Down at East India Dock. Turns out a good tune on 'is tin whistle as well. Couple of years an' he'll fill out. Got my bone structure, you see. All the Woods are big men. Brawny. Lanky long sod now but you wait and see. You could be proud of 'im, gal.'

'Leave 'er be, Bill. She never came looking for a husband. What was it you wanted to do, lovely? At the biscuit factory. Work on the belt?'

'Well . . . I was hoping there might be a vacancy in the offices. I'm trained at note-taking and trusted with the post.'

'Oooooh . . .' crooned the man, shaking his head. 'Clever as well as pretty. Funny, that is, the way clever people are led to this door. I knew from the minute she stepped fru that door she was clever!'

'I'll find out for you, dear . . . about work and that . . . and you pop back sometime on yer way 'ome from wherever you've bin and I'll give you the wink if there is anyfing going.'

'She gets biscuits cheap, you know. Not all of 'em there get that, do they, Poll?'

'No. Only the inspectors – which is wot I am now. I go round making sure ginger goes into the nuts and jam goes on the tarts!' She roared, enjoying her own quip.

A sudden burst of laughter from the man startled Maria, who was by now wondering whether everyone in this street was as cheerful and optimistic as this family, who were only just above the poverty line – not that they would see it that way.

'She's a comical cow!' He laughed. 'Has me in stitches, I can tell you. Oh yes, I could tell you a few things, as a matter of fact.' Wiping a tear from the corner of his eye with a clean piece of cotton rag, he sighed happily and then said, ''Course, he's not the only son, but I was rather 'oping to get rid of the serious one first. The only trouble is that the other three are all away on 'oliday, if you get my drift. Silly buggers, thought they could work a tight plan between 'em. First time they've strayed and to that I cross my 'eart. Eh, Poll, they've never bin in trouble wiv the law before, 'ave they?'

'No,' said the woman, sadly, 'not to our knowledge they 'aven't. Too ambitious, my boys, that's the trouble.'

'I should say they are.' The man sniffed and looked at Maria as if he had known her all his life. 'Counterfeit coins. Half-crowns. Fencing 'em for one of the big boys. Silly bleeders. Still, only got twenty-eight months and so they'll be out . . . in good time. Don't like it in there, though, do they, Poll? No. They'll stick to the straight and narrow now. Well . . . the straight and narrow as I see it. Counterfeit half-crowns?' He drew breath. 'Too ambitious, that was their trouble. Mind you, they cut a very good impression in the courtroom. Apologised like true gentlemen, they did.'

'Well, you've bin really kind inviting me in and if you don't mind my coming back to find out about—'

'*Mind?*' roared the man. ''Course we don't *mind*.

But before you go . . . 'ave they nailed that bloke who lives above the stable yet? A gentleman fallen by all accounts. They say he did that woman in.'

'Not to my knowledge, no,' said Maria, feeling uneasy. 'I don't think they've even questioned him yet, so how come the rumour's spread already?'

'Ah, well, they wouldn't need to interrogate the man, would they? Clever, you see.' He tapped his temple with one finger. 'Brainy. But then they would 'ave to be, wouldn't they? Oh, yes. I said to Poll, no smoke without fire. He's the one. That's wot comes of letting strangers in. And by that I mean people from a different *walk* of life. It's not as if he was one of them from Whitechapel or Bethnal Green. Aldgate, mind . . . no . . . very low sort of a person lives there, in my opinion. Lots of Jews as well but they tend to stick together, don't they?'

The door to the living room suddenly opened and the lanky son stood there, his droll expression unchanged. 'I'm goin' out. D'yer want me to walk the lady 'ome?'

'No!' said Maria, a little too much alarm in her voice. 'No, I wouldn't dream of it. I've enough to thank you all for already.'

'There's bin a murder.' The lad sniffed. 'You don't wanna get strangled. That's the worst way to die. Ain't that right, Dad?'

'That is right, son. No flies on you.'

'Oh, I'll be fine,' said Maria, rising from the chair. 'I'm not gonna let someone intimidate me. I've walked by myself through these backstreets since I can remember. I'm not changing now for no one.'

'She's got a point there, son. Why don't you take the girl to the penny Odeon instead? In a week or so, to let 'er get used to the idea. It's a dump and the singers can't sing and the jugglers drop their balls but it's a laugh. We all need a laugh now and then. Even you, son.'

'D'yer wanna go to the Odeon, then?' The lad's long pale face showed no sign of emotion one way or another. 'Tomorrer night?'

'I can't. I'm sorry . . . I've a widowed mother and a small brother and sister to look out for. Maybe in a year or so, eh?'

'Yeah, all right,' he said. 'Next August. That'd be all right, wouldn't it, Dad?'

'I should fink so, son. It's wot I originally suggested, as a matter of fact.'

'Mum?'

'Yes, son. Sounds just the ticket. You'd make a nice couple walking out together. Look all right, arm in arm.'

'Would we?'

'Oh, yes, son. Definitely.'

'Right, that's settled, then.' He held out his hand to shake Maria's. 'The name's Dick, Maria.'

'Oh . . . pleased to meet you, Dick,' said Maria, a touch bemused.

'Well, ain't that nice. Lovely. All nice and formal and proper. See your young lady out, then, son.'

'No! I wouldn't dream of it. Now that we're friends . . . all of us . . . I think I should see myself out. That's the way we do things in Kelly's Yard. Always have.'

'Oh?' said Polly. 'Well, I should fink we could go along with that.'

''Course we can,' said her husband. 'Dick? You agree with that, do yer?'

'It's all right. Yeah. That should be all right.'

Relieved to be out of the house, and with the name of the person she was to see at the biscuit factory promised to her, Maria could not wait to get home. Much longer and she felt sure she would have found herself promised to the son.

On her way home she caught sight of Steffan carrying a shopping bag, on his way back from the local Jewish grocery shop. She felt her heart go out to him. He looked so alone. He was by himself and so was she, and so where was the difference? She certainly didn't long for company. It was the shopping bag. It was a young man carrying a shopping bag. It didn't look wrong, just sad . . . and he was in no hurry. It was as if he had all the time in the world to kill on this quiet Sunday. She had no trouble whatsoever in catching up with him.

'I was just thinking about you, Mr Tremain,' she said, smiling broadly.

'Oh, hello, Maria. Are you well?'

'I am, thank you. And you?'

'All the better for seeing your friendly face.'

'Oh, you old softie,' she said, slipping her arm into his. 'It's such a lovely day now there's a breeze in the air. Perhaps we should go for that walk a bit later on. Down to the beach by the tower?'

'That would be lovely. I've just got to prepare

something for my father to eat. He's probably returned by now. He stays out on Saturday nights and when he does show his face he's always famished.'

'Well, you should tell him to cook 'is own meal. You're not his slave, are you? It's not fair. Why should you—?'

'Maria,' he said, stopping and looking at her. 'I do it and I don't mind. It keeps the peace, and anyway . . .' His expression suddenly changed to one of embarrassment. 'I . . . prefer to see him fed and bedded. Keeps him out of my way and in fairly good temper.'

'And,' said Maria, making amends, 'he's your father, and no matter what he's done or how he treats you, you love 'im? I understand that, Steffan. And I admire you for it.' She smiled. 'Come on . . . let's get the old goat fed.'

Back in the rooms above the stable, Mr Tremain had given up trying to ignore a fierce tapping on his front door, and in a particularly facetious mood was about to open it and have fun with whomever it was. It was in fact Detective Inspector Barcroft of Scotland Yard.

'Mr Tremain?'

'Senior, dear boy, senior!'

'My humble apologies, sir. May I come in?'

'Well, if you really think you'd prefer this stinking hovel to the fresh air, then be my guest, Officer.' Sporting a bumptious grin, Tremain stood aside and made what could just pass as a theatrical welcome as he floated a hand through the air while bowing. 'Welcome to my humble abode.'

'Thank you, Mr Tremain. And it's Detective Inspector Barcroft.'

'Oh, I do beg your pardon, Inspector Barcroft. I fear I have been so long in these dreadful parts that the brain has slipped a little, but not, I am pleased to say, my manners. Would you care for a refreshing drink, my good man?'

'No, sir. Not while I'm on duty, thank you.'

'Oh? You don't drink tea while on duty? I find that terribly hard to believe, Mr Barcroft.'

'Tea would be most acceptable, sir. I was under the impression you had an alcoholic beverage in mind,' the inspector murmured sarcastically, staring into the face of his host, who was obviously a drunkard.

'Ah, now . . . tea . . .' Mr Tremain looked around the messy area that passed as a kitchen. 'Well, of course, what can one expect from a greedy son who will cling to his father's coat-tails!' He turned to the inspector and sported a very sorry face. 'My son has used every last tea leaf. I could offer you a small gin with a slice of lemon, sire?'

'No thank you, Mr Tremain. So,' Barcroft said, sliding his notebook from his pocket, 'your son lives with you and has done so since you were released from Marshalsea Prison. Is that correct?'

'It is indeed, Your Lordship. How clever you people are. It grieves me to think that you must waste your talent trudging around this ghastly place in search of the killer of a common whore. It is an insult to your intelligence.'

'Common whore, sir?'

'Well, yes, Officer, are they not all common sluts? How a gentleman can touch one is a mystery to me. Ghastly creatures spreading disease, as if there were not enough rats to do the work for them.'

'So . . . you've never been with a prostitute, then, Mr Tremain?' The inspector looked him straight in the eye, his face expressionless.

'Well . . .' Tremain said, waving a hand in the air. 'When I was a very young and inquisitive man. But it was by introduction, mind you. Oh yes. A lady from a very private and select house of assignations, sir. Not a common whore.' Tremain filled his empty glass and gingerly sipped his gin as if he were not accustomed to alcohol, feeling that he might have unwittingly talked himself into an uncomfortable position.

'And what about your son, Mr Tremain? Did he follow in your footsteps, or does he have a young lady whom he wishes to marry?'

'My son? Marry?' A faint whiff of stale alcohol clung to his breath as he spoke. Pulling his double chin inward, he smirked. 'I shouldn't think that very likely, sir. Oh, I don't think so. I shouldn't think he'd know how to go about the business even if you gave him twenty-six clear instructions written boldly on white paper. No . . .' He chuckled with pursed lips. 'The lad is a little on the queer side, I am mortified to have to confess. Not the usual run-of-the-mill chap, I'm afraid. Strange sense of what is enjoyment and what is not. Would much prefer to paint a picture of a woman naked than see or touch one, from what I can make out. Not that he has an affection for those of the male species who frequent houses such as the one found in the notorious Cleveland Street. No. I believe that my son,' he said, scratching the tip of his nose, 'is and always will be non-sexual.'

'So he isn't particularly fond of women, sir, is that what you imply?'

'He isn't particularly fond of anyone, sir. I implied nothing, I merely stated a fact. So if you will pardon me, *Inspector*, I tell you point blank. He does not like women.' Tremain sipped his gin delicately and sighed. 'Do you know . . . I think they actually repulse him. Of all things! To be repulsed by a woman?' He placed his glass down on a dust-covered side table and smiled up at the police officer. 'Would you like to see one or two of his drawings? This will back up *all* I have said.' He placed a hand on his heart. 'I tell you no lies, sir.'

'Perhaps later, Mr Tremain. Once I've interviewed you.'

'Interviewed me? Ah. Oh, well then, go ahead, dear boy . . . ask away and ask whatever comes into your mind. And *I* shall answer to the very best of my knowledge.' He grinned.

'If you could tell me where you were on the night of the murder, sir?'

'Which murder might that be, Inspector? In these parts they are many and close between.'

'The murder of the woman whose body was pulled out of the river, sir. The penny farthing case? You must have read about it in the newspapers. They made quite a headline of it.'

'Oh, that,' Tremain said, flapping a hand. 'Trash.

They will print anything to double their print run, Inspector, as you must be painfully aware. The silly woman probably lost her balance and fell in the cut . . . to swallow all the fishes up!'

'No, sir, she was strangled before she went into the river.'

'Well – I – never! Strangling herself while riding a penny farthing *and* while driving it into the river? Now that *would* make a headline, wouldn't you say?' He emptied his glass and roared with laughter while nodding rapidly, overexcited. 'Yes, indeed! That would sell newspapers!'

'So you can't remember where you were on the night of the murder, is that what you are saying, sir?'

'Inspector . . . one day is much the same as another to me. I come home from my place of business, I eat a little something to keep the wolves away from the door, I sleep. I get up the next day . . . and so on. I am controller of a very, *extremely*, busy railway station. My day—'

'Yes, sir,' the inspector cut in, agitated by this infuriating man. 'We know where you are employed. In fact we know all there is to know about you.'

'Ha! Not so!' barked Tremain. '*Where* was I on the night of the *murder*? You do not know *that*, sir!' He grinned. 'You cannot know that . . . because even *I* don't bloody well know!'

Grinding his teeth and giving Tremain a look that could kill, the officer had to will himself not to lose his temper. He was deliberately being goaded, and it was all very well to know this but it was not always easy to *ignore* it. 'Will your son Steffan be home soon, Mr Tremain? I would like a few words with him.'

'On this extremely serious matter of a woman having been murdered? Yes, I expect you do. Hard to say . . . with a bit of luck he might not come in at all.' Tremain was sporting a different expression now. His lips curled down like those of an ageing judge passing sentence. He resembled a bulldog. 'He might arrive any minute or any hour. You never can tell. Likes walking, you know. Walks all over the ruddy place. Limehouse, Wapping, Whitechapel, Aldgate, Shoreditch. Day and night when he is off duty . . . he likes to walk!'

'At night too, sir?'

'Oh yes, at night too. From dusk until dawn, if it takes his fancy. I told you, Yer 'Onour, he is not the run-of-the-mill sort of a fellow. Odd. Distinctly odd. His mother wouldn't listen. Up to me, I would have given him away at first sight.'

'Just the one son, is it, sir?'

'Too bloody damn well right only one. One too many, if you ask me. Odd fellow is that one too, make no mistake of my tone, sir. I mean every word. Harmless enough, though! Oh, wouldn't harm a bird on a penny farthing!' Tremain rocked with laughter. 'His mother bloody well adored him! But then she's a bit odd too.'

'These paintings—'

'*Drawings*. I think I said *drawings*, Officer. *Drawings* mostly and *some* paintings. Tight little bugger wouldn't pay out for paint if he could avoid it. He'd sooner cut me and use the blood from the wound rather than pay out. Are you sure you won't have a drink, Sergeant?'

'Not while I'm on duty, sir, thank you. If I could take a look at the drawings which you've brought to my attention—'

'I?' Tremain placed a hand on his chest. 'I brought them to your attention? Why, I've—'

'Yes, sir. You've mentioned them, which is more than enough. So if you would oblige.'

'Well, if I must entertain you, then I must.' Tremain grinned. 'I shall have to find a clean dinner knife to slide between the lock. The boy is very private, Inspector. A very *private* person. But I'll say nothing if you will do the same, mmm?' He pushed his face a little too close to the detective inspector's. 'We'll take a peep *together.*'

'No, I'll leave you to fetch them through, sir. It shouldn't take long. You've given me a lead so I'm obliged to follow it.'

'A lead?' Tremain chuckled, opening a drawer and removing the piece of cutlery he needed before deliberately dropping it to the floor in order to secretly pour himself a large gin from the cupboard below, which did not go unnoticed by the officer. 'How very inspiring.' He grinned, sipping his drink. 'May I offer you a glass of water? It's not bad as water goes.'

'No, thank you, sir.'

Tremain put down his glass and walked over to his son's bedroom door. 'Can't say I blame you. Boring bloody taste. So! Would you like me to join you on this so-called murder case?'

'So-called, sir?'

'Well . . .' Tremain hooted triumphantly. 'There we are! What do you know. I can pick a lock too.' He pushed the door open with his foot. 'I'm wasted at that bloody railway station, lad. Wasted. Never too old, mind, to change professions,' he said, looking dolefully into the officer's face. 'I'll take your job if you'll take mine, what? You might even end up driving a chuff-chuff.' He roared with laughter.

'The pictures, then, sir, if you please.' The officer was clearly losing patience.

'Oh dear.' Tremain sighed as he entered his son's bedroom. 'We cannot crack that exterior of yours, can we? You know,' he added, deliberately looking into the officer's face, '*you* shouldn't take yourself quite so seriously, Detective Inspector. You could have a little more fun with people, you know.' With raised eyebrows he made an effort to stare the man out in a rather worldly, knowing and incredibly patronising fashion.

'I don't have a warrant to search the premises, sir, so if you would be so kind as to hand the drawings to me. The ones you'd like me to look at.'

Lifting the lid of an old but clean tin trunk, Tremain pushed it back so that it landed with a decisive clunk against the wall. He then stood aside, smiled graciously and, with mock gallantry, waved at the contents. 'Be my guest.'

'Thank you, sir,' the inspector replied wearily. 'That's very hospitable of you.'

'Take the bloody stuff away with you if you wish. I tried to discourage this sort of thing when he was a boy but his mother let him do exactly as he wished. If her beloved boy wanted something, then he got it.'

Carefully lifting one picture at a time so as not to touch anything other than the corners of the paper, the inspector glanced briefly through the drawings in silence. Once he had had a brief look through the pile, he lifted them out of the trunk and tucked them under his arm. 'I would like to take these away to look at them at leisure, if that's all right with you, sir?' He spoke more formally now, so as not to mislead Tremain concerning the gravity of the situation. This development was clearly of importance to the case and procedure had to be followed.

'So long as you don't fetch the ghastly things back, Constable, you can do what you bloody well like with them.' Tremain chuckled.

'Thank you, sir. I'll see myself out.'

Before Steffan's inebriated father could answer, the officer was out of the door, going down the wooden steps and striding purposefully through the yard, quite aware that he was being stared at but glad to be rid of the insufferable drunkard.

'Well now,' murmured Angel as she placed the last of her matchboxes into a container, 'could that be evidence of something that he's taken away, Olly?' She glanced at her husband and raised an eyebrow.

'It don't look none too good, wife,' he said, rubbing his chin thoughtfully and staring after the man. 'It don't look too good at all.' He turned slowly and artfully checked the rooms above the stable. In the open doorway he could see the shabby gentleman, a look of bewilderment as to what was happening on his highly coloured face. He was swaying slightly, and it didn't take a genius to see that he was, as usual, drunk.

'What do you fink he was carrying?' said Angel, too concerned to be frivolous on this occasion, as a small chill ran down her spine.

'Who knows? Who in the world knows?'

In the same frame of mind as his wife over the officer taking away what he could only assume to be evidence, Olly was deeply worried. It was even more troubling because the elder of the two men living in the rooms, it appeared, was still a free man. Did this then mean that it was the young man whom they were watching closely? The young man who had recently befriended Maria and Daisy? The young fellow he had sold the perfume bottle to and then contrived for him to give it as a gift to Maria? Olly was tempted to go up those wooden steps and ask the gentleman point blank what exactly was going on. But Olly, being Olly, decided against rushing in, and instead went inside the stable to his chair, to sit quietly and consider this latest episode.

'It's not looking so good, Angel, is it?' Coming out of his house, Jacob Marcovitch was slowly shaking his head. 'There's a bad feeling in this yard. Something big is coming. Something's not right.'

'You really think so, Jacob? Perhaps it's just you worrying over your Sophie that's put you in that frame of mind?'

'No. No, I don't think so. She's tired, that's all.

But I've told her now. No more mattress stuffing. It's enough. There's other work she could do from home instead of that.' He waved his hand dismissively and looked solemnly at his wife's best friend. 'She doesn't have to work so hard any more. I keep telling her. Trapping rats doesn't pay a fortune but I've built up a regular trade now and things are not so bad. The boys can look after themselves with what they earn at the box factory. She won't stop being a worrying mother, that's the trouble.'

'So she'll have a nice rest, then. That's good. That's what she needs. But you know what, Jacob?'

'No. Go on.' He sighed, 'You're gonna tell me in any case.'

'She wouldn't know what to do with 'erself if she never stuffed them bleeding mattresses and I'm no different. I've bin making matchboxes for so long it's in my blood.' She looked up at the tall, skinny man. 'I'd miss it. Can you believe that? I would actually miss making these bleedin' boxes!'

''Course you would, and I'd miss my rats. Because they're not such bad little fellers, you know. Not their fault they pick up disease.'

'So you think Sophie'll pick up soon, do you, Jacob?'

''Course she will!' he said, rallying himself, raising his voice deliberately, making light of a situation that was not as it appeared to be on the surface. 'We can count our blessings she's gone quiet for a while. I don't remember the last time she lay down during the day or kept her mouth shut for longer than ten minutes. It's a ruddy miracle. And God knows I could do with one of those where she's concerned.'

'I can hear you out there, Jacob Marcovitch! Every word of it!' roared Sophie from within.

'And you think I don't know that!' he yelled back, grinning broadly. 'See . . . she's perking up already, worse luck.' His attention was suddenly caught by a young lad sauntering into the yard, hands in pockets and whistling.

'This is Kelly's Yard, innit?' said the tall, skinny lad, who had a stoop.

'It is, young man. And what can we do for you?'

'Nuffing, really. I just popped in to see a friend of mine. Maria. Gotta make arrangements, ain't we? That's all right, innit?'

'Possibly,' said Jacob, not giving an inch. 'Depends on what kind of arrangement you're after.'

'We're gonna meet up next August and go somewhere. Can't remember where now but I will. I normally do,' he said, scratching the side of his straight thin nose.

'But this *is* August,' said Jacob, enjoying a little bit of banter with this lad, who didn't appear to be all that bright.

'I'm not talking about this year, am I? Next year. Should be all right.'

'If you say so,' Jacob replied non-committally.

'She's a nice girl.' The lad looked around, hands still in his pockets. 'Nice little place you've got 'ere. It's all right, innit?'

'Very generous of you to say so,' came the mildly

sarcastic but amused reply. 'We think so. What's your name?'

'Dick. Short for Richard. Cor, stable's a bit whiffy. Be all right if I come and clear it out? Won't charge or that. I'll just 'ave the horse shit. I can shift that. Good for gardens and yards and that. My old grandfather grew the best carrots out of horse shit. Fit for royalty, they was. Be all right, won't it? If I take it?'

'You'd best check that with Olly Black, young man.'

'Them flowers look nice growing up that wall. Was it always like that, the wall?'

'No, lad. Mrs Bertram planted it. It's called honey-suckle.'

'Is it? Fink she'd plant one outside our 'ouse?'

'Ask her.'

'I will.' He grinned, admiring the climber and nodding. 'Mrs Bertram? Is she Maria's mum?'

'She is.'

'That's 'er 'ouse, then. Tell 'er I'll come back tomorra. Sorry I couldn't 'ang around. Be all right, won't it?'

'Tell me something,' said Jacob. 'Does your mother ever get a headache?'

'Well, stone me, how did you know that? She don't mind, though. Sympathy comes wiv it. I can give anyone an 'eadache! Give you one, if you want.' His eyes twinkled as he spoke.

'You already have,' mumbled Jacob. 'How will you shift the muck?'

'Got a wheelbarra, 'ave yer?'

'Charlie the cart-pusher keeps one in there.'

'I'll borrow that, then. Be all right, won't it . . . ?' His voice trailed off as if his question had really been a statement of fact, rather than a request, but his eyes held the gaze of another.

Feeling relieved at the sudden pause in the chatter, Jacob followed the lad's gaze. He was looking up at the rooms above the stables and at Tremain, who was in the doorway peering down into the yard at nothing in particular, occasionally glancing at the lad.

'Is he your chum?' said Dick cautiously, a more serious expression on his face now.

'He's our neighbour.'

'But not your chum?'

'Not particularly, no . . .'

'Is he Maria's chum?'

'Your Maria?' Jacob laughed. 'I shouldn't have said so. Why?'

'Don't spread it but she wants to keep well away from 'im. Maria.' He tapped the side of his nose, spun around on one heel and sauntered back out of the yard. 'See you later on in the week!' he called back, cheerful and happy-go-lucky again.

'Yes,' Jacob said to himself, 'I don't doubt it.'

He instinctively looked up at the rooms above the stable and quietly studied the mysterious Tremain. There was no reason to take the lad's caution seriously, but even so he could not get the words out of his mind – 'She wants to keep well away from 'im.' True enough, he hadn't said much, and it was clear to anyone that he was a little simple, yet the fact that he did not waste his words bothered Jacob.

The lad may have seemed slow but he was sharp enough to restrict his choice of words to necessities, a transaction of facts and no more. Why, then, had he deemed it necessary to issue such a warning?

'Strange sort of fing to say, wasn't it, Jacob?' said Angel, who was never far out of earshot of any conversation. Spreading a few matchboxes to dry, she went on, 'Do you think he knows something we don't? Saw something perhaps that we should have seen?'

'I doubt it,' Jacob said, keeping his tone nice and even. 'Shouldn't worry yourself over it. The lad's an idiot,' he concluded decisively.

Catching Tremain's eye as he stared down at him, Jacob tipped his hat and nodded. The response was a leering smile before the man turned and went inside his lodgings. Try as any of them might, they were not going to draw Tremain out, and Jacob wasn't the only one who wanted to know the reason for his constant desire to snub and keep his distance.

Behind closed doors in the privacy of his rooms, Steffan's father rubbed the dusty window with the sleeve of his jacket and peered out in the direction of the half-moon alleyway leading out of the yard. The strange-looking lad was familiar but he couldn't quite place him. The sight of his son walking into the yard arm in arm with a girl he deluded himself into thinking was a whore pushed thoughts of the young lad out of his mind.

'That's it, son.' He leered. 'Sow your oats and reap

your diseased harvest later.' Throwing his shoulders back, he roared with laughter.

'How's Sophie, Mr Marcovitch?' asked Maria, slipping her arm out of Steffan's. 'Is she still in bed resting?'

'She is, sweetheart, but picking up. She'll be all right.' He nodded.

'Roses!' yelled Sophie from inside the darkened room. 'Put roses on me grave! Every summertime.'

'You see? She's on the mend, all right. Please God she'll stay put for at least one more day!' He said this loud enough for his wife to hear. 'She drives me mad!'

'I'll pop in, shall I?' enquired Maria, although it was much more a statement than a question.

'Please yerself. She'll only go over her funeral arrangements. She wants us to wrap 'er in a cloth and chuck 'er in the river.'

'And throw rose petals in after me, don't forget! And a bunch of roses on the day forever after!'

Laughing, Maria waved a hand at Steffan, who was also smiling and was by now on his way up the wooden steps to his rooms. Unbeknown to him, and to all in the yard, the wheels of justice had been irretrievably set in motion, although only one man living there had any inkling that Steffan was about to be arrested on suspicion of murder.

7

---◆---

The humidity of the night hung thickly in the air.
Tossing and turning in her bed, with beads of sweat
trickling down her face and neck and soaking into
the sheet below her, Maria was struggling to escape
from her nightmare. She lay restlessly, dreaming of
crowds of people dressed in black, carrying swords and
long-bladed scissors and chasing her, her small brother
Willy and Steffan. All three of them were desperately
screaming out to each other, though try as they might
no sound would come out of their terrified mouths. In
all the tumult and confusion they had lost each other,
and the sound of church bells and the clatter of hoofs
on uneven stones all around them was deafening. If
they had been able to cry out they would not have
been heard.

She awoke suddenly to the sound of chains rattling
and coach wheels coming to a stop outside, and in her
confused and emotional state was about to run when
she realised that her nightmare had somehow bled into
her first waking moments. As the fog of her dream
lifted, she saw she was in her bedroom, safe, with
her five-year-old brother sound asleep on his mattress
beside her. Glancing over at Daisy, who was as usual

dead to the world, she relaxed back into her pillow and waited for her heartbeat to slow down. As she lay there trying to compose herself, she could hear the sound of very low voices and horses settling down coming from outside the yard in the cobblestoned street.

Half listening, with little concern about events taking place outside at such a late hour, her curiosity was then piqued by the quiet sound of urgent whispering and footsteps in the yard. She carefully eased herself up and peeped through the gap in the curtains to see what was happening. No one could have been more shocked than Maria when she saw two uniformed policemen caught in the moonlight. Another man in a cloak and deerstalker trod carefully with them across the worn stones and crept up the wooden steps to the rooms above the stable. Leaning on the window ledge, fixing her eyes on the space below the steps, she waited, fully expecting a ruckus of some sort.

A short while later she heard a door creaking open and then a shuffling sound and a low murmur. Her heart was pounding in her chest as she watched and waited with bated breath to see what would happen. In sheer amazement she looked on as the two uniformed officers held Steffan of all people firmly by each arm. Maria felt as if a bolt of lightning had struck her body. She could not believe her eyes, gripped by utter disbelief at the arrest of the wrong man, firmly convinced that it was a ghastly mistake – a misunderstanding at best.

Losing no time, she flung aside her bed sheet, wrapped it around herself, crept out of the room so as not to wake the children, then scurried down the narrow stairs and out of the house. Once in the yard she ran quickly through the half-moon passage to see them bundling her friend roughly into the police coach. Leaving all decorum aside, she grabbed the arm of the gentleman in plain clothes and stared into his face. 'You've made a terrible mistake,' she whispered urgently, assuming they had arrested Steffan for the penny farthing murder. 'He's not the one you should be arresting,' she added hurriedly and without thinking. 'It's his father!'

The only explanation she could think of for this midnight activity was a grim one. If the police had come to the yard, or more specifically to the 'Tremains' lodgings, surely that could mean only that it was to do with the murder. After all, it was generally known that the police had interviewed Steffan's father, and that they had stayed long enough to arouse suspicions in the yard.

'Madam, this is official business and I would thank you to kindly return to your chamber!'

'But, sir,' she pleaded, her throat almost dry, 'you have the wrong man! He wouldn't harm a fly! I know him! You're making a terrible mistake! I beg you with all my heart, please take notice of me. Please!'

'It's all right, Maria,' said Steffan, his voice no more than a whisper. 'Don't worry.'

'No,' she insisted, 'this is wrong!' Maria punched the side of the coach. 'You mustn't do this to him! You mustn't! Why are you taking him away? How dare you!'

'Madam, I must warn you . . .' came the stern voice of one of the officers.

'Leave it be, Maria,' Steffan urged. 'Go back inside. I've done nothing wrong. The truth will out, I promise you.' His words may have been full of confidence but the tone of his voice was dull and monotone. He was clearly in shock but trying to regain his composure.

Allowing one of the policemen to pull her away from the coach, she held Steffan's gaze and willed her eyes to convey a message. *I won't desert you.*

The sudden slamming of the coach door sent a shudder down her spine, and with her eyes still on Steffan as he looked at her forlornly through the window she placed a finger to her lips and gently kissed it as tears streamed down her cheeks. Slowly nodding at her, Steffan clenched his jaw as he forced back his emotions.

Turning to the officer in plain clothes who had not got into the coach, she asked, 'Where are they taking him?'

'Arbour Square police station,' replied the inspector she had spoken with previously in her home. There was a hint of compassion in his voice but no sign of sympathy on his face.

'And will he come home tomorrow? After you've questioned him?'

'No, Miss Bertram.' His answer was accompanied by a hardened stare. 'We'll discuss that tomorrow evening. I shall call on you at eight. I trust you will be home from business by then?'

'Yes, sir,' said Maria, the worry evident in her

voice. 'But why should you be calling on me? I don't understand.'

'You have made a very serious accusation against Mr Tremain senior. I cannot ignore that in the circumstances. Until tomorrow evening, then,' he said, tipping his head. 'Goodnight to you, Miss Bertram.' With that he turned and walked away into the gloom.

Standing in the middle of the dark and isolated street, Maria watched as the coach pulled away and disappeared into the night, to Arbour Square, where Steffan would be locked in a cell until arraigned to the courtroom. Stunned by it all, she walked slowly back into the yard as if in a trance, and as if pulled by some magnetic force her eyes seemed to raise themselves up to the rooms above the stable. The silhouette of Steffan's father standing at the window sent a bolt of sheer terror straight through her. He was looking down at her, and although she could not see his face she glared up at him. She was fully aware he must have heard her as good as accuse him of murder, but her anger overcame her fear of him, and seemed to form a protective shield around her.

Once back inside her house, she dropped down into the armchair and stared at the floor, her mind blank, her body numb. She could hear the creaking of floorboards from above and hoped that it was her mother coming down and not one of the children. She fixed her eyes on the winding stairs and breathed a sigh of relief when Liza did appear.

'What's happening, Maria?' she whispered, not fully alert. 'Has Sophie taken ill?'

'No,' Maria murmured, 'they arrested Steffan. He wouldn't hurt a fly. I know he wouldn't. I don't understand it. Why did they come and take him away? I don't know what's happening . . .' Her voice trailed off as tears welled in her eyes and threatened to spill over once again.

'According to Angel an officer took some papers away earlier on today, from their rooms. That's all I know, sweetheart.' Liza yawned. 'I can't tell you any more than that.' Slipping her arms around her daughter, she held her tight, patted her back and silently tried to comfort her. Something she had not done in a very long time.

'It's just police procedure, I expect,' she eventually murmured, rubbing her eyes and then stretching. 'A lad came looking for you earlier apparently. I meant to tell you but forgot. I think he was the son of the woman you went to see about working at the biscuit factory.'

'Oh, very likely.' Maria sniffed. 'I thought he might come round. He's harmless enough and funny. He'll make us smile if nothing else does.'

'Peculiar, is what Angel thought. Anyhow . . . she said that the lad saw Mr Tremain in his doorway and out of the blue said you were to keep away from him. They think he recognised him from somewhere.'

'Why didn't you say so earlier?' Maria reproached her gently. 'That could be really important. He might *know* something.'

'I told you, I forgot. Besides, Maria,' said Liza, gently stroking her daughter's hair, 'we mustn't jump to conclusions over Mr Tremain just because he drinks too much. It's hardly uncommon, now, is it?'

'It's not only that! It's everything. He's just a horrible man. The way he behaved and how he carries on now; and he's been in prison. Would you want to be alone with someone like that? From what I can gather from Steffan's intimations, he goes with prostitutes all the time and always has done.'

'Well, that's not out of the ordinary, Maria. It happens all the time. The man has painted a none-too-good picture of himself, granted, but . . . well, the police must have had a reason for taking that lad away. I think you might 'ave bin a bit too trusting, sweetheart.'

'I can guess what happened,' murmured Maria, crossly, a little more fire in her face now. 'To think that that man, Steffan's own flesh and blood, his own father, might have told lies to cover himself. The police officer's coming to see me tomorrow after work. We'll find out more then.'

'Coming to see *you*?' Liza pulled back and stared into her daughter's face, full of concern. 'Why?'

'Because when I went out there I said that it was Steffan's father they should be taking away,' she admitted begrudgingly.

'Maria! You never did say such a thing? Surely to goodness you never said that?' Liza's hand flew to cover her mouth, as if somehow she could hold Maria's words back.

'I did say it, Mum. And he replied that I'd made a very serious accusation, and no, he didn't look too happy about it. But I don't care. I know I'm right about Steffan and I'll prove it. One way or the other I will prove his innocence. They can't just arrest him like that. They can't!'

'Well, love, I hate to say it, but it seems that they just did.'

The next morning, on her way to work, Maria forced herself to concentrate on what she might say to Miss Drake to soften the woman, enabling her to retract her resignation without losing her dignity. At Bollards respectability was high on the list of expectations where staff were concerned, so getting the right balance was all-important. To remain at the firm was now one of her main objectives. She was still dazed by Steffan's arrest, and although it felt as though part of her world had collapsed, she had the strength of mind to recognise that she must carry on and not go to pieces. She would be no use to Steffan, let alone her family, if she let that happen.

Her priority, for today, was her job. She had to find out as much as she possibly could about the plans that had been drawn up for a building to supersede the yard. Having been awake on and off all night, disturbed as to what Steffan might be going through, she had to draw on her inner strength to appear sharp and efficient. Her apology to Miss Drake had to sound sincere, and her story as to why she wished to withdraw her notice convincing. She would say that her mother had changed her mind, had said that it was wrong of her after all to uproot the family, and that she didn't want to be the cause of her daughter leaving such a good and reliable firm as Bollards.

Arriving in the building ten minutes early, she went directly to Miss Drake's office and knocked firmly on the door, willing herself to be strong and positive yet defensive and compliant. It was almost predictable that the sound of the steely voice ordering Maria to enter would turn her into a quivering wreck within seconds. Bracing herself, she turned the brass handle and pushed open the heavy door.

'Good morning, Miss Drake,' she said, showing as much respect as she could muster under the circumstances. 'I'm sorry to disturb you so early but there is something important I have to say to you, if I may, and if you can spare me the time.'

'Well,' Miss Drake snapped coldly, folding her arms to emphasise her impatience, 'since it is in *your* time, Miss Bertram, and not in the company's, I can give you five minutes.'

'Thank you, madam. I do appreciate it. I realise that this is your special time of peace and quiet before the day begins.'

'You are rambling, Miss Bertram,' said the woman, easing herself down into her chair. 'Please be brief,' she continued, rapping her fingers on the desk.

'I apologise. I will come straight to the point. I beg to withdraw my resignation. My mother was very angry with me for putting her desire to move away before my post here at Bollards and without telling her of my intention to hand in my notice. So I wish to withdraw my resignation.'

A slow, self-satisfied smirk spread across Miss Drake's face, and for a few seconds it seemed that she had lost her dour façade. Quickly regaining her composure, she replied coldly, 'Do not grovel, Miss Bertram. It belittles you and your act is not entirely convincing. Did you not get the position you applied for?'

'I've not applied for another position,' Maria murmured, swallowing her pride. 'I fully appreciate that you might already have someone in mind for my job—'

'Your *job*, Miss Bertram?' The woman leaned back in her chair and narrowed her eyes, the smirk still faintly on her lips. 'You make it sound as if you were employed in the factory loading bay and not in the offices.'

'Am I to take it, then, that I may not withdraw my resignation?' Maria was by now struggling to keep her self-control. This woman was infuriating, but if her plans were to be brought to fruition she had to stay calm. 'If I may not withdraw it I fully understand and I shan't waste any more of your valuable time,' she said.

'As I have already said, this is *your* time and not that of the company, Miss Bertram.' Miss Drake opened a ledger, picked up her quill and continued without looking up. 'I accept the withdrawal and will thank you not to come into this office again unless you have something of real importance to report. You now have three black marks on your record. Another and you will find yourself dismissed without a testimonial but with a damning reference.'

'I understand. Thank you. From now on I will be an obedient employee and go about my work in silence.'

The hint of sarcasm in Maria's voice went undetected. Once outside the personnel office, she leaned on the wall and drew breath. She had done it. She had bought herself more time in this company. Now she could relax a little and go about her duties effecting a happy albeit false disposition. She knew what she had to do. To bring any acting ability she might possess to the fore and to put on a show of being proud to be employed in an archaic, unfriendly firm. She would also appear to obey the rules to the letter, as if she agreed with them wholeheartedly. As far as Mr Clarkson was concerned she was going to have to use her guile to walk a very fine line: smiling at his cheap asides, listening to his confidences with regard to Miss Drake, and feigning ignorance should he make suggestive advances towards her. This was not something that she would consider in the normal run of things, but there was too much at stake to do otherwise. Her resolve to expose the secret plans of this company was going to have to be put on hold until the time was right for her to give it her full concentration. To her mind now her most important task was to do all she could to help Steffan. Kelly's Yard and its future were going to have to wait a while longer.

Once inside her small private place in the post sorting room she relaxed and went about her business, wiping all her worries from her mind. She could not afford to make a mistake now and give Miss Drake a reason to give her notice. To Maria it was obvious that the woman had accepted her withdrawal for one reason and one reason only – she did not want to have to go through the business of finding and interviewing others for her post.

Startling her, the door of the post sorting room suddenly burst open. It was Mr Clarkson, and he was sporting a by now familiar sickly grin. 'Just had a word with the tyrant,' he whispered, overly familiar. 'Glad to hear you're not leaving. Good girl. Excellent.' With that and a sly wink he was gone, leaving Maria to stare at the closed door.

Smiling nervously, she wondered whether this middle-aged gentleman truly believed that there was anything remotely attractive about him which would turn a girl's head. For some reason the sight of him this morning, after all that had happened during the night, removed any fear that she had harboured. She was no longer afraid of this man. She couldn't see that she had done anything wrong; certainly she had not encouraged him to behave so familiarly towards her. However, if going along with his fantasies was simply a means to an end, to her working her way into the architects' department, she would string him along, but still at arm's length.

With her thoughts now returning to Steffan and his plight, she knew which of her priorities was the most urgent. She not only believed he was innocent – she knew it. Whether or not his father was involved in the so-called penny farthing murder was up to the authorities to investigate and was no concern of hers.

Immediately after work that day, Maria went directly to Arbour Square police station, where Steffan was being held, hoping to be able to speak up for him. On seeing the official-looking building she suddenly felt her stomach lurch. This was not quite what she had expected, and the sudden feeling of nausea caused her to lose confidence. Staring at the entrance to the police station, she imagined Steffan locked behind bars, and she wasn't sure she could face either seeing him in that situation or being turned away without a reason being given.

Forcing herself forward, newly invigorated, Maria managed to push all her trepidation aside as she walked boldly into the station and up to the desk and asked whether she might speak to Detective Inspector Barcroft.

The desk officer looked blandly up at her from his desk. 'May I ask the nature of your business, madam?'

'It's to do with the penny farthing murder and the young man you've locked up.' An uneasy silence filled the room as Maria summoned the courage to continue. She was regretting coming in as fear crept over her. 'I just wanted to have a word about Steffan Tremain.'

'Yes?' The officer fell silent again.

'Well . . . finding the right words, sir, is no easy thing. I—'

'May I ask your name, madam?'

'Maria. Maria Bertram.'

The desk officer glanced at her left hand. 'That would be Miss Bertram, would it?'

'Yes, sir. It would.'

'If you would care to wait a moment I'll see if the

gentleman is in the building.' He gave her a nod and a faint smile and left her with an assistant desk officer.

'He shouldn't keep you long,' said the slightly more amiable man. 'His patience is a little stretched, mind. You're not the first to come in with information, and most of it so far has been time-wasting. There are lunatics who post their letters of confession and vindictive neighbours who come in their droves when a murder is committed to damn an enemy. It soon wears thin.'

'I don't expect to take up too much of Mr Barcroft's time,' she said curtly, wiping her sweaty palms down her skirt.

'It's Detective Inspector Barcroft, Miss Bertram. You would do well to remember that.' He gave her a fatherly wink and turned back to his work.

'I will, Officer. Thank you.'

No sooner had she settled herself on a wooden bench for a long wait than the door opened and the officer beckoned her inside. Her stomach still churning, she nervously followed the man into a narrow corridor where there was a door with the detective inspector's name on a plaque. Once inside, with the door closed behind her, she again regretted having come, and was totally at a loss as to what she might say.

His hands behind his back, Detective Inspector Barcroft was looking out of the window at something going on in the exercise yard. 'Please take a seat, Miss Bertram,' he said, indicating clearly by his tone that this was to be a brief visit. 'I don't usually see people impromptu like this, but since we've already met at your mother's house it seemed only polite to return the hospitality. Secondly, this will save my having to come and see you later this evening. I'm surprised you didn't wait until then. Would you like a glass of water?'

'I would, sir. Thank you. I came because I couldn't bear to think of my friend locked up with no visitor to at least give him something to feel better about. I'm his only real friend and he has little family to speak of.' Her words were to the point, but her voice gave away the fact that she was very nervous in these surroundings.

As he turned to face her, Barcroft's face relaxed into a smile. 'I remember the first time I entered such an office as this . . . when I came as a young peeler, as we were then called. A bobby on the beat.' He poured her a glass of water from a glass jug. 'My throat was very dry then too.'

'I must admit,' said Maria, taking the glass from him, 'now that I'm here I'm not quite sure what to say to you.'

'Then let me help you. Please take a seat,' he repeated, waving a hand at a chair opposite his desk and then sat down himself. 'I presume you wish to talk to me about Steffan Tremain?'

'Well, yes . . . but it seems foolish now.'

'Why would that be?'

'Because really and truly, sir, I have nothing to say other than that I don't think he is capable of harming anyone, never mind strangling a woman and pushing her and her bicycle into the Thames.'

'A testimony is never ignored, Miss Bertram,' Barcroft

said, looking directly into her face. 'Especially when it comes from someone who has never been in trouble with the police and is employed in the offices of a respectable company such as Bollards.'

Surprised that he should know where she worked, Maria sipped her water and waited for him to say something else. But he was expecting her to speak and the expression in his eyes made this very clear. 'Sometimes, sir,' she said, in a quiet voice, 'sometimes you just know someone. I suppose I am only going on instinct but—'

'And what of his father, Miss Bertram? What do your instincts tell you about Mr Tremain senior?'

'That he has a cruel streak and that he takes too much gin. But then that's not instinct, sir, it's fact.'

'Mmm . . .' Barcroft clasped his fingers together and narrowed his eyes. 'A cruel streak?'

'Well . . . from what Steffan's told me—'

'Exactly. From what the man's son has told you. The man's son, Miss Bertram, is being held in a cell on suspicion of murder. That is not exactly a testimony that I—'

'But it's not just that, sir! It's . . . it's the way he is. The way he ignores everyone in the yard. Never ever looks us in the eye—'

'Well, what else would you expect from a gentleman of his class? That he sit and gossip with the women?'

'No, of course I wouldn't expect that, but—'

'Tell me something,' Barcroft said, cutting in, 'has Steffan Tremain ever shown you his drawings? His works of art?'

'No . . . he's told me about them and promised I could 'ave a look one day but we just never got round to it. He said they're not landscapes or anything like that and that they might not be to my taste . . . but that was all.'

'And you think you know enough about him to waste my time and yours?'

'I don't think I am wasting your time, sir. He is innocent, I know it. May I see him?'

'This is not a sanctuary, madam, where visitors may come and go as they please. If all you have come to tell me is that Steffan Tremain is an innocent man, then I must ask you to leave, unless of course you have something of importance that will throw light on the case we are investigating.'

'I do have something important . . . to ask.'

'One question, then, but an answer to it is not guaranteed.'

'Would it be possible for you to give me his grand-parents' address so that I can tell them what's happened?'

'We have already informed the prisoner's father that he is under arrest. That will suffice. Now if you don't mind—'

'Please, sir. Please contact his grandparents in Saffron Walden. You may get a clearer picture of what Steffan is like.'

'I'm sure I would, Miss Bertram. But we cannot spend time looking for that kind of picture. We are looking for a murderer. Can you blame the deceased woman's parents for pushing for action?'

'No,' murmured Maria, casting her eyes down. 'Is there *any* possibility at all of my being granted a visit to see my . . . the prisoner? Two minutes would be enough. He doesn't have many friends and—'

'You may have five minutes,' Barcroft conceded, a little more gently. 'But you will not turn up here again without an appointment, is that understood? If you wish to speak with me you must write in.' With that he rang his desk bell and waited in silence for the desk sergeant to arrive. This he did within seconds. 'Please show Miss Bertram to Cell Five and lock her in with prisoner Tremain and yourself.'

'Yes, sir,' said the sergeant, looking from his senior to Maria.

Rising, Maria smiled and thanked the detective inspector. 'I promise not to come uninvited again, sir. I wasn't sure of the rules—'

'No. We don't print the procedure on the outside walls for obvious reasons. We do not want any Tom, Dick or Harry coming in as if this were a hotel. Goodbye, Miss Bertram.'

'Goodbye, sir, and thank you again.'

As she followed the sergeant through to the cell block, Maria's heart was beating so fast she felt as if it would burst, and when she was shown through a heavy iron door into a long narrow stone passageway with cells on either side she felt light-headed and giddy. When they arrived at Cell 5 she clenched her hands into fists and braced herself so as not to lose courage. The clanking sound of the heavy key turning in the lock made her go cold, and when she saw Steffan slumped on a narrow bed, which had no more than a grubby thin mattress, it was all she could do to stop herself from holding out her arms to him. He looked so pathetic as he sat staring down at the stone floor. She wanted so badly to hold him close and comfort him, but knew that if she did so she would burst into tears, and that was not her reason for being here. She had to be strong for his sake. As far as she was concerned Steffan needed to be cheered up and not cast down into a more depressing mood than he was already in. He gazed up at her as if he were seeing a ghost from his past. His face, drawn and grey, held no expression whatsoever.

'Hello, Steffan,' she said, forcing back tears that were welling at the backs of her eyes. 'I dreamt you would be coming home soon, and you can bet Sophie's last shilling you will be!'

'Maria?' he murmured, peering at her. 'Is Sophie here too?'

'No, silly. I was just saying what she always says. About her last shilling.'

'They let you come in to visit me?'

'I took pot luck and it paid off.' She moved closer and sat down next to him. 'Only five minutes, though. That's all I'm allowed. Are they feeding you anything?'

'Nothing that I'd want to eat but I'm not exactly hungry.' He raised his eyes from the floor again and looked at her. 'I didn't do what they've arrested me for, Maria.'

'I know that. Mum said they took some papers away. Were they your drawings?'

'Yes. My father led them to the trunk. They were a mixture of my paintings, sketches and the like. Why did he do that? What was he trying to prove? Does he hate me that much?'

'Of course not. He's just a very sick man. But listen to me. The minutes will fly.' She lowered her voice almost to a whisper. 'Tell me your grandparents' address in Saffron Walden.'

'No. I don't want them to know about this. It would break their hearts. They're not getting any younger. I feel so ashamed and yet I've done nothing wrong.' He slowly shook his head. 'It would devastate them. My father in prison and now me? It would break their hearts, I know it.'

'But they would *want* to know. You can't not let them know, Steffan. It's not fair. You've got to give them the chance to help you. Please. Please tell me.'

'No. I don't care what happens to me, Maria. Try and understand. They've questioned and questioned and questioned me until I feel like saying I did it to stop the questions once and for all. I can't take this kind of treatment. I just can't. I thought I was lonely in the room next to the prison but it doesn't compare to this. I'd rather be dead. Let them hang me and be done with it.'

'And what about me? I've to live with that, have I? I don't have many friends, Steffan. I don't have any. Only the women in the yard. You're my only friend.'

He brushed away a fly from his shoulder, avoiding her eyes. 'Just because I like to paint pictures they call me a murderer. It was a particularly macabre sketch that to me was art. One of the officers said I had been drawing my fantasies until I was ready to make them real.' He managed a sardonic smile. 'Can you believe *anyone* would think such a thing?'

'Please. Please tell me where they live.'

'No, Maria. I don't want them to be hurt any more. Best they grow old not knowing what's become of me.' He turned again from her searching eyes. 'They believe here that I strangled a woman. That I strangled her and then pushed her into the river. They actually believe that I would do something like that. As if I could do such a thing. But now they have me thinking that if people believe I'm capable of it . . . it's as horrible as if I am capable of it.' He turned and peered into her face. 'Does everyone in the yard think it too?'

'No. Of course not. Look, I don't have much time, Steffan. Five minutes is nothing. Please tell me where they live! If not I'll ask your father. I won't give up. I won't.'

'Go away, Maria,' he murmured, turning away from her. 'Go away and don't come back. Imagine I've had a fatal accident. That I'm dead. I don't want to live any more in any case . . .'

'Daisy said if I don't get the address she'll bleedin' well climb in a winda and find it 'er effing self.'

Unable to stop himself smiling he slowly shook his head. 'She wouldn't do that.'

'Wouldn't she? Wouldn't she, Steffan? You're sure about that, are you? And don't think she won't do it while your dad's in there because she will. She'll hold scissors to his neck to get what she wants. She's wild

over this. Worse than me. And Willy cried in his sleep
as well as being sad before he dropped off. Everyone
in the yard sends their good wishes and tells you not to
worry.' This was a white lie but she was desperate.

'They hardly know me, Maria,' he said, again avoiding her lovely eyes. 'They know nothing about me.'

'You saved our Willy, don't forget. You can't lie
down and die now. They wouldn't let you. Please,
Steffan. Please just give me this one thing. The
address.'

'Time's up, miss,' said the officer, himself somewhat
moved by this scene. And this man had seen women
sobbing for their husbands and children, begging for
their fathers to be let out. 'We must go now.'

'It's called Three Chimneys. Anyone will tell you
where it is.'

'Time to go,' the officer repeated, his officious voice
bringing home the reality of this situation. Swallowing
a lump in his throat, Steffan mouthed the words 'thank
you' to Maria and turned his face away.

'We will get you out of here, Steffan. You shouldn't
be locked up. Daisy reckons she's gonna find out who
did it. She's already been to see Wilkie Crow and told
him to get his arse moving.'

'Just go, Maria,' said Steffan quietly, covering his
head with his hands. 'Thank you for coming. It will
help me get through the nights.'

Thank you for coming. Steffan's parting words min-
gled repeatedly with Maria's thoughts until she realised
that she was home and walking through half-moon
alley and into the yard. It was deathly quiet but she did

not notice because her mind was elsewhere. It wasn't until Daisy came out of the house in a sullen mood that she realised something else was terribly wrong. She looked at her sister, waiting for her to announce some bad news, but Daisy was reticent, which was out of character. Looking around, Maria focused on Sophie's house. The door was shut and that was unusual too.

'She can't breathe properly so we've all got to be quiet while she gets some rest,' said Daisy sulkily. 'Everyone's acting like she's dead. I asked the poor doctor when he came out and he said she'd be all right wiv peace and quiet. He only said that to stop us from playing spinning top.'

'Who's with 'er now, Daisy? Is Mum in there?'

'And Angel. Mr Black and Olly 'ave gone to get her sons from the tavern up West India Docks. She might not go fru the night.'

Numbed by Daisy's casual account of something so grave, Maria fell quiet. Totally lost for words. When, out of the corner of her eye, she saw movement above the stables, she just knew that Steffan's father would be watching. She could feel his eyes on her. She could feel his eyes boring into her flesh. Shuddering, she ignored him, went to Sophie's front door and quietly tapped. It was Liza who appeared, with her finger to her lips. Taking her daughter to one side, she whispered, 'She's very poorly, Maria. The doctor thinks that dust from the flock and feathers has gotten into her lungs over the years. She's inhaling hot vapours that Angel made up for her from coal and eucalyptus.'

'Daisy said—'

'I know. I heard her.' She looked across at the eight-year-old and scowled at her. 'The doctor said that Sophie would need watching through the night and that's just what we're going to do. Me and Angel. She'll pull through providing we can get her to cough up the dust and phlegm. We've been taking it in turns to pummel her back. We've soaked 'er back and chest with linctus oil.'

'But it's like a morgue, Mum. It's so quiet.'

'Which is how it should be when someone's ill. She's very poorly, Maria, but she won't die. She might 'ave done had me and Angel not been forceful enough. We've sent the men out on errands and messages to get them out of the way. Their fussing around her made it worse.'

'So they've *not* gone to get Sophie's three sons because it's urgent, then?'

'No. They've gone to *report* to the three sons. We gave strict instructions for them not to come back for a while and when they do they're to sleep on the straw in the stable. We've put the bedding out there already.' She glanced across at Daisy, who was now on the doorstep, elbows on knees, her hands cupping her face. 'Daisy's been waiting for you to come home. She's been pacing this yard non-stop.'

'Why?'

'Because she listens to what everyone is saying. And they're saying that no woman's safe now. Willy asked her if she thought you'd bin strangled on the way home from work and she started to cry.'

'Where's Will now?'

'On his mattress as quiet as a church mouse.'

'I don't know what's happening in this place,' said Maria, beginning to lose all hope of things getting back to normal. 'It's as if someone's put a curse on all of us.'

'Don't talk like that, Maria! That's tantamount to blasphemy. Sometimes things do seem as if an ill wind's never going to stop blowing, but it does. Nothing, good nor bad, lasts for ever.' Liza slipped her arm into Maria's and walked her slowly to their front door.

'Just one week of *good* would be nice.' Maria slowly shook her head. 'What next? What's going to happen next, Mum?'

'I've got the shits as well,' Daisy quietly mumbled, moving aside to let Maria and Liza into the house. 'I fink I've bin poisoned by bad chocolate and toffee. I might die of it.'

'Take no notice of Madam,' said Liza. 'She's attention-seeking agen. Eat your supper, Maria. It's on the table with a tin plate over it. We must all keep our strength up now. You're right, things are happening in this yard and we must keep our spirits up. It's the only way.'

'Will you and Angel be sitting with Sophie till morning, then?'

'On and off. Just to give Jacob a chance to get some shut-eye. The man works hard and he must be up very early. He'll want to be by her side all the time, of course he will. We'll just see how it goes. The poor man's beside himself with worry and tries not to show it.'

'I dropped in at Arbour Square on my way back to visit Steffan,' murmured Maria. 'That's why I was late. I didn't forget that Sophie was ill. I promise.'

'Arbour Square?' Liza was shocked. 'But they never let you in, surely? Why would they? You're not a relative and that young man's suspected of murder.'

'They allowed me five minutes and no more. He didn't do it. I know he didn't.'

'None of us can know anything for sure,' said Liza, picking up a hair brush from the window ledge and eyeing her eight-year-old on the doorstep. 'We're in the dark over this.' She glanced up at the rooms above the stable. 'What must his father be going through?'

'That's what I'd like to know,' said Maria. 'If anyone's violent around here, he is.'

Watching her mother step towards her, and already on her guard, Daisy said, 'You ain't gonna brush my 'air at a time like this? That's bleedin' wicked.'

'It's got to be done, Daisy. Look at it. Come inside and be quiet. I'll take it slowly.'

Taking one step back, Daisy spun around suddenly and ran for her life, knowing what she had to do. She had to go and see Wilkie and borrow his big scissors!

Watching from his lodgings, Tremain smiled before turning away from the window, admiring the girl for having mettle when his own pathetic son was sitting in a prison cell, and all because of his soppy drawings. Looking around the room, he grimaced and then shuddered. With Steffan not there to keep it tidy and clean it was a disgrace. Worse than that, his gin bottle was empty and there was no money in his pocket. Cursing, he took a greasy knife, went into Steffan's room and took hold of his tarnished black tin box, which he had taken from its hiding place. With trembling hands caused by his desperate need for alcohol, he prised for all he was worth to no avail. Jabbing beneath the lock, he cursed until he was red in the face, and then threw the money box across the room, smashing it against a wall and yelling, 'Selfish little bastard!'

Rage overcoming all else, Tremain left the rooms, slamming the door shut behind him, and stomped down the wooden steps and out of the yard, heading for Tobacco Dock to see the man he considered to be a money-tosser. Someone who had a brain the size of a pea. He had already procured thirty-four guineas from him and another five now would suit him nicely. With no thoughts for anyone or anything else, he blindly staggered on until he saw Wilkie outside his usual haunt, talking to the whore's young sister from the yard.

Never missing a trick, Wilkie had seen him coming from a distance. By now he had managed to talk Daisy out of chopping off her hair. 'Run along 'ome, Dai,' he said, his voice gentle but authoritative. 'And if you come back in the morning and give us a report on Sophie, still wiv every hair on yer head, I'll treat you to tuppence. Can't say fairer than that, can I?'

'You could say frupence, Wilkie. I mean to say . . .' She sniffed, wiping her dribbling nose with the back of her hand. 'I'm doing wot you want, ain't I? I'm leaving me 'air be. And I'll need more than two bleed-ing pennies to buy a nice chunk of coal tar soap to wash it wiv.'

'All right, but for thrupence you'll 'ave to run an errand for me tomorra. Deal struck. Now go on 'ome and leave me be. I've got business to attend to.'

'Can't I 'ave a little glass of beer 'fore I go?' she said, putting on her astonished expression. 'I've come all the way to get yer advice an' I can't 'ave a sup of your beer?'

'No! Off you go!'

Shrugging and rolling her eyes, Daisy turned to leave. Mr Tremain was now only a few feet away. Peering up at him, Daisy curled her top lip. 'You know what, mister? We fink it was you who murdered that woman and not our friend. You've stitched up yer own flesh and blood, you bleeding geeza!'

'Charming child.' Tremain sniffed, waving her away with a limp hand and an expression that could easily have been his downfall had Wilkie not been there to give Daisy a look which needed no accompanying words. Turning away from him, prolonging her sneer, she spat at his feet and sped off.

'I shouldn't be living amidst these people, Wilkie.' Tremain sighed, slumping down into a chair next to him. 'What *am* I doing here, dear boy?'

In a flash Wilkie saw the opening he had been waiting for. Tremain was obviously in a talkative mood and Wilkie needed all the information he could get on this man.

'Well, it's funny you should ask that, Gent, 'cos I

was only just sitting 'ere finking to m'self the very
self-same thing. What would a gentleman of standing
like Mr Tremain be doing in these parts? Of course,'
he said, leaning forward, eyes wide and innocent, 'we
realise full well that you must 'ave fallen on hard times,
and no need for explanations on that side of things.
Enough said.'

'Well, yes, you have a point there, and I would be the
first to say you are a wise man, Wilkie, and considerate
to boot. However, now that you ask, I did not fall on
hard times, I was *pushed*, and by, of all people, my very
own dear wife. Not that it was entirely her fault, sir, no.
Mental illness is a cruel, cruel thing.'

'Ah. So she lost 'er mind, did she?'

'Worse. Much, much worse. She bankrupted me to
boot, Wilkie, and there you have it in a nutshell. I was
left to look after our only son and with not a penny to
my name, and I shall tell you something else. I had to go
into the debtors' prison because of it! Can you believe
that? She gave thousands away to a scrounger who she
believed herself to be in love with. A scrounger who, of
course, once the money was gone, disappeared into the
night with no word and no hint of having been there.'

'Dear oh dear oh dear.' Wilkie sighed, shaking his
head for reasons he would keep to himself. 'That is
the worst I've heard so far. Dreadful, that. But there.
That's women for yer!' He paused for a moment and
then said slyly, 'I expect that's why you've turned to
our girls. As a comfort.'

'Indeed. Indeed, indeed.' Tremain sighed melodra-
matically.

Taking a risk, Wilkie pursued his line of questioning. 'It's a wonder you never turned against women, to my mind. I've known men do that, you know. To be scorned by love *can* bring on attacks of revenge.'

'Can it? I wouldn't know about that. Didn't feel anything, to be perfectly honest. And as far as the women down here go . . . if we must sneeze, then we must. It's no more than that, I'm afraid. I merely come here to relieve myself in order not to become . . . shall we say, a frustrated old man?'

'I can understand that sentiment.' Wilkie nodded thoughtfully. 'Yes, Gent, I can see your point. In short, you feel nothing for women. No love, no hate, no resentment, nothing.'

'Exactly.' Gent slowly turned his face to his companion. 'You think that a little odd?'

'I don't really think about it at all, my friend. It's not the sort of thing a man broods over now, is it? I was just a little curious, that's all. Now I'm not any more.' He grinned broadly and swallowed the rest of his ale in one go.

'Now then, my very good friend. To business. I'm prepared to borrow on the same terms. Ten guineas, if you please. I was going to say five, but why come back again next week and waste your time? Yes, ten would do nicely.'

'I'm sure it would.' Wilkie chuckled. 'But your limit has reached the little red line, my man.' He looked at Tremain and waited.

'Oh, we needn't worry about little red lines, dear fellow. Indeed not. In the not so distant future, and

I speak of months, not years, I am to come into my inheritance. You must have guessed that I come from a very wealthy family. My father has a terminal illness, I am unhappy to say.' The expression on his face changed accordingly. 'I received a letter no less than three days ago from my mother. She begs that I return to the fold. We had an almighty row, you see . . . when they found out that I had let my wife be in charge of our finances. They were totally unforgiving at the time and furious when I went to prison instead of exposing her as the real bad debtor. But' – he tipped his chin proudly – 'I am a gentleman and I have high principles. I am also a proud man. I would rather have hanged than let it be known that a wife of mine was a fraudster, a cheat and a liar. No, sir, I would not let that get out into the public domain.' He stopped and then looked pleadingly into Wilkie's face. 'I trust I do have your undivided confidence on this matter? Because, you know, I do consider you a friend, even though we are of different breeding.'

Wilkie grinned at him, winking. 'Well, I am glad to hear that, Gent. Very glad indeed.'

'Ah! You are a *lucky* man, Wilkie Crow! To be so very gladsome in this dire world is a gift. I commend you. Now then, why don't we say ten guineas and be done with it. Or fifteen if you would prefer it. You have a business to run, after all, and a man's profit is a man's purse.'

'Well, that's very commendable, Gent. Very commendable. But business is business and until you pay your bill, my friend, my arm's bent backwards, if you get my drift. Thirty-five guineas is maximum. And you've had thirty-four.'

'Thirty-four guineas! Indeed I have not borrowed that much, my friend! No, sir! You are mistaken!'

'And you wouldn't be the first to have said that, Mr Tremain, but I must say I am surprised by it. I 'ad you dahn for an intelligent man. Someone who would've kept a running account of what he owes.'

'Wouldn't dream of it! I trusted you implicitly to keep a straight record.'

'And now?'

'Now I say you must be mistaken, Mr Crow! I say you have made a mistake with your arithmetic, sir!' Catching the look of anger in Wilkie's eyes, he quickly changed his expression and lowered his voice. He had been backed into a corner, and must appease his only source of quick cash. 'I mean to say . . . surely you are mistaken? Or have I, in my misery and loneliness, spent more on women to comfort me than I imagined? Do you think this might be possible, Wilkie? I cannot believe it of myself but I am open to criticism if I *have* behaved so badly.'

Without a word, his face expressionless and with his pipe gripped in the corner of his mouth, Wilkie pulled a small notebook from his pocket. Flicking through until he came to the appropriate page, he held it out for Tremain to view, keeping a firm grip on it.

'Gracious, is that how many times I have borrowed from you? I *am* astonished!'

'Well, I don't know why, Gent, because you initialled

every entry. I would 'ave thought you would 'ave noticed the list growing.'

'No,' Tremain said, slowly shaking his head. He then placed a hand on his heart. 'On my father's grave—'

'He's not dead yet, Gent. Let's not wish the poor old bastard away before he's gone cold.'

'A manner of speech, my friend, a manner of speech. So then . . .' He groaned, leaning back in his chair. 'I must go and see the old codger for an advance on my inheritance.'

'It would seem so, my man.'

'Ah well . . . if needs must then I shall go with cap in hand. At least that will put a smile on his face. I dare say he has been waiting for this.'

'Well then, I shan't keep you, sir.' Wilkie grinned. 'Let's say we meet here tomorrow at midday. That should give you time to get to Essex and back. Because that is where you said your family 'ome was, if I'm not mistaken?'

'Indeed you are not mistaken, Wilkie. You forget and miss nothing. I commend you.'

'It's a pleasure to do business with such a gentleman,' said Wilkie, offering his hand.

'I couldn't agree more,' replied Tremain, shaking it wholeheartedly. 'I shall be here tomorrow at, shall we say, five o'clock in the afternoon.'

'Five o'clock it is.' Wilkie nodded.

Wilkie watched as Tremain walked somewhat unsteadily along the dockside, satisfied that he had gleaned enough from their contrived conversation to satisfy him. This man, useless waster though he be, was not a murderer. 'Yes,' murmured Wilkie, 'you are many things, my friend, but you don't have it in you to end a life. That is no compliment, it is merely a fact.' His next step would be to have the man tailed the following day to see whether there was actually a mansion or rich parents.

So, wondered Wilkie, as he pulled himself up from his chair, why would a gentleman deliberately point the finger at his own son? Although he was beginning to see this as pure speculation now. The fact that Tremain had shown what he believed to be childish drawings to a police officer, no doubt when he was out of his head with booze, proved nothing. This was a mystery that Wilkie had found intriguing, one which he felt satisfied that he had solved as being nothing more than very stupid behaviour. The stupid behaviour of a drunk, which was not uncommon in this part of the world. He had seen enough men behaving like silly boy lemons in his time while under the influence.

He watched in amusement as Tremain staggered off in dire need of another drink. He knew that the Gent was mean spirited, but he had believed there was money in the background. If his instincts were wrong, and he didn't think they were, Mr Tremain, like others who did not pay their debts, might well meet his Maker floating down the Thames.

Now fuelled by anger, Tremain was trying to think where he might borrow a little cash to pay something back to the loan shark, in order to borrow more from him. Having already decided that he was far too distraught over his son's arrest to go into work, he could now spend time looking for the key to Steffan's cash box. Running through his mind the places where it might be hidden, he soon came to the conclusion that he would most likely have it with him and would not have run the risk of leaving it overnight in his trouser or coat pocket. The trembling of his hands worsening, he wondered whether he might try another tavern out of the area, where he was sure to find another moneylender. But this thought was discarded since he had nothing, not even a cheap watch, to put down. Swaying and cursing aloud, he continued on his way back to the yard.

Having penned a letter to Steffan's grandfather, there was little else that Maria could do other than post it and hope for a reply. She had explained all that had happened, giving her high opinion of their grandson and relating how lost and abandoned he had appeared on her visit to him in that awful cell. Her only hope now was that these people from an entirely different class to herself would not simply see her as someone hoping to worm her way into their world and dismiss her as nothing more than a peasant from the worst end of London, of no breeding and with a low reputation. Setting off for the post office, she came face to face with Mr Tremain on his way in through the half-moon alley.

'Ah!' he said, almost blocking her way, deigning to talk to her for the first time. 'The young lady who is to become my daughter-in-law!' He pressed one hand against the crumbling wall to steady himself. 'You do realise,' he slurred, 'that one day I shall give everything to that lad of mine. Every penny, mind! Directly I have sorted out my financial affairs. Oh, yes!' He hunched his shoulders and splayed his hands, swaying as if he were on a boat. 'Alas . . . until then I have not a penny to my name. Would that I could bail out my dear, dear, beloved one and only son.'

'I'm sorry, Mr Tremain, but I have urgent business elsewhere. I—'

'*Urgent* business? My, my, how very important that sounds. Well, now . . . I don't suppose you could help out a friend? A small loan? So that I may get my son out of that dreadful prison. I believe they have taken him to Newgate! They will have locked him in the condemned cell! A stone dungeon, eight feet long by six feet wide, with a bench, a Bible, a prayer book and nothing else.'

'Your son isn't in Newgate, sir, he is in Arbour Square police station, in a cell which has a decent enough bed.'

'And how would you know that, mm?' A silly grin spread across his face, and Maria couldn't help noticing that the whites of his eyes were yellow and the lids red rimmed. His breath reeked of pipe tobacco and gin.

'Because I went to visit him, sir. They seem to be treating him quite well, and there's no charge of murder. He's only there to answer questions. They don't really believe he murdered that woman. They have an older man in mind. An eyewitness has come forward,' she added, fabricating her story for her own reasons.

Ignoring her, Tremain grinned. 'So what about that small loan, then? Mmm? Half a guinea would do.'

'I'm sorry, sir, but we are a poor family and only just make ends meet. Why not go and see Mr Crow in Tobacco Dock? He would willingly give you a loan, I feel certain of it.'

'Bah!' screeched the man, flapping a hand at her. 'Silly woman!' he yelled. 'You know nothing of the world! Nothing!'

'Sir, if you please . . . one of the women in the yard is very ill. If you could see your way to going quietly it would be much appreciated.'

'If I could see my way?' he sneered. 'To go quietly? I'll make as much noise as I bloody well like!'

'Oi. What's this? Shouting at a lady? That's not right.'

Spinning around, Maria was mortified to see that the young man, Dick, had returned once again. Before she could say anything, the lad told Tremain to stop being rude to his girlfriend. Then, pushing his face close up to Tremain, he squinted and stared at him. 'I've seen you before. You know it. I know it.'

'Have you indeed?' said Tremain, backing away. 'Well, I do apologise, *boy*, but I did not and would not register the likes of you, no matter where or when we passed each other by. I do not, under normal circumstances, speak to idiots, but since you addressed my future daughter-in-law as your girlfriend I am graciously giving you the time of day. Furthermore,

I am now telling you to go away and leave my son's fiancée alone. Unless, of course, you have five shillings to loan me until I can get to my bank?'

Turning to Maria, the lad, stony faced, spoke in an over-familiar tone. 'His son's fiancée? He's took you for someone else.'

'He knows exactly who I am and he has not made a mistake, he is simply telling an outright lie! Now, if you will excuse me I have an errand to go on!' She pushed her way through the pair of them and strode out of the alley, angry and a touch nervous – she wasn't quite sure which of the two unnerved her the more.

'Now do you see what you've done, you foolish boy?'

'You live in this yard, do yer?' said Dick, studying the man's face.

'I *lodge* here, boy! There is a huge difference. A week or so and I shall be living back in my house in the country! Away from the likes of you!'

Dick shoved his nose close to Tremain's face. 'Ah. Thought so. You're one of them.'

'One of what, may I ask?'

'Drink from the minute you wake up till you go to sleep agen. Yeah, I can see it now. You're a red-face. That's wot we call a drunk round our way. It's funny. You all smell the same.'

'Much more from you, lad, and I'll land a punch on that thin nose of yours.'

'Bin drinking long, 'ave yer?'

Tremain waved a hand wildly in the air. 'Be off with you!'

'So you don't recognise me, then?'

'Away, boy, away!'

'Well, that's good. I'm pleased about that. 'S'one fing about drunks. Can't remember nuffing. Not from one hour to the next, never mind one day to the next. I recognised you, though, didn't I. See?' He tapped his temple. 'Sharp as a fox, me. Gotta get up early to catch Dicky-boy.' He grinned broadly and then broke into a strange babble of laughter. 'Stay drunk!' With that the lad spun on his heel and sauntered off.

'Ignorant common people,' mumbled Tremain as he staggered through the yard. 'I should not be here!' he yelled, turning in a circle, addressing anyone and everyone. '*I* was born in a mansion house, with a nanny to see to my every need! *I* was born to mix with royalty, not the scum of the earth! *I* am from a long line of aristocrats!' Splaying his arms theatrically, he began to recite, overly loud and melodramatic:

> 'With blackest moss the flower pots
> Were thickly crusted, one and all!
> The rusted nails fell from the knots
> That held the peach to the garden wall.
> The broken sheds look'd sad and strange:
> Unlifted was the clinking latch;
> Weeded and worn the ancient thatch
> Upon the lonely moated grange!'

Standing as if he were exhausted after giving a dramatic performance on stage, Tremain awaited his applause. He did not have to wait long. From an upstairs window a cracked old flower pot came flying through the air to crash at his feet. From another window came the familiar voice of Daisy. 'Go and jump in the bleedin' river and drown yerself!'

Cursing and grumbling, Tremain staggered up the wooden steps. Once inside his rooms he slammed the door shut and collapsed on to his unmade, dishevelled, grubby bed. Staring up at the lopsided ceiling with its numerous damp stains, he was pervaded by self-pity with no thought to spare for what his son might be going through in his lonely prison cell. Weeping loudly for all he had lost and all he could no longer have, he placed his hands together and begged the good Lord to send him just one bottle of gin. 'I have suffered aplenty and I have suffered long. Spare me this one request, I beg you. Send your messenger with just one bottle before sleep takes me. I dare not sleep, Lord, for fear that when I wake every tavern and public house will be boarded for the night!'

Dragging himself up from his bed, he began to search frantically for the key to the money box, muttering about how he could not be out-foxed, how he would find the key and have the last laugh. Before very long he was sweeping things from rickety shelves, turning out drawer after drawer, the contents sprawling on the floor. On and on he went until the rooms were in utter chaos, with his and Steffan's mattresses dragged halfway off their iron steads and nothing in its right place.

Finally, having exhausted every possible option regarding his son's hiding place, he slumped to the floor and lay half on, half off a mattress, pulling a moth-eaten grey blanket over his face. Willing himself not to fall asleep, he closed his eyes and found that the face of the simpleton who went by the name of Dick was floating through his mind. 'I know you, boy,' he mumbled to himself, 'and you know me . . . from where, that is the question!' With the back of his hand on his forehead, he cried out: 'I must be away from this filthy, smelly ditch before I go completely insane!' That said, he fell immediately into a drunken sleep.

8

A week is a very long time and drags slowly when you are waiting despondently for something to happen. Maria was by now beginning to think that Steffan's continuing imprisonment meant that the police authorities believed they had their murderer. She had found it difficult to concentrate at work and the atmosphere whenever she came across John was cool, which confused her. Fickle though he had already proved to be, pledging his love for her and then turning his back because she had not gone along with his wishes for her to leave seemed strange. Thinking back to their first time walking out together, she recalled the way she had felt then. That spine-tingling challenge of breaking Bollards' rules and the fun and laughter they had enjoyed when exploring the ancient buildings by the river seemed a lifetime away. She could hardly believe that he was the same person. It was almost as if there were two of him. Two very different personalities entwined in one.

As for Mr Clarkson, he continued to behave as if they were kindred spirits, always giving her a suggestive smile with a certain expression in his eyes that caused her to feel as if he could see through her clothing. Miss Drake, characteristically, stood each morning on guard watching for latecomers and behaved as if Maria were invisible whenever she saw her.

Leaving the building on this particularly hot and humid early August day, and making her way home, she wondered how Steffan was faring. She missed him more than she had thought she would, and had been angrier with his father when she had seen him than she ought to have been. Strolling along Commercial Road, preoccupied with her thoughts, she was surprised to hear John call her name. Turning slowly, she waited for him to catch up with her. Red in the face and a little out of breath, he stood before her. 'Maria. You walk far too quickly,' he said, smiling at her.

'Do I? I didn't realise. I was miles away—'

'Well, at least I caught you up. How are you?'

'I'm all right, thanks. And you?'

'Very well but . . . but I'm confused, Maria. You said you would stop working at Bollards. That you wouldn't ask to stay on. I don't understand.'

'No . . . I said I would probably stay. You frightened me into it at first, saying all those things about Mr Clarkson, and so soon after a woman had been murdered almost on my doorstep. I didn't lie to you. I'm sure I said I would stay when we were in the park.'

'But I thought you would have changed your mind once you knew my position at Bollards – that I'd broken confidentiality by telling you about the plans for the yard. Especially since I told you how I felt.'

'That you loved me? Is that what you mean?'

'Of course that's what I mean. Did it mean nothing to you?' He looked genuinely hurt.

'Oh, John . . .' Maria sighed. 'Of course it meant something. It meant a lot. But I was confused and it came as a surprise. I had no idea.'

'I wouldn't have said anything yet but I was trying to explain why I wanted you to leave. I knew I was in love after our very first time together. Did it mean so little?'

'No. It was a lovely thing for you to say. No one's ever said anything romantic to me before. It was lovely and I enjoyed the memory for days but . . .' She stopped there and shrugged, unable to say what she meant.

'But what? If you don't feel the same I'd rather know.'

'It's not that. It's just that . . . well, I didn't quite believe you. I thought you was saying it so I would leave. I thought you were more concerned about being found out or in case I stormed into your office and let the cat out of the bag.'

He pressed his hands into his face and slowly shook his head. 'You don't know me at all, Maria. I'm not like that. I just couldn't bear the thought of us being under the same roof and my not being able to smile at you or touch you.'

'Well, maybe you shouldn't 'ave lied to me in the first place. You got me to hand in my notice because of Mr Clarkson when all the time it was for another reason—'

'Yes! It was because I loved you! Is that such a bad thing?'

'I don't know. I don't know anything any more. My life used to be so straightforward but now . . .'

'Now? Since we became sweethearts, you mean?'

Staring into his face, Maria could hardly believe her ears. 'Sweethearts? I . . . I don't know what to say, John.'

'But you can see my point? Look at the position I'm in now. I daren't risk breathing in your company, let alone smiling at you.' He paused for a moment and then showed a different expression, one that bore resentment. 'And what about the plans for Kelly's Yard? Are you saying you don't care about that any more? Or do you intend to make trouble?'

Maria was flummoxed. She didn't know what to think or say. Covering her sentiments, she offered a tired smile. 'Well, Kelly's Yard is not exactly a palace, is it? I expect they'll find somewhere for us to live. We're a fairly resilient bunch and if it comes to it and we're not happy we'll stand up for our rights. I'm not so worried any more – in fact I've put it out of my mind. It won't happen for a very long time yet. Unless, of course, you know different?'

'No. No, I don't know any more than I've already told you.'

'Well, there we are, then.' She smiled. 'We can forget all about it.'

'Yes. Yes, it would be good if we could do that. Forget I ever mentioned it. Do you think you could manage that?'

'Well, I can't promise not to get angry again, but if I do I doubt that I'll come bowling into your office and rip up the plans in a temper.'

'You mean you've really thought about such a thing?' he said, staring into her face.

'Of course I have. Wouldn't you?' A small voice at

the back of her mind was telling Maria to stop talking like this.

'Well, I hope that doesn't happen, Maria, for both our sakes.' His face set, he tipped his hat, bade her farewell and turned away.

Watching him striding along towards an omnibus, Maria felt that any possible romance between them had just sailed down the river. Continuing on her way home, and thinking it through, she could see that John had been worried, and that when he had said once again that he loved her she had not responded in the way she should have.

'Silly fool,' she murmured, half smiling. 'I'll make it up tomorrow after work.' If he could snatch a few clandestine minutes on the way to his omnibus then so could she. If only to apologise and get him to stop worrying over losing his job. She wondered whether he had really fallen in love with her, even though his reasons for telling her to leave Bollards had not been entirely honest, to say the least. One thing she did know – attractive though he was, and in spite of everything else, including their first wonderful afternoon out together, his charm and his confidence, she knew that he was not the one for her. When it came to love and all the feelings that this sentiment brought to the surface, it was Steffan who was in her heart and no one else. The thought of never seeing him again should things go that way was something she could not bear to contemplate. This was her secret. This was something she would tell no one.

*　　*　　*

Arriving at his stop in Camden Town, John Cunningham walked slowly through the backstreets with much on his mind. Convincing Maria that he loved her was not going to be a problem in so far as he could tell. Their brief time together this evening, he believed, had almost eradicated the doubts she had been harbouring since he had admitted that he had wanted her to leave the firm for different reasons to the ones he had first given her, and that was the most important thing. His object now was to fully sway her and win back her trust one hundred per cent. If she had left Bollards and his plan had come to fruition he felt sure that they could have shared a life together without anything getting in their way and without mistrust and exposure darkening his doorstep.

Why Maria had first reminded him of his mother, who he was very close to and who meant so much to him, was a mystery. He could see now that on the face of it they were nothing alike, and he would have his work cut out trying to bring them together and to like each other.

Turning into Shoemaker Street, he decided not to dwell any longer on Maria and Bollards for the time being. He went down the stone steps of number 11, to the basement rooms where he lived with his mother.

Going quietly in through their front door and along the dreary passage, which had grimy, ornately framed paintings on either side and a large oval mahogany mirror on the end wall, he felt secure again now that he was back in his own world. Safe and secure.

He went into the living room, which was crammed
with old furniture: faded and worn velvet-covered
chairs, framed mirrors on every wall and vases, glass
bowls and framed photographs everywhere. Easing
himself down into his elaborately carved chair with
its frayed tapestry cover, he leaned back and closed
his eyes, waiting for his mother to arrive with his cup
of tea and two biscuits.

'You're a quarter of an hour late, John,' she said
when she came into the room. 'You're never this late.
I thought there might have been an accident.'

'No, I—'

'I expect it was the girl,' she interrupted rudely. 'The
one you've been to the park with on two Sundays. You
don't have to lie to me, John. You never have and I
would not have you start now. I'm too old to be lied to.
Your father had me live a long and silent lie.' She went
back into the kitchen and returned with a tray set with
two cups of tea instead of the usual one and placed it
down on a side table. Easing herself into her armchair,
she looked directly into his face. 'I didn't expect you
not to fall in love, but just remember all the warnings
I've given you and how I've not been wrong so far.

'I thought your father loved me but we both know
how wrong I was. Pity I hadn't seen the light before the
stable door had been left open and the horse bolted. Be
very careful is my message. Now I've said my piece I
shall leave it there and thank you to do the same.'

'I shan't be seeing the girl again,' said John, his face
set and determined. 'Well, not intimately. Of course, I
shall have to see her during working time when we can

hardly avoid it. She betrayed me and put my position at work in jeopardy. That's the reason I'm late and why I forgot to buy our newspaper. My mind was occupied when it shouldn't have been. I should have known it would turn out like this. It always does. Your warnings are never far off the mark.'

'Well, that's something,' said his mother, sipping her tea. 'A lesson has been learned and you'll be the better for it.'

'Yes. I realise that now.'

'We can trust no one in this world, sadly. No one. Would you have believed your own father could have been a philanderer and a born liar?'

'I don't remember much about him, Mother. You know that.'

'Then we'll leave it there. But there is something else I need to talk about. The prostitute that you said too much to. This girl from your offices lives close to where she met her end.' His mother sipped her tea, her eyes fixed firmly on his face.

'She's not talked about it other than to mention it in passing. But you are right to ask.' He raised his eyes to her. 'I laid myself wide open when I put my trust in Maria. She has already put me in a precarious position, has she not? She promised faithfully that she would leave Bollards and now she tells me otherwise. She can't be trusted not to try and bring about my downfall.'

'You cannot afford to trust anyone in these times! How often have I said so? How many times must I say it?' Shaking her head fiercely, she went on, 'At least you learned *something* from the last one. Had the article been written by her you would have been in serious trouble. Trouble I could not get you out of.'

'Yes, I know. And yes, I did learn something, but clearly it was not enough. I'm finished with all women. Prostitutes too. I pay for their services and pay well and *still* she tricked me! She would have written that article and seen me damned for it without a care nor any feelings of guilt. I thought she might be lovely, like her name. Rose. But no, she was simply the thorn!'

'Did you burn her journal that you found, like I said?'

'No, but it's hidden well. Besides, they have no reason to come searching here. They have her diary and that will be enough to convict the man who betrayed her twice.' The room fell quiet, which was not unusual when mother and son were thinking things through.

'The notes she wrote after I confided in her,' murmured John, 'with regard to the plans for Shadwell, were not mentioned in her private diary but her journal. That evidence is hidden well. She must have been out to blackmail me, Mother. Why else would she want to write down things I had told her in confidence? It was lucky I found her journal.' His expression suddenly changed and there was a different look in his eyes, one of hostility, as he brought to mind all the woman had written down. 'There wasn't much, granted, but my name was on the page and beside it was the name of Bollards and the address. It was easy to put two and two together. Farther down she had written "Tobacco

Dock, land purchase", so what does that tell us? The name meant nothing to me but the connection was clear. My name, the name and address of the place I work, Tobacco Dock and, most damning of all, *land purchase!*' He glanced at his mother. 'Doesn't all of that add up to one thing? Blackmail. Blackmail or exposure and my downfall.'

'Good,' she said, slowly nodding. 'At last you are heeding my words. By now you must be convinced,' she added, looking directly into his face. 'That you must trust *no one*. That I have *not* exaggerated.'

'How can I not be convinced? I told two women too much and each of them were ready to expose the company I am loyal to and to hell with me. I am wondering now if I've been right all along and people *are* out to get whatever and whoever they can – if they see a profit in it.'

The woman sighed. 'I would sooner that you had not arrived at the same thought I have had to live with all these years, but better you arrive at it now than later on in life when it might well have been too late. Yes. Better sooner than later.'

'So you can see the way my mind is working? That the girl has left me no choice? That she is forcing my hand?'

'I saw it before you did, my son. But never mind. At least you will not be obliged to do it again. Lessons have been learned. You've come through your severest tests, and at a young age, John. Wisdom is there for the mastering and you have learned well and you've learned fast. I'm satisfied that when I go from this earth I shall leave you capable of living a contented life until we are reunited. This is a deeply troubled world but you will cope with it now, I feel certain of that. And that's been my one concern since the day you were born. Continue to visit your paid women in this area. Why look farther afield when all you need is on your doorstep? We can afford the guineas but we cannot afford another broken heart. Mine was enough for the both of us. Self-preservation, my son, is next to godliness.'

'Did you manage to sell anything today?' said John, his mood having swiftly changed.

'I purchased and I sold.' She smiled. 'The widow Phillips in Boot Street sold me her silver candlesticks, which I passed on to Mr Cohen at a good profit.' She nodded, pleased with herself. 'It's boiled bacon and carrots for supper.'

After a few days of waiting for word from Steffan's father, Maria came to the conclusion that there was no need to rush things. Her friend had spent a week of his life in a cell, and all things considered that really was no time at all when a lifetime stretched ahead of him. She was convinced that he would soon be set free. For reasons unknown to her, the worry over him being hanged for this murder had subsided. He was innocent and therefore, as far as she could see, there could be no evidence to convict him of murder. No, to her Steffan was a young man with a lifetime ahead of him, and she felt certain that once his grandparents appeared on the scene they would take him back into the fold. His father, however, was a different kettle of fish. He would either continue to live over the stable, an innocent although alcoholic man, or he would be justifiably hanged for murder. If he was the murderer then he would be found out in the fullness of time.

Without knowing why, Maria felt strongly now that the truth would come out and that Steffan would be released. Whoever it was who had strangled the poor woman who came looking for her lover would eventually be smoked out of the woodwork if he was local. Apart from the police, and those in the neighbourhood who wanted to know whether they had a murderer in their midst, Wilkie Crow was watching and listening, and so too were his men, but still there was a worrying fear in and around Shadwell and Wapping. The murderer, not generally believed to be the young man who had been locked up, was still on the loose, and possibly still on the prowl.

In a lighter mood than she had been of late, Maria made her way to that part of the yard where three clothes lines stretched from one wall to another, her washing basket on her hip, and began to peg clean wet clothes out to dry. Relieved that she was not having to search for new employment and would shortly be starting her part-time work in the flower market, she hummed a tune while she worked, unaware that Olly, from his chair in a corner of the stable, was watching her.

'Now that's what I call white,' he said, gently rocking to and fro. 'Washing day is Friday, I thought,' he added, raising an eyebrow. 'I thought it was a lovely meat pudding bubbling away in that tin bath.'

'Is that right, Mr Black?' She laughed. 'Well, you'll be pleased to know that your Angel slipped your Sunday shirt in and your long johns. In this weather we sometimes need to do an extra boil up of our whites – Sunday or not.'

'So that's where my underpants got to. Just as well it's not a cold day.'

'We would have yanked them off you in any case.' She laughed again.

'Well, Maria,' he said, drawing on his pipe, 'I can't tell you 'ow good it is to see a smile on yer face agen. We've all cheered up a bit, it would seem, and I fink we know the reason why.'

''Course we know the reason why. Sophie's pulled through the worst and the sun's still shining for us. This 'as bin a good summer, and my washing's going to dry in no time.'

'So I'd best not mention anyfing on the downhearted side, then? Is that right?' He kicked the floor to rock himself to and fro. 'I mean to say . . . no point in pouring cold water on your sunny self, now, is there?'

She knew exactly what he meant. 'Steffan's all right, Olly,' she said, pegging his long johns on to the line. 'I can't tell you why I'm saying that but it's what I feel inside. I bet you he'll be back in this yard in a day or so. I bet you that little green powder bowl he will be.'

'You don't 'ave to risk yer money gambling, Maria. I'm only asking threepence for it. To you, that is. Anyone else and I'd charge a shilling, so I would.'

With the last of her washing hanging to dry, Maria joined Olly in the shade and sat on the edge of his display table, which he had not yet set up. 'What would you say if I told you I know something that I can only tell to someone who I really trust not to go mad over it?'

'Can't promise I won't,' he said, sniffing. 'Won't promise nuffing till I know I can keep the pledge.' He tapped his pipe on the side of his chair and wiped the inside of it. 'You must do as you fink fit, my girl.'

'I'm being serious now. Really serious. I know something and I don't think I can keep it to myself, but if I tell the women they'll go mad. I know they will.'

'Go on, then, if it's that serious. You've got my word. It'll be between the two of us.'

Taking a deep breath and hoping she was doing the right thing, Maria began her story from when John Cunningham first told her of the plans for the yard. Through it all Olly said nothing. He listened, filled his pipe, nodded now and then and was thoughtful once she had finished. Respecting his silence, she waited, with a sense of having shifted some of her burden and with no regrets for having offloaded it.

'And you say that your job at Bollards is safe and the governors 'ave no inkling that you've found out about it?' he said, keeping his eyes down, concentrating his thoughts entirely on the matter in hand.

'They couldn't possibly know. John Cunningham wouldn't dare let it slip for fear of losing his job and getting into serious trouble over it. He's broken the rules of confidentiality, let's not forget.'

'Well then, in that case . . . you've done the right thing in clawing back your position there.' He looked up at her and smiled. 'Ain't it nice to know that the likes of us can 'ave a spy in high places, eh?'

'You want me to be a spy, then?' She laughed. 'And you think I could manage it?'

"Course. You're our Maria! Our pride of the yard!'

'So you agree that we should keep quiet over it?'

'I do, Maria. I most definitely do. But you must keep your ear close to the ground, your eyes peeled and furthermore . . . you've got to stay on very good terms with this young man, Cunningham. That you *must* do. You're a clever girl and I know you'll be able to wheedle things out of 'im.'

'Well, that might be difficult, Olly. He says we can only see each other if I leave the firm. He's frightened in case we're seen together. He won't even give me so much as a glance never mind smile at me these days. We're only just on polite speaking terms now . . .'

'That's understandable. Yes.' He became pensive again, and then murmured, 'But really and truly . . . you've no choice. You've got to try and win the chap back. I'm not saying you've to be sweet'earts. No.' He began to rock on his chair again, concentrating. 'Can you fink of anyfin that you've got in common with the lad? Somefing you both enjoy . . . like goin' to one of them free museums, for instance?'

'No. He'd smell a rat if I suddenly got that friendly.'

'Mmm. So he's not as daft as he sounds, then?'

'No. I think he's rather cunning, Olly.'

'Where did you say he lived?'

'I didn't. Camden Town. He lives with 'is mother—' Her face suddenly lit up as an idea struck her. 'His mother! He went to Petticoat Lane to spy out the place for 'er. She wants somewhere other than Camden where she can buy cheaply to sell on where she lives! Old things, Olly! Second-hand and antiques!'

'Is that right?' He beamed. 'Well, well, well, wot a coincidence!'

'You're the *one*! You're the one that could draw John in!'

'Yes. Oh, yes. I know the way a dealer's mind works.' He grinned. 'But *you* must draw 'im in, Maria. Fetch 'im to me. Bait 'im.' He glanced around at his various fruit crates which were packed with curios. 'Sometimes we have to bait wiv silver to get the gold,' he said, rubbing his chin thoughtfully. 'Yes, that's wot we must do, Maria.'

Inspired and excited, Olly was up and shifting packed boxes. 'I've just the fing tucked away,' he said, chuckling. 'Just the fing.'

Digging deep into one of his rickety old crates, he pulled out a small parcel wrapped in old newspaper and tied with string. 'This will do the trick.' He opened it to reveal a Georgian silver and blue glass cruet set. 'This,' he said, with a certain amount of pride, 'is my very best find of all finds, Maria. It was in wiv a load of old junk and as black as coal. Now you look at it.'

'It's beautiful, Olly. Really lovely. But it must be worth a lot of money.'

'It's for when me and Angel can't work so much.

I've a few bits put by going up in value all the time. Yes, it's for the day when we can't make ends meet, Maria, put it that way.'

'Well then, we mustn't risk losing it.'

'We won't lose it, darlin'. No. This 'as got my name on it,' he murmured, before giving it a little kiss. 'And you know . . . my luck's changed a bit of late. I don't know why but I'm not gonna question it. I've found some good junk and I've sold quite a bit. I'm prepared to take the risk wiv this.' He stared out at the yard. 'I don't wanna leave this place, Maria. It's bin my 'ome since I was a lad. A baby in arms, in fact. And now . . . it's not only puttin' a roof over my 'ead, it's givin' me the chance to earn a few bob so Angel can ease off working so much.' He looked into her face; his eyes a touch watery. 'D'yer get my drift?'

''Course I do. I feel exactly the same. This is our home, Olly. And I don't care who smirks at me for saying so but we are like family in this yard, and long may that go on. Family 'ave their differences, don't they. So if a little row breaks out now and then it's only natural.'

'That's right. It's only natural. 'Course . . . if they find us a nice place—'

'Cottage almshouses set around a green,' she cut in. 'We might just accept it, Olly, mightn't we?'

'We just might at that, Maria, we just might at that.' He grinned. The smile quickly dissolved, however, when he saw that in the entrance of the yard an elderly couple who were clearly not from these parts and had the aura of the well-to-do about them were standing quite still and looking around themselves, flabbergasted. 'We've got company,' he murmured.

Turning to see who had arrived, Maria knew immediately who these people were. Placing her washing basket on the chipped white enamel-topped table, she wiped her damp hands on her skirts and approached the couple, noting that the gentleman was now focusing his gaze on her. 'Excuse me, sir,' she said, offering her hand, 'my name is Maria Bertram and I was wondering if—'

'Yes,' he said, eyeing her from top to toe. 'I had a feeling you might be the young lady who wrote to us.' He took her hand and gave a polite nod. 'Is there somewhere we may talk in private?'

'Well, yes . . .' she murmured, half turning and looking up at the rooms above the stable. 'The door to the rooms where your son and grandson live is not locked. We could go up there. As far as I know, Mr Tremain senior is not at home.'

The gentleman, nodding graciously, turned to his wife and offered a faint encouraging smile while placing an arm around her waist and gently urging her forward. 'Come, my dear. The sooner this is over and done with the better.'

Looking around, the grandmother could hardly believe that things had come to this, and she now fully realised why they had not been able to track down their grandson. He had been living the life of a vagrant, she felt sure of it, going from one camp to another. It had been no less a task than searching for a needle in a haystack looking for him in this overcrowded part of London, which was bursting with the homeless and forgotten people.

'Are you certain that no one is home?' she asked, on the verge of breaking into tears, raising a trembling hand to her face. 'My son isn't in?'

'I'm certain of it,' said Maria, 'but if it makes you feel better I'll go and check.'

'Oh, would you, my dear? I should so appreciate it.'

'Of course. It's no trouble.' Maria turned from them and was relieved to see that Olly, in his wisdom, had disappeared into the depths of the stable. She ignored the two or three curious faces which were by now peering out through smudged window panes. Pushing the front door of the rooms open, she quietly called for Mr Tremain, even though she could tell by the stillness that no one was there. Without Steffan there to keep it clean and tidy, the place smelt of unwashed clothes and stale food and was a disgraceful mess. Empty gin bottles could be seen scattered about, mostly on the floor, showing beneath chairs and a small kitchen table.

Moving on to the small veranda, she beckoned for Steffan's grandparents to come up. The grandmother glanced from Maria to her husband and looked to be in a swoon, but with his strong arm about her she graciously allowed him to guide her up the wooden steps. Once at Maria's side she spoke in a whisper. 'Is there a chair, my dear?'

'Yes,' said Maria, smiling fondly at her. 'But I must warn you that the rooms are a shambles, which is not usually the case. Your grandson keeps the place tidy and clean, but of course . . .' Her words trailed off, for she did not want to mention the fact that he was in a cell right then. His grandparents already knew that from her letter and hardly needed to be reminded.

Herding them both inside, Maria pulled forward the only comfortable armchair and offered it to the grandmother. 'I'm not usually this fragile, my dear,' said the lady, excusing herself. 'It's all been a bit of shock, you see.'

'Of course it has, madam. I—'

'Oh, please. Please call me by name, my dear. It's Mrs Tremain.' Leaning back, as if all her strength had been used up, the woman drew breath and slowly shook her head. 'How long have they been living like this?'

'Stop fretting over it, Grace,' said the grandfather, brushing the seat of a hard-backed chair with the back of his hand. 'We've found them and that's all that matters. Now perhaps we shall be able to get on with our lives without worry.'

'Without worry!' moaned Steffan's grandmother. 'My poor boy is in a police cell. How can I not worry?'

'He shouldn't be in there,' said Maria, firmly. 'And I'm certain they'll have to release him soon.'

Clearing his throat and taking a deep breath, Steffan's grandfather shook his head. 'Grace, my dear, I believe we have at last found our angel of mercy.' He turned to Maria and smiled, holding back his own tears and swallowing the lump in his throat. 'We are indebted to you, my dear. Please . . . if you would be so kind, tell us the whole story as you know it, from the beginning to the end.'

'Your son and grandson 'ave been living in the yard for almost two years, sir. For most of that time Steffan kept himself very much to himself, but more recently we became friends. I can't say the same for your son, though, Mr Tremain. He'll have nothing to do with any of us in this yard, but it didn't matter. In this part of the world we live and let live. Most of us are too busy surviving to worry over nothing.'

'I can understand that sentiment, my dear. And as for my son, I have no wish to know more about him. I can see from the debris in this room that he has not changed and no doubt has worsened. It would please me if you were to say that he is not here today because he is at business somewhere, but I fear that will not be the case.'

'No, sir. As far as I know he doesn't work at the railway station of a Sunday, and he usually rolls into this yard some time in the afternoon after staying out of a Saturday night.'

'Well, that makes sense,' said the gentleman, bitterly. 'You need not be embarrassed, my dear, I am only too aware of his habits. Wine, women and song would be a pleasant way of putting it. But there. Let us not waste time. We are here to rescue our grandson, who we have dearly missed since he was taken from us by his father.' He returned his wife's emotional smile and nodded. 'We have found him and it's thanks to you, my dear. No doubt the authorities would have done so but you saved us from a worse shock. I dread to think of them turning up on our doorstep. 'We're not altogether sure why Steffan did not get in touch with us but—'

'He was almost ready to, Mr Tremain. I can vouch for that. He was waiting for his twenty-first birthday, and he'd been saving so he could present himself in a way that wouldn't upset you. He's much better off now than when he first came to London.'

'That sounds like my grandson,' said the old gentleman, his voice almost strangled with grief, the heartache of the past six years showing on his face.

Keeping a firm grip on her own emotions, Maria said, 'Do you remember when your grandson was small and he liked to draw and paint?' She had to move quickly on in case Steffan's father returned earlier than usual and a row broke out.

'Of course. Drawing was his love.'

'He was very talented,' added his grandmother, pride instead of grief now shining from her eyes. 'So talented.' She looked up and spoke with hope in her voice. 'Is he still painting, my dear?'

'No. And I'm sorry to say it was his drawings that caused them to arrest him.' This short statement was to the point but there was an urgency in Maria that she could not explain. 'Mr Tremain, your son, showed the drawings to the police while Steffan was at work. He was drunk at the time.'

'And that is *all* they have against him?'

'Yes, sir. That and no more. So you see—'

'Then our lawyer will have him out within twenty-four hours.' The gentleman stood up, his energies renewed, the worry gone from his face. He suddenly looked more his age and not so much an old man. He was, after all, no more than sixty-two, and apart from the grief he had suffered over losing his one and only beloved grandson he had lived a comfortable life. 'Our coach awaits us, my dear.' He smiled, holding out a hand to his wife. 'We may return to Essex in a happier frame of mind.'

'But, my dear husband,' she gasped, 'surely you can't mean that we're not going to visit my grandson? Surely you want to see Steffan?'

'Of course I do! But there has been an awful mistake and he will be released and back in our fold within days. Why distress ourselves and our grandson by going into a dreadful cell where he would certainly hate us to see him? No. We've waited this long, we can be a little more patient. We shall leave for Saffron Walden immediately.' He turned to Maria. 'You will be rewarded for your kindness. I shall—'

'There's no need for that, sir. I did not write in order to profit by it. I am in full employment as a clerk and shorthand copyist. I am also entrusted with the company mail, both business and private.'

'Ah. I can see I have offended you, my dear. I apologise.'

'All I want is to see my friend out in the fresh air and as free as he is entitled to be. He's suffered enough already. Did you know he lived in conditions much worse than these and worked as barge-cleaner and rat-trapper when his father was in prison?'

'No. We have managed to find out nothing of his

whereabouts since he was fourteen,' said the grand-father, choking back his sorrow once again.

'Well, I'm sure he'll tell you everything himself. I just wanted you to know the reason why I felt so sorry for him, having to suffer all over again with it being no fault of his own.'

'His poor mother will be so relieved,' murmured Steffan's grandmother. 'Relieved and overjoyed. She wrote to us explaining why she left in the first place—'

'Maria doesn't want to hear all of that, my dear.'

'It's all right,' said Maria. 'He told me what hap-pened and that his mother said he was to stay by his father's side so she would be able to find 'im when the time was right.'

'Foolish advice,' said Mr Tremain, 'but at the time she had enough on her mind. Our son has much to answer for.'

'He's been saving the little he has over each week so as to go in search of her one day. I think he intended to go to his maternal grandmother in Loughton as his first port of call.'

'My dear,' said the grandmother, gazing into Maria's face and sighing with relief. 'You know so much about him.'

'We've really only been friends for a few weeks but we hit it off straight away,' she said, blushing and low-ering her eyes. Close to shedding a tear herself, Maria stepped outside the rooms and waited. She wanted them to go. She had to try to forget Steffan because she knew in her heart that very shortly he would be free and soon after that he would have gone from her life.

So, in the quiet and still of the evening, knowing that eyes would be on them, Maria said her goodbyes, certain she would not see the couple again. They thanked her and wished her and her family well. 'There is one thing, sir,' she said, before they turned away. 'I believe that Steffan's father has a debt to pay down in Tobacco Dock. It would be wise to see it settled, if you don't mind my saying so.'

'A moneylender,' murmured Steffan's grandmother. 'He finds them wherever he goes.'

'Mr Crow is a good man at heart. He helps those who need it and he profits by those who can afford to borrow. Please don't think badly of him.' She cast her eyes down, adding, 'If you do nothing else for your son, I would advise that you do see to this in your own time. I have a feeling he may well up and leave without a word now that Steffan is not here to see to his every need. If that should be the case I will write to you and tell you the amount owed and where you might send the money.'

'Thank you again, my dear,' said the grandfather. 'We have much to thank you for.' As he turned to his wife the gentleman's expression immediately changed. There was a look of stark horror on the grandmother's face, and she was staring wide-eyed at the entrance to the yard. Steffan's father had appeared, dishevelled, in need of a shave, and was pressing one hand against the wall to steady himself. Clearly he had only just managed to get this far and was ready to collapse from too much drink and lack of sleep.

'*Owen!*' Steffan's grandfather's voice echoed around

the yard, and any murmuring from within was silenced.

Slowly lifting his head, Tremain peered at his father and then turned his eyes towards his mother, doing his utmost to focus. Either from shock or total intoxication he was not able to utter one word. He stared from one to the other.

Turning to Maria, Steffan's grandfather squeezed her arm. 'Thank you, my dear. I shall be in touch.' With that he strode towards his son and had short, sharp words with him.

'I don't know if I can face this, my dear,' murmured the grandmother, almost as if she were talking to a close relative, a daughter. 'I feel so dreadfully sick.'

'Let me help you to your coach,' said Maria, sorry for the woman and confused at suddenly intruding on their grief. 'Take my arm. We'll walk very slowly. You can talk to your son once you're all on board.'

'Will he come with us, do you think?' she said, looking into Maria's face for an answer to all her problems. 'I don't think he will. I don't think his father will entertain it.'

'Look.' Maria nodded towards the men. 'Your husband has already seen to it.' With a firm grip on Tremain's arm, the gentleman was half supporting, half pushing him through the half-moon alley. 'It'll all turn out for the best now, I'm sure of it.'

'Oh, I do hope you are right, my dear. I do hope you are right,' said the woman, happy to be guided along.

'Well, well, well,' murmured Olly, rocking in his chair.

'What a strange turn of events.' He removed his cap and scratched his head. 'Who would 'ave thought it? Who would 'ave thought that the upper classes would be so dependent on our little Maria.' He began to quietly chuckle and then roar with laughter when he saw her coming back into her domain, head held high and in complete control.

'It's not over yet, Olly,' she said, coming into the stable. 'Stop gloating.'

'I'm not, Maria. I'm not. Go and put a kettle on your mother's fire and I'll sneak some tea from Angel's hiding place. This is a time to celebrate if ever there was one. I'm proud of you, sweet'eart. Very, very proud.'

'That's all very well, Olly, but what am I supposed to do now?'

'Concentrate on more important things. On this yard and the dark cloud looming over it.' He sniffed and leaned back. 'Where's that little silver cruet set?'

'In my apron pocket safe and sound.'

'Well, you know what you have to do tomorrow when you're in them offices.'

'You don't have to remind me. I know what to do.'

'Good. Now then. Tea. I'll just go and see what kind of a mood Angel's in. It's too quiet in this yard for my liking. The nosy sods 'ave bin peeping out, watching. But where are the neighbours now, eh? Now that the posh nobs 'ave gone?'

'Shivering in their bleedin' boots!' Daisy had come out of the house. 'Who was they, Maria, and what'd they want? Mum sent me to ask yer, so don't tell me to shut up!'

'Lying mare.' Olly grinned. 'Yer mother's in with Sophie! Angel an' all. Gossiping and drinking tea behind my back, no doubt. Go an' 'ave a butcher's, Daisy. And bring a bit of life into the place, will yer!'

'I ain't goin' in there! I don't like tea! It stinks! Willy'll 'ave a cup, though. Fetch it in, Ria. We're looking fru our picture books.'

'*Your* picture books, is it? I don't think so,' said Olly, in lordly fashion.

'They stink of mould but they're all right. I s'pose you want 'em back when we've finished wiv 'em?'

'You can bet your last tuppence I want 'em back! Cheeky cow. Money don't grow on trees, you know. I can get a few coppers for them on me rounds. You look after 'em and no smearing anyfing nasty on one single page!'

'We're starving 'ungry in there, Ria. All right if we 'ave our bread and jam now?'

'I should think so. Don't go too heavy on the jam! Damsons might grow on trees but not in our back yard!'

Turning away, Daisy grumbled loud enough for them to hear, 'Them rich people would 'ave adopted me, I reckon! I should 'ave come out earlier. Stuck in this dump wiv you lot!'

The roar of laughter from Sophie's house proved that Daisy's voice was pitched high enough to carry. Before she had had time to go inside and slam the street door good and hard, the familiar voice of her favourite nagging neighbour rang through the air:

'One two three, one two three, who'd want that
    kid,
Rat's tails for hair where all the fleas hid.
But let's not despair 'cos she's wiry all right,
Someone might take 'er who likes a good fight!
One two three, one two three, Daisy, my love,
Come and see Sophie and give us a hug!'

'You can't even bleedin' well sing in tune!' roared Daisy, before kicking the door shut with her boot.

'See wot I mean, Maria? It's up to you now, cock. We can't let them chuck us out of our yard.'

Shrugging, Maria untied her apron, folded it and laid it on Olly's little table. 'I'm goin' for a walk down to the river. If we do get a shower, take the washing in for us.'

'What about my cup of tea, Maria?'

'Daisy. Get her to move herself. It's time you sorted 'er out. Dad would 'ave expected it of you!'

'Crafty cow,' murmured her neighbour to himself. 'She's gettin' 'er own back and I'm not sure which is worse. Saving this yard or taming that little mare, Daisy.'

Smiling as she strolled along, Maria had a sense that things might work out. She had a reason for going to see Wilkie Crow. She wanted to bring him up to date on Mr Tremain and Steffan and to let him know that his debts would be paid by the grandparents. She also felt in the mood for company. She was missing out on something and wasn't quite sure what it was. Pleased though she was that she had done all that she could for now for Steffan, she was aware that by having done so she would very likely lose a friend. Someone who had become almost inexplicably close to her in a short space of time. She needed to cheer herself a little. Maybe she would accept a drink from the chieftain today. Yes, thought Maria, today I will try my first taste of ale and let my hair down. Suddenly it had dawned on her that she hadn't had much fun in life, and it was time that she did.

9

After a long spell with no rain, the sudden storm which broke on this early August morning before dawn was a welcome relief. Even the homeless, sleeping rough with no roof to cover them, welcomed it too, enjoying the warm shower which cleaned and freshened not only their bodies but their clothes too. A midsummer storm such as this was nearly always followed by blazing sunshine, so the worry of the clothes on their backs not drying out was no worry at all, and the very most was made of this free wash-and-dry day. Railings and brick walls along Maria's route to work were strewn with jackets, old blankets and sheets which would soon be steaming under the blazing sun. Thinking of this she was suddenly reminded of Olly's idea for fixing up their own makeshift shower to be turned on and off freely, and made a mental note to speak with him about it after work. He had been so excited by his plan that she now felt a touch guilty at having pushed it from her mind.

With a renewed determination to do everything she could to find out more of what was going on in the architects' office, and how far along the road the planners were with their scheme to demolish half of

Shadwell, Maria felt as if she were shedding an old skin and emerging all the stronger for it. Gone were any fears about the short, fat philanderer, Mr Clarkson, breathing hotly over her, and the intimidating Miss Drake, whom she now saw as a woman making the most of her lonely spinster life. With regard to John Cunningham, she wasn't certain as to his motives but could see no harm in playing the little game that Olly had suggested in order to keep him interested so as to find out more. Steffan still wasn't free, but the case against him was so flimsy that she was confident of his release.

With the small silver cruet set deep in her skirt pocket, wrapped in black cloth, she went about her business in the post sorting room efficiently and in a lighter mood than she had been in of late. In her other pocket was a note that she was to slip to John when delivering the mail to his office. She had kept her message short, sweet and to the point. It read:

> *Dear John, A neighbour has come across a trunk full of what he considers to be old junk and he wishes to sell it. Here is a piece I withdrew as an example for you to see. Would your mother be interested in buying these old-fashioned bits and pieces? Let's meet after work in the coffee house if the answer is yes. If the answer is no, then bring it to the sorting room when no one is about. Maria.*

Later that day, when John pushed a reply into her hand on passing her in a corridor, she felt sure he had taken the bait, and after a fairly hectic day she left Bollards wondering whether it was the right thing to do to allow him to take home the silver. Olly had made it clear that she was to let him, but John could so easily say that he had mislaid it or that someone had picked his pocket. He had fabricated the truth before, and her trust in him by now was fragile at best. Waiting for him in the coffee shop, Maria was beginning to half hope that he might refuse the Georgian cruet set, uninterested. At least he had agreed to meet her, so their friendship could be revived, which was the purpose behind Olly's idea, after all. The main reasoning behind all of this was to get information, and if she had to be devious to do so, then so be it.

As she watched the busy street, full of people coming and going on their way home, her heart sank when she realised that Dick had caught sight of her through the window and was smiling broadly. She didn't need this interruption. Apart from everything else, Steffan had crept into her thoughts again. Into her thoughts and into her heart.

'Hello, Maria!' He beamed as he approached her table and pulled up a chair. 'Don't like the idea of you being all by yerself an' lonesome. Bit sad, are yer?'

'No. I'm waiting for a friend,' she said. 'He should be here any minute.'

'Well then, I'll keep you company till he arrives. Did you want a biscuit to go wiv that coffee? I've just got a bag of broken ones from Muvver, who, by the way, ain't stopped talking about yer. Fancies us gettin' married, she does. Said we'd give 'er beautiful grandchildren. What d'yer reckon to that?'

'I'm not thinking of getting married for a very long time yet,' she said, managing to keep a straight face and masking her impatience.

'That's wot I said. I said we'd prefer to wait a couple of years. I might be doin' all right by then. My foreman reckons I'm after 'is job.' He winked and grinned at her, showing uneven teeth. 'I reckon he's frightened, you know.'

'Oh, look!' said Maria, somewhat relieved. 'Here's my friend now!'

Twisting in his chair to see John Cunningham coming in, Dick narrowed his eyes then turned back to Maria. 'This is 'im, is it?' He sniffed, a probing tone to his voice.

'That's right.' She smiled and waved a hand at John. 'We've a few things to discuss about work.'

'Ah . . . so he works at Bollards as well.' He spoke as if he'd found a missing part to a jigsaw puzzle. 'Don't wanna work at the biscuit factory as well, does he?'

'No. He likes it where he is.'

On arrival John looked uncomfortable in the presence of this strange young man and behaved almost as if he weren't there, but Dick was pleased to have a chance of seeing him close up.

'I'm sorry to be late, Maria,' John said. 'I had some drawings to deliver to the directors' rooms.'

Sucking air through his teeth, Dick raised an eyebrow. 'Sounds a bit important, don't it.' He flicked the end of his nose and then scratched his cheek. 'I'd best be goin', Maria.' He pulled himself up from his chair and looked again at John, a little more studiously this time. He knew for certain now that this was the young man he had seen with Maria. Someone he later realised he had come across before in unpleasant circumstances. 'Look after 'er, friend. Never know who's about these days,' he added, pointedly. He then turned to Maria and said, 'I'll be passing back this way in ten minutes or so. Wait an' I'll walk you 'ome.'

'No, that's all right, I—'

Dick raised a hand to stop her. 'No arguing on this one, Maria. I won't be goin' out of me way. So you just wait for me 'ere.' He turned back to John. 'I'll trust you to see she does wait for me. Right?'

'Well, I think that's really up to Maria.'

'No. It's up to you. If she's not 'ere when I pass by I'll come looking for yer. It's that simple.' He clicked his teeth, winked and spun on his heel.

'Strange chap.' John smiled. 'Who is he?'

'Oh, just someone I know,' she said. 'I'll wait for him, it'll be easier. He'll only come to the yard if he can't make sure I'm home safe. He's a neighbour's son.'

'I see you've finished your coffee. Would you like another?'

'Not really. But you have one.'

'No . . . I should be on my way, Maria. May I take home the cruet set to show my mother? I'm sure she will be interested in buying your friend's bits and pieces. I was going to ask if you'd like to come with me. It's only twenty minutes on the coach.'

'I would like that, John, very much, but Mum'll be worried if I'm that late home. Maybe tomorrow after work?'

'Yes, that probably would be better. I don't suppose you could make your own way to the omnibus? It stops just up the road in front of the milliner's. Best if we're not seen leaving or walking along together.'

'Good idea.' She smiled. 'And you don't have to worry any more over my being upset about the plans for the yard. I think it might all be for the best in the end,' she lied convincingly.

'I'm sure it will be.' He smiled. 'Everything works out for the best in the end,' he added, no longer trusting her. 'But I expect you'd like to be kept informed along the way?'

'Well, that would take a load off my mind. I mean . . . it could be next month, next year or in five years that we're evicted without a word.'

'That's right,' he said, his feelings confirmed. She *was* being friendly just to use him as a spy. 'But you know, Maria, with something as explosive as this, I don't think you should let anyone know that we're seeing each other. And especially that you're coming to my home tomorrow. We could both end up in a lot of serious trouble. This country takes company espionage very seriously.'

'I know. I'll tell Mum I'm going to a music hall to see a show with a friend from work. That should be all right, shouldn't it?' She decided to go along with his cloak-and-dagger theatricals.

'I should think so,' he said pensively. 'Although, on second thoughts, it might *not* be a good idea for you to come to my house. Anyone could be on that bus. Someone from Bollards. It gets fairly filled with people. We could be seen together without knowing it.'

Astounded that someone could so easily put their own welfare before anything else, she opened her mouth to say something, but he stopped her, raising a hand.

'Even though my mother would be interested to see the cruet set, I don't think it fair to involve her in all of this.' He withdrew it from his pocket and pushed it across the grubby table towards her. 'Tell your neighbour thank you but my mother's no longer buying and selling.'

Maria was by now beginning to feel on edge over his behaviour and couldn't think why he would suddenly change his mind over the silver or what might be going on in his mind. 'So we shouldn't meet up agen. Is that your meaning?'

'No. Of course not. We could meet somewhere else. In the Black Boy tavern perhaps? Or the Plough Inn on Mile End Road?'

'I've never been in either of them, but why not? Close to Millionaires' Row, are they?' She smiled, doing her best to act natural although irritated by his self-assured manner.

'Not quite, that's closer to Bow. But we could find a tavern there if you'd prefer.'

'No. Mile End'll be fine.' She was at a loss as to his motives, but she knew what hers were so decided to go along with him. 'Let's say tomorrow evening, then. Directly after work?'

'Good. But I think we should make our separate

ways there and keep it our secret. I'll not tell my mother if you don't tell yours,' he added, smiling.

'A secret between two is better than one between three,' she said, covering her true feelings of umbrage at this ridiculous subterfuge – and all because of his precious job! Why he wanted to socialise with her at all was a mystery, but she would wheedle as much information from him as she could and report back to Olly. After all, what had she to lose by it?

Once he had left, with an air of satisfaction about him, Maria pondered as she waited for Dick. She did not have to wait long. His smiling pale face warmed her. He was a peculiar chap but harmless. 'Ready, Maria?' he called from the open doorway.

'As ready as I'll ever be, Dick,' she said, rising from her chair.

Slipping her arm into his, she strolled along with one thought in mind, to be honest with this young man so that he would not get the wrong idea. 'So, we're friends, then, Dick. I'm pleased about that because I like your family and I know Mum will take to you. My sister Daisy's a minx but I've a feeling you're a good match for her any day of the week.'

'How old is she?' he asked ponderously.

'Eight.' Maria laughed. 'A bit too young for you.'

'You're not, though.' He sniffed.

'No, but I don't want to lose you as a friend and I do need a friend to confide in. My heart lies with someone else who loves me.'

'Not that bloke I just saw you wiv?' he said, a worried look crossing his face.

'No. Someone else, but it's a secret.' She was enjoying a moment of fantasy, thinking of Steffan. 'I'll tell you in the fullness of time.'

'Sounds all right. But if it don't work out I'll marry yer. Do you agree wiv that?'

'No. You shouldn't marry a friend, there's no gain in it. So long as I'm here for you if you're in trouble and you're there for me when I want someone to listen. Do you agree to that?' she said, repeating his phrase.

'I s'pose so. But keep your eye on that bloke I just saw you wiv. Keep yer wits about yer.' He winked.

Amused by his way of giving her advice, she hid a smile. 'Why d'you say that?'

'Friends give advice and friends take it. That's all right, innit?'

'Well, yes, but you left a message in the yard for me to stay away from Mr Tremain as well. Don't make a habit of it, will yer? Am I to stay away from every man?'

'Only if I say so.'

'Whatever you say, Dick, whatever you say.' With a person as affectionate as this lad, how could she hurt his feelings and tell him to mind his own business? He was harmless as far as she was concerned. Harmless and lovable, reminding her in some ways of her little brother, Willy. 'Now let's get home before Mum starts to worry where I've got to.'

'I was in your yard earlier on,' he suddenly said. 'Looking for that bloke above the stable. Goes by the name of Gent down Tobacco Dock . . . did you know that?'

'No, but the cap fits.'

'I need to 'ave a chat wiv 'im rather urgently as a matter of fact.'

'Well, you're out of luck. His wealthy parents took him back into the fold, from what I gather.'

'Maybe so.' Dick sniffed. 'But he's back. Turned up early afternoon by all accounts, blind drunk. 'Is old man arrived in the afternoon in 'is own private little carriage. Must be a millionaire, eh?'

'He's back?' Maria could hardly believe it. 'Why would he want to come back?'

'Looked very 'appy be all accounts. Singing at the top of 'is voice. His old man wasn't so pleased, mind you.'

'No, I bet my last shilling he wasn't. And I bet he's given the rotter money to pay off his debts and more than necessary. Well, I s'pose it proves one thing. No one, not even a man whose brain's sodden with gin, would come back to a place where he's committed murder. So the gossips are wrong agen.'

'He never strangled that woman,' said Dick. 'P'raps he just likes it in Shadwell, living wiv us lot. Just goes to show, don't it? Bit of a compliment really,' he added, pushing back his shoulders with a touch of pride. 'He admires us, see? Can't put the bloke down for that, Maria.'

'So why're you interested in 'im, then?'

Tapping the side of his nose, he grinned at her. ''Cos I can vouch that he never killed that woman. Pretty soon we'll 'ave the real culprit on the end of a rope.'

Stopping short, Maria peered at him. Now he was beginning to make her feel edgy. 'Well, come on, then. Tell me what you know.'

'Nar, can't do that. Wilkie says to keep me mouth shut. Me mouth shut and me eyes wide open. Yep. Me and Gent the drunk will see 'im to the gallows. 'Cos we was witnesses. I knew I'd seen 'im somewhere in dodgy circumstances but couldn't fink where it was at first. Then it came to me and I was straight down to Wilkie. Right pleased wiv me he is, I can tell yer.'

'You're having me on.' She chuckled. 'And I'm not falling for it. You and Steffan's dad? A peculiar combination, if you don't mind my saying so.'

'Not really. Class ain't everyfing, you know. If I was born rich I might be Prime Minister for all we know, and Gent born poor might be a street beggar. Your sweetheart'll soon be released.' He gave her a sideways look. 'Wilkie'd vouch for it but you mustn't let 'im know I've bin blabbing to yer. I take my advice and instructions from Wilkie Crow. He's a good bloke. Got brains. He tells me step by step what to do. And I'm doing it. Enough said.' He stepped up his pace as if he were on a mission.

'So I've to go and see Wilkie if I'm to find out more, then?'

'No! Mustn't do that. He'll string me up for telling yer! This is all 'ighly confidential. But don't you worry, it's all in hand. Be a good kid and do as I say. Go to work and that. No harm'll come to you, never you fear. I'll see to that.'

'What d'yer mean, Dick? No harm'll come to me. Why should it?'

'Manner of speech, Maria, manner of speech.' Realising that he had said too much, Dick gave her a reassuring smile. His orders from Wilkie were to keep his eye on things and his mouth shut. 'I tell all the ladies that now we've 'ad a murder. Keeps 'em nice and easy knowing I'm there for 'em.'

Arriving at the yard, and having thanked Dick for seeing her home, Maria could see no sign of Steffan's father. Outside her front door, however, sitting next to Angel, was Sophie, quieter than usual but with a little colour back in her cheeks. Instead of being surrounded by all the paraphernalia that went with mattress-making she was pasting advertising labels on to small soap boxes.

Approaching her neighbours, Maria felt a warmth surge through her. Returning here after a day spent in the austere surroundings of Bollards was a pleasure.

'That's more like it, Sophie.' She smiled. 'Easier than rolling and tying them mattresses, I bet.'

'I don't know why I never tried somefing like this before, Maria, but there we are. None of us are too old to change direction, are we?' She looked from Maria to the rooms above the stables and then at Angel. 'You gonna tell 'er or shall I?'

'As if you'd let me finish a sentence.' Angel sniffed. 'Go on. I'll fill 'er in on the bits you miss out on. Your mother's squeezing lemons . . . compliments of Olly, who 'ad a pick-up from Spitalfields this morning and picked up a crate of lemons while he was at it.'

She laughed. 'Your muvver's making lemonade for all of us.'

'The shabby gentleman's back,' said Sophie, unable to contain herself. 'We thought we'd got rid of 'im at last, but no, in he strolls, 'appy as a sandboy and as drunk as ever. We've 'ad a couple of songs out of 'im, mind. Ain't got a bad voice. And he's not a bad-looking chap really.'

'He got down on one knee and proposed to 'er, Maria. That's why the ugly man is suddenly a handsome prince.'

'Did either of you get a chance to talk to Steffan's grandfather?' said Maria, wanting to get down to the nitty-gritty.

'How did you know he was here?' Sophie was disappointed – she had been saving that bit for later.

'Someone told me on the way home. Well, did you, then?'

'Well, no, we never actually 'ad a conversation wiv the man,' said Angel, 'but he did leave a message for you. He said to tell you that his grandson has been released on bail and he's been taken back to Essex. That's all he said. Just that. They drag away the lad we was gettin' to know and like and leave that thing up there behind.'

'He never 'ad no choice, Angel. The man didn't wanna leave,' said Sophie. 'He yelled that this was 'is home now and this is where he'd stop. That don't sound like someone running away from the law, does it?'

'I don't know any more, Sophie, and I'm past caring,'

said Maria. 'He'll end up in a lunatic asylum the way he's going. Is Daisy about? It seems too quiet.'

'None of the kids are about. They're down the river. A ship's in from the West Indies and there's talk of coconuts going begging,' said Angel, chuckling. 'You've never see anyone run so fast. If they can't shift the bleedin' fings they can't be much good, can they?'

'Rotten, more like,' said Sophie. 'I 'ear say them merchants of the West India trade are multimillionaires, owning sugar plantations, slaves and ships. People like that don't give fings away.'

'Well, we mustn't criticise 'em too much, Sophie. They give the men plenty of work and that's somefing.'

'Yeah. But 'ave you seen them that work in Blood Alley? Go 'ome of a night with more sore and weeping flesh showing on their hands than skin from heaving them overloaded sugar sacks.'

'And speaking of which,' said Angel, eyeing her friend, 'it's time we stopped working if we're to stick to our new rule of not overdoing things.'

'My thoughts entirely.' Sophie sighed, pleased to have someone else say what was in her own mind. She was tired and ready for a ten-minute lie-down before she began to prepare supper.

Glad that Sophie was back in the fold, Maria left both women to it. She knew that Olly was out on his rounds since his beloved carthorse was not in the stable. She would return his piece of silver later. Above the stable she could hear Mr Tremain talking loudly to himself. His voice rising by the second, he was soon yelling and swearing. Looking up, she could see a shaft of daylight coming in through a gap in the stable ceiling and couldn't understand why. The boards above her were not exactly tight but she had not noticed daylight coming through before. Stepping out of the stable, she peered up at the rooms and now could see why this was happening. The dark, heavy cloth which had previously hung at the windows was no longer there. She was startled by a sudden loud crashing noise, which was followed by the man yelling at the top of his voice: '*Spawn of Satan's black witch!*'

Maria glanced around the yard, expecting her neighbours to be in their doorways or at the windows, smothering their laughter and enjoying the show, but instead there was a deathly hush. Flinching at more crashing sounds from above, she trod cautiously up the wooden steps to peek through one of the badly cracked, grimy windows. Tremain had lowered his voice to a snarl as he kicked anything in his way into one corner of the room. Slow and heedful, Maria pushed open the door and watched as the man, who looked out of his mind, continued to kick things about, more slowly now, as though almost worn out.

Staring at him, she suddenly said, 'Is there anything I can do to help you, Mr Tremain?'

Spinning around, he glared at her. 'You? Help me?' Leaning back with his hands on his hips, he began to quietly laugh at her. 'A peasant offering to help a king?'

'Why did you come back?' she asked. 'Why didn't you stay with your parents?'

'Madam, I do not need their help! Kindly leave my abode! Away with you! Away, I say!'

She stepped into the centre of the room and slowly turned around, considering the mess and feeling sorry for this tragic man. 'Do you want me to help you to clear up?'

Slumping into a chair, Tremain lifted his eyes to her and spoke in a low voice. 'I do not need help. I shall be a rich man again one day. Rich. Do you hear? A wealthy gentleman of means. Until then, I shall remain here, living the way that the poor must live. If I am to help them in the future when I am lord of the manor then I must live the way they do to truly know their plight.

'Come and see me in a calendar month. Tell all the poor and needy in this court to come to me then.' He looked around, slowly nodding. 'My castle far from here is being prepared for complete restoration, and all of you here in the yard will be given private quarters. You may pass that message on to my people. Tell them I shall take them away from poverty! Now be gone with you and fetch my supper. Send a message immediately to court that I summon the jesters, the dancing girls and the musicians! There is to be a celebration in the courtyard!' He suddenly sat up and stared maniacally. 'Away with you, woman of no virtue and little flesh! Send me three voluptuous *full-bodied*, lusty prostitutes!'

Pitying Steffan even more now that his father was obviously suffering from serious delusions on top of his drunkenness, Maria focused on the iron money box on the floor with a small crow bar lying next to it, which she guessed had been taken from the stable below. Following her line of vision, Tremain looked contemptuously at the box and sneered. 'The court fool has thrown away the key or hidden it in these rooms where even he himself will never find it. Only an idiot would do such a thing. Far better he be locked away in the tower for good and be fed only on stale bread and water. Let the jailer know it!'

'If you're referring to Steffan, Mr Tremain, I know he's been freed from his cell and is back with his grandparents in Saffron Walden. Soon he'll be reunited with his mother as well.'

'The whore is most likely *dead*, wench!' He clasped a hand to his head and groaned. 'Must I be surrounded by imbeciles?'

'Why do you say that?'

'Say what, madam?'

'That your wife is most likely dead?'

'I beg your pardon but I did not say that! I said the whore is dead. Strangled and thrown into the river with her bloody penny farthing!'

Maria felt as if he was about to unwittingly confess. 'Whoever did it must have had a reason, I should think,' she said, baiting him warily.

'Indeed. She was a bloody whore, wasn't she! Would that I had strangled the bloodsucker. Would that I had!' Falling quiet, he gazed down at the floor. 'I saw him, you know. The wretched soul must have had more to lose than others like myself who she threatened with blackmail. But what does it matter? He did us all a favour. She was no more than a bloodsucker!' He raised his eyes and sported a look of self-satisfaction. 'I suppose you could say that I was the hand behind the hand that rid the streets of her. Yes, indeed . . .' He smirked, leaning back and drumming his fingers on the arm of the chair. 'It was *I* who was the reason she came by the river in the first place and he, your murderer, who engineered her coming for his own reasons and his own benefit. I was the carrot he dangled. Not that I knew him, you understand. But he knew of me. The whore spared nothing . . . except of course the truth.'

Shuddering at his ramblings, Maria felt herself go cold. 'You shouldn't say such things, Mr Tremain. Someone might believe you.'

'Oh? And you are an expert on what one should say and what one should not say? Away with you. I tell you, I saw him! And once he had kicked the body into the river . . . in went the bicycle! Splash!' He splayed a hand. 'And that, my dear, is when I took him by the collar.' Taking his pipe from his pocket, he cupped it in the palm of his hand. 'Once he explained that the whore knew too much about certain things to do with his profession, I could see that he had had no choice but to get rid of her. He had in fact done me a great favour. His reputation was at stake by all accounts. Reputation indeed. My purse was at stake! Blackmail was on her mind at the very least! I shall inherit everything when my parents die and foolishly in the past I told her of this. And that, *madam*, is a far worse state of affairs!'

'Of course it is, Mr Tremain. Your friend did the right thing by you from the sound of it.' Maria had heard enough, but she felt that she was so close to getting the name of the murderer that she had to go on. 'Have you managed to secure a good hiding place for him?'

'*I?* Good gracious, woman, no! We only happened across each other by chance. He is no more than a stranger to me! We met in Tobacco Dock where that money-sucking scoundrel who goes by the name of Wilkie Crow hangs out! Had I the strength I would put my hands to his neck, make no mistake!'

'I'm sure you've nothing to fear from Mr Crow, sir. He minds his own business.'

'Yes,' said Tremain, not listening to her, having changed tack yet again. His lordly aura was back. 'I could see that young man who strangled her in prison! With the snap of a finger.

'She came to hunt me and bring about my downfall but found another who brought about her own end.' He was staring out at nothing, grinning. 'You see, my dear, justice will out in the end. The woman let just *one* too many lovers into her bed. The wrong one, as it turned out!'

He suddenly roared with laughter. 'The inexperienced fool imagined himself in love with her and she with him.' Rolling his eyes, he slowly shook his head. 'A whore in love with a client. I ask you,' he said, addressing Maria as if she were an old and trusted friend.

'He told her things that could so easily have seen him in the courts and prison. He held information that would very much surprise you, my dear.' He leaned back again, closed his eyes and quietly chuckled.

'Would surprise quite a lot of people around here.' He continued to chuckle and stare down at the floor, back in his own private, empty world.

'Mr Tremain,' said Maria in a nervous voice, 'if you know who murdered that woman, why don't you tell the police so that they may clear your son's name once and for all?'

'To teach the snotty little bastard a lesson, that's why! He's too bloody pathetic to commit murder, you silly girl. And there's no evidence. Chief detective bloody constable and officer in charge of the case fell for it as well!' Again he roared with laughter. 'I led him to the silly bloody drawing for a joke and he followed like a lame dog on a fucking lead!'

Backing out of the rooms, having heard more than enough to clear Steffan's name should it need to be cleared, Maria went down the steps, leaving the madman to himself. Once in the yard she leaned on the stable wall in order to calm herself. There was a horrid sick feeling in the pit of her stomach. Waiting for it to pass, she gripped a wooden peg wedged into a hole in one of the supporting timbers and took in long, slow breaths of air, but flashing lights were flying through her head, and suddenly they turned into a trillion white stars and she had the sense of falling from a great height and in slow motion before everything went black and she slumped to the floor.

Coming to in a daze, feeling awful and confused, Maria, deathly white as she looked up at the sky, took a few moments to realise that she had fainted. Easing herself up, she rested on her elbows and waited for the second rush of giddiness to pass, then got to her feet and leaned against the stable before very slowly inching her way towards her house. Once inside, she staggered to the narrow staircase and dragged herself up the stairs and on to her bed, where she almost immediately fell into an exhausted sleep.

Busy in the tiny back kitchen, Liza had only realised that Maria was in the house when she heard her going up the stairs, and so had no idea that she was unwell and not simply resting. The lemonade had been poured into three jugs and was now cooling as she went proudly to deliver two of them filled to the brim to Angel and Sophie. This special treat would be much appreciated by her two neighbours.

Once she had found Maria on top of her bed, heavy-eyed after waking, she realised that her growing worries of late over her daughter had not entirely been without foundation. She could see that Maria was paler than usual and very quiet, but asked no questions and simply went about her normal routine. She had been aware that the woman's murder and then Willy's near-abduction had upset and unnerved her daughter, but had no idea of all her other worries to do with Bollards.

Later that evening, with the sun setting over the yard and her younger children put to bed, Liza slipped out of her house, leaving Maria curled up on the armchair, quiet and resting.

Finding Olly at the back of the stable, brushing down his horse before mucking out, Liza approached him and, choosing her words carefully, asked whether he had spoken to Maria, and whether he had any thoughts as to what might be troubling her. He had, since her husband had passed away, stepped in as a kind of father figure when there was a need for one.

Olly, down on one knee, listened to Liza but continued brushing the back leg of his beloved mare. Quietly chuckling, he rolled his eyes at the woman he had known most of his life. 'Well . . . if you can't fathom that one out, Liza, I'm a Dutch 'erring.'

'Well then, you are, Olly, because I can't fathom it.'

Olly pulled himself up and cupped his pipe, which was fixed in the corner of his mouth. Puffing on it and narrowing his eyes, he looked into Liza's face. 'You really need to ask me what's up wiv 'er?'

'Well, all I'm trying to say is has she said anything to you that she wouldn't tell me for fear of worrying us? Me and the children, that is.'

Giving her a friendly, incredulous look, he raised an eyebrow. 'No, she's said nothing to me but . . . well, I would 'ave thought you'd 'ave guessed it as well as me.'

'Guessed what? I wouldn't be asking if I knew. Stop beating about the bush. I'm worried!'

'The lad who's now gone from 'er life . . . that never entered your mind?'

Liza became thoughtful and then, as if the sun had suddenly risen, said, 'Steffan? You think she's missing him? Surely not.'

'Well, that might surprise you, Liza, but not me.

I've seen the way they look at each other. She may not realise it 'erself but experience tells me otherwise. If I was a betting man I'd put my last pound on her being in love with that young feller.' He puffed on his pipe and waited, amused by the expression on Liza's face. 'She is a grown woman, Liza.'

Lowering her eyes, a little embarrassed at not having seen what might well have been before her eyes, Liza became more pensive. 'In love with the lad? Well, yes, I s'pose that's possible – but to feel faint over it?'

'Well . . . the shock of 'im being arrested in the first place might be coming out now. I should leave 'er be and wait.' He smiled, turning back to his carthorse and the work in hand.

'Wait for what exactly?'

'For when he comes back to claim 'er.'

'Oh, now you go too far. He won't be back and I should think his father will be away from here shortly. No. You're wrong there, and I wouldn't want her hopes raised over it, neither.'

With his back to her, and leaning over his carthorse, he murmured, 'You think I would do that, do you, Liza? I'm not one of your gossiping women. You asked my advice and opinion and I've given it.'

Knowing that she had offended her friend without meaning to, she laid a hand on his shoulder and gently squeezed it. 'I'm sorry. I never meant it like it sounded. You're a good man and much more than a neighbour to all of us, whether you realise it or not. My children see you as a replacement father and I for one don't know what I would 'ave done without you and Angel when I lost my husband. And you know how much he thought of you.'

'That's all right,' Olly said, 'that's all right. No 'arm done.' Keeping his head down, he willed her to go before she managed to completely break through his barrier and have him shedding a tear.

'I'll consider what you said while I'm in bed, Olly. I should think you've hit the nail on the head, as usual.' She gave his mare a pat on the rump and bade them both goodnight, adding, 'It'll all come out in the wash, eh, Olly?'

''Course it will,' he replied, 'it always does.'

It was not without a little trepidation that Maria made her way through the back streets of Stepney and into the Mile End Road the following evening, but as soon as she passed the brewers' alms-houses, which surrounded a lovely green fenced with ornate iron railings, she stopped ruminating as to John Cunningham's true motives. Her mind was now filled with a picture of her family and neighbours happily living somewhere similar. She suddenly felt a strong moment of clarity. If she were to discover for certain the date of their impending eviction from Kelly's Yard, the public protest could begin and she could see all of her neighbours settled in a similar place. So caught up in her fantasies was she that without realising it she had reached the Black Boy Inn.

'Hello, Maria.' The familiar voice of John broke into her thoughts as she idly looked into a shop window. 'I hope I've not kept you waiting too long.'

'Of course not,' she said, covering the fact that she was a little on edge.

'Good. Shall we go into the Black Boy, then? Or would you prefer to walk along to the Plough?'

'Let's go in. I'm quite dry after the walk,' she said, stepping back from a two-horse carriage which was pulling to a halt.

Taking her arm, John guided her inside the smoke-filled place, where the tall, lanky proprietor and his rotund wife were sitting round an unlit fire laughing as a man so short as to almost be a midget performed tricks with playing cards, seemingly pushing one through his left ear and pulling it out from his right.

The customers were being entertained by various artists from a travelling circus which had stopped en route from Kent to Cambridge. Another artist in colourful jester's costume was performing his act of swallowing a dozen sixpenny coins one after the other while balancing a half-crown on his nose, while his partner, wearing different bright colours, was pressing the bridge of his nose to make a convincing show of drawing water. It poured into a tiny copper jug as if it were coming from a tap.

'Well,' said Maria, laughing, 'it's lively, I will say that for it. And fun.'

'Perhaps we should go somewhere more quiet,' replied John, a serious expression on his face.

'No! This place is wonderful! Of course we must stay!' She nudged him and indicated a far corner where it was quieter and where there was a small table with two chairs. 'We'll go over there where we'll have bird's-eye views,' she said, unable to stop giggling at everything going on around her.

Not particularly amused by the antics of the travelling performers, John showed Maria to the table and then went to order their drinks. By now, even though she was pleased to be in this place, Maria knew she was sharing the evening with the wrong person. She imagined herself here with Steffan, who she felt sure would be as entertained by the goings-on as she was. Glancing at John's face and his set expression, she wondered why he was here at all. He showed no sign of pleasure at being in her company.

'We'll have the one drink and then go, shall we?' she said on his return.

'I think so,' was his dull answer. 'I prefer it down by Wapping embankment. In the Prospect of Whitby. Maybe we'll go there. There's far more atmosphere . . . especially after dusk with lamplight reflecting on the river.'

'Sounds as if you already had that in mind,' she said, sipping her gin and aromatic bitters.

'Well, yes, it came to me on the way here, as a matter of fact,' he said, gulping down his drink, almost as if he couldn't wait to get out of this crowded place which he had assumed would be quiet. 'I'll go first or would you prefer to?' he said, emptying his glass. 'Either of us could follow in five minutes or so.'

Resisting the urge to laugh at him and his silly secretive mood, she shrugged. 'I don't really see any point in us going separately . . . unless of course a reason's cropped up?'

'Well, as a matter of fact it has,' he said, thinking quickly. 'I've seen someone who works in Bollards but as yet he hasn't seen us, I don't think. I'll slip out the side door.' With that he made a shifty departure, leaving Maria somewhat confused and disappointed. She would have preferred to have stayed here in this inn and watched the free entertainment going on around her. The mood in the bar was charged with energy. Catching the eye of a portly gentleman sitting by himself and giving her a leering smile, she was angry at having been left like this, and decided that once she had caught up with John Cunningham she would give him a piece of her mind and then go directly home. He was a strange fellow, and there was no space in her life for such people. For Maria, life was complicated enough without having to try to fathom what someone was thinking all the time.

Walking through Stepney Green on her way to Wapping, and half thinking that she might cut through to Shadwell instead and not bother with John, her mind was yet again filled with thoughts of Steffan and how happy he must be now that he was back with his grandparents in the country. So wrapped in her thoughts was she that she was taking no notice of anything going on around her, and could have no idea, or reason to think, that she was being followed, and indeed had been since she left Kelly's Yard earlier.

Arriving in Wapping with night falling, she couldn't help thinking how eerie this area was in near-dark. With its imposing tall warehouses, its shops boarded for the night and its gloomy narrow courtyards, it was all a bit cheerless, and there was a feeling of rank oppression in the air. In this small corner of East London there were no street lamps. Low voices could be heard as vagrants, young and old, families and single people, curled up on the pavements, bedding down for the night. Averting her eyes from the drawn faces, which showed no hope and which possibly welcomed death as a long-awaited sleep, she continued on her way, quickening her step, by now frightened of what she could not see in the shifting shadows. Regretting having agreed to follow John to the Prospect of Whitby, indeed having agreed to meet up with him at all, she was still in two minds as to whether or not to turn off and go in another direction. She would much rather be back in Kelly's Yard among friends and in familiar surroundings. Shadwell at night was a far friendlier place than Wapping could ever hope to be.

'Maria!' The urgent, hushed voice of John from a dark alley caused her to draw breath. Stopping in her tracks, she narrowed her eyes and looked around, but in this gloom it was difficult to make anything out. 'John?' she called quietly, afraid of the sound of her own echoing voice. 'Where are you?'

Stepping out from the narrow alley, he beckoned her towards him with a wave of the hand. Once she was close enough he whispered to her that the gentleman from Bollards who had been in the Black Boy had been following him and was still around somewhere.

'But this is silly, John!' said Maria, tired of this nonsense. 'We've done *nothing* wrong!'

'Let's not argue over it now,' he urged. 'Now that

we've been seen together this will be seen as treason in so far as the company is concerned. Come through here – it branches off in two directions and is a better lit and safer place once we're through the passage. We can go our own ways once we're through the alley.'

With no other thoughts but to get away from this madman, Maria slipped into the long, narrow, arched alley and hurried through in his tracks. She was startled when they came out into a dark, dead-end timber yard. Spinning around to face John, she found herself looking into an almost unrecognisable face. His expression was very strange and his eyes were boring into her. Stunned and almost frozen to the spot, she flinched as his hand came swiftly to her face and cupped her mouth. 'I should have known not to get involved with you,' he snarled. 'Why would you be any different from the others?' With one of his hands pressed hard against her mouth, the other gripping her neck, she knew that she was staring into the face of a deranged person and a murderer. In one sweeping recollection of all that he had said before and the way he had behaved, it sank in. John Cunningham was the one who had murdered the woman found in the river.

'We could have avoided this,' he whispered tightly. 'You didn't have to be like the others. You're no different or better than the whore on the bike who wanted to bring me down. You shouldn't have withdrawn your notice to leave Bollards,' he continued, all the while his hand squeezing tighter and tighter as he watched her eyes bulge and her face redden. 'That's when I knew you were out to bring me down! You bitch of a—'

The sudden echoing sound of running feet coming from the alleyway stopped him dead. Spinning around to see a dim light from a policeman's lantern showing in the gloom, he let go of Maria and, in panic, looked around to see that he was trapped. Trapped in this yard and by his own doing!

To the sound of shouts and louder footsteps, Maria sank into dark oblivion in the dank and putrid gutter of this warehouse yard while chaos reigned about her. John Cunningham, in the grip of two officers, was protesting his innocence and insisting that this was a prostitute with whom he had been about to engage in business and who had in the process tried to steal his purse. As his voice trailed off and he was carted away, Maria's friend Dick kneeled beside her and gently stroked her face, saying, 'Come on, Maria, you're safe now. He's gone. The police 'ave taken 'im away. Wake up or they'll cart you off to the 'ospital. You don't want that, do yer? Wilkie Crow'll be 'ere soon. Your friend wasn't gonna let the loony go too far.'

Slowly raising her heavy eyelids, Maria tried to focus and say something but her throat felt swollen and dry. Seeing Dick's friendly face and that of Wilkie appearing above him, she just barely managed to nod before she passed out again.

'She'll be all right now,' said Wilkie. 'You did good, lad. Excellent.'

'But we weren't quick enough in, Wilkie. He could 'ave finished 'er.'

'No, son. It takes more than that. The timing was all right and she'll be as good as new once she's over the shock. From experience I'd say the police wouldn't 'ave arrested that bloke on your word as a witness to 'aving seen 'im throw the penny farving into the river. And as for the drunk, who on God's earth'd take notice of 'im in court? No . . . Maria might 'ave gone through a nasty experience but time's a good healer an' all. She'll be all right. And from what you told me, she's soft on that poor bastard, Steffan, who they 'ad marked as a chief suspect, so that'll make up for it, eh?'

'Yeah.' Dick sniffed. 'S'pose you're right. And we was protecting 'er anyway, wasn't we?'

''Course we was. Left to itself this could 'ave bin a very different ending, son. The nutcase 'ad 'is sights set on 'er in any event. And who knows 'ow many more women he might 'ave done for?'

'Or might 'ave killed in the future.'

'Exactly.' Filling his spare pipe with tobacco, Wilkie handed it to Dick. 'That one and mine was the only ones my grandfather puffed from. Now it's yours, son.'

Taking it from his guru and settling himself down next to Maria while they waited for one of Wilkie's men to fetch a stretcher, Dick lit the pipe in the cup of his hand and drew on it for the very first time, establishing the fact that Richard Young, known locally as Dick Young, was no longer a lad but a grown man. A man who had saved the life of Maria Bertram. A local girl much admired and loved.

A week later, on a warm afternoon, out of her sickbed and relaxing in a Bath chair supplied by the charity hospital, Maria was reading one of Olly's second-hand books. The women, having exhausted all speculation as to why a seemingly healthy young man from a fairly privileged background would want to go around strangling young ladies, were now focusing their attention on the recent startling news which had broken in the press. Their yard was really going to be pulled down, and within eighteen months or so. A petition had been sent to Bollards as a starting point, demanding that they all be rehoused locally and in decent accommodation, preferably almshouses set around a green, which were becoming the mode.

The fact that an employee of the firm involved, working on the plans for that part of Shadwell, had murdered, among others, a woman who had threatened to publicise the information given to her during pillow talk after they had had sex had already deeply embarrassed the directors of Bollards. Not only had someone working in their offices strangled to death Rose Cranfield but he had also attempted to murder Maria Bertram, another of their employees.

On the doorstep next to Maria sat her brother and sister, who had not left her side since her terrifying ordeal. 'D'yer reckon he'll be hanged in front of everyone, Dai?' whispered Willy to his sister. 'Will we be able to chuck rotten stuff at 'im?'

'Bleedin' well better not put 'im out in the open! He'll get 'is wotsits ripped off and—'

'That's enough, Daisy,' said Maria, not looking up from her reading.

'It's no more'n he deserves,' she said, curling her top lip.

'Go and read the Bible and then come and tell me that.'

'An eye for an eye is wot I 'eard,' Daisy said, narrowing her eyes. 'And a toof for a bleedin' toof.'

Ignoring her wayward sister, Maria continued to read, but was suddenly aware of the hush that had come over the yard. Her mother, Angel and Sophie, who were sitting outside enjoying a cup of tea, had stopped talking . . . Her instincts telling her that something was up, she was instantly terrified again, wondering whether John Cunningham had been freed. Glancing up, she could see that they were all looking in the same direction, towards the entrance to the half-moon alley. Her stomach churning, she saw that standing there, in a new and fashionable frock-coat with matching trousers, carrying a silver-topped ebony cane and looking not only handsome but debonair, was Steffan. The silence of the yard added to this magic moment. Even Daisy and Willy were struck dumb.

Smiling, and with eyes only for Maria, Steffan flicked the brim of his hat cheekily and stood his ground, waiting for her to get out of the Bath chair. Passing her book to Daisy without taking her eyes off him, Maria eased herself up and walked slowly forward, longing to be held close by him. 'Well, don't you look the gentleman now,' she said quietly, looking into his watery blue eyes.

'And don't you look as beautiful as ever,' he returned.

'I suppose you read all about it?' she said, a touch self-conscious.

'I did, Maria. Can we go inside your house? I feel as if I'm on stage,' he smiled.

''Course we can.' She slipped her arm into his and together they walked slowly into the house, away from their audience.

'Well, Liza,' said Sophie, a broad smile on her face, 'it looks as if the old saying is right – what goes round comes round.'

'I'm not sure what you mean,' murmured Liza, gazing at her open doorway, deeply moved by the sight of her daughter and Steffan walking arm in arm with eyes only for each other. Olly's words came back to her. Her wise old friend was right after all.

'Well, correct me if I'm wrong,' said Sophie, 'but didn't you once tell us that your husband's ancestors were from the gentry?'

'That's right,' said Angel. 'Nuffing wrong wiv your memory, is there? It was way back, though, and it's took a bleedin' long time in coming. Sixteenth century, wasn't it, when the first of 'em settled in Shadwell?'

'It was, Angel. Walter Bertram fell in love with a local clergyman's daughter and settled here.' Liza slowly turned to face her friends, pinching her lips and desperate to hold back her tears. She murmured, 'I can't believe what I just saw.'

Chuckling, Sophie blew her nose. She too had been touched by the scene. 'Not that I imagine that young man would want to settle in this yard. I should fink your 'usband's wishes might well come true, Liza. You might all end up living in the countryside.'

'No. No, I don't think I want that now. Look at them

two scruffy little urchins on my doorstep. They love living close to the river, and I know that Daisy'd miss Wilkie. And things are different now what with steam trains and the like. We can move about, can't we? Visit them who choose to live miles off.'

Sophie slapped her knee, laughing. 'Same old Liza! Use yer kids as an excuse not to go when all the time she knows full well that she couldn't bear to leave London 'erself!'

Looking up at the sky, Liza cleared her throat before saying, 'Same old Sophie, the witch who can read minds.'

'She never 'ad to tell me!' said Angel, poking a finger into her own chest. 'If anyone's got a sixth sense, I have! I know full well what you want, Liza Bertram, and if I'm not wrong it's wot all three of us ladies want. A nice little almshouse wiv a bit of a green to sit out on and roses growing up our walls.'

'Honeysuckle,' said Liza.

'Roses,' repeated Angel.

'Ivy,' chipped in Sophie. 'Ivy that's a pretty green in the summer and red in the autumn. That's wot we'll have!'

'What about a little of each?'

'Whatever you say, Liza, whatever you say. You always 'ave the last word, in any case.'

'No she don't,' said Olly, coming out of the stable, having heard every word. 'I do. And what I say is this. Alms'ouses are all very well but I won't agree to it and nor will me or Angel sign any more petitions over it unless there's a stable attached.'

'Silly bugger,' moaned Angel, ''course there won't be a stable attached. You'll 'ave to find one near by and pay rent for it. You can afford it.' She turned to the other two women. 'He made a packet out of that penny farving case and even more, Liza, when that poor unfortunate man fell in the river!'

'All right, all right,' said Olly, flapping a hand. 'Leave it there, woman. Leave it there.' With that he went back into his stable and resumed polishing two brass fenders he'd picked up for next to nothing.

Maria and Steffan had drawn two chairs as far from the open doorway as they could and spoke almost in whispers, so that Daisy and Willy, who were straining their ears, would give up and go away. 'I wouldn't expect you to say yes straight away, Maria, but if you could consider it . . .'

'I don't have to consider it, Steffan.'

'Oh. Well, I can't say I blame you. Two of us from my family have been imprisoned now so—'

'That's not what I meant.' She smiled, her hand in his. 'You've just asked me to marry you and you asked in the most wonderful way possible and I would have said yes straight away but . . .'

'But what?'

'You haven't said that you love me. Surely that must—'

He sighed, his body relaxing. 'Is that all? Of course I love you. I think I must have even before we started to talk to each other. I adore you, Maria. I love, worship and adore you.'

Pulling her hands from his, she raised them to her face and took a deep breath, her eyes staring out over the tips of her fingers at Steffan's searching blue eyes. She was desperately trying not to cry. Not now. Not at a time like this. But all the while she was silently ordering herself to control herself, the tears were trickling down her cheeks.

'You silly thing,' murmured Steffan, swallowing the lump in his throat. 'Fancy thinking I didn't love you. Now it's my turn. Do you love me, Maria, and if so will you please do me the honour of being my wife?'

Pinching her lips together, she nodded furiously, trying to say everything that was in her heart and mind through her eyes. Her lips trembling, she opened her arms to him, and as he stood up he slowly drew Maria to her feet and held her tight, kissing her neck and sending delicious waves of ecstasy through her entire being. Then, slowly moving her face until their lips were together, she kissed him, and they were no longer in that small room but in a heavenly place shrouded in light gold and sky blue.

Outside, on all fours and peeping in, Willy was giggling behind his hand on seeing his big sister in the arms of Steffan and kissing him. Daisy had no time for all that. Hands on hips, she was standing in front of the three women, a defiant look on her face. 'If this means we're gonna 'ave to go an' move into the country wiv them posh old people who came round I'm soddin' off! Running away, an' I don't care if I get murdered, freeze to death in the winter or starve! I ain't going to the boring country!'

'I shouldn't fink they'd want you anywhere near 'em,' said Sophie. 'I wouldn't do.'

'Well, in that case, Sophie Marcovitch, I fink you're not as nice as Angel and you're an' old cow after all!'

With that she flounced out of the yard to give Wilkie Crow the good news, her version to be embroidered with a certain amount of poetic licence. She would tell him that her sister was going to marry a bloke from a rich family and they were going to live in one of the grand houses that had been built around a romantically lit square.

'God 'elp the man who marries that one.' Angel chuckled. 'I feel sorry for 'im, whoever it is.'

'Feel sorry for me,' said Liza, 'if no one'll take her on.' Turning her head, she saw that Willy was eavesdropping and marched over, dragging him away with one finger on her lips, her eyes forbidding him to make a sound.

'You naughty boy,' said Sophie, loving it.

'Never mind naughty,' snapped Liza, 'he's taking leaves out of his sister's book and I'm not having that!' She pushed him inside Sophie's house and told him to sit quiet and not to cry. Willy murmured, 'Don't bleedin' care anyway! I'll run away wiv Daisy and sod all of yer!'

They all three doubled up. It was Angel who noticed that the door to Liza's house was slowly closing. This she kept to herself.

*   *   *

Maria and Steffan were facing each other across the small kitchen table. 'I would rather come back to the rooms, Maria, until it's time for you all to move out,' said Steffan softly. 'My grandfather's packed my father off to a relative in India who owns a plantation. He can drink and lord it over the workers and he'll love every second of it.'

'But you surely wouldn't want to live above the stable now? Now that you're a proper gentleman!'

'Yes, I do. Once I've had the place cleared of everything and painted. I'll need someone to help me choose the right kind of furniture, mind you. Furniture that will fit into a cottage in Saffron Walden, where I shall be living once I've enough saved from my salary as manager of my grandfather's estate. The cottage I'll be living in with my lovely new wife.'

'Steffan, don't. I'll start to cry again.'

'That's all right. Cry yourself dry before you meet my mother and grandmother. Tomorrow we're taking a trip to Loughton, where they're both living. If you're up to it.'

'I will be. I feel so much better already. I'm very happy. And I love you.'

Liza, Sophie and Angel felt sure that Maria was receiving a proposal of marriage. Sophie could not resist leaning towards her two best friends and singing in a hushed voice:

'One two three, one two three, what do we see,
Maria and Steffan, a bird and a bee.
The wonder of love is a wonderful thing,

Small chubby babies is what it will bring.
One two three, one two three, the bells will
   soon ring,
For our lovely couple and we'll loudly sing,
One two three, one two three, he *will* be her king!'

That evening, with the red setting sun reflecting in the
river, life in Shadwell went on as usual, some people
settling down under their blankets in the streets while
the restless ones strolled through courts, passing lads
and men who sat cross-legged under street lamps playing cards or shove-ha'penny. Oil lamps glowed from
cracked windows to the echoing sound of footsteps as
shift workers came and went in silence. And down by
Tobacco Dock, outside his favourite tavern, Wilkie
Crow sat smoking his pipe, gazing into the murky water
of the Thames, where oyster boats and other vessels
were moored up for the night and gently rocking in
the waves, causing ripples to spread outwards. Wilkie
was content. Despite the murder and the attempt on
Maria's life right had been done and the mood along
his part of the river was back to normal.

As he cast his eyes up to the lopsided black weatherboarded buildings, basking in the glow of the last rays
of the glorious red sun, he sipped his ale and sighed.
To some folk this little oasis, as he had come to think of
it, was just a filthy, smelly part of the slums of London.
To him it was his little bit of heaven. 'Long may you
remain as you are, Tobacco Dock,' he murmured,
raising his glass to the river. 'Long may you remain
as you are.'

*An extract from WHERE SPARROWS NEST
by Sally Worboyes*

I

─────◆◆◆─────

1952

On this clear early August morning, as she watched her
belongings being lifted and stacked on to a rickety old
truck that looked as if it might not make the short
distance to her new home, Edie Birch felt a sense of
dread and anxiety wash over her, wakening feelings that
she had so far managed to keep at bay. Combing her
fingers through her sun-streaked brown hair, she told
herself to be strong and that she was on the brink of a
new beginning. A new life.

Having burned the candles at both ends with all of
the sorting and packing that goes with moving from
one home to another, she was tired and low on energy
and felt as though it hadn't just been boxes she'd been
packing but parts of her life that she had somehow been
storing away. Now, with most of the work at this end of
the move over, she had to use every bit of will-power
to maintain her usual feisty spirit and hold back the
now threatening tears. The floodgates must not open
yet. Until now she had managed to shut her emotions
away, deep inside, keeping them under lock and key
until she was ready, or able, to open the door and let
them out. Perhaps later, alone in her bed, with the long
night stretching ahead of her, she would allow herself

the luxury of crying into her pillow.

In this determined mood she was reminded of two
of her mother's sayings: *Never wear your heart on your
sleeve* and *Shed not one tear in public else a flood will
follow*.

Turning her back on the house that had been her
home and safe haven since birth, Edie leaned against
the crumbling brick wall and closed her eyes, berating
herself for not having the will-power to suppress her
fear of the unknown. This row of terraced slums in
which she had been living was infested with mice and
damp, she reminded herself, and without any of the
modern comforts she would enjoy in her brand new
flat. Common sense told her that the move was the
best thing she could have hoped for, but her heart
was wishing for something else: wishing that the clock
could be turned back to when she was a child and
living here with her younger brother and her parents,
that things had gone differently.

Glancing along the war-damaged street, scenes from
the past floated across Edie's mind: the hopscotch, the
skipping, the ball games and, best of all, the world
of make-believe. Focusing on what used to be her
favourite play area, a forbidding derelict building with
a morbid history, which, of all places, should have been
blown to smithereens, she smiled at the irony. But then
again, she mused, the sinister Victorian workhouse had
also been to her a weird and wonderful, haunting place
where fantasies were created. A place she had often
crept into alone to explore with a mix of terror and
thrill urging her on.

Edie lifted her pale face to the sun, which was emerging from behind a cloud, and thoughts of the future returned. What if she didn't like the people she would from now on be living so close to? Or what if they didn't like her? Worse still, what if they didn't take to the no-nonsense side of her nature? Having lived in this turning all of her life, she was not only leaving familiar ground but neighbours who had, over the years, become close, more like an extended family, rallying round in times of trouble, comforting her mother through the dark times when her father had seemingly disappeared into thin air.

As the memory floated across her mind yet again she wondered if it would ever stop haunting her. It had been an ordinary Sunday morning and an ordinary errand. Her doting father had gone out as usual to buy his Sunday newspaper, a sixpenny bar of chocolate for her mother and a bag of pink and white sugared coconut chips for her brother and herself. She could see the expression on his face now, the strange smile as he stood in the doorway – a smile that said everything but had meant little to her at the time. How could she possibly have imagined, all those years ago, that she would never see him again?

On that Sunday, and for days and weeks afterwards, Edie the child had not been able to fathom why the neighbours were consoling her mother and speaking in hushed voices. There hadn't been an accident. No sudden heart-attack. No murder. Her father had simply not come home from the errand. Thankfully, her mother had, in her wisdom, chosen to tell the truth without frills or fuss. The man Edie had thought she knew so well had in fact been leading a double life. Her father had been seeing another woman for as long as he had been married to her mother, and the woman had had his child, a son. He had ended up choosing one life to lead, and it wasn't with them.

Now, in the wake of leaving the only home she had known, Edie wished that her brother, Jimmy, was by her side. He had offered to take a day off work to help her move but her determination to cope alone had put paid to that. Her firm insistence that he mustn't lose a day's pay and that she could manage had put his mind at ease and a smile on his face when he had said, as he had many times before, 'Too bloomin' independent, that's your trouble, Sis.'

In a way he was right and she knew it, although her independence had not come from choice but necessity. Once the reality had sunk in that her father was not going to return all those years ago her mother's depressions had worsened and her happy-go-lucky nature had vanished. In consequence Edie had been thrown into adulthood before she had reached her sixteenth birthday, when she had not only to care for Jimmy and her traumatised mother but hold down her job as machinist in a local dress factory, working all the hours God sent.

Two years after her husband had gone from her life, Edie's mother had still not got over the pain of losing the man she'd loved and trusted to another woman. Over and over she had asked the same question: how could he abandon us? It was obvious to all those who knew her that she was losing her grip on life and reality, and that she had all but given up until she finally lost the will to live. It came as no great shock to her neighbours when she took her own life.

To Edie and Jimmy, however, her suicide had come as a devastating shock and neither of them had been able to get over it. The only saving grace had been that the tragedy of losing their mother had brought brother and sister closer than they had ever imagined they could be.

Now in her early thirties, with most of her possessions on the back of a truck and her old life shut away behind a paint-peeling brown door, Edie forced herself to look on the bright side. A new life was stretching out before her, full of possibility. Peering along the turning, she saw a smart removal van pulling away and smiled inwardly. It was followed by a truck filled with the Cooper family. Showing a hand as they passed, she smiled gamely back at the mother of four, whose expression somehow pushed Edie's blues away. Even though they all knew, as they bravely waved cheerio, that they would most likely never set eyes on each other again, there was a look of optimism on Mrs Cooper's tired and lined face, and determination on her husband's. They had chosen to take up the offer to move out of London to Harlow and a brand new terraced council house, and they had not been the only ones to opt for different surroundings.

More East Londoners wanted a new way of life closer to the countryside. Some families were heading for Norfolk, or Basildon and Dagenham in Essex. It was a time of change, but although there was a sense in the

air of better things to come away from the 'Smoke', Edie
felt safer in London – her familiar home ground. Safe
and at home. Even if her new neighbours would all be
strangers in the beginning, at least she would still be in
the city of her birth.

Not only had she lost both parents, she was a war
widow – at least that was how she saw herself. She
had certainly come through enough grief to realise
that it was futile to hang on to a shred of hope that
her husband Harry would be found alive now. She had
spent too many nights when younger hoping that her
father would return to keep a torch burning for her
husband.

The main priority of Edie's life now was to be amid
people she knew and trusted, shopkeepers, stall-holders
and neighbours. Finding someone to take Harry's place
was not an option. He had been her first love and
would be the last. She had her daughter Maggie, her
brother Jimmy and her great-aunt Naomi, the flamboy-
ant seventy-year-old who had spent all of her working
life, since the age of twelve, around actors in the worst
and best of British theatres. A widow herself, having
lost her husband in the First World War, Naomi had
been the one to show Edie the way forward when the
devastating telegram arrived in 1942 telling her that
Harry was missing, presumed dead.

According to the War Office, the rescue boat on
which he was stationed had been detailed to search
for survivors who had been aboard an allied war plane,
which, while crossing the mountainous region of
Turkey, had crashed close to Kemer. The rescue boat,

on arrival into the region, had gone into a sea severe and rough with waves reaching monstrous heights. The last radio SOS message from a crew member had been on the rocky coastal shore near Oludeniz. The boat had capsized in the area and the crew were listed as missing, presumed dead. No survivors had been found and there had been no trace of the wrecked boat on the shore.

'Better to be loved by one good man than by a dozen wasters,' had been Great-aunt Naomi's few words of comfort to Edie, which were followed by unbending advice: 'First, have as many lovers as you want, my darling, and second, never, *never* marry twice.'

Edie had taken the second piece of advice, but as for having many lovers – here she differed greatly from Naomi. Edie had loved Harry deeply and had married young. Her modest wedding day had been wonderful and she was content with her memories. After her marriage, and before the Second World War had broken out, the couple had lived in Edie's family home with Jimmy, who had regarded Harry more as a real brother than an in-law. The two had spent hours fishing in the Cut, a narrow river that flowed from Essex through Hackney and down into the Thames at Wapping.

Feeling a little easier now as snapshot scenes of better times flew across her mind, Edie brushed away rust coloured dust from her skirt, which had come off the crumbling brickwork of a house ready for demolition. As she turned her front and back door keys in her hand, worn-out and familiar thoughts were crossing her mind. That maybe Harry was alive. That maybe he had been captured by the enemy while trying to make his way home. That maybe he had been taken to some God-forsaken prisoner-of-war camp and would one day return. That she would wake up in bed to find him lying next to her, softly snoring.

'Penny for them, Edie,' came the slow voice of the coalman who today was clean and spruced up to the nines. 'I hope you're not having second thoughts.'

'Of course I'm not, Ben, but . . .' she slowly shook her head, pinching her lips together. '. . . I can't help thinking that some of us won't see each other agen. After all these years.'

'Don't be mad. We're not all trotting off to live wiv the carrot crunchers, thank God. Don't worry, we'll all be rattling against each other like bad pennies, in the eel shop, the markets, down Brick Lane, in Balmy Park . . .'

'Maybe so, but I think I might miss this old house,' she shrugged, 'once it's been flattened with the rest and it's too late to do anything about it.'

'Well, I shan't miss mine,' he chuckled, continuing on his way. 'You women, you make me laugh. It'll take a cleverer man than me to fathom you! A clever man and a lifetime twenty furlongs too long!'

Laughing at his strange rhetoric, Edie shook off her nostalgia and went back into the house where her removal man, Mr Crow, was struggling with her old settee. 'You're sweating like a pig, Mr Crow,' she smiled. 'Leave that for a minute and I'll make us a cup of tea. I expect you're ready for one.'

'Ooooh,' he said, lowering the end of the piece of

furniture he had been heaving and dragging along. 'That lad of mine's bin gone for half an hour,' he puffed, wiping sweat from his brow with the back of his hand. 'You wait till he gets back. I'll give 'im what for. Popped off to get me some Golden Virginia. You can bet yer bottom dollar he's slipped into the Carpenter's Arms for a pint. Left an old man to it. Lazy little bugger.'

'You're not so old, Mr Crow. What about a nice cup of tea, then?'

'Can a duck swim?' he laughed. 'Four sugars, if you don't mind, dear. I'm sweet but not sweet enough.'

Edie looked from his rosy face to the tatty old sofa. 'You know, Mr Crow, I'm sick of the sight of that fing. I don't think I'll take it to my lovely new flat. Don't bother with it. We'll leave it behind for the mice.'

The old boy pushed back his cap and scratched his head. 'Sure about that are you, ducks? They don't make 'em like that nowadays you know. Well sprung, that is.'

'Maybe so, but it's old, it smells of damp, and them springs you're talking about don't half dig in your bum.'

'Well, then, you put a coupl a cushions on top. You don't wanna go getting in debt. Bloomin' tallymen wait on street corners for you women and your fancy ideas of buying this, that and the other.'

'Even so. We'll leave it behind.'

'Well, if you can afford new, buy from a factory and sod the middle men. Go into Johnny Carpenter's shop floor and tell 'im I sent yer. You can't miss 'is place –

it's slap bang on the end of the other furniture makers' just off Columbia Road.'

'Ah, but will he give it me on tick?'

'Probably. But you'll end up paying more'n the cost in the long run.'

'Well, I don't 'ave much choice, do I? Us lot hardly have bank accounts to draw from.'

'That's true,' he sniffed. 'Very true. Tell you what. Come and 'ave a look round my yard in Tobacco Dock. I don't only moonlight with moving families from one place to another. I clear the odd 'ouse and office now and then. You'll find summink that takes your fancy. A couple of quid for a settee. Can't be bad, can it?'

'Depends on the state of it.'

'Oh, I don't waste floor space on rubbish. No point. This old one of yours wouldn't find its way into my yard. I could find an 'ome for it, mind. Some poor old bugger'll be pleased to 'ave it for four or five bob. I'll dock that from the price of a decent one. How'd that suit yer?'

'I'd need one straight away. Don't want to sit on orange boxes for weeks on end.'

'Well, you wouldn't do, would yer? Tell you what . . . once I've moved you in I'll come back and fetch this and the rest of the rubbish you're leaving behind and drop by your flat tomorrer with a settee you'd be proud to let your neighbours see. That suit you, will it? I'll only charge a dollar for all the manoeuvring and let's say two quid for the bit of furniture.'

'It's a deal. But if I don't like it—'

'You'll like it,' he said. 'It'll give you a few years' wear and it'll be a darned sight better'n this old fing.' He looked into her face and grinned. 'Four sugars for me, then. I'll load that tea-chest up while yer brewing.'

Back in the scullery, Edie filled the kettle and smiled. The people in this part of London would be the same no matter where she moved to. Wheeling and dealing was a way of life.

She was so deep in thought she didn't hear her daughter arrive. 'You ain't taking that bleedin' old settee, are yer?' groaned Maggie, her hands firmly on her bony hips and her green eyes glaring. 'Flea-bitten old junk needs—'

'I'm not taking it! And where'd you skive off to? There's your clothes to be packed into a tea-chest yet.'

'Went and 'ad a look at the flat. Peeked froo the winda. Kitchen looks like a palace. Don't know what all the fuss's bin abaht. It'll be like living in one of them American films. Fresh paint everywhere, sparkling white sink and silver taps. Cupboards on the walls all brand new and painted cream. And you could eat off that stone floor it's so clean. Mice won't be able to chew froo that, will they? And they definitely couldn't get up them stairs.'

'Maybe they'll use the lift,' said Edie, tongue in cheek.

'That's a point.' Maggie raised her thick ginger eyebrows. 'They could sneak in every time the door's pulled open. I went up and dahn six times to check it works properly. I don't want you gettin' stuck in there.'

'Oh . . . and I didn't think you cared, Maggie Birch.'

'I don't.' The wily fourteen-year-old shrugged. 'But you might 'ave the shopping bag wiv yer and I'd starve to death while you suffocated.'

With her back turned to her daughter, Edie smiled inwardly. 'So you like the flat, after all. That's good.'

'They've put up an enamel sign on the stairs. "No spitting." As if we'd spit!'

'I'm pleased you like it, Mags. Makes a big difference to me. You did say before you thought it was more like a prison or a lunatic asylum than somewhere to live.' Edie was relieved that her cantankerous daughter had had a change of heart.

'I never said that. Aunt Naomi did. Anyway, it wasn't finished when we went to 'ave a look, was it? And there was mud and builders everywhere. Got grassy areas round the block of flats now. You could sit out there wiv yer new neighbours and gossip – jus like when we went hop-picking that once.'

'I don't think so.'

'Uncle Jimmy's right. You *are* a snob. Never liked it, did yer?'

'No, I never. Tin sheds with a hole in the ground for lavatories. Straw to sleep on and cooking on a camp-fire. It was like the poor living in the Dark Ages.'

'I might go wiv Uncle Jimmy and Aunt—'

'You will not! No more time off school – and that's final!'

'You're *allowed* by the School Board to go!' growled Maggie, turning away and peering into the back of the removal truck. 'The country *needs* us to pick 'ops.'

'I'm sure it does but you need *education* and in my books *that*'s more important.'

Ignoring all of that, Maggie sniffed and looked her mother in the face. 'There's a Tarmac playground, you know. One for each block of flats and a big cement one for them who're gonna live in the cottages and maison-ettes. Some boys was already playing football on it.'

'Sounds all right, then.'

'Course it does. Should 'ave moved out of this dump years ago.' With that, Maggie eased the brace off her teeth, tossed it over her shoulder then pushed a hand through her thick red hair. 'Don't need that any more. They're straight enough now.' The wolf-whistle from one of the boys playing football had left its mark.

'Don't be too hasty now,' said Edie, as she cupped her daughter's face. 'The dentist thought another month.'

'I know, but look at 'em. They don't stick out any more and the gap where he took that one out has nearly gone. You can 'ardly see it.'

'That's true.' Edie didn't really think so but she had to admit that Maggie was smiling properly for the first time in ages and the improvement from when she first went for treatment on her teeth was as good as she had hoped for. Giving her daughter's flushed cheeks a little squeeze she winked at her. 'I said you'd turn into a swan and I bet you do.'

'No, I won't, Mum. Stop pretending. So I don't 'ave to wear the brace any more, then?'

'No. And do you know what else?' said Edie, slowly removing Maggie's National Health glasses. 'I think it's time you got yourself a Saturday job so you can save to buy a nicer pair of these.'

'But I only need 'em for reading. So it'd be a waste of money. No one sees me when I'm in me bed, do they? And I couldn't care less about being called Four Eyes in class.'

Moved by this sudden change in her daughter, Edie went quiet, carefully choosing her words. Maggie had been hiding behind her glasses since she was six years old, pretending she couldn't see properly without them. The school nurse knew differently, and so did the optician, but Edie had long since given up trying to persuade her that she had lovely eyes and should show them off – lovely sloping green eyes and thick, nicely shaped eyebrows to match her healthy head of lustrous copper hair, just like her father's.

'Too lazy to get yerself out of that bed of a Saturday morning, eh?' she managed to say, inspired by the new look of confidence on her daughter's face.

'I never meant I wouldn't try for a Saturday job. I meant I'm sick of wearing these fings all the time. I ain't gonna waste me money on another pair, am I, when I need some new clothes? And you've got other fings to buy off the tallyman. New curtains and that.'

'That's true,' said Edie. 'That is *very* true.' She nodded thoughtfully. 'I saw a notice in Woolworth's window and in the fabric shop down Bethnal Green Road. They're looking for Saturday girls.'

'I'm not working in bleeding Woolworth's!' declared Maggie, and then, in a quiet voice, 'I'll try the curtain shop though.'

'Whatever. Go and pack the rest of your things into the tea-chest I've left in your room.'

Maggie turned away from her mother, sullen. She had been excited when she inspected the new flat that was to be her home, and relieved when she had seen that others in her age group were arriving in lorries and trucks. The expressions on some faces seemed apprehensive and that, in a strange way, had boosted her confidence. The mix of people she had seen moving on to the estate had surprised her. In the street where she lived the neighbours had been white and mostly Church of England. Jewish and Catholic families tended to live in separate areas, or at least that was how it seemed to Maggie. They certainly moved in their own circles, the Catholics using certain pubs and churches, while the Jews had their own markets, shops and synagogues, the Anglicans here, there and everywhere. Apart from the Turkish barber shop and the Maltese café at the end of the turning, foreigners seemed few and far between in Stepney. But today she had seen a West Indian family moving on to the estate, had spoken to a fair-haired woman with a strange accent who turned out to be Polish, and had laughed furtively at an Irish Catholic, who had sat on the wall of her tiny front garden continuously crossing herself and asking Mary, Mother of Jesus, to help shift a mountainous pile of furniture off the pavement and into her house. Her husband, like other husbands moving on to the council estate, was offering his custom to his new local and believed it the duty of the removal men to carry everything into the house. Removal men who had been paid between five and ten shillings for the deal of carting their belongings from one place to the other and no more than that. The discovery that hardly any men were waiting at the houses at the other end to help unload had not gone down too well, and the women had had to take the flak. Maggie had witnessed more dramas in the couple of hours she had spent wandering around the Barcroft council estate than she had seen in her whole life in this back-street.

The last thing she had done before she pulled herself away from the bustling place was help an Italian woman carry a pram filled with kitchen pots and pans up three flights of stairs. The woman didn't believe or trust that the lift would take her safely to where she wanted to go. Her sixteen-year-old son, carrying a blanket box on his broad shoulder, had been one reason why Maggie had offered to give a hand. He was the handsomest boy she had ever set eyes on – and he had flashed a smile and winked at her.

'I s'pose I've gotta let Mad Woman keep my rabbit?' said Maggie, her thoughts nipping from one thing to another, as she watched a mouse scouting for crumbs in the doorway leading into the scullery.

'Just try taking it back from 'er now,' chuckled Edie. 'And don't you think it's time you stopped calling your aunt Naomi Mad Woman? It was all right when you was little but you're fourteen and—'

'She likes me calling 'er that and, anyway, she *is* mad. The theatre work never made her bonkers – the film studios did. She said so.'

'Oh, whatever . . .' sighed Edie, pushing a hand through her hair. 'I can't see her settling on the estate, though. Too clean and clinical. I s'pose you popped in to see 'er?'

'Course I did. She's all right. Finks 'er neighbours are old and boring but she likes it all right – now that she's draped her Chinese shawls everywhere and put her pictures and photos up. She was really beautiful before she turned into a prune.'

'And a very good actress, according to the reviews in her scrapbook. So Naomi's settled in. That's good.'

'She's planted seed potatoes in 'er bit of garden already and she's nicked some plants from the old-boy-next-door's garden.'

'I don't wanna know,' said Edie. 'Come on. Time's marching forward. It'll be afternoon before we know it and the nights are drawing in. I planned for us to be all settled in by nightfall. I'll be ready for my bed by then, that's for sure.'

'I won't. I'll be in the flat next door watching their television. They've got a brand new nine-inch. Oh, and I think you might 'ave to go round to Mad Woman tomorra. She's goin' up the rent office to cause pandemonium. She reckons they're charging 'er ninepence over the top. You've gotta argue it for 'er.'

Edie slowly shook her head. 'I knew it was a mistake to persuade 'er to live on this estate. Why didn't I listen to myself instead of you?'

'Because she's family!' Distracted by more mice scampering around the fireplace, Maggie gazed around the empty room as a wave of panic rushed through her.

The moment had finally come, and once she was out of this house she would never see this room or her bedroom again. The bedroom that knew all of her secrets and had listened to her crying softly into her pillow. She spoke in a broken voice: 'Do you fink they'll pull this house down straight away, Mum?'

'Course not,' said Edie, sensing that her daughter was feeling the same as herself – a bit on the low side and with past memories swimming through the mind. 'They won't demolish till everyone's gone from the turning and some will stay put for as long as they can. Five or six don't want to move from their roots.'

'So they'll just board ours up, then?' said Maggie, avoiding eye-contact.

'No. They don't do that any more. Tramps and down-and-outs must have somewhere to sleep. And there were enough of the poor sods from the first war never mind the second. Better they camp out in these old places than in doorways and parks. Let's 'ope they'll be in here over winter – and the next come to that.'

'Mad Woman said that life's like a roller-coaster.'

'It is. Ups and downs. An even life, if you can get it, is the best you can hope for.' Edie gave a gentle tug to her daughter's long pony-tail, which was scurfed back and tied with a strip of rag. 'Welcome to the real world, Mags.'

'What's that s'posed to mean?'

'Time'll tell. This month next year you'll be looking at things differently. My little girl will 'ave turned into a young lady.'

'And we'll be settled in our new 'ome.' Her eyes shut

tight, Maggie slipped her arms around her mother's soft, warm body. 'We'll be all right, won't we? You'll meet some new friends and you won't miss Dad so much.'

'I'll never stop missing him, sweetheart,' whispered Edie, with a tremor in her voice, 'but at least I won't be lonely with all them people around me. Let's hope our close neighbours'll be as good as the ones in this turning. I think we're both gonna take time to settle down but we'll like it. I know we will. We'll love it,' she said positively. 'And now we need to get a move on. It's time to go, Mags. Time to put the last of our things on that truck. Mr Crow's a good man and knows that this is a bit emotional for us but . . . he's got a living to earn and time is money.'

'I know,' murmured Maggie, and then, 'Promise me you won't cry?'

'I won't if you don't. We'll be brave soldiers for each other, eh?'

Maggie nodded and managed a weak smile. 'I can't wait to sleep in my new bedroom or soak in that gleaming white bath.'

'Nor can I,' said Edie. 'Nor can I.'

Two hours later, Edie was standing in her sparkling new kitchen with the afternoon sun streaming through the window and on to her face, while the smell of fresh paint and new pine timber lingered in the air. The décor throughout the flat had a spring-cum-summer feel to it. Doors and picture rails had been painted fresh apple green and walls emulsioned cream. It was airy and bright, with no hint of the smells and atmosphere she had lived with for so long and had got used to – damp, mustiness and the gloomy dark. To close the door for the last time on Cotton Street had seemed an impossible task. Now she was glad, really glad, to have done it.

Catching Maggie's expression as she came into the kitchen, Edie knew that she had made the right decision in choosing this second-floor flat. It was almost as if their name had been on it before the paint was dry. The face of her only child, who was on the brink of adolescence, was glowing. The adventure of new beginnings during the past few months had now turned into solid reality. All thoughts of things going wrong in so far as Edie was concerned were diminishing by the second. Gone was the nagging worry that if they hated living here there would be no turning back. Edie no longer wanted the option of a second chance to change her mind. New housing was in demand and people like Edie, whose homes had suffered major or minor bomb damage, were desperate for the new flats or cottages on offer. And even those whose homes had not been damaged wanted to move out of the slum dwellings. The working classes had had enough. They had had it with showing the stiff upper lip, of making do on bread and cheese, of being freezing cold in the winter and of being looked upon as if they were third-rate citizens who smelt and didn't care if they had hot water to bathe in or not.

Most, if not all, wanted new, decent places to live where they could hold up their heads and be shown some respect. Some were even determined to climb the sanctimonious class ladder and grin into the faces of those horrified to have the working classes at close to touching distance. There was a distinct air of determination and an atmosphere so thick you could feel it. Determination, indignation and pride. Poverty would no longer be tolerated. Men and women were beginning to march forward, not to save King and country, but themselves, their children and their children's children.

Waiting in her new kitchen for Mr Crow to arrive with her belongings, Edie gripped the rim of the sparkling white sink with its pine draining-board and looked through the window at the light blue sky with its sprinkling of cotton-wool clouds. The echo of talk and laughter on the staircase outside was music to her ears. Especially since the laughter was interspersed with swearing coming from two dockers struggling with an oversized, overflowing trunk filled with bedding. 'Home from home,' she murmured delightedly, then went out of the flat to glance at the two men as they struggled with a bulky piece of furniture. Her neighbours might have found the manoeuvring easier had they been of similar build, but the elder, was short and round while the other, a man in his mid-twenties, was tall and broad. Leaning on her elbows on the balcony Edie viewed the comings and goings below while being entertained by these two men and their banter . . .

'Gawd, Jack . . . This can't all be pillows and sheets! I reckon Laura's got the Crown Jewels hidden in there!'

'All my half-crowns that I can't find more like! Nicked all me notes, didn't she? Save for a rainy day and it gets blown on daft machines. What do she want with a vacuum cleaner in a brand new place? Broom'd do!'

'It's 'er house-warming present to 'erself, Jack. She's not stopped talking about it for weeks so don't start moaning when 'er and Liz get back from the shop with it. Anyway, me and Lizzie put 'alf towards it so you're only fifty per cent out of pocket. Stop yer moaning.' Taking a rest when they'd reached the top of the flight of stairs, he wiped his brow. 'I'm not as young as you, don't forget. Must be a lot of half-crowns in there to make it weigh this much.'

'Stop *your* moaning Bert,' mocked Jack, as he grinned his handsome smile. 'Let's get this out of the way and slide off for a pint. Laura, Liz and our Kay can fetch all the bits and pieces up once they get 'ere.'

'Hold on a minute, if you don't mind!' came the magisterial shriek of a woman on her way to the third floor. 'We've all gotta use this staircase, you know!'

Glancing sideways at Bert, Jack covered a smile. 'Sorry, love,' he said, trying to sound sincere and gallant as he moved aside to give her space. 'You don't 'ave to walk up, you know. That's a smart old lift we've got.'

'If I want to take the lift I'll take it. If I choose to walk up I will.' She stared into Jack's face, weighing him up. 'I've seen you before?'

'Might 'ave done, luv. Dunno.' Jack scratched the tip of his ear and glanced sideways, catching Edie's eye. Giving her a flirtatious wink, he turned back to the other woman and showed a concerned face. 'Need 'elp with your bags, love? Cos Bert 'ere—'

'Oh, yes! Your face looks familiar! I've seen it. I get

the East London paper every week, you know.' Her eyes narrowed, as she looked accusingly at him.

Knowing full well what she was alluding to, Jack thanked his lucky stars that his name had never been in the court columns. 'Mine's the *News of the World.*' He sniffed, turning his face to give Edie another little wink, as she turned the bright new keys to number forty-one, Scott House, in her hand. Relieved to find that although this block of flats was a far cry from what she had always been used to, the people were no different.

'I might 'ave guessed you'd read *that* paper,' said the woman from the third floor, 'all filth and gossip. Any beer parties and I'll report yer! Mark my words!' That said, she climbed the next flight of stairs. 'The name's Sarah James, *Mrs* James to you, and my 'usband is George. He works for the railway in the offices, so watch yer step!'

With a hand cupping his mouth, Bert just managed to hide his laughter; his eyes, however, were glistening. Making sure the woman was out of earshot he released a muffled burst of laughter. 'She's a bundle of joy, ain't she?'

Jack let out a low moan as he half turned to include Edie in the conversation. 'There's one everywhere you go!'

'Looks like it,' she chuckled.

'I reckon we can handle 'er, though. The name's Jack, by the way, and this is Bert.'

'Pleased to meet you both. Mine's Edie.'

'And don't think I never heard that because I did!'

came the high-pitched voice of their neighbour from above. 'I'm not deaf!'

Pulling faces, the men went quietly about their business. 'I thought Carlton Square was bad enough,' murmured Jack, 'Gawd 'elp us if we've made a mistake . . .'

'I told you not to take a place on an estate, but you wouldn't listen,' said Bert, lifting his side of the trunk. 'Still, that bleached blonde we saw earlier should perk up yer Percy.'

Struggling along the balcony towards their flat, Jack bore a grin but a nervous worry was starting to nag at him. Women. Women next door to him. Women above and below. And far too many for his liking. The rooms he and Laura had moved out of overlooking a small tree-lined square, were far more romantic, to Jack's way of thinking. He had flirted with more than one pretty lady while hidden by the shrubs and wrough-iron fence. When Laura had been at work and he hadn't, he had also slipped into one or two other rented rooms for a little bit of loving on the side. Their rooms, the top half of a Victorian house, had been cramped but at least it had felt more secluded than this estate. The fact that they had been only a five-minute walk from Stepney Green Underground station, which he often used, was another advantage.

'Fat chance of a bit of the other with all these windows,' grinned Bert, reading his mind. 'But, then, it's not the windows you need to worry about, Jack, mate, it's the balconies. I've seen flats similar to this and rows of 'ousewives leaning on their elbows on every floor enjoying the view. Nuffing'll be missed, I'm telling yer. Wink at one of the women and another'll spread the word that you're cocking 'er. You'll 'ave to live like a saint now, mate. No more sneaking in and out of back doors. You're gonna miss Albert Square—'

'Carlton Square. I've told you enough times it was never called that.'

'And I'm telling you it was! Way back. My great grandmuvver knew what she was talking about. Ask any of the neighbours when you pop back for a cup of tea. It was changed when young Queen Victoria met 'er Albert and fell in love. They changed a lot of squares from Albert to summink else. Political, my old granny reckons.'

'Load of rubbish,' said Jack. 'Anyway, I might not need to pop back. I fancy the one in number forty-one. Little cracker she is.'

'Oh, leave off. Poor cow's a war widow, according to Liz. She bumped into 'er when they first come to view. Any'ow, she's out of your class, mate, she is. Out of your class.'

'Don't let Laura 'ear you say that. Did Lizzie catch 'er name? I never did.'

'Cos you was looking and not listening. It's Edie. And the kid's called Maggie.'

'Edie, eh? Sounds all right. Nice and soft. Which is 'ow I like 'em.'

'Well, you would do, wouldn't yer?' said Bert. He arrived at the flat door and lowered his end.

Taking a breather, Jack leaned against the balcony wall and pulled his tobacco tin from his pocket.

'Edie . . . yeah, that name suits 'er.' He ignored Bert's disparaging response. To Jack, life was too short to miss opportunities – especially when they came wrapped in a lovely feminine parcel.

'I ain't listening and I'm taking no notice of yer. Should be ashamed of yerself,' sniffed Bert, wiping his brow with his handkerchief. 'Talking like that after all your Laura's bin through.'

'I'm not talking about now, Bert. Give it a few years.' He winked, saying, 'Anyway no 'arm in dreaming, is there?'

'More'n you think, mate. More than you think.' He dug deep into his trouser pocket and pulled out his Zippo lighter before Jack could ask for it.

Lighting his roll-up, Jack drew on it and raised an eyebrow. 'And Laura's not the only one cut up over what 'appened. I'm not made of stone, you know. I loved baby John as much as she did.'

'I know that. Just don't act like nuffing's 'appened. It's not clever and it don't do none of you any good. Not you, not Laura and not Kay. Never mind my Lizzie. She still cries in her sleep over it.'

'That's it, Bert. Rub it in. Rub the salt right in! I was just trying to look on the bright side, that's all. Strike me dead for it if you must, though. Take me dreams away and gimme a razor blade.' He said, berating his brother in law. 'Life's too hard to get too soft.'

Bert answered with a short nod. He and Jack were close and he knew him well enough to realise that it would take him a long time to get over the loss of his baby son. This pair were best friends and worked as a team. Even so, Jack didn't seem to have control of his dick, as far as Bert could tell. It seemed to have a mind of its own. His very own water diviner.

The sight of another lorry pulling into the grounds, but no sign of Mr Crow and her belongings was causing Edie to feel nervous. Maybe there had been an accident. Or perhaps his old truck had finally given up the ghost. Telling herself to be patient, she watched as three families alighted from the lorry and ran all the good things through her mind to calm herself: lights at the flick of a switch, hot water at the turn of a tap, a fireplace fitted with a gas poker to get the coals burning quickly. The brand new grey and white flecked gas stove in the kitchenette.

A natural blonde was stepping down from the back of the latest lorry who looked about the same age as Edie. It was Jessie Smith, mother of two: the lively thirteen-year-old Billy and shy ten-year-old Emma-Rose. This family was about to move into their flat on the top floor, the fourth. Jessie's assumed husband Max, unable to take time off from work, was not here to help her. But, then, Max Cohen hadn't been as eager to move in here as Jessie and the children.

Max Cohen's hopes and dreams of owning his own house in Golders Green had been dashed but his aspirations were not yet dead. An accountant by profession, he had realised, when the Second World War had finished, that his business would take a nose-dive. Most of his clients had moved upwards and onwards, to other territories, the West End in particular where there was more money to be earned, where more and more nightclubs were opening with wealthy owners at the helm who would require protection against rival and jealous club owners. Not all of Max's clients were of this ilk by any means, but most of those who were honest businessmen found that after the war the buildings in which they had run their business were no more than a pile of bricks and rubble.

Now, employed as an accountant for a small wine and beer merchant, Max's one ambition was to work for himself again, to rise from the ashes. He had spoken openly of his discontent at being employed instead of running his own business, but the hurt he felt because his beloved Jessie had not filed for divorce from her husband Tom, whom she had been separated from since the end of 1945, he had always kept close to his chest. Why she hadn't set the wheels in motion to end her broken marriage was something only she could explain. The fact was that she had never stopped loving Tom, even though he had been an unreliable and reckless husband.

Now, standing in the Tarmac grounds, Jessie looked around herself, feeling light inside. The sun streaming down on to her face, she closed her eyes and thought of her comfortable bed up there on the fourth floor, up in the sky and away from the world, with all of the hustle and bustle and worry of a so far troubled life.

Before the war Jessie had had too much to cope with: the discovery of her twin sister, Hanna, whose existence had been a tightly kept family secret; her engagement to

Max Cohen had been broken, thanks to his interfering sister who did not want a Christian marrying into their Jewish family; and her new romance with Tom Smith just weeks afterwards had introduced her to a world of petty crime, which eventually led to the police turning up at her door and a search of her house for stolen goods – stolen goods which Tom had hidden in *her* wardrobe.

Now, with all of the worst behind her, Jessie felt she could look forward to a peaceful, untroubled life and concentrate on bringing up her two children within the confines of this safe council estate, which had a village feel to it. Looking around herself with the warm sun on her face, she was convinced that she and Max could settle down and continue to bring up Billy and Emma-Rose without the never-ending strain of having to worry or look constantly over her shoulder for trouble brewing. She glanced across to the grassy area and low wall surrounding the flats and cottages, which had new young trees planted. She imagined a rug spread out and a picnic basket. She could see her children playing there with others from the estate. She pictured herself sitting on her rug with other young mothers, out of their homes and taking a break, chatting about their children, schools and their hobbies.

Her ten year old Emma-Rose tugging on her sleeve brought her back into the present, the real world and the task in hand. Tired from all of the packing and carrying, she gazed into her daughter's innocent face. Emma-Rose's pale blue eyes squinted against the sunshine as she shifted her weight from one thin white leg to the other while screwing up the material of her summer frock with both hands. 'Can – can – can I – can I—' rushed Emma, excited and anxious to get out her words in lightning time '—can I go in the lift?'

'Calm down, sweet'eart. We've got a lifetime of going up and down in it.'

'But I want to go in it *now*! Uvver children are going in by 'emselves! Why can't I?'

'*Them*selves, Emma. And I never said you couldn't, sweet'eart.'

'Well, can I, then?'

'If you must. If you can't wait for me.'

'Not by meself, though. Billy can take me up and fetch me down.'

'It's a very busy time for everyone and the lift's gonna be in demand . . .' murmured Jessie. She turned to Billy, who was peering at a steam train rushing by on the track above the arches. It had caused a flock of sparrows to flee from their dark nesting-place. He seemed to be in a world of his own.

'Billy, why don't you go up in the lift with Emma and train-spot from the fourth balcony?'

'If you want,' he said, his eyes focused on the railway line, his attention undisturbed.

'Only five minutes, mind. I'm gonna need you to help. Both of you. There's a lot of fetching and carrying to do.'

'I know that,' was his mumbled answer. 'I don't want 'er watching wiv me later on, though. I won't get five minutes' peace . . .'

'I wouldn't want to stop up there with yer!' snarled

Emma, her skinny neck stretched and face pushed forward. 'Trains are boring.'

'Good.'

'Go on, then, scarper,' said Jessie, 'and be careful. No climbing down the drainpipe, Billy.'

'Who said I was gonna?' The guilty defensive tone in his voice gave him away: his mother had guessed exactly what he was thinking. Glancing up at the front balconies and catching the eye of Edie who smiled and nodded, Jessie returned the neighbourly gesture.

Stepping out of the way of her neighbours, who were already carrying things off the lorry, tiredness hit Jessie like a wave. Her legs were aching and she felt as if there were grains of sand behind her eyes. Stifling a yawn and knowing that her belongings would be last off the lorry – they had been picked up first – she went inside the building. The echo of her footsteps on the stone stair-case, the gleaming white tiles on the lower half of the walls and the painted green iron hand-rail reminded her of the London Hospital, and she shuddered. Towards the end of the war she, like many local women, had been a voluntary helper, going in to do whatever she could for the victims of the blitz on the East End.

When she arrived at the second floor Jessie instinc-tively popped her head round the corner to where Edie was leaning on the balcony, waiting for Mr Crow to arrive with her furniture. 'Have you moved in?' said Jessie, above the excited buzz that was coming from all corners and from people of all ages.

'Not yet. I'm waiting for my things to arrive. I bet the dilapidated old truck's broke down.'

'Are you pleased with it, then?' said Jessie, nodding at her neighbour's open front door, all tiredness draining away as her excitement grew.

'I love it,' said Edie. 'I've got a flask of tea inside if you fancy a cup.'

'That was clever. Now, why didn't I think of that? I'll pop back down in a minute, if that's all right. Can't wait to get inside my flat now. I'm up on the fourth floor, right at the top. God help me if that lift ever breaks down. I can't imagine—'

The sudden shrill voice of Sarah James, ringing through the block, stopped Jessie in her tracks. The woman was scolding Billy. She listened to see if he was going to cheek her. The woman's voice, louder now, continued. 'And you can tell your mother I told you off as well! Bloody nuisance! You break that lift and I'll report you to the caretaker! Then you'll know what being in trouble means! Now, clear off to your own balcony!'

The rapid sound of hurried footsteps on the stairs was a sign that the fear of God had been put into both Billy and Emma-Rose. Eyes on the staircase, Jessie waited until the pair emerged from above, a look of sheer terror on that faces. 'It's all right, kids!' she said, deliberately loudly. 'Slow down, Emma, or you'll fall and break your neck! No one's gonna hurt either of you.'

'I'm not living 'ere!' screeched Billy. 'They've put all the mad people up the top! I'm not living up there!'

'He's right, he's right, he's right!' puffed Emma, grabbing Jessie's arm and shaking it. 'A lady's sitting in the kitchen sink wiv the curtains open and she's singing wiv no clothes on!'

'And that other women tells *everyone* off!'

Covering a smile, Jessie turned to Edie. 'Sounds like we're in for some fun.'

'Just what I was thinking,' said Edie, looking over the balcony and catching sight of Mr Crow's dilapidated truck being manoeuvred round a lorry and two vans. 'My furniture's arrived at last. If your son wants to run down and fetch up two kitchen chairs . . .' she said, looking down at Billy.

'Course he will. I'd best go upstairs and see what's what.' Jessie tousled her son's hair, 'You'll give the lady a hand, won't you?' The expression on Billy's face and his curled lip said it all: fetching and carrying couldn't have been further from his mind.

'Well . . . if you was prepared to help my daughter Maggie to help Mr Crow bring up our furniture,' said Edie, her voice persuasive, 'I'd give you a silver tanner.'

At the thought of earning sixpence, Billy raised an eyebrow. 'I would 'ave 'elped anyway, but if you fink it's worf a tanner, it must be.'

'Right, then,' said Jessie, amused by his expression, that of a young businessman. 'I'll leave Billy in your hands. Come on, Emma. You stop with me.' She took her daughter's hand. Her nervous daughter, who still had a look of worry in her eyes.

Easier with her hand firmly held by Jessie, Emma-Rose peered up at Edie, the afternoon sun on her snow-white hair. 'Have you got any children like me? I'm ten.'

'Well . . . Maggie's fourteen and she's not got your lovely hair and blue eyes but she's a *bit* like you . . . but more like yer brother.'

'Like Billy?' Emma screwed her nose, aghast at the thought.

'That's right. A bit on the cantankerous side. And right now she's gonna be yanked from the back balcony to help your brother fetch my things up.'

'What back balcony?' said Emma, narrowing her eyes.

'One like this only out the back. She's watching some boys down below racing on their rickety old go-carts.'

'She don't really look like our Billy, does she?'

'Come on, you,' said Jessie. 'Let's go up and see where we're gonna put your bed. The men'll be fetching it up soon.'

Going rigid, Emma-Rose pulled back, her eyes wide. 'Wot about that woman sitting in the kitchen sink? Billy said she probably kidnapped girls and locked 'em in cupboards.'

Jessie looked from Emma-Rose to Edie. 'What on earth have we let ourselves in for?'

'Time will tell,' chuckled Edie, and then, a more serious expression on her face, 'It's gonna be a lot different from living in a quiet turning. A lot different.'